THE
PRIVILEGE

THE
PRIVILEGE

D.W. Buffa

Copyright © 2021 by D.W. Buffa

Cover and jacket design by 2Faced Design

ISBN 978-1-947993-97-6

eISBN: 978-1-951709-53-2

Library of Congress Control Number: available upon request

First hardcover edition May 2021 by Polis Books, LLC

44 Brookview Lane

Aberdeen, NJ 07747

www.PolisBooks.com

POLIS BOOKS

Chapter One

San Francisco has always been a place without rules, where nothing is forbidden and everything is allowed. People came from all over, drawn, in that marvelous phrase of Robert Louis Stevenson's, by "all the winds of heaven' to a place where they could live whatever life they chose to live. In the Gold Rush, when men got rich overnight it became the new Babylon where everything was for sale. In 1906, when the earthquake leveled the city, and fire destroyed the buildings still standing, people knelt in prayer, and then lined up at a table where Gianini, who founded the Bank of Italy, which later became the Bank of America, gave out money to anyone who wanted to help rebuild. In the 1940s, when movie stars wanted to have a good time, the Southern Pacific railroad, whose owner lived in one of the mansions that dominated Nob Hill, started the Starlight Express to come up from Los Angeles on Friday afternoons and go back Sunday night, so Errol Flynn, among others, could go on a weekend drunk in the most wide-open town in the country, a place where the police, for a price, could always be counted on to look the other way. When the Second World War brought sailors back from the Pacific, a lot of them decided, from their first sight of the Golden Gate Bridge, never to leave.

In the 1960s and 1970s tourists, and not just tourists, lined up around the block to get into places like Big Al's in North Beach where the drinks were watered and the sex acts were live, where a showgirl like Carol Doda could become famous for no other reason than her gigantic silicon breasts. It was a place where by the end of the twentieth century a straight couple could be asked to leave a gay bar because they had been caught kissing. It was the world gone crazy, and enjoying every minute of it; the only thing thought shocking the suggestion that anything in San Francisco could be shocking at all. Except when it was a murder trial, and everyone tried to pretend that infidelity was an unforgivable sin, and that it must have been the reason why Justin Friedrich had murdered his wife.

"Everyone knows him," Albert Craven assured me. "That's why everyone is so shocked - and so intrigued."

'Everyone' meant the few hundred socially connected people who formed the city's financial and cultural establishment. The number may have been even smaller; perhaps as few as a hundred, the names listed as contributors to every important charitable appeal.

"I don't know him; I had never heard of him," I remarked, smiling in advance at how in Craven's mind it was my own fault if I did not know anyone. "You know everyone in San Francisco," I remarked, before he could say it. "You know more about them than they do themselves," I added. "So why would I want to spend my time with people when I could learn so much more about them from you?"

With a slight, understated grin, the kind that acknowledges, without pretension, as it were, the nature of his achievement, his total grasp of the essential elements of the social world in which he moved, he pulled his shirt cuffs into their proper place below the sleeves of his dark tailored suit.

"Justin Friedrich," he explained, sitting pin stripe straight in the wingback chair in front of my desk, "had never been arrested, much less convicted, of a crime; any crime, even a minor traffic offense. It never would have occurred to him to break the law. He never had to. Everyone can talk all they want about equality, but Justin Friedrich knew only privilege. He attended only private

D.W. Buffa

schools, and when he finished prep school, he enrolled at Yale like his father and grandfather before him and graduated somewhere in the middle of his class. No one thought him unusually intelligent, certainly no one confused him with a serious scholar; but neither did anyone think he wouldn't be a great success in life. He was interested in what others were interested in; reasonably good, but not more than that, in the sports like golf and tennis and sailing that occupy the time and attention of young men of wealthy families like his own. A solid, if not a brilliant student; good, but not exceptional, at the leisure time activities of the young and well-connected rich. Exactly what you would expect. His marriage to Allison Brewster, whose family was as much a part of the city's establishment as his own, a marriage that, two years later, ended not in divorce but murder, seemed to follow the same, predictable path."

"The same predictable path?"

Craven stared through the rain spattered window at the leaden gray sky. He was always more cheerful when the sun was out. The dark days of winter reminded him, I think, of how much closer he was to the end, than to the beginning, of the time he had left.

"Yes, exactly," he replied, with a brief, apologetic smile as he came back to himself. "The marriage was a disaster. The ruling passion, the cause of the attraction, what brought them together, was not love or even physical desire, but money. Difficult to believe, in one sense; perfectly understandable, if not particularly admirable, in another. They had as much money as anyone, and a good deal more than most, but it was not how much they had, it was the comparison with what others had, where you ranked in the scale, that made the difference. It was all a question of what, or in this case, who, you looked up to. Together, almost everyone looked up to them. They lived in one of the most expensive buildings in the city, up on Russian Hill with a view of the bay and the Golden Gate and almost everything else worth seeing. Their apartment took up two whole floors. They kept a sailboat - a yacht by any other name - at the Yacht Club at the Marina. They had everything, and none of it was enough. They hadn't liked each other very much when they married; they had come to hate each other by the time, just last week, Allison Friedrich was murdered, supposedly by her husband."

"Supposedly? She's found shot to death on their sailboat. He's the only one there. They had been fighting earlier in the evening, hit her hard enough to knock her down. But you don't think he did it?"

"No, I don't."

"Because you know him, and he's not the kind of person who would...?"

"We've met, at various social events, but I only know him because I know the family. I don't think he did it because it doesn't make any sense. What reason could he have had to kill her?"

"There doesn't have to be a reason. Anger, jealousy, rage - He had been drinking, gotten quite drunk, from what I've read."

Pressing his lips tight together, Craven shook his head at his failure to explain adequately what he meant.

"They hated each other too much for that."

"They hated each other too much...?"

"It was all about the money. What I said before: not how much they had, but whether, together, they had more than the other rich, privileged people who make up the only world they know or think important. They didn't love each other, they didn't get married to be with one another; they got married to be a famous couple, the center of other people's attention. Allison Friedrich was probably having an affair six months into the marriage, if not before; Justin Friedrich was guilty of infidelity with who knows how many women. Neither of them cared what the other did. They lived their own, private, lives, while they performed in public the part of the wealthiest young couple in town. Does that sound like a marriage in which the husband kills the wife out of jealousy or rage?"

"It sounds like a marriage in which either one of them might kill the other out of disgust."

Lifting an eyebrow, Craven granted the possibility.

"Disgust with themselves, you mean. Perhaps; but that would require a depth of feeling I'm not sure either of them ever had, or was ever capable of having."

It was that remark that kept echoing in my mind when I first met Justin Friedrich to discuss whether I would take his case. He walked into my office, as relaxed and comfortable as if he had come to talk to the family lawyer about a minor change to the family trust. His manner, if slightly formal, was polite and impeccable. He reached across my desk to shake hands and looked me straight in the eye. With his brownish blonde hair and pale blue eyes, with his finely drawn features, it was not only easy, but almost inevitable, to imagine him leaning against a white railing fence on a polo field after he had finished playing for the day, a cold drink in his hand and a Porsche convertible a few short steps away. He was young and rich and good-looking, and as ignorant of what really happens when you are accused of murder as anyone I had ever met.

"I'm innocent, Mr Antonelli. I didn't murder Allison. I don't know who did."

There are no second chances in a criminal trial. You ask a question and, whatever the answer, you don't get to ask it again. If you are not ready to live with the decisions you make, if you are not prepared to act immediately on your own judgement, there are a lot of things you can do as a lawyer, but trial work is not one of them. Three short sentences and, without being able to give a reason for my decision, I knew I was going to take his case. It was only later that I came to realize that I had made a mistake, and that someone whose innocence I never doubted was going to spend the rest of his life in prison.

Most murder trials are conducted in near empty courtrooms. A prosecutor and a lawyer for the defense go about their business under the guidance and direction of a black-robed judge, while twelve citizens of varying degrees of ability and intelligence listen and observe the witnesses called by each side, and if there happens to be someone sitting on the public benches chances are that it is a lawyer with a few minutes to spare before his scheduled appearance in another courtroom just down the hall. Most murder trials involve the poor, and the victim, and the accused, everyone involved, are people whose names mean nothing to the public and, sometimes, not very much to themselves. The crime might make the late night news, but in the normal run of things that is the last anyone hears of it. The trial passes unnoticed. But money gives even death a different meaning. The Friedrich murder trial was the lead item on the nightly news and the front page story in the morning paper. The courtroom, like a successful Broadway production, was always sold out.

"They should charge admission," suggested Albert Craven, as I dropped my briefcase on the floor next to my desk and settled into my chair.

I had just come back from court, where I had given my opening statement. Craven had come in behind me, so quietly I had not noticed he was there until I heard the bare whisper of his voice. It made everything sound like a secret, a secret he could not wait to tell you.

"They really should, sell tickets, at least for every trial in which you're involved. Nothing else is free anymore. When I was a kid, you could go to the zoo, you could go to the aquarium, to the DeYoung Museum, to anything in Golden Gate Park, and you didn't have to pay anything. Now, you pay for everything."

"Even for things you haven't done," I remarked, with a weary cynicism that reflected perfectly what I felt.

"Your opening? It didn't go well? I find that hard to believe."

I shrugged it off. I had told the jury what I needed to tell them: a preview of what I suggested the evidence would show; or, rather, what the evidence would not show. That was the problem. There was no evidence I could point to that was directly helpful to the defense. All I could tell them was that the evidence the prosecution was going to present was not anywhere close to what was needed to prove guilt beyond a reasonable doubt. It was all I could do, and it was not half as good as it needed to be.

"The trial hasn't even started," objected Craven, trying to cheer me up. "You've picked a jury - a good one, from what you told me. The trial starts tomorrow, when the prosecution calls its first witness."

It would have been unkind to disagree. And so I told him he was right, that the trial had not started and that, as I must have told him at some point in every trial since I joined his firm, you never knew what was going to happen, but that something unexpected almost always happened and that, when it did, it often turned everything upside down. I felt better for telling him that, not because I believed it, but because after years of trying cases I had acquired the useful habit of convincing myself that what I knew was utterly impossible might, just this once, actually be true. Like nearly every law, even the law of contradiction has its exceptions.

The only real hope I had was the prosecutor herself. Samantha Ferguson knew what she was supposed to do, and she knew how to do it. She was methodical, relentless, no detail too small to escape her attention, and all of it organized with logical precision into a straightforward and compelling presentation. When you read the transcript of a trial - any trial - she had prosecuted, you were immediately impressed; when you sat in a courtroom and listened to her, you remembered that half the force of an argument comes from the person who speaks the words you only later read about. Samantha Ferguson was dull, lifeless, without, it seemed, emotion of any kind; her only obvious quality a stern implacability that might make you fear her but could never make you like her. Tall, five foot eight or five foot nine, she had long arms and the large, grasping hands you might see on a sharecropper's daughter. Her eyes were large, dark, and sullen; her voice harsh and unforgiving. She called the first witness for the prosecution with her usual cheerless enthusiasm.

"Would you please state your full name for the record?" she instructed. She stood at the end of the jury box, directly in front of the witness stand.

"Edward Alan Kendricks."

"How are you employed?"

"I'm a police officer with the San Francisco police department."

"Were you called to the scene of a possible shooting at the San Francisco yacht harbor last New Year's Eve?"

Kendricks was in his mid-thirties, with close cropped hair and an off-center nose that made his left eye look larger than the right. Well over six feet tall, his waist, wrapped tight by the thick black belt of his uniform, seemed ready to burst,.

"New Year's Day, a little after two-thirty in the morning."

"What did you find when you got there?"

"The victim, Allison Friedrich, was laying dead in the bedroom of the sailboat she and her husband owned. She had been shot, twice, once in her head, once in the heart."

"And was the defendant also on the boat as well?"

"Yes, he was there. He said he had been asleep on the sofa in the living room. That is the first room you come into," he explained, talking to the jury, "when you go on board and go below deck. He said he woke up when he heard the noise, and that someone then rushed past him. It was dark, and he could not see his face, but that whoever it was still had the gun in his hand."

"What was the condition of the defendant when you arrived?" asked Ferguson, as she began to move around the front of

12

the courtroom in long, looping strides.

"Condition?"

"It was two-thirty in the morning. He told you he had been asleep. His wife had just been murdered. Was he in a state of shock? Was he sobbing, was he angry; what, if any, emotion did he show?"

Hendricks closed one eye and left the other half open as he remembered what he had seen. He tried to be careful.

"Not in a state of shock. He was not sobbing, he did not seem angry. Dazed," he said, brightening at the discovery of the right word. "Dazed, but I couldn't tell you the exact cause: whether it was because of the death of his wife, or because, as he told us - my partner and me - he had had a lot to drink and had been sleeping it off. He said that was the reason he had been sleeping where he was, instead of in the bedroom with his wife."

"What else did he tell you, officer Kendricks?" asked Ferguson, still walking back and forth. "What else did the defendant say about why he was not sleeping in the bedroom?"

"He said they had been at a party that night - New Year's Eve - at the Fairmont Hotel and that his wife had left early, and that when he got back to the boat, where they had decided to spend a day or so sailing around the bay, she had already gone to bed, and he did not want to wake her."

Stopping at the far corner of the second counsel table, Ferguson fixed the witness with an intense and relentless gaze.

"He told you that there was an intruder, and that the intruder had murdered his wife?"

"Yes, that's what he said."

"Did you find any evidence to support that claim?" she asked, taking a step forward and managing to make that single step seem important. "Was there any evidence that someone had broken in: anything left behind, anything at all?"

'No, nothing."

One more step, matching, as it seemed, a new link in a chain she was about to hang around the defendant's neck.

"Did you find the gun, the weapon used to murder Allison Friedrich?"

"No, we did not."

"How far would the defendant have had to go to get rid of it by throwing it into the bay?"

I was on my feet, shouting an objection. The question assumed that the defendant had a gun. The prosecution had not introduced any evidence to prove that he did.

Walker Nyland had been on the bench for less than a year, but thought himself too intelligent to be taught anything by experience. He batted my objection away like he might have done a fly.

"I said I object!" I insisted vehemently, refusing to take my seat before I had an answer.

"The prosecutor knows what she is doing."

"That's it? That's your ruling? - The prosecutor knows what she is doing? Thank you, your Honor. It's always good to know in advance that an appellate court will have at least one reversible error!"

"Do you want me to hold you in contempt, Mr. Antonelli?" he fairly shouted, bristling at my unexpected defiance.

"No, your Honor. I want you to hold me in at least the minimal respect with which a trial court judge is supposed to treat any lawyer who raises a legitimate objection to a question that, under the law of evidence, is never supposed to be allowed."

Nyland was short and slight of build, with graying hair and small, insolent eyes. He spoke with admirable efficiency, brief and to the point, when he talked with jurors or when he talked about the law; he spoke forever when he spoke about himself. I said something I should never have said, and did not regret for a moment that I had said it.

"If your Honor is so eager to join the prosecution, it should be easy to find another chair at Ms. Ferguson's table."

His eyes went wild. He picked up his gavel, ready to hammer me and my objection to perdition, but then, with the gavel raised high above his head, he caught himself. There were too many people in the courtroom, too much coverage of the trial. He set the gavel down on the bench with a smile, as if he had only meant to get my attention.

"Your objection is noted, Mr. Antonelli. Ms. Ferguson, perhaps you could rephrase your question."

"Yes, your Honor; I"ll be glad to," she replied, as solemn, as grim-faced, as before. "Officer Kendricks, given the size and configuration of the sailboat, about how long would it take someone who was inside to get up on deck and dispose of a gun, or anything else, by throwing it into the bay?"

"Maybe thirty seconds, if that long."

"Thank you. Your witness," she said, looking for the first time, and that only briefly, at me.

"What time did you receive the call telling you that there was a report of a possible shooting?" I asked, as I slowly rose from my chair.

"A little after two-thirty, New Year's Day morning," replied Kendricks. He was leaning forward on his heavy arms, looking at me with those two unbalanced eyes of his.

"That is what you said on direct, but I wonder if you could be more specific. What was the exact time you received the call from dispatch? I see you have your notebook with you. Perhaps its recorded in there."

He opened it and found the page he needed. He scratched the side of his face, took a long, deep breath and looked up.

"Two forty-two."

"And you arrived there at what time, exactly?"

He again consulted his notebook.

"Two fifty-three."

"Eleven minutes. You testified, in answer to the prosecution's question, that it would have taken 'maybe thirty seconds, not more than that,' for someone on board the boat - it is called, by the way, 'Bay Wind' - to go up on deck and throw the murder weapon into the bay. Do I remember that right?"

"Yes, that's right."

"Then let me ask you a question the prosecution did not ask: How far could someone go in the eleven minutes it took you to get there if they had a car parked right there, next to the Bay Wind, the way the defendant, Justin Friedrich had? Far enough that you wouldn't have known he had been there? Eleven minutes, Officer Kendricks, at 2:42 in the morning with nothing but empty streets and empty highways. What would you estimate: five miles, six, even ten in the kind of fast sports car Justin Friedrich drives?"

"I don't exactly know; but, yes, far enough we wouldn't have seen him."

"But he was there, wasn't he? - Waiting for you, waiting for someone to come to help. He did not leave because - isn't it perfectly obvious? - he did not have anything to run away from."

That at least gave the jury, and everyone else, something to think about. I looked at the jury, treating them with the serious respect they deserved, letting them know that they needed to ask themselves the same question I had just asked: Why would someone who had just murdered his wife never think of leaving?

Samantha Ferguson asked only one question on re-direct.

"When I asked you to describe the condition, the demeanor, of the defendant when you arrived, what was the one word you used?"

"Dazed."

One word, and the jurors, who had been leaning forward, intensely interested in the suggestion that the fact Friedrich had not left might be proof that he had not murdered his wife, sat back in their chairs, freed from having to think too far into things. None

16

of them had committed murder, but 'dazed' might be exactly the state they would be in if they had ever done so. Justin Friedrich was not some hired assassin, some cold-blooded killer; he was not on trial for murdering a stranger, he was on trial for murdering his wife. Everyone could understand how that could happen: an act of passion, not something he had planned far in advance. Precisely because he was not a hardened criminal, a professional killer, his failure to leave the scene of the crime could now be construed not as proof of his innocence, but of his guilt. Samantha Ferguson had reason to be pleased with herself, as she announced she was through with Office Kendricks.

For the next several days, the prosecution put on the witnesses needed to establish that Allison Friedrich had died from two bullets fired from a .38 revolver. The technical details of death and ballistics, the angles of entry, the position of the body, the photographs taken at the scene, passed from one juror to the next, all the dismal requirements of the prosecution's case for homicide, were handled with thorough competence. There was very little for me to do, except sit there all day and try to appear confident that nothing about the violent death of Allison Friedrich had any bearing on the ultimate outcome of the case. Sitting next to me, in the chair closest to the jury box, her husband seemed astonished he was even there. He followed the testimony of each witness with the same eager curiosity with which he would have observed the trial of someone he did not know.

Finally, the prosecution was finished with all the technical details and at the beginning of the second week moved to the question of motivation. Allison Friedrich had been murdered, murdered, according to the prosecution, by her husband. But why he had he done it on that particular night instead of some other time? Justin Friedrich and his wife had been married a little more than two years. He could have killed her any time he wanted in the relatively short history of their marriage. The opportunity, as the prosecution and the police always like to talk about, was always there, every day, every night, they were together. It had not happened. Why now? What happened that led Justin Friedrich to decide that the woman with whom he had lived for two years should now die?

The first witness called by the prosecution when we started again Monday morning provided part of the answer.

Chapter Two

"Were you having an affair with Allison Friedrich?" asked Samantha Ferguson.

"I'm not sure I would put it quite like that," replied Anthony Bulwer.

In his early forties, Bulwer was soft-spoken, polite, a man who moved easily in the crowd, so long as it was a crowd at a reception or some other elegant, expensive event. He did not seem entirely comfortable in front of a mainly middle-class jury and the staring eyes of several hundred strangers in the audience.

"How would you put it?" asked Samantha Ferguson, a little irritated at his attempted correction.

" Allison and I had known each other for years. We were good friends."

Ferguson had just begun one of her long reaching strides. She stopped abruptly and with a warning glance asked with impatience, "You weren't having an affair with Allison Friedrich? Which is it, Mr. Bulwer? We don't have all day."

"Yes," he admitted, reluctantly but without embarrassment. "If you want to make it that kind of simple choice."

Had he not been her witness, if she were cross-examining a witness for the defense, Samantha Ferguson would have been apoplectic at his failure to give a direct answer to a direct question. But he was her witness, and all she could do was try to burn a hole through him with as piercing a stare as I had ever seen.

"We'll try this again. You're a witness, Mr. Bulwer, a witness for the prosecution, a witness in a murder trial. You are -"

"Objection!" I cried, jumping to my feet. "The prosecution gets to ask questions, not tell the witness how to answer them."

Whenever Walker Nyland was stymied, which was often, he pulled back his upper lip, exposing his front teeth, as he sucked in air, like a mouse showing disdain for the mousetrap he has just robbed of bait.

"Well, I don't think she is really doing that; but, yes, all right - Perhaps, Ms. Ferguson, you might rephrase your question."

"I'll try, your Honor; but as I hadn't asked a question, I am not quite sure how to go about rephrasing it," she said, drily. She turned back to the witness.

"Were you sleeping with the victim, Allison Friedrich?"

"Yes, once in a while, but -"

"You were sleeping with her. Did her husband find out about this?"

I was back on my feet, but Ferguson, catching her error, changed the question.

"Did Allison Friedrich tell you that her husband knew?"

"Yes, he knew. But," he added quickly, as if it made a difference, "she said it was all right, that they had an understanding."

Anthony Bulwer was not a willing witness. He resented this intrusion into his own private life. He had probably been less than forthcoming when, as part of her trial preparation, Ferguson interviewed him. He would have volunteered nothing beyond what he had to tell her in response to what she asked. This was the first she had heard anything about an understanding. Her surprise banished caution.

"Understanding? What kind of understanding?"

Bulwer did not like the patronizing way she was treating him. He returned her condescension with some of his own.

"An understanding that she could lead her life anyway she wanted, and he could do the same thing. They were married to each other, but monogamy wasn't part of the bargain. They both understood that; they both wanted that. So, yes, counselor, I slept with Allison. As I say, we had been good friends for a very long time."

She stared at him for a moment through half closed eyes, and then moved to another line of questioning.

"Did you attend a New Year's Eve party at the Fairmont Hotel?"

"Yes, I did," replied Bulwer, as he reached down to pick lint from his pants.

"Would you tell the jury what happened that night?"

Bulwer threw back his head and laughed.

"I had a lot to drink, and had a really good time!"

Samantha Ferguson had enough.

"Permission to treat the witness as hostile, your Honor?" She did not wait for Nyland's fumbled response before she bore in. "You were at the Fairmont Hotel on New Year's Eve - correct?"

"Yes, that's correct."

"There were several hundred people there - in the Venetian Room - correct?"

"That would be my guess."

"You had a lot to drink. Isn't that what you just said?"

"Yes, I drank a lot that night. It was New -"

"And you weren't alone in that, were you?"

Bulwer blinked twice. He was not sure how to answer.

"A lot of people were drinking, drinking champagne, including the defendant, Justin Friedrich - isn't that true?"

"He probably had more to drink than I did. That's true. He was quite drunk by the time that he and I -"

"'He and I.' Yes. You got into an argument with each other, a heated argument, didn't you?"

"An argument, yes," he replied, reluctantly.

Ferguson had remained in the same place, in front of her

counsel table, and in the same position, staring hard at the witness. She now took a step forward, and with her hands behind her back, allowed herself a brief smile. The witness could relax. They were no longer enemies.

"Would you please tell the jury, Mr. Bulwer, what happened between you and the defendant at the Fairmont Hotel on New Year's Eve."

No one, it is safe to assume, had ever subjected Anthony Bulwer to anything like what, at the practiced hands of Samantha Ferguson, he had just endured. Now that it was over, he acted like someone who has just walked out of the dentist's office: too grateful it was over to resent the pain.

"It was a few minutes before midnight, everyone who wasn't sitting at their table drinking champagne was on the dance floor. I was dancing with Allison. Justin - I'm not sure if he was still at the table or if he was dancing with someone else - but the orchestra stopped playing and everyone started the countdown to midnight and the new year. When the bell started ringing and it was midnight and the old year was finished, everyone on the dance floor kissed whomever they were with. I kissed Allison. That's when it happened. Justin grabbed my shoulder and pulled me away, and then he grabbed Allison by the arm and started dragging her across the dance floor back to their table. He was calling her every name in the book, and she was screaming right back at him. Everything seemed to be happening in slow motion, the two of them fighting with each other, everyone watching and wondering what was going to happen next."

"And what did happen next?" asked Ferguson in a calm, understated voice, her eyes full of fabricated encouragement.

"When they got to the table, Allison twisted free and shoved him away from her. He was off balance and it was enough to throw him backward into the chairs. She shouted that she was leaving, that so far as she was concerned he could get himself a room in the hotel."

It was my turn, but instead of rising from my chair, I spoke for a moment to Justin Friedrich, a short, whispered conversation with my hand on his shoulder that had as its only purpose the impression of my confidence in him. I wanted the jury to believe that I would not come in such close contact with someone I thought guilty. Everything has an effect.

"You testified, Mr. Bulwer, that you and Allison Friedrich were old friends. You didn't tell us how old. How long had you known her? Some years before she was married, isn't that right?"

"She was probably still in high school when we first met."

"But you weren't in high school then. You were - what? - ten years older."

"I knew her family. And yes, I'm nine or ten years older."

"How old was she when you first started sleeping with her? I assume she was not still in high school?" I asked, in as pleasant a voice as I could.

There was a moment's hesitation. He did not want to answer, and I understood why. That was enough, that slight hesitation, to tell the truth he did not want to admit. I let him think I was doing him a favor by not asking again.

"All I really want to know, Mr. Bulwer, is did this affair begin before, or after, Allison Friedrich married her husband?"

"Before."

"And it continued, did it not? It never stopped - correct?"

"Yes, but as I tried to explain before, we weren't together all that often. Only once in a while. We were more friends than lovers, if I can put it like that."

"You weren't just friends with her, though, were you? You were also friends, quite good friends, with her husband, the defendant, Justin Friedrich."

"Yes, we were very good friends."

With my arms crossed over my chest, I stared down at the

23

floor, and then, lifting my head, fixed him with a stare of utter disbelief.

"Very good friends, but still sleeping with his wife? Very good friends, such good friends that, as you testified earlier, he knew, and did not mind, that you were sleeping with her. That must have been convenient!"

"Objection!" exclaimed Ferguson. "If Mr. Antonelli wants to comment on what the witness testifies, he can do that in his closing argument."

Walker Nyland's mouth began to twitch. He shook his head as if he disagreed, and then with a wave of his hand seemed to dismiss his own decision.

"Ask a question, Mr. Antonelli," he said, finally and with evident relief.

"It's your testimony that the defendant knew all about your affair with his wife, but that he did not care because they had an understanding. Is that correct?"

"Yes, that's right," he replied, shifting uneasily in the witness chair.

"But despite that, you had to ask if he knew. Isn't that a little odd? On the one hand, they have this 'understanding,' each of them free to do whatever they want: sleep with you, sleep with someone else. And yet, somehow, after all these years in which you were carrying on this 'once in a while' affair, she never mentioned this, never told you there was nothing to worry about, that her husband, your friend, your 'very good' friend, really did not mind, until, years after it started, you decided for some reason to ask if he knew?"

"I know it must sound strange, but it did not seem strange at the time. Just because there was this understanding between them, it did not mean it was the kind of thing you go around talking about."

"You mean that despite their 'understanding,' there were

24

things they did not want to know?"

"Yes, that would be right."

"Things they wouldn't want other people to know about, things they would not want to become so flagrant it might cause the kind of rumors that lead to scandal?"

"Yes, exactly."

"Which would explain," I insisted, my eyes cold and determined, "why Justin Friedrich became as angry as he did when he saw you kissing his wife in front of a few hundred of your other wealthy, entitled friends! Why he might have become so angry that he hauled her off the dance floor, so angry that he stayed behind and let her go back to the Bay Wind alone. But she did not go there alone, did she, Mr. Bulwer? She went there with you!"

Bulwer almost came out of his chair.

"How did you know about...?"

I did not know; but given their history, given what had been going on between them that night at the New Year's Eve party, it was not hard to guess what happened.

"But you didn't make it there, did you? You didn't know how much time you had before Justin decided he had had enough to drink and wanted to come back, how much time you had before he decided he should try to make things right with his wife. You drove her from the hotel to the yacht club, and you stayed there, in your car, and then, when you were finished - But you didn't finish, did you? Because you wanted her to leave with you, that night, leave her husband, not just for that night, but forever, leave her husband and live with you - isn't that right, Mr. Bulwer?"

"No, I never -"

"No more questions. I'm finished with this witness," I announced, shaking my head in contempt for what I had heard. Then I changed my mind. "There is one other question. You weren't the only one she was sleeping with, were you? She had other lovers, didn't she?"

"As I say, they had an understanding...."

Friedrich was not happy with what I had done, and when I visited him that night in jail he let me know it.

"You made her sound like a tramp, a whore who slept with anyone who happened to come along."

I did not really care what he thought. I was trying to save his life. I was not concerned with his sensibilities, and I certainly was not concerned with his dead wife's reputation. I was tired, exhausted, by the uphill battle to win a case that seemed all but unwinnable.

"She was sleeping with your good friend, Antony Bulwer; sleeping with him before your marriage, during your marriage, sleeping with him whenever the two of them happened to be in the mood, and you don't like what I'm doing? You'd rather I not cast doubt on your murdered wife's virtue? I'm afraid you have rather missed the point of that little exercise in cross-examination you witnessed today in court. The best, and maybe the only, hope you have is if everyone thinks she slept with every guy in San Francisco. Good God, I hope they think she was a tramp, a whore! Because if she was, and if you knew it, knew it and for some reason really did not mind, then maybe, just maybe, they might believe you could never have been jealous enough to murder her!"

"I didn't murder her!"

He said this the way he always said it, as if a simple declarative sentence was all the proof anyone would need to know he was innocent. Though he had no religious beliefs of any kind, though the mystery of existence vanished in his refusal, or rather inability, to even recognize the question, he reminded me of one of those honorable medieval knights who, believing in all the everlasting torments of hell, never doubted that a lie, the breaking of their solemn oath to tell the truth, would take them there without any possibility of reprieve. He was innocent. That was the simple truth. Hs word ought to be sufficient, or, rather, enough to convince

26

the world that the evidence, when all of it was finally discovered, would prove it.

"The gun. If we found the gun, that would prove I didn't do it, wouldn't it? I've never owned a gun, I've never fired a gun. I've never even held one in my hands. The gun - someone had to buy it. There has to be a record of that, doesn't there? It would prove, whoever bought it, that it wasn't me!"

Unless of course the gun was stolen, or sold under the counter. There were thousands, millions of them, in circulation. The chance that there was a record of the sale - if the gun were ever found - that would show who purchased it and when, was about as likely as the real killer rushing into court to save an innocent man with his confession. It could happen, but no one was going to stay up nights waiting.

"We have to forget the gun. It will never be found," I told him with complete assurance. "You didn't kill your wife, remember? Someone else did, and they took the gun with them, probably got rid of it somewhere miles away, if they got rid of it. We can't find the gun and, worse yet, we have no idea who the real killer is. There is a question hanging over this trial, a question we can't run away from. The killer killed her, but he didn't kill you. It makes your story seem incredible, something you made up at the last minute, after you came to your senses, after you came out of that 'daze' the police say you were in. Why would someone murder your wife and not murder you? There is only one reason I can think of, but we've been over this before and…."

"I can't think of anyone who would have wanted to murder Allison and make it look like I did it. You don't think whoever he was came to rob us, went into the bedroom…? Maybe in the dark he did not notice I was there; maybe in the dark he didn't think anyone was there. Allison wakes up, he panics, shoots her, then runs away, so scared he doesn't see me when he leaves."

There were bigger boats, yachts the size of houses, that

seemed a more likely target for a robbery than the sailboat where Justin and his wife were spending the night. It was not a robbery. That much I was certain of. Which meant someone had gone there to murder Allison, and either had not expected Justin to be there, or had wanted him to be there. Justin had arrived almost two hours later than his wife. Had the intruder been there the whole time, waiting until he came? Had he followed Justin from the hotel? And why? What reason had anyone to do this?

"The prosecution is going to put on witnesses to testify that you were as guilty of infidelity as your wife ever was. Ferguson is nothing if not thorough. She's going to hammer away on the theme that your marriage was nothing but a farce, that money was all that held it together, that you hated your wife and that she hated you, that you finally reached a breaking point, that you had been drinking all night, were in a rage about what she had been doing with Bulwer at the New Year's Eve party, that all you could think about was how to get rid of her. But intertwined with that is another possibility: that one of you became involved with someone, had an affair, and that the husband or the wife of whomever it was found out about it and decided to take their own measure of revenge: murder one of you and blame the other."

I left him to ponder what I thought a possibility as unlikely as the sudden discovery of the missing gun, and spent the rest of the night going over everything I had on the witnesses the prosecution, starting the next morning, was going to call. As I had warned Friedrich, they were all variations on the same theme, an orchestrated attack on the way he had lived his life in a world in which there was no measure to anything except what you could afford to spend.

I have never met a female undertaker, but if I ever do I imagine she will look a lot like Samantha Ferguson. I do not know if she was born with that mournful expression in which her mouth turned down at the corners and her lifeless eyes seemed darker the deeper you looked into them, or whether the years of seeking justice for homicide victims had given her such a close sympathy with death, but there were times when she rose from the counsel table to begin her examination of a witness when I could almost hear the dirt fall from her hands and shoulders as she climbed out of her grave. Perhaps it was none of this, but only my own sense of impending failure that made death, and everything about it, so vivid.

"The prosecution calls Alex Lindsay."

Agile for his size, which was considerable, Lindsay stepped up to the witness chair. Balding, with a short trimmed beard that covered a double chin, he nodded to himself as he surveyed the watching crowd. He glanced at Friedrich, gave him a serious smile, and then, ready for whatever he was asked to do, turned to Ferguson. She asked him a series of questions that established that he had been acquainted with the defendant and the defendant's wife. He had known them both from before their marriage.

"Were you surprised when they married?"

"Surprised? Yes, I suppose I was," replied Lindsay, in a gravel throated voice. "Justin, I thought, was in love with someone else. And Allison - well, I'm not sure she was ever in love with anyone."

"Not in love with Justin Friedrich when she married him?"

"I don't know; I can't really answer that."

"After their marriage, did they seem happy?"

Lindsay seemed to think the question almost juvenile. He did not think she was serious; worse, he thought it funny.

"Aren't marriage and happiness a contradiction in terms?"

There is a scene in an old movie, one I saw as a kid, a scene I never forgot. The House of Usher with Vincent Price, in which a woman, buried alive in a coffin locked up in chains, breaks free. I expected that now.

"Do you know where you are, Mr. Lindsay?" asked Samantha Ferguson in a voice like cold steel. "Do you think you are back at your country club where some of your rich empty-headed friends laugh at something as pathetic as that? You're in a court of law, Mr. Lindsay; a witness - if not a very intelligent one - in a murder trial. No one cares who you are, and certainly no one cares who you think you are," she went on, moving close to the railing on the jury box. "The only thing anyone cares about, Mr. Lindsay," she said, her voice rising and becoming more menacing with every word, "is whether you can answer truthfully the questions you're asked, or whether I have to ask the court to find you in contempt so you can spend a few days in jail thinking about whether you might actually be capable of a straight answer!"

I almost stood up to applaud. Lindsay looked shell-shocked. Ferguson walked away from the jury box and as she passed behind me I heard her mutter, 'rich bastard,' under her breath. I half suspected she said it on purpose so I would hear.

"All right, Mr. Lindsay, we'll try once more. Did they seem like a happy married couple?"

"No, I guess not."

"Would you explain to the jury what you mean?"

"It was more like an arrangement. They went places together, all the usual social events. They never missed anything. But, as far as I know, they never traveled anywhere together, anywhere they would be alone."

"Did you ever see either of them engage in an act of physical violence against the other?"

"Yes, once. It was at a wedding reception, down on the peninsula, a place in Atherton. Everyone was leaving. Justin and Allison were waiting for their car. They started arguing about something and then, suddenly, Justin hit her, hit her hard on the side of her face, knocked her to the ground. I don't think he meant it, because as soon as it happened, he was kneeling down beside her, telling her how sorry he was, that he didn't know what he was doing, that he had had too much to drink."

"Didn't know what he was doing. Had too much to drink,"

repeated Ferguson, as she looked directly at the jury. "Sounds familiar, doesn't it?"

Before I had a chance to object, she was asking the next question.

"To your knowledge, Mr. Lindsay, was the defendant, Justin Friedrich, involved with any other women during the course of his marriage?"

Lindsay bit his lip and leaned back in the witness chair, reluctant to talk about the private lives of other people.

"You are under oath, Mr. Lindsay," she reminded him, in an impatient sing-song voice. "Answer the question."

"Yes, he was often seen with other women. There was no secret about it. But whether he was having an affair with any of them, that's something I wouldn't know."

Alex Lindsay was only the first in a long line of witnesses called to prove that Justin Friedrich did not love his wife. After nearly a week of this, the answers had become as tedious as the questions.

"I should have thought, your Honor," I began, rising to object to what had been an endless assault on the defendant's character, "that even Ms. Ferguson, whom I know is an able prosecutor, might have thought that implicit in a charge of murder is at least the possibility that the defendant did not like her very much. Yes, I know, " I went on, before Ferguson could object to my objection, "you want to show everyone that the defendant must have killed her because he did not like her. If that is your theory of human behavior," I added, as I smiled knowingly at the jury, "I'll make sure to lock my doors tonight on the chance that you might decide to act on your own, all too evident, feeling."

"That's enough!" declared Judge Nyland, leaning forward on his arms, determined, as it seemed, to prove he could, at least on occasion, be decisive. "Mr. Antonelli - Do you have an objection, a serious objection, you wish to make?"

"Yes, your Honor. The testimony of this witness is redundant, repetitive, and goes over the same dull ground covered by the last five witnesses called by the prosecution."

"Ms. Ferguson,"he said, pleased with his new-found confidence; "I tend to agree. Do you think you might move things along?"

And so it went, day after day, until, finally, at half past three on a Friday afternoon, the prosecution was through with its case. Nyland adjourned the trial until Monday morning. I had the weekend to figure out a defense. After the jury had left, after the spectators had gone, I spent a few minutes with Justin Friedrich, and then, promising I would see him tomorrow, I walked out of the courthouse into a mob of reporters.

Chapter Three

I had just come out the door, wondering how I was going to navigate my way through the dozens of reporters who, while they were shouting questions at Samantha Ferguson, were, some of them, already moving toward me, when someone put his hand on my arm and pulled me back. It was not done with force, there was nothing abrupt or rude about it; it was more the kind of gentle restraint with which a well-meaning friend might guide you away from an obstacle you had not noticed.

"Might I have a word?" asked a stranger.

I knew immediately that I had never seen him before; he was not someone you would ever forget. A blind man would have known it; his voice was that distinctive: cultured, sophisticated, and with a distance about it that was remarkable. It carried, that voice of his, a feeling, a sense of independence, but independence of a very unusual kind. It was not arrogance; it was far more than that: the unquestioned assumption of a capacity that was not measured by any comparative standard. His sense of himself, if I can put it like this, was not relative, it was absolute. The understated elegance with which he dressed - dark gray suit and dark gray tie - only enhanced the effect. Each movement - the way he gestured with his hands, the way he held his head at just the slightest angle when he looked at you - suggested the habitual efficiency of a man who, because he always knew what he was doing, was never in a hurry. There are some people you see every day and, if suddenly asked to describe them, you cannot remember anything about

33

them. This stranger, whoever he was, had within three seconds created an indelible portrait in my mind.

"What can I do for you?" I replied as, before I knew it, we were shaking hands.

"I know you must be terribly busy. I won't take any of your time. But I wonder if I might make an appointment? I'm afraid I may be in some trouble. I may need a lawyer."

"You've been here, watching the trial?" I fumbled in my pocket for a card.

"Yes, every day. It's extremely interesting. Though I imagine from your perspective it is extremely difficult."

I was not sure what he meant.

"Difficult?" I asked, as I handed him my business card.

"Difficult, if your client is really innocent. The case against him seems pretty solid." He smiled apologetically. "I'm sorry; I shouldn't have said that. I don't know anything about what happens in a trial. That is the reason I've been coming. I thought I should try to learn something about what I might myself be facing. The other reason is to see if everything I had been told about you was true."

He glanced at my card, told me he would call my office, and then, without another word, turned and walked away. It was only then that I realized I had not gotten his name.

I waved away the questions of the reporters and jumped into a cab. It had become part of a settled routine, a cab ride from the courthouse to Fisherman's Wharf where I caught the ferry across the bay to Sausalito where I now lived with the woman who in a moment of inspiration I had asked to divorce her husband and marry me. She had a name that, even had you never heard of the once famous song she was named after, you could never forget: Tangerine. And if the name caught your attention, her face stopped traffic. Literally. I had seen it happen often enough. Green light, red light, no light at all, and if she was standing on the sidewalk

34

waiting to cross the street, you could only hope there would not be an accident, one car running into the back of another, as everyone tried to get a better look. There was no end to the comparisons that kept getting made. It became a kind of game to decide which famous movie star she most closely resembled, the one constant the conclusion that there really was no comparison at all. Every day when I got off the ferry, she was there to meet me. Except today, when she was waiting for me at Fisherman's Wharf.

"The ferry was just pulling out," she explained in the soft, breathless voice that made me forget everything but her. "So I got on board so you wouldn't have to make the trip alone."

It was late in the afternoon on a late winter day, but the sun was out and there was not much wind. She was wearing a yellow silk scarf around her head, dark glasses and a blue wool jacket with the collar turned up. Holding my hand, she passed unnoticed in the crowd as we moved through the ferry to the outside deck in back. We sat on a bench and watched the city fall back in the distance as the ferry plowed long white furrows in the gray waters of the bay.

"I just met someone," I remarked. Sitting next to me, Tangerine wrapped both hands around my arm. "He came up to me outside the courthouse when I was leaving."

"Who was he?"

"I have no idea. He said he thought he might need a lawyer and wondered if he could make an appointment. I gave him a card."

She looked at me, knowing there was more to it than that.

"It was not what he said, it was him. Everything about him. His voice, the way he spoke, the way he held himself, the way he moved. If you were at a dinner, or a cocktail party, and you did not know anyone, he is the one you would remember."

"And he needs a lawyer?" she asked, lowering her dark glasses just far enough to tease me with her eyes.

"Apparently I've been auditioning for the part. He told me

he had been watching the trial, that he had been there every day."

"Why do you think he needs a lawyer? Do you think he murdered someone?"

She was still teasing. She could read my reaction, what I had felt in that brief meeting with the stranger who wanted to see me. Murder would have been the last thing I would have thought, and she knew it.

"If I had to guess, he doesn't want me to represent him for anything he is accused of doing. It's more like some government investigation into whatever business he is in. And if that's the case, I probably can't help him. I don't handle white collar cases."

"That's where the money is," she laughed.

"Who needs money?"

"Everyone. Except you and me."

The wind kicked up, and the cool air snapped across our faces, and we did not mind at all. Tangerine huddled closer as we watched the city skyline draw away until it seemed to break loose and float free, an island in the water. High above the Golden Gate Bridge, glowing in the orange light of the late day sun, a thick bank of fog seemed to grow taller and taller, a dark gray wall climbing straight up to the blue dark sky.

We left the ferry in Sausalito and with seagulls chirping at our feet got into Tangerine's car and drove through the narrow, winding streets to the chocolate shingle-sided home, high on the hillside with a view across the bay to San Francisco where everyone is a dreamer and dreams never die.

"Do you want to talk about the trial?" asked Tangerine, after we had finished dinner and were having a glass of wine.

"It's a disaster. There's nothing more to say."

"It isn't a disaster. There's a lot more to say. You haven't started yet. Monday? Yes?"

It was not thinking about what I was going to do Monday when I had to call my first witness. I was thinking about how little

36

was really under my control, the limitations that, before this trial, I had always managed to ignore. I looked at Tangerine and, throwing up my hands, started to laugh. Then, as the laughter died away, I got up from the sofa and walked over to the sliding glass doors that opened onto the back deck and, shining in the distance, the city lights of San Francisco.

"I hate to lose. Do you know why? It isn't vanity, it isn't because winning somehow sets you apart," I remarked, staring out across the bay. "I'm not a fool. I know that winning, especially cases I was supposed to lose, made my reputation. It's the reason people come to me for help, the reason I've become well-known: Joseph Antonelli, the lawyer who never loses. It's all nonsense. Some of the best lawyers I ever knew, great ones I watched when I was just starting out, before I had any idea about everything that was involved, did some of their best work in cases they lost. There is a limit to what you can do: you can't make up evidence; you can't made evidence disappear. All you can do is take the evidence, whatever the evidence is, and use it to tell the best story you can, the story that puts your client, the defendant in a criminal case, in the best light possible. You can't save a guilty man from what he did; if he's guilty all you can do is try to show there is still some doubt that the evidence against him is good enough to prove it. When you get right down to it, its a little like saying, 'We all know he's guilty, we all know he did it, but it doesn't matter: the only thing that matters is that the prosecution can't prove it!"

I turned from the window to Tangerine's waiting gaze.

"That's all I do: defend the guilty on the argument that it is the only way to make sure the innocent go free. There is a line I've used in so many trials I can't remember the number. It's a famous line from Blackstone."

"Blackstone?" she asked, mocking her own forgivable ignorance with a gentle smile.

"William Blackstone, Commentary on the Laws of England, in four fat volumes, the first of which was published in 1776. Every lawyer used to read it; Blackstone was Lincoln's legal education. No one remembers that anymore; no one remembers Blackstone. Take it even farther if you like: no one remembers the 18th century."

"The line - Blackstone's line?" taunted Tangerine. "What was it?"

"I don't remember," I deadpanned. "It goes like this: 'It is better, under our system of justice, that ten guilty men go free than that one innocent man be found guilty.' Well, damn it," I remarked, with a quick grimace, "I've got the eleventh man. Justin Friedrich is innocent and he is almost certain to be convicted. Where is the justice in that?"

"The trial isn't over," she reminded me again.

"That's what I told Friedrich today, just before I left. It's interesting what has happened to him - tragic, really - the deterioration, the way he has changed. People who live privileged lives don't always think they're privileged. Why would they? It's what they have always known. He assumed - he had never had any reason to think otherwise - that crime, that murder, only happened to other people. Sure, you could have told him that people were sometimes convicted for things they had not done, and he would probably have agreed. But he would have been thinking of people without money, without education, poor and unfortunate; he would not have been thinking about anyone in the circles in which he moved. If someone like that were falsely accused of something, the lawyer - the expensive lawyer they could afford - would sort it all out. And now, suddenly, after all this time in jail, after seeing for himself how the court system really works, after listening to witness after witness, some of them friends of his, people he has known his whole life, talk about him as if the fact he is on trial for the murder of his wife fits perfectly with what they know about his marriage and his character, he has come face to face with the realization that there is every chance he is going to spend the rest of his life, not on the golf course with his friends, not playing tennis, not out sailing on the bay, but in a prison cell in San Quentin. It may not seem so on the surface, he looked pretty much the same way he did when I first met him, but inside he's aged twenty years or more. The boyish innocence is gone; he has become cynical, jaded, and as angry at the world as anyone I've seen."

Tangerine came up to me, put her arm around my neck and kissed me on the cheek.

"The trial isn't over, Antonelli. Something will happen, something will change. Isn't that what you told me - in every trial something happens no one expected, something that changes everything?"

She was trying to make me feel better, and she did, but not about the trial and what I knew was going to happen, about her, the knowledge that whatever happened, whether I won or lost, nothing would change between us. In a world in which everything seemed to have become provisional, in which not just the old standards, but any standards, had disappeared, in which everything was measured by success and success measured by money, if I could count on nothing else, I could count on her.

"Whatever happens in the trial," she whispered to me later that night, as she switched off the lamp in the bedroom, "I'll still be with you - unless, of course, you lose."

"I knew the first time I saw you, that night at Albert Craven's place, that it would last forever."

"The night I waited outside in my car, hoping you would run away with me; the night you thanked me for the one block ride and drove home by yourself."

"If you keep going," I reminded her, as I pulled her close, "you'll get to the first night we spent together, when you told me you would always be faithful, 'at least for a week,'

"And then, right after that, I told you, Joseph Antonelli,

39

that, if you wanted, each week would be renewable."

The weekend slipped by. We went for long walks in the afternoon and in the evenings had long, quiet, candlelit dinners. I tried not to think about the trial, but it was always there, just below the surface, questions I could not answer tugging at me like impatient children who think that if you only stop to listen you will understand what they are trying to tell you. Sunday night I felt like a child myself, a child who hated school. I did not want to wake up. I did not want to go to court.

It was cold and wet, a morning for umbrellas and overcoats and quick sure-footed steps on the slick steep sidewalks that ran down the city's hills. I got out of the cab in front of the courthouse and made my way inside. Friedrich was just being brought into the courtroom. Dressed in a suit and tie, he did not look like a prisoner, but neither did he look like someone who was free to come and go. His glance was furtive, running one way then the other as if he were on his guard, afraid someone might suddenly attack him from the side. When I talked to him, quickly reminding him what we had covered when I visited him in jail two days earlier, on Saturday morning, he had to make an effort to keep his eyes on me. And even with that effort, it did not work. When the door at the back opened and the crowd of spectators and reporters rushed in, he jumped at the sudden noise.

"It's all right," I told him. "There is nothing to worry about. Remember what we talked about. Look at me when I ask you a question, look at the jury when you answer. Don't worry," I went on, bending closer and looking him straight in the eye. "It's all right if you forget, if you look at me instead of them. You're going to tell the truth. A jury can tell when you're doing that. That's all you have to remember: tell the truth, whether I'm asking the questions or the prosecutor is. If you don't know the answer, just say so. You'll be a little nervous at first. Don't worry about it. Everyone is nervous." I paused for a moment before I smiled and added with more confidence than I felt, "You have a great advantage over people who don't tell the truth: you can't get caught in a lie."

The prosecutor was at her table, the judge took his place on the bench, the bailiff brought in the jury, and I had now to begin the case for the defense. I stood up, ready to call my first witness, when I noticed that the court reporter was wearing open toed shoes and, kicking one of them off, had left it laying on the floor.

"You might want to put your shoe back on," I remarked in a voice quiet enough that the court clerk might be the only one to hear it. "This is a murder trial, not a day at the movies."

It startled her. She threw me an angry glance, but quickly, before anyone could notice, slipped her bare foot into her shoe.

"Mr. Antonelli?" asked Nyland, wondering why I had not called a witness yet.

"The defense calls the defendant, Justin Friedrich," I announced, in a voice that echoed off the walls.

I began with the only question that mattered and which, by itself, meant nothing at all.

"Did you murder your wife?"

Justin remembered. He turned to the jury. He did not hesitate, but neither did he rush to answer the way the guilty often do to disguise their duplicity.

"I didn't kill Allison," he replied in a strong, clear voice. "It's true, what some of the prosecution's witnesses said - I'm afraid we did not always like each other very much. But murder her? No, that would have been impossible. We never even discussed divorce."

With my hands shoved deep in my pockets and my shoulders hunched forward, I stood in front of him, near the end of the jury box, and asked him to tell the jury in his own words what had happened that night. I did not stop with that, however. I wanted right from the beginning to shift ground, to get out in front of the jury, not what they had heard from the prosecution, but what really happened.

"Tell the jury what happened, the night your wife, Allison, was murdered, shot to death by an intruder who came onto your sailboat in the middle of the night."

Samantha Ferguson was screaming an objection before the last words were out of my mouth.

"There is no evidence of any intruder! The defense attorney isn't asking questions, he's testifying, he's -!"

Nyland ignored her, and with a quick sideways motion of his head made her stop.

"The witness may answer," he ruled. Satisfied with his own performance, he nodded twice for emphasis and then sank back in his chair.

"We sometimes spent the night on our sailboat. As you have heard - as you could see from the photographs Ms. Ferguson showed you - there was plenty of room. It's berthed at the Marina - the San Francisco Yacht Harbor. You heard testimony that Allison and I quarreled . That's right, we did. We did that quite a lot, and that night, New Year's Eve, we were at a party, a large party, at the Fairmont. There was a lot of drinking. I did a lot of drinking, and I didn't behave well. Allison was dancing with just about every man there, and I didn't like it very much. As I say, I had been drinking, quite a lot, and finally I just couldn't take it anymore. I went out on the dance floor, grabbed her by the arm and pulled her away, just the way you heard. She started calling me all sorts of names, which only made me more determined. When we got back to the table, I told her if she was going to dance with everyone in the place she should start selling tickets. She grabbed a drink from the table and threw it in my face, and then she pushed me, pushed me as hard as she could and I stumbled against a chair and fell down. I knew it was my fault, and I tried to apologize, but she did not want to hear it. I was upset, angry, embarrassed. I left, but I didn't go back to the boat, I stopped in the hotel bar and drank some more."

Staring at the jury with the lost look of someone who wishes more than anything that he could take it all back, do things differently than he had, he took a moment to collect himself.

"I finally got back around one-thirty in the morning. Allison was asleep. I was drunk. I could barely walk straight. I left Allison alone in the bedroom and went out to the main cabin, took off my coat, loosened my tie and must have passed out on the sofa."

"You fell asleep. When did you wake up, and why did you wake up?" I asked, as I pulled my hands out of my pockets, crossed my arms and looked at him with intense interest.

"About an hour later, around half past two. I only know that because of what happened. I heard something; I wasn't sure what it was, but it woke me up. Then I heard a second noise, and I knew what it was. I thought I must still be drunk, that it couldn't be what I thought it was - a gunshot. And then someone bolted past me. It was dark; I couldn't see. All I could see were shadows. Someone was running away, outside, off the boat. Everything was moving in a kind of haze. I got up, went back to the bedroom, and turned on the light. That's when I saw her - Allison - her head was on the pillow, blood was pouring down her face."

That was his story, his version of what had happened, the night his wife, Allison Friedrich, had been murdered. Now I had to take him back through the testimony of the prosecution's witnesses, the case, the open and shut case, of the prosecution.

"According to the prosecution's witnesses, you didn't call the police when you found your wife murdered. Someone else, someone who heard the gunfire, called them. Why didn't you?"

It was a question he had asked himself, a question to which he had never found a sufficient answer. He was honest enough to admit it.

"I don't know," he replied, still puzzled, not so much by the decision he had made, but by the absence of one. He had not decided anything; he had not thought about anything. "I didn't know anything. None of it seemed real. It was like a bad dream: you know it's a dream and you keep waiting to wake up."

There was a change of expression, a glimmer of recognition, the memory of something that he, alone of all the people sitting in the courtroom, had experienced, different than what he, and they as well, would have expected. He turned to the jury.

"We think we know what we would do in a situation like that. We think we know because we have seen it so many times, on television, in the movies: someone discovers a murder victim, laying the floor - laying on a bed - and the first thing that happens is someone starts screaming and the police are called. Unless, of course, the murderer is standing over the body, and then he doesn't make a sound, and he certainly doesn't call the police. He gets away or tries to hide the body. But it isn't like that. I just kept looking at her; I kept thinking it was all a bad dream, that any moment Allison would be wide awake and so would I. I never thought about calling the police; I never thought about anything. Then, when she didn't move, when I started to remember someone running past me, when I started to realize that it had really happened, that I had not dreamed it, hadn't imagined it, I heard the sirens. The police had come."

I stood there in the silence that followed, letting the jury think about what Justin Friedrich had said, and, of equal importance, how he had said it. I let them consider what was implicit in what he said before I asked the question that would bring it out into the open.

"You didn't call the police, and you didn't leave?"

"No, I didn't do anything. I just stayed there."

"You didn't try to run away, to escape, before the police arrived?"

"Escape? I had no reason to escape. I hadn't done anything."

There was one more issue that had to be dealt with.

"Your wife was murdered with a gun. You heard the prosecution's witnesses. She was killed with a .38. Do you own a gun of that description?"

"No, or any other gun. I've never owned a gun."

"Have you ever used one? On a gun range, or anywhere else, at any time?"

"No, never."

"No gun was found at the scene; no gun was found anywhere. The prosecution insists that after you shot your wife, you got rid of the gun by dropping it into the bay. My last question, Mr. Friedrich, is this: Did you shoot your wife and then get rid of the weapon?"

"No. I did not have a gun. I did not use a gun. I've never even fired a gun. I did not murder my wife. I did not murder Allison."

I asked questions as if I were perfectly confident not only in what the answer would be, but that every answer proved beyond even the possibility of a doubt that Justin Friedrich could never have murdered his wife or anyone else. I tried to convince myself, as I listened to Samantha Ferguson begin her cross-examination, that the jury just might possibly find Friedrich's unsupported word more compelling that all the prosecution's undisputed evidence. Ferguson did not have to convince herself of anything.

"You were alone on the boat with your wife - correct?"

"Yes," replied Friedrich, with an earnest innocence that Ferguson treated as a performer's overacting.

"You were drunk, passed out, and you heard a shot - two shots - but you still weren't sure what they were, and then someone - in the shadows, I think is how you described it - ran past you. Then you found your wife murdered, shot to death, in her bed. Is that the story you want this jury to believe?"

"It's not a story, it's the truth!"

With a long, calculated look of perfect disbelief, Ferguson

let the jury know what she thought of that.

"But you didn't call the police. You waited because - what was it? You thought it might be a bad dream? But it wasn't a bad dream, was it? The police came, and they found you there, alone with your murdered wife,. But they didn't arrive - did they? - before you had time to get rid of the gun, throw it into the bay, and then, in the drunken haze that, by your own admission, you were in, invent this bizarre and utterly unbelievable story of an intruder, the real killer, who killed your wife and for some reason did not kill you!"

"I didn't invent it! It's true!"

"Was anything taken, anything stolen?"

"No, not that I know of."

"Did your wife have any enemies, anyone - besides you - who hated her so much they would want to do her harm?"

"No, I don't think so."

Ferguson was pacing back and forth, stopping only long enough to fire the next question.

"So someone - this intruder in the shadows - comes on board your sailboat at two-thirty in the morning, not to steal anything, because he doesn't steal anything; and not because he is some kind of homicidal maniac on a killing spree, because you're right there, the first one he passes on the way in and the one he passes on his way out, and he doesn't even touch you. He only murders your wife, a woman sleeping in a closed door cabin where, unless he had gone there expressly to kill her, unless he knew the layout of the boat, unless he had tracked her movements, he would not have known was there? Tell me, Mr. Friedrich - tell the jury, tell us all - does that make any sense at all?"

There was no answer to this. All Justin Friedrich could do was repeat his denial, insist again that he had not murdered his wife. The jury wanted to believe him. I could read it in their faces, the way they watched him, hoping, as it seemed, that he would

46

find something to say that would suddenly cast everything in a new and better light. They wanted to believe him, but when he finished his testimony, they looked down at their hands, shifted position in their chairs, disappointed by his failure to explain away the prosecution's relentless recitation of the evidence against him.

Justin Friedrich was going to be convicted of murder and there was nothing I could do about it. I knew it, and so did he. I tried to tell him that the trial was not over, that there was still a chance. He looked at me with the withering contempt of someone who has just learned that his whole life has been a fraud.

Chapter Four

"The trial isn't over," insisted Albert Craven, when I came back from court.

I tossed my briefcase on my desk and with my hands on the small of my back stared out the rain streaked window. It struck me as almost funny that he had chosen the same phrase to offer encouragement that, a few days earlier, Tangerine had chosen, and that less than an hour ago I had used with Justin Friedrich. It was quintessentially American, this notion that the game is never over until the clock runs out, that it doesn't matter how far behind you are, there is always the chance that somehow, some way, you can still win.

"It is forty-eight to nothing, a minute to play. You really want to bet that the final score is forty-nine to forty-eight?"

Craven, who had followed me into my office, sat at an angle, one leg crossed over the other, one arm thrown casually across the corner of the wingback chair. He lifted a wispy eyebrow and gave me a look that was not the least bit sympathetic.

"You aren't that far behind. You'll pull it out. You told me Friedrich is innocent. Couldn't the jury see that for themselves when he testified?"

I could only shake my head. He had practiced law longer than most lawyers had been alive, he had known all the great ones, had been friends with perhaps the greatest civil lawyer in the country, Melvin Belli, and he was as innocent as Justin Friedrich in his belief that only the guilty were convicted. Albert Craven had in his long career made only two brief appearances, in a courtroom and had thrown up after each of them. He sat there without the slightest doubt that because I almost always won, I could not lose.

"Friedrich did fine, better than I was afraid he might. It's odd, really," I said, as I sat down in my chair, "but what I told him before he took the stand was true: It's easier to tell the truth than to lie. You don't have to remember all the details of an invented story. He's innocent, he didn't murder his wife. The jury believed him, or they wanted to. You could see it in the way they looked at him, the way they accepted what he was saying. They wanted to believe him, and they did, while he was telling them what happened. But then, when Ferguson - she may not be very likable, but she is as methodical as they come - went through her cross-examination everything he had said began to seem forced, contrived, a desperate attempt to explain away what could not be explained: his wife murdered by an unknown, and unseen, intruder, a dark shadow in the night, who did not murder him. They would like to believe him. He doesn't seem like the kind of person who would murder anyone. That's what they were all thinking, but then, by his own admission, he was drunk, they had a fight, she threw a drink in his face, he fell into the chairs at the table, and all in front of a couple hundred witnesses. He's drunk, he's been in a fight with her, and neither one of them are what you would call normal, decent people. They cheat on each other, sleep with other people about as often as they change clothes. Of course he killed her. No other possibility makes sense. When he first began testifying, everyone on that jury was curious, interested, sympathetic, eager to hear what he had to say; when Ferguson finished with him, the sympathy was gone. They looked like twelve judges prepared to pass sentence."

"The trial isn't over," said Craven, persisting in the belief that somehow innocence, even tainted innocence, would triumph in the end. His belief should have been contagious - hope is always the last thing to die - but I had become fatalistic.

"I have a few more witnesses to call, a few people who saw him that night, when he was drunk, when he argued with his wife. They aren't going to be able to add much. He didn't own a gun, so far as any of them knew. He did not have one on him at the New Year's Eve party. There was security; everyone had to pass through a metal detector. He's going to be convicted, Albert. He's going to spend his life in prison, and I get to spend mine wondering what I could have done to stop it from happening."

Craven got up from his chair and gave me a long, solemn look

"Something will happen," he assured me, with the generous certainty that makes the impossible seem not only conceivable but inevitable.

He had reached the door when he remembered.

"You have an appointment. He's waiting down the hall. Would you like me to bring him in?"

I did not know I had an appointment. My secretary took care of that. I glanced at my datebook and there it was, an appointment for six o'clock. I did not recognize the name.

"Thanks. Don't bother." I reached for the phone and buzzed my secretary. "I'll have Millie bring him back."

Craven let go of the door and stepped back inside.

"Who is he? He seems familiar, but I couldn't quite place him."

"I don't know. Someone who needs a lawyer." I glanced again at the name in the datebook. "Redfield. James M. Redfield."

"Redfield," he mused. "He looks more European than American, and he pays a small fortune for what he wears. He bought the suit he's wearing at Wilkes-Bashford, here in the city, or Saville Row in London. His shoes are custom made, his shirt is tailor made. Everything is understated. He doesn't dress to make an impression. But he does - make an impression, I mean."

Craven liked nothing more than to describe the small detail

by which you could define, in advance, as it were, what someone was like. He had an eye for this sort of thing, the brush strokes which, once you noticed enough of them, revealed before you saw all of it, the full portrait.

"He holds himself with close to military precision, the way the member of an old aristocratic family would have been taught from childhood to walk and sit and stand, every movement measured, everything tightly composed. When I walked past him, he watched me as if he were judging me. He doesn't move his eyes, they stayed fixed, straight forward; he moves his head. And yet, I must tell you, his eyes are perhaps the most interesting thing about him. They seem to look right through you."

Suddenly, I remembered.

"I've met him. The other day, just outside the courthouse. He asked if he could make an appointment. Apparently he has."

James M. Redfield - James Michael Redfield, as I learned he preferred - looked taller than he was. It was, as Albert Craven had suggested, the way he held himself, though it seemed to me not so much like a soldier as the statue of one, every part of him in perfect proportion with every other. It was the same thing when he moved. He walked from the door to the chair the other side of my desk, a distance of nearly thirty feet, and if he had put a ball the top of his head it would have been in exactly the same position as when he entered.

"It's good of you to see me, Mr. Antonelli," he said, after we had shaken hands and he had taken the chair. "Especially after a day like this one must have been for you."

His voice was quiet, undisturbed, the voice of someone not easily, if ever, stirred to anger. It had, as I remembered, something of the quality of a brush drawn slowly over a smooth flat surface, or, perhaps more accurately, the brush of a jazz drummer's drum, rich, vibrant, but still the background, if the essential background, of other, more important things, in this case the thought, the emotion, of what it helped express.

"Especially after a day like… Are you talking about the trial?"

"Yes, the trial. I was there again today, part of the crowd. As I told you before, I wanted to watch the trial; I wanted to watch you. Let me explain," he went on, sitting with his legs crossed. He held an attache case in his lap. "I may be in some difficulty; I may require the services of an attorney. I try never to do anything without adequate preparation. From everything I was able to learn, you're the most qualified attorney I could hope to find. I haven't spoken to anyone else; I hope I won't have to. I have watched you in this trial, defending Justin Friedrich, and I am as certain as I know you must be that he is going to be convicted."

That was exactly what I thought, but it did not mean that I liked hearing it from him, someone, a spectator, who, so far as I knew, did not know anything about the law.

"Are you a lawyer, Mr. Redfield? I asked, coldly.

"No, of course not. I'm sorry, Mr. Antonelli; perhaps I should not have said what I did. Given everything I have heard about you, I wouldn't be surprised if you somehow manage at the last minute to find a way to win after all. I wouldn't be surprised at all. It's just that today, watching his testimony, listening to what the prosecution did on cross-examination, it just seemed to an outsider like me that the odds are not very good."

He was right about that as well, and there was no reason not to acknowledge it.

"It's a difficult case. But you didn't come to see me about the Friedrich trial. You have, as you put it, some difficulty of your own?"

"I didn't quite say that. I said that I may be in some difficulty. It isn't yet certain that I will be. But I don't think it advisable to wait until it is - Do you?"

He asked this with genuine interest, but, more than that, as if the question were one of general application and not specifically about his own situation, whatever that situation might turn out to be. There was a scholarly detachment about the question, an objective aspect to his inquiry. He might have been a reporter, an extremely intelligent and well-educated one, asking about the kind of advice a criminal defense lawyer normally gives a prospective client.

"If you think there is a real, a serious, chance that you might be in trouble, then, yes, it's generally a good idea to retain counsel."

I closed my eyes and bit my lip to stop myself from laughing. I sounded like one of those pompous slogan spouting lawyers who give legal advice on television.

"The real question, Mr. Redfield, is have you broken the law, have you committed a crime? If you haven't, why waste your money?"

He seemed to think this almost ironic, and, once again, he was right.

"Justin Friedrich certainly needed a lawyer."

I was tempted to tell him that it had not done Justin Friedrich any real good. Instead, I reminded him of something.

"He was arrested and charged with murder. You haven't been arrested, you haven't been charged with anything, have you?"

"No, but, as I say, I may be in some difficulty, and for that reason I should think it only makes sense to be prepared."

"What is it you think you may be in difficulty about?"

He did not seem like someone who could be led by his emotions; he never would have done something on impulse. If I had to guess, I probably would have said, what I mentioned to Tangerine after that brief meeting on the courthouse steps, some sort of intricate financial scheme that had unraveled.

"You'll have to forgive my ignorance, Mr. Antonelli, but before I can get into that, before I can discuss any of this with any kind of specificity, I need to make sure of a couple of things. Would you tell me if I am correct in the belief that there is something called the attorney-client privilege, and that it means that nothing I tell you can ever be revealed?"

"That's correct. Whatever you tell me, I have to keep secret. I can never tell anyone, anyone at all, unless you were to authorize me to do so. The privilege belongs to you, the client - it doesn't belong to me, the lawyer. You also need to know what the privilege doesn't cover. It doesn't cover anything you might tell me about the future. If a client tells his lawyer that he is going to commit a crime tomorrow, or right after he leaves his office, or at any time in the future, that is not privileged. Not only can the lawyer reveal what he has been told, he has an obligation to do so. If you tell your lawyer you're going to go kill the mayor tomorrow at city hall, the lawyer better call the police. Does this answer your question?"

"Yes, thank you. I have only one more. Does the privilege exist only after a lawyer agrees to represent a client?"

"It starts immediately, the first conversation someone has with a lawyer about the possibility of the lawyer taking the case."

"The privilege covers our conversation, the one we're having now?"

"Yes, of course."

"So I can confess all my crimes?" he remarked, with an agreeable smile. "If I had any to confess."

He had come to see me because he thought he might be in trouble, and he had, if you took at face value what he said, spent a considerable amount of time investigating whether I was the one he should ask to represent him in whatever trouble he might be in. There had been others who had tried to find out what they could about me before they asked if I would help. This was different. Whatever difficulty he thought he might be in, he did not seem to be especially worried about it. It felt more like a conversation I might have with another attorney, one like Albert Craven who had never practiced criminal law or tried a case in court, a conversation about the various procedural requirements that a criminal defense lawyer had to be careful never to violate. I began to wonder if he was worried at all, whether there really was some difficulty he might have to face; I began to wonder whether he had come to see me just because he thought it might be interesting to see what a criminal defense lawyer was really like.

"What do you do, Mr. Redfield? Do you live here, in the city?" I asked.

I pulled out from a desk drawer a new legal pad and jotted down his name. I thought this might get his attention and force him to tell me whether he wanted to proceed.

"No, I don't live in the city; I live down on the peninsula, near Woodside. What do I do? - You mean, how I make a living? I own a company, a high-tech company. We produce very high end electronics used to increase the volume and speed of various kinds of communications. We do very well: billions in sales every year, with a growth rate three, and sometimes even four or five times, the rate of most of our competitors. Strictly between us, Mr. Antonelli, I am at least partly responsible for the fact that a great and growing part of our population, not just in America, but especially in America, can no longer talk with intelligible coherence."

Astonished, I could not help but laugh.

"So far as I know, Mr. Redfield, while no doubt a serious problem, what you have just described is not a crime."

"No, but perhaps it should be. Kill one person, they call it murder and either kill you in turn or send you to prison for the rest of your life. Destroy the language, and therewith the ability to think, of an entire generation - and who knows how many generations into the future - and they call you a genius, the savior of the planet, give you the Presidential Medal of Freedom, if not the Nobel Prize, and think it only fair that you have more money than

God!"

"You could always give it away," I said, with a shrug. It seemed a simple enough solution to what few others thought a problem.

"I have," he replied, with a shrug of his own. "Most of it; not all of it. I still have too much. The house in Woodside: the cost of that alone would probably feed a thousand families for fifty years. It is utterly obscene, as unforgivable as it now seems to be inevitable. Everyone now thinks of everything as a means to the only serious question: how to make things faster because speed of movement has become the only way to become rich. Matter in motion, Mr. Antonelli - it is the only thing we still understand. There is an old line, written in the 18th century, I think; but it is even more applicable today: 'People used to talk about virtue and morals, now we only talk about business and money.' I've decided to do something about that, Mr. Antonelli. I give some of my money to those in need, and....Well, the other thing, there will be time to talk about that later, if you agree to represent me."

It was this strange dichotomy, what many would regard as the contradiction, between how he had lived his life, what he had achieved, the enormous wealth he apparently had, and his disdain for those who had acquired something similar, the way he spoke about what he called the obscenity of an arrangement that gave everything to a few and next to nothing to everyone else, that most intrigued me. I did not know what he had done, or if he had done anything at all, but if he had committed a crime, it seemed certain to be far more interesting than most of those whose commission had caused me to defend someone before.

We talked for quite a while, nearly an hour, and then, as he was getting ready to leave, he went back to what he had said at the beginning, that remark about what I must be feeling after what had happened in court.

"The prosecutor, that woman, Ferguson: Her cross-examination would have been difficult for anyone to overcome, wouldn't it? It all comes down to the gun, doesn't it? The fact it was never found. If Friedrich is telling the truth, the intruder, the killer, would have taken it with him. Thrown it away, sometime later perhaps, but never would have left it at the scene. And if the prosecution is right, if Friedrich did it, he of course would have thrown it in the bay just like she said."

"If the gun had been found, we might have been able to trace it back to the owner," I mused. "We might have been able to show that it did not belong to Friedrich, that he had never had it. The gun might have been all we needed. It might have saved Justin Friedrich from...."

Redfield was watching me with unusual interest. I had the feeling I was missing something, that watching the trial he had seen something I had not noticed.

"What? What is it you think I might have done; what is it you think I could still do?"

"Nothing. I'm not a lawyer; I don't know the first thing about how you - how anyone - tries a case. No, I was just reacting to what you were saying: how one piece of evidence can change everything, turn what seems guilt into innocence. It is the specific detail that has always fascinated me, the way sometimes just the slightest change can make the biggest difference. I don't know why that should surprise me. If you aim at something a long way away - launching a rocket, shooting an arrow, or going for a walk in the forest - a mistake at the beginning, just a few inches, and you miss by miles. The beginning is everything, don't you think, Mr. Antonelli? Know that, know what happens at the start, you usually know how things will turn out in the end."

He had kept an attache case in his lap the whole time we talked. It was locked, which seemed to suggest an usual degree of caution or the presence of something valuable inside.

"I want to leave a check for your retainer," he remarked, as he turned the tumblers on the two locks on the case.

I thought he was reaching for his checkbook, ready to discuss my fee. Instead, he pulled out a blank envelope and handed it to me. I was not sure whether to open it or wait until I was alone. He caught my hesitation and decided for me.

"I think you'll find it adequate," he said, as he reached again inside the leather case. He handed me a gift wrapped package. "This is something I wanted you to have. I'm not a lawyer, Mr. Antonelli, but watching the trial I thought you might find it useful."

Clients paid me for my services. That was business, an agreed upon price for what I did. It was always an arm's length transaction, as impersonal as I could make it. I was willing to be someone's lawyer; I was not willing to be their friend. The distinction was not only important, it was essential: I had to be able to act with complete independence, without regard to how they might feel about the decisions I made.

"Thank you, that's very kind. But I really can't. It's not...."

"Yes, I know: it isn't done," he said, as he got up to leave. "But you may find that you will want to make an exception this time."

He left the package on my desk, told me he would be in touch, and then turned and left.

First a retainer that we had not discussed, then a gift he thought I would not want to refuse. I did not know what to make of it. Just as I started to reach for the package, Albert Craven burst in, as excited as I had seen him.

"Redfield! Why didn't I think of it? Do you know who that was?" he asked, shaking his head in wonder.

"One of the more interesting clients I've ever had, from what I know so far. Why? You look like some star struck teenager who has just seen someone famous."

"Famous?" he laughed. I thought he was going to sit down,

but he began instead to parade up and down the room. He could not stop shaking his head. "Famous, yes; but not the way of other famous people. No one knows him, no one has ever seen him; there aren't any photographs. There are, but they're all out of date, taken when he was barely out of college. James Michael Redfield! And he was here! I walked right past him," he remarked, baffled apparently by his failure to have somehow realized that the famous James Michael Redfield was sitting just outside his office. "No one has ever seen him. Did I just say that? Tell me something," said Craven, stopping at the bookcases that lined the long wall opposite the windows that looked out at the bridge and the bay. "Did he look around the room, was he drawn to these, did he spend any time examining this old library of yours?"

It seemed an odd question, but then he was always interested in the kind of detail that other people too often missed. There was something, but it was not what Craven had assumed. I had not thought of it until he asked about the books on the shelves, books of history and philosophy and literature, part of the library I had inherited, years before, from a wise and learned judge who taught me the great difference between the demands of justice and the requirements of the law.

"Leopold Rifkin's library," I head myself say. "Not mine. I have it on loan, so to speak. But, no," I said, "Redfield did not look around the room; he did not look at anything. The entire time he sat in that chair and his eyes never left me. But I would not doubt for a minute that when he left he could have described everything in here, including what is on those shelves. Not the titles - he was too far away for that - but that there were more than law books, that there were leather bound books, single volumes, multi-volume sets, and in several different colors. I would not be surprised if he could tell you that there are four Persian rugs and what part of Persia each of them came from. You had the feeling that he could take everything in at a glance. The strange thing is that until you asked about it, I had not noticed. I did not notice anything while we were talking except what he was saying and how he was saying it. But why did you ask about the library?"

He came across to the chair and put his hand on top of it. He was extremely serious and seemed in doubt.

"They say he has read everything, that there isn't anything of importance ever written he has not studied, studied and understood. But like everything else said about him, there isn't any way to know how much, if any, of it is true. What did he tell you? Yes, I know, you can't tell me anything that is confidential…. He wants you to represent him? That means he must have done something…. But never mind that, what did he tell you he did, where he lives?"

I could not understand why any of this could be so mysterious. He ran a high-tech company on the Peninsula. There were hundreds of them.

"He has an electronics company which apparently does very well. He lives near Woodside. It did not sound like any of this was any great secret."

Craven stood behind the chair, resting his arms on top of it. He was not so much astonished, as amused.

"Everything about James Michael Redfield is a secret. Howard Hughes was a publicity hound compared to him. He leads such a reclusive existence it has never been entirely certain that he actually exists, that he isn't a made-up legend. I wasn't kidding. No one has ever seen him; you're the first, as far as I know, to have talked to him."

"He said he had been in court every day, watching the trial."

"Completely anonymous, part of the crowd. I didn't mean it quite literally when I said no one had seen him; no one who sees him knows who he is."

"And just who is he? There must be some reason why he seems to be the subject of so much discussion."

Craven stepped around the chair and sat down. He was not sure where to start.

"There are stories, strange stories, the kind that precisely because they are so incredible make you think they must be true. Redfield runs a company, as he told you, an enormously successful company in terms of the money it makes. A lot of people became rich buying stock when the company was first publicly traded. Even that was done - the public offering - in a way that had not been done very often, if at all, before. He kept fifty-one percent and put only forty-nine percent on sale. His control is absolute. But the financial part - sales numbers, profit margins, the corporate structure - what everyone concerns themselves with, doesn't tell you anything about Redfield and whatever it is he is doing: The company isn't really a company at all; it's more like his own private country."

"Private country? What do you mean?"

"Rumors. Some of them stranger than anything you have ever heard. What isn't rumor is that, like some of the bigger, and best known, technology giants, Redfield's company does not have a bunch of office buildings. It has them, of course, but they are part of what everyone now likes to call a campus. I'm not sure who started this, but it undoubtedly was an attempt to emphasize that this was just like college: a place of research and learning in which everyone, teacher and student both, make a contribution. Redfield, according to the rumor, has taken the idea farther, much farther, than that. Everyone who works there is enrolled for five years, just as if you were there to get both an undergraduate degree and a one year master's program. This is where it gets interesting. It is like going away to college, far away. You don't leave; you live there. The campus is on a thousand acres, up in the hills behind Woodside, the other side of Skyline Road. It's gated. Only one way in or out. They are not college students, of course. Most of them have graduate degrees before they start. Most of them, probably all of them, were offered top dollar to go to work for Google, or Apple, or Microsoft, or one of the other places where young men and women go expecting eventually to make millions. They make more with Redfield, but, and this is what makes everyone wonder, if the rumor is true, what Redfield is really all about: everyone who works there is paid exactly the same salary. Communism for capitalists, you might say. You are rich the day you start, but you'll never be richer than anyone else who works there. Five years, then you're finished, and another class enters. There must be a reason for this, but all anyone can do is guess. But five years! Five years in which you never leave."

"Never? Not at all? Weekends, holidays, summer vacation?" I asked, more intrigued than ever.

"If you leave, you can't come back. And even then, you can't talk about what goes on there. Every employee signs a non-disclosure agreement. That hasn't stopped the rumors. Some of them must have talked. There are stories that Redfield only comes out at night, that after everyone works all day, doing whatever research and development goes on there, after everyone has had dinner - they take all their meals together - Redfield lectures, for hours at a time, and that he does this completely in the dark. No one sees him; they only hear his voice."

"What does he lecture about?"

Craven pursed his lips and stared down at his hands, for a moment lost in thought. I remembered what Redfield had told me: that his company helped increase the speed of communications and how that helped destroy the language and the possibility of coherent thought, and I remembered thinking that there was some deeper meaning in what he said.

"How to change the world," said Craven, looking up at me with a puzzled expression. "Or so the rumor says, because, again, no one knows for sure."

"Except those who have spent five years listening to all

those lectures in the dark. Don't you think it a little strange that no one has ever left the place, angry, disgruntled, or just changed their mind about being there; left and gone public, gone on the record, about what goes on there?"

Craven's eyebrows shot up. A smile moved quickly across his mouth.

"You tell me. You just spent an hour with him. Would someone break their word with him?"

I was not sure. All I knew for certain was that Redfield was now a client, and that, as he had first been careful to understand, I could never tell anyone anything he chose to tell me.

"You and I keep secret what people tell us. We don't have a choice. The privilege is absolute. If you sign a non-disclosure agreement, listen to what everyone around you thinks is something that can never be repeated to an outsider - maybe."

"But that can't be why he needs a lawyer: to enforce some non-disclosure agreement," observed Craven, with a shrewd narrowing of his eye, as he pushed himself with both hands up from the chair. "Are you going to represent him?"

"I suppose I am. He hasn't been charged with anything, and if he has done anything he didn't tell me about it. But he left a retainer - and that," I said, pointing to the gift wrapped package on the front corner of the desk.

"It looks like a box of candy," said Craven, with a smile. "Take it home and give it to Tangerine."

I picked it up, weighing it in my hand. He was right: it could have been a box of candy, though it seemed rather unlikely.

"Why don't you open it and find out?" asked Craven. "Unless you think it might be a bomb."

For some reason, it struck me as funny.

"That would be one way to cover the check," I remarked, as I began to unwrap it.

"Is that what I think it is?" cried Craven, as his hands flew to his face and he took a step forward to get a closer look at the cover of the cardboard box.

Slowly, carefully, with the strange sense as of a tragedy foretold, I lifted the lid of the box. There it was, a .38 revolver and, more importantly as it would turn out, a sales receipt. I read it first to myself and then out loud.

"It was purchased," I explained to an astonished and bewildered Albert Craven, "at a Palo Alto gun store at nine o'clock on New Year's Eve."

James Michael Redfield had not given me a gun for self-protection; he had given me the gun used to murder Allison Friedrich, the gun that her husband, Justin Friedrich, who had been getting drunk at Fairmont Hotel on New Year's Eve, could not possibly have purchased.

Chapter Five

It was all about winning. Ballistics tests proved that the gun Redfield had given me was the one used to murder Allison Friedrich. The receipt proved that it had been sold while Justin Friedrich was at the Fairmont Hotel where, three hours later, he fought with his wife in front of hundreds of witnesses; where a dozen people, including the bartender, were willing to testify that they had seen him drinking in the hotel bar until almost two o'clock in the morning. The clerk of the gun store in Palo Alto swore that he had not seen Justin Friedrich that night or at any other time; the store surveillance camera showed someone in a hooded sweatshirt entering, and leaving, at the time the gun was sold. You could not see his face, but he was younger and had a completely different build than Justin Friedrich. Samantha Ferguson, however, would not hear of it when I suggested that she drop the case and dismiss the charges. It was, she insisted, a matter for the jury to decide.

There was nothing for it but to introduce the gun and receipt into evidence, call the ballistics expert to the stand, and then the gun store clerk to verify the time and place of the sale. Three witnesses seemed to me sufficient to prove, what the prosecution's own witnesses had said, that the midnight kiss between Allison Friedrich and Anthony Bulwer had started a minor riot. The bartender's testimony was enough to show that the defendant had not left the hotel until between 1:30 and 2 a.m. and was not sober when he did. Samantha Ferguson was not impressed, or so she claimed in her closing argument to the jury.

"The sudden, last minute discovery of the murder weapon, the kind of thing you might expect in a movie: the sudden, dramatic scene in which the defense lawyer finds the gun just before he calls his last witness, however convenient it might be, changes nothing. The only thing we know now we did not know before is that someone other than the defendant purchased the gun. That certainly does not prove that the defendant did not use it. The gun was purchased more than four hours before Justin Friedrich left the hotel. Someone bought it for him and waited outside the hotel, or waited in the parking lot near where the Friedrich's kept their sailboat. Or, perhaps, - and each of these alternatives is possible - left it by pre-arrangement on board the boat where Justin Friedrich would know where to find it. What we know is what we have always known: Justin Friedrich hated his wife; Justin Friedrich had been humiliated by her in front of a few hundred of his wealthy friends; Justin Friedrich had been drinking, and he kept drinking, and when he could not drink anymore he went to where he knew she would be sleeping and murdered her in cold blood."

I let the jury know, or rather I let them believe, that I took exception to the prosecution's implied suggestion that there was something not quite right about the sudden production of the murder weapon. There was a certain irony in the fact that, though I knew the defendant was innocent, I was now compelled to conceal at least part of the truth. I told the jury that, "it was left at my office," and let them assume, the only thing they could assume, that it had been left by someone I had not seen and did not know. Then I tore Ferguson's argument apart.

"Despite what the prosecution wants you to believe, the gun proves, and proves beyond even the possibility of a doubt, that Justin Friedrich is innocent, that he did not murder his wife. He did not buy the gun. Someone else - the real killer - bought the gun while Justin Friedrich was at a New Year's Eve party he did not leave until nearly two o'clock in the morning. The prosecution tells you that he still must have done it. You're told that whoever bought the gun must have given it to him. The prosecution does not know how, or when, this was done - only that it must have happened this way. He got it when he left the hotel; he got it when he got back to the boat. It was waiting for him in his car; it was waiting for him on the boat, concealed in a place where only he could find it. Somehow, we don't know how, and we certainly don't know by whom - We don't know this, by the way, because once they arrested Justin Friedrich because he was there, on the boat, waiting for the police to arrive, no one, not the police, not the prosecution, ever thought to investigate what might really have happened, who might actually have been the killer - somehow, the defendant gets the gun ."

Pausing, I looked at each juror one by one. With a knowing smile, I took the last, decisive step: proof there was only one verdict possible.

"Somehow, the prosecution tells you, the defendant got the gun. What did he do with it?"

Walking across to the clerk's table, I picked up the cellophane bag in which the gun was held as an exhibit.

"All through the trial, what did the prosecution keep telling you? - That the defendant murdered his wife and then threw the gun into the bay. Ms. Ferguson was very clear about it. She made a point of asking the police officer - Officer Kendricks - how long it would take to get from inside the cabin up to the deck, how long to throw the gun away. Remember the answer? - Not more than thirty seconds! This is the gun, the one the prosecution insisted had been thrown into the bay. How then did it get here? Did someone go diving for it? And if they did, how, after it had been in the mud and saltwater of the bay, did they ever manage to make it look as brand new as the weapon that we now know was used to murder Allison Friedrich? Justin Friedrich did not murder his wife. And this gun proves it."

The jury was out for less than thirty minutes. Justin Friedrich was a free man. The murder of his wife now, suddenly, a crime that had not been solved.

The mystery was not what everyone thought it was. The question was not who murdered Allison Friedrich. James Michael Redfield had killed her, or had someone do it for him. If that is what happened, it was no ordinary murder for hire. Redfield had made sure that the murder weapon, the gun, would not be thrown away, and that it would be kept somewhere where it could not be found. He had done the same thing with the time stamped receipt, a receipt which contained the time and place where the gun had been purchased. The meaning was clear: Killing Allison Friedrich was only part of the plan. He wanted her husband to be blamed, blamed and then exonerated. This was the only possible conclusion. It had not been some sudden sense of remorse; he had not become conscience stricken at what he had done. He knew what he was doing from the very beginning. It was all part of his plan, whatever that plan might really be. He had kept the gun, he had kept the receipt. He wanted Justin Friedrich to be blamed, to undergo all the humiliation, all the tribulations, of a trial, a trial in which he would face the seeming certainty of conviction; a trial in which, Redfield knew from the beginning, he would provide at the last minute the evidence needed to make sure Friedrich was acquitted.

What possible reason could he have had for doing this? Why did he want Allison Friedrich dead? Why did he want her husband to suffer through a trial in which there would seem to everyone, including especially Justin Friedrich himself, no possible way to avoid a lifetime in prison? It was inexplicable, diabolical; nothing about it made sense. The questions followed me whatever I did and wherever I went. I could not escape it. What did James Michael Redfield really want?"

If Redfield had not murdered Allison Friedrich, he had arranged it. This was not the first time I had someone else's guilt on my conscience. I carried with me a lifetime worth of other people's secrets, my memory a catalogue of violence - murders, rapes, and thefts - crimes that had gone unreported, crimes that had never been solved, all of them things I had learned from the men and women I had represented in the past; confessions made with the full knowledge that they could never be repeated, that whatever they told me, however bestial, however shameful, was protected by a privilege that was more sacrosanct than anything they ever had with their priest. Confess to your priest, you are required to do penance; confess to your lawyer, the lawyer is required to help you avoid paying any penalty at all.

This was different. Redfield was different, not just from any client I had had before, but from anyone I had met. He had not confessed to anything; he had not asked me to represent him for a specific crime he had committed, something he thought might soon lead to his arrest; he had not talked about any criminal act at all. Now, when I looked back on it, I realized that the only serious discussion we had was about the question of privilege. He wanted to make sure I could never reveal to anyone anything that passed between us. He wanted to make sure that I would become the silent accomplice in whatever he chose to tell me about anything that had happened in the past. What else had he wanted to make sure of?- That he could use me to get the gun into evidence at the last minute, stopped by the privilege from telling who gave it to me?

"It's been a week since the Friedrich trial," Tangerine reminded me. "If this is how you celebrate victory," she laughed, "I don't think I'd like to see you after a defeat."

I had been lost in thought, staring out the window of the restaurant where we were having dinner. Her voice, as magical as the moonlight on the bay outside, made me forget everything but her.

"I'm sorry. It's just that, whatever this was, it was not a victory."

"You won. Justin Friedrich was acquitted. You proved his innocence. You didn't save someone who was guilty; you saved someone who was innocent, someone you thought was almost certain to be convicted. Remember? How is that not a victory?"

It was eight o'clock on a Saturday evening. We were having dinner at the Spinnaker, a restaurant in Sausalito we often came to because, built on pilings over the water, it had a three sided view of the bay and, looking west, San Francisco, a shiny bright harlequin dancing in the night. Waiters were bustling from table to table serving seafood and whatever anyone wanted to drink. There was noise and laughter all around. Outside on the bay, just a few yards from where we sat, a forty foot sailboat, its sails lowered, motored slowly past, one of the last to come in. Tangerine reached under the table for my hand.

"You won; you saved an innocent man. Why have you been so upset?"

I picked at my Crab Louie, then put down my fork and smiled.

"If we were married, I might be able to tell you," I laughed, quietly.

Bewildered, all she could do was shrug her shoulder and with an impish grin dare me to explain.

"The privilege," I told her.

"The privilege? What privilege...? Oh, I see: how privileged I would be married to you!"

My index finger in front of my mouth, I studied her the way I would anyone who had told such an obvious, incredible, world record lie. Except it was not a lie. For reasons that only made sense to her, reasons which were not reasons at all, Tangerine was actually in love with me. That did not mean she would miss the chance to accuse me of arrogance.

"It would be a privilege, an honor, the greatest prize I could ever hope to win; it would be...," she went on, her eyes sparkling with the sheer fun of it. She bent closer. "It would be the next best thing to what we do every night in bed together."

I ignored her.

"The privilege. The lawyer-client privilege, the husband-wife privilege; the privilege that stops me talking about what someone - a client...a wife - tells me in confidence."

She had not gone to law school; she did not need to: she was anything but dull-minded. She grasped immediately what it meant, and what it did not mean.

"But even if we were married, you could not tell me what a client told you."

"That's true; but if I did it anyway the privilege - the husband-wife privilege - would prevent you from telling anyone that I violated the lawyer-client privilege."

"What you're really telling me is that someone - a client - told you something you can't tell anyone else, and that it has something to do with the Friedrich case. It must be something about the gun. I'm right, aren't I? You know where it came from, who had it, but that means, doesn't it, that you know who did it? But you can't tell, because...?"

She suddenly stopped and looked up. Someone was standing behind me. I turned and looked around.

"I hope I'm not intruding. But I saw you sitting here and I just wanted to come over and say hello," said James Michael Redfield. He put his hand on my shoulder. "And you must be Tangerine. It's true, what they say," he remarked, with a polite, respectful smile. "You are the most beautiful woman I've ever seen." The smile changed. He seemed to scold himself for a breach of etiquette. "Perhaps I shouldn't have said it quite that way. My excuse is that, in this instance, the truth is too obvious to permit disguise."

Tangerine had seen the way my eyes had gone cold the moment I saw who was standing behind me. She acknowledged Redfield's compliment with a brief, cautious smile.

"I don't want to intrude," he repeated; "but, as I say, when I saw you sitting over here…."

He was waiting for me to make the first move. I had recovered from my initial surprise and wondered what he would say in front of someone else, without the privilege to protect him. I did not believe this was nothing more than a chance meeting.

"This is James Redfield," I said, introducing him to Tangerine. "He lives down near Woodside and runs a very successful high tech company. Do you often come to Sausalito?" I asked, as, at my gesture, he sat down at the table.

"Not as often as I would like." He was sitting across from Tangerine; I was sitting between them.

"But you decided to come up this evening?"

"Yes. Strange we should be having dinner in the same restaurant. But then, chance rules almost everything, don't you think?"

"Like what happened at the Friedrich trial," I remarked, casually, as if I were only giving evidence of my agreement.

"The gun," he said, quick to see my point. "Yes, of course - you're right. I don't think anyone expected anything like that to happen."

Turning to Tangerine, I explained that Mr. Redfield - I insisted on calling him that, insisted on maintaining a formal distance - had been a frequent spectator at the trial. I did not need to tell her more than that.

"Do you often watch trials, Mr. Redfield? - Or only when Joseph Antonelli is the attorney for the defense?"

"That was the only one. And yes, in answer to your question: I watched that one because of Mr. Antonelli. I had heard he was very good; there are some who think he is quite simply the best there is - I now include myself in that category. I'm not a lawyer, of course, and so I wouldn't know about everything that is involved, but watching, the way I did, day after day, it was just remarkable what he did: ask a question, then, whatever the answer, ask the next one, and the one after that, ask them for hours, never lose track of where he is going, never give a witness the chance to stop and think whether what he is saying now is consistent with everything he has said before. It seemed to me - and, again, I don't know much about this kind of thing - you didn't have anything on your side." He was looking at me now in a way that seemed completely serious. There was nothing ironic, nothing to suggest the double meaning of someone with whom you share a secret. "The prosecution had everything. The case seemed open and shut. And then…."

"The gun," I interjected. I started to repeat what he had said earlier: that so many things happen by chance, when Tangerine asked a question of her own.

"You haven't told me the reason why you wanted to see a trial in which Joseph was the defense lawyer. Did you know Justin Friedrich, or his wife, Allison? Was that the reason?" she asked, as she pushed aside her dinner plate and wrapped her long, elegant fingers around the stem of her wine glass.

"No, I didn't know either of them." He paused, searching, as it seemed, for the right way to express something that had just occurred to him. "I knew them only by reputation. You couldn't open the Sunday paper without seeing their picture at some social event."

The waiter removed our dishes and I asked Redfield if he would like something to drink. He said he had to get back to his own table, where his friends were waiting. But he did not seem in any rush to go.

"Why do you think it happened?" asked Tangerine, appearing to be genuinely interested. "You were there, at the trial. If Justin Friedrich was innocent, who do you think did it instead?"

"Whoever did this," he suggested, "wanted it to end exactly the way it did. This is just my opinion, of course; but how else explain that it was only when the trial was almost over that the gun miraculously showed up? Whoever left it at your office, Mr. Antonelli, it doesn't seem likely that it was some good Samaritan who stumbled across the murder weapon with the sales receipt conveniently attached. Whoever it was, it seems obvious that he could have done the same thing, got it to the police, before the trial even started. Why did he wait, why did he want a trial? Why would anyone want someone to go on trial when he had no intention of letting that same man be convicted?'

"I'm afraid that doesn't get us any closer to an answer, Mr. Redfield," Tangerine reminded him, with a tight, enigmatic smile. She was sitting on the edge of her chair, alert, and intensely interested, though less in what he said, than in who, and what, he really was. "Who did it, who murdered Allison Friedrich?"

"And I'm afraid I couldn't answer that," he replied. "But you asked me that question because I was there, watching the trial. There were several things that struck me about it that might have some bearing on the question of why Allison Friedrich was murdered and her husband put on trial. It was early, when the prosecution witnesses were talking about the kind of marriage the Friedrich's had, how everything was about money, how it was all an arrangement, so that they could be at the very top of the social scale. Infidelity, for them, was a way of life. There was nothing admirable about anything they did, and, more than that - and I wonder, Mr. Antonelli, if you noticed this - none of the witnesses called by the prosecution, none of those who knew them, even once expressed their own disapproval. I found that enormously interesting. It proved something I have long believed: there are no standards anymore, no agreed measure of what is wrong and what is right. I'm not some backwoods moralist," he added, looking first at Tangerine, then at me. "But I have some understanding of what happens when, as someone once put it, 'everything is permitted.' Everything breaks down, everyone is left to his own devices; there is no common bond that holds at least the center together."

Redfield waved his hand, dismissing what he had said as a matter of no importance, and showing by that very gesture how important he really thought it was. It was the easy manner of a seasoned diplomat, announcing in the same breath that war between your two countries was about to be declared and that there was nothing in the world he prized more than your great and lasting friendship.

"You're suggesting someone murdered Allison Friedrich and made sure her husband was put on trial because of the way they lived?" I asked, searching his eyes to see if he was serious.

"Why not? What better way to show how corrupt things have become."

He turned to Allison, moving, the way he always did, not just his head, but his whole body. Everything about him was measured, controlled, and without obvious effort.

"Did you ever read Tolstoy's War and Peace?"

"Yes, but quite some time ago."

He was impressed, and did not try to hide it. He studied her with a new, and a different, appreciation.

"And Anna Karenina as well. But that was also quite a while ago. Why do you ask?"

"Most of us think of War and Peace as this big, sprawling novel about love and war, the great exploits of the Russian aristocracy in he days of Czarist Russia, the military genius by which Napoleon was defeated. And if we have only seen the movie," added Redfield, with deliberate understatement, "it is all about romance. But those who read it when it was first published in the 19th century had a different understanding. What those readers saw was a Russian aristocracy rotten to the core, hollow men bored with life, driven by their own shallow dreams and ambitions, the only thing important whatever ascendancy they could claim over others of their own, useless, class. They did not believe in anything worth defending. The picture Tolstoy painted proved, to those who read

War and Peace when it first came out, that Czarist Russia was a mere facade, a worm-eaten structure, that would fall at the first hard push. War and Peace, which we think a tribute to the Russian aristocracy was Czarist Russia's obituary."

"You're comparing Tolstoy's War and Peace to the murder of Allison Friedrich?" I inquired, curious what kind of connection he might try to draw.

"To the trial of Justin Friedrich, if you leave aside the obvious differences. Tolstoy wrote a novel; someone committed murder. But both the novel and the murder reveal the corruption that sooner or later will destroy a way of life. Wouldn't that explain why the trial was as important, perhaps even more important, than the murder? Without the trial the murder was nothing more than another crime. The trial tells the story, and what better way to tell it than a trial in which both the victim and the defendant are extremely rich and socially prominent? The whole country was interested."

Redfield gazed out the window at the lights of the city glowing in the distance across the dark waters of the bay. His eyes narrowed as he concentrated on the thought, the strange, insidious thought, moving through his mind.

"I'm sorry," he said, looking at Tangerine. "It doesn't make sense, does it? Why go to such extremes to prove what everyone already knows, or rather, accepts?" With a quick sideways motion of his head, he dismissed this as insufficient. "That's not right. It isn't a question of what everyone accepts. That would assume that anyone thought there was anything particularly wrong, or even out of the ordinary, about what people like the Friedrich's do when they have enough money to do whatever they happen to want at any given moment. For most people, the trial was just another form of entertainment, a reality television show, the only difference that someone had actually been killed. The question would be how to cure the corruption when corruption is everywhere, how convince an audience that there is something wrong about the corruption described in the story you are trying to tell? There is only one answer, isn't there? Whoever did this doesn't care what everyone thinks or believes; he has a different kind of audience in mind."

"A different kind of...?" asked Tangerine, fascinated, and alarmed, by what Redfield was saying.

"The careful readers, the ones who saw beneath the surface of what Tolstoy wrote, the ones young enough to still want more out of life than material comfort. The ones who -"

"Who listen to your lectures late at night?" I interjected.

I had hoped to throw him off, to make him wonder how much I knew. He looked at me as if he could not have been more pleased.

"Yes, you're exactly right. I do that occasionally; try, in my own limited way, to bring some light into the darkness."

"And you find that examples - what went on in the Friedrich trial - helps with that?"

"Examples are always helpful, especially extreme examples. That was one of the reasons," he explained to Tangerine, "I was at the trial: to see for myself the story that would be told. And, of course, the trial itself provided another example of what I was talking about earlier."

Tangerine gave me a quick, searching glance, and then looked across at Redfield.

"The trial, if you're right, was a necessary part of this dreadful, murderous scheme, because without it there was no way to show the corruption, the way these people lived their lives. But the trial did more than that, didn't it? It showed some kind of corruption of its own. That's what you mean, isn't it?"

Redfield could not have been more impressed. For a moment, he could only stare, as if she were outside all known experience.

"Yes, Mr. Redfield," I said, "she is. What you're thinking:

that no one who looks like that should be able to think like that. What you don't realize is that she has an advantage that neither you or I ever had: she did not go to college, so she doesn't have to struggle with that otherwise insurmountable barrier to the free working of intelligence. Now, why don't you finish what you were saying? What is it, what was it about the trial, that you think - or, rather, what you think the killer thinks - is another proof of all our present day corruption?"

He looked at me as if he were certain that if I only thought about it a moment I would know the answer on my own.

"You, Mr. Antonelli! You're the best example there could possibly be. I don't mean that you're corrupt. Not at all. In fact, I think you may be one of the few really honorable men I have met. It's one of the reasons you are so good at what you do. Jurors - I watched them - trust you; they admire the way you work. That is the problem. Justin Friedrich could afford you. I know you some-times take cases without a fee, but if Friedrich had not been able to afford you, if he had had some run of the mill defense attorney, or, if he had not been able to afford even that, if he had had a court appointed attorney, what chance would he have had - in a case in which there was no one to save him at the last minute? What would you call a system in which innocence and guilt, life and death, de-pend on what you can afford, if not an example, a flagrant example, of corruption?"

"And you think that whoever murdered Allison Friedrich and made sure her husband would be put on trial did all this to show not just that the Friedrich's and what they represent, but the justice system itself are, as you suggested Tolstoy was revealing about Czarist Russia, 'full of hollow men and rotten to the core'?"

"Yes, Mr. Antonelli; that is exactly what I am suggesting. There is no other explanation. But now," he said, as he got to his feet, "I've taken enough of your time. I really must get back to my friends."

I watched him make his way through the crowded restaurant, watched him walk out the door. He had not even bothered to pretend that he had not come alone. There was no one waiting for him at another table. He had no friends.

"The privilege?" exclaimed Tangerine, with a grim, knowing look.

"The privilege."

We were not in a state of shock by what had happened, more like a state of exhaustion, or at least fatigue. We did not want to move. I ordered us each another glass of wine and for a long time we sat there in silence.

"I didn't know you read War and Peace," I said, finally, if only to get us back on balance.

The solemn, thoughtful look vanished and her beautiful marvelous eyes began to dance with mischief.

"Neither that nor Anna Karenina; though I think now I might. Did you think I would tell him the truth, let him think me some illiterate, empty-headed fool?"

No one would have thought that had she never learned to read.

Chapter Six

Among the great mysteries of San Francisco one that will probably never be solved is how many times Albert Craven has been married. His most recent marriage was to a woman who, though not nearly as old as Albert, was well past middle age. It was hard not to like Isabel. She told me once that they were the perfect pair: she had made enough money in her own various, but unnumbered divorces to balance out most of what Albert had lost in his. It was difficult to quarrel with a woman as sensible as that. They seemed to fit together in other ways as well: She liked to talk, and no one had a greater talent than Albert to make you think that what you were saying was the most interesting thing he had ever heard. Though it had not yet caused any serious disruption in their otherwise seemingly well-ordered life, the one point of friction was his reluctance to change anything and her restless eagerness to change absolutely everything. They had been married less than a month when he came home to find that their house in the Marina had been painted a different color, and, a few days after that, the same thing had been done with all the rooms inside. He finally drew the line when she started suggesting that he might want to change the way he dressed.

"Thank you, Joseph," he said, when he greeted Tangerine and me at the door. "You wore a tie." He kissed Tangerine on the cheek and added, "Certain persons were trying to tell me that I would be the only one."

"Look!" cried Tangerine, as she turned around to point at

the Golden Gate Bridge glowing reddish gold in the evening sun. But she was not pointing at the bridge, she was pointing at something else. "Our house - high up on the hill. You can see it from here if you know where to look." Squeezing my hand, she turned to Craven. "It's all because of you. if you hadn't invited me to that dinner party last year, I wouldn't have met the famous criminal attorney and started acting a little criminal myself."

"Criminal?" he laughed. "What did you do that was criminal?"

"He never told you? - How I waited for him outside and tried to kidnap him He never told you how he refused to run away with me, a married woman?"

Shrugging his small, sloping shoulders, Craven turned up his palms.

"Refuse to run away with you? Why would he tell me anything about himself as absolutely stupid as that? Impossible!" he laughed, as he led us inside.

"It's a rather eclectic gathering," he remarked, as he shut the door behind us. "I'm on the board of a number of places, and so, once in a while, like tonight, I invite a few of those who head these places to dinner. I have no idea how they'll get along. That's why you're here," he said, with a sparkle in his aging eyes. "Everyone likes to talk about crime. Even better," he added, taking Tangerine by the arm, "I can now introduce them to a real criminal."

I have never been very good at meeting new people; I am perfectly awful when it comes to remembering names. Whatever instinct I may have for taking the measure of a witness, deciding on first impression, as it were, how they had to be approached, it always took much longer to get any real sense of the kind of socially prominent people with whom Albert Craven moved with such apparent ease. Perhaps it was because none of them were under oath and were free to embellish what they said in whatever manner

they thought most advantageous to themselves. When you contra-
dict a witness on the stand, it shows a talent for cross-examination;
do that with a guest in someone's home, you are marked as rude
and inconsiderate. - Unless you were one of Albert Craven's dinner guests, and then, so far as he was concerned, the evening was
ruined if you did not say exactly what you thought. Not everyone
who was invited to his home in the Marina was invited back, and
not everyone who was wanted to come. Dinner at Craven's was
always interesting; tonight it almost became a riot. It started with
a question that, if I have heard it once, I have heard it a thousand
times.

"Tell me, Mr. Antonelli: how do you justify doing what you
do?"

There were twelve us at table. Rupert Kramer, the director
of the museum of modern art, had a brusque manner and sharp,
skittish eyes. He glanced quickly at the other guests to gauge the
reaction to what he assumed would be a line of argument he could
easily win. I pretended not to understand what he meant.

"What I do? Justify? - You mean explain? I think I know
what you're asking: how can I explain what Tangerine is doing
with me, how explain what a young, beautiful woman could possibly want with...? Luck, Mr. Kramer; good luck for me, perhaps
not such good luck for her."

I was sitting across from a woman in her late forties or early fifties, Sophia Gambarini, the wife of Giuseppe Gambarini, who
was for the year guest conductor of the San Francisco symphony.
With full, voluptuous lips and enormous almond shaped eyes, she
could have been an Italian film star in the last years of a long career.
The moment they were introduced, she became attached to Tangerine who, it seemed, reminded her of herself when, at the same age,
she had probably seduced half the men in Palermo.

"Wouldn't you agree, Mrs. Gambarini?"

"Sophia, please. Yes, but only half of what you said," she

remarked, as a smile floated over her mouth. Her voice was warm and inviting, as if you were sitting right next to her and she was whispering something she wanted only you to hear. "Good luck for her as well. But then," she added, throwing a teasing glance at her husband who sat two places down from mer, "I have always had a thing for Italian men."

With her elbows resting on the table, she folded her hands together. She wore two rings on each of them.

"I was told you also were Sicilian, but the way you avoid Mr. Kramer's interesting question is more what a Florentine would do."

"A Florentine?" asked Tangerine, laughing as they exchanged a glance that made them seem like old friends or near relations, an older and a younger sister. "You mean, evasive?"

"Misdirection, of the kind Machiavelli himself would have approved."

"Except, of course, he's been caught!" cried Tangerine, happily.

"But only by us; not poor Mr. Kramer, who is still waiting for an answer. Let me ask it for him. How do you justify defending people for crimes you know they have committed? Or, to be as direct as you Americans like to be: How do you justify, how do you excuse, convincing a jury to find someone innocent when you know they are guilty?"

"I've never had to face that particular difficulty," I somehow managed to say with a straight face. "All my clients have been innocent."

With half-closed eyes and a marvelous smile of willing duplicity, Sophia Gambarini nodded.

"All your clients, and all your women?"

Tangerine laughed so hard she spilled her drink.

"All but one," she said, with a purely evil smile

"Really?" asked Sophia. "You've only known one? I

thought only my husband told lies like that."

"I've never lied," protested Giuseppe Gambarini. He looked down the table at his wife. "I've always told you the truth. You can't say someone is lying about things he can't remember - can you, Mr. Antonelli? You're the lawyer here. Perhaps you might be willing to add me to your list of always innocent men you defend."

With a glittering smile that, by itself, brightened the room, Sophia Gasperini tossed her napkin at him.

"Can't remember? Italy is full of women who do. Can't remember? This from a man," she went on, more animated, more gleeful, with each taunting word she uttered, "who thinks he can put me in my place, keep me on my toes, by quoting a line from Lorenzo d'Medici - Lorenzo the Magnificent - who ruled Florence a mere five hundred years ago, a line I cannot find in any book, a line I think he made up, his own scandalous autobiography put in the mouth of a man dead so long no one can prove Lorenzo never said it."

"The line...?" I asked, when she was smiling at her husband with such magnetic intensity I thought she had forgotten.

"The line Lorenzo the Magnificent supposedly spoke when he lay dying: 'I have known many women in my life; my only regret is that I did not know more!' Unbelievable! But every time he says it, you should see the way he gets all puffed up." She bent toward him, sitting across the table, a few places away, and wagged her finger. "Too bad you can't live your life backward: You could turn all your romantic failures into successes after all you learned from me!"

"Yes, but best of all," he replied, with a cunning grin, "is that I'm such a slow learner, it would be years before I could graduate."

The way they looked at one another in the brief silence that followed, you could almost hear the squeaking of the mattress springs.

"You wanted to know how I could justify defending someone I know is guilty?" I said, suddenly. I decided to get it over
with, give Rupert Kramer a response, though not the one he expected to hear.

"Yes; I'd like to know how you can do that."

"I've been to your museum; I've seen a number of the different exhibits. I'm not a great fan of post-impressionism. But you
won't bar me from your museum, will you?"

"No, but I don't see what that...."

"I'm no an artist, but if I were, and I had painted, or sculpt-
ed, something you wanted to acquire for the museum, would you
ask me whether I was a liberal or a conservative?"

He threw up his hands, dismissing the suggestion as too
absurd to deserve a reply.

"In the one case, you don't want to know anything except
whether I can pay the entrance fee; in the other case, you don't
want to know anything except whether I have something you want
to buy. We do the same thing. I don't decide whether someone is
guilty or innocent; that is up to a jury, after they have heard all the
evidence. I'm there to make sure that no one gets convicted without the kind of evidence the law requires."

Kramer was not convinced, which in a way was more interesting than it usually was when someone accused me of being
morally obtuse, if not criminal, myself. I had often, perhaps too
often, used the example of a physician, a surgeon, who tries to save
the life of someone shot by the police after he had murdered a half
dozen children in a schoolyard. No one accused the surgeon of
aiding and abetting a criminal. This was more interesting because
of who Rupert Kramer was.

"Correct me if I'm wrong, but modern art doesn't know
any rules. Everything, and anything, is art, in your understanding,
if someone - the artist - says it is. Am I wrong?"

If I had asked him what time it was, he would have taken a moment to think about what he wanted to say. It made everything he thought about seem important. Ask him if the sun will come up in the morning and you were likely to get something like, 'Based on everything we know, it would seem probable that....'

"I wouldn't say you were wrong, exactly," he said, after due deliberation. "Modern art is all about creativity; it is about getting people to see things, to interpret things, for themselves. A work of art, if it is any good, enables people to find their own meaning in it. It isn't what the artist believes that you should think or feel when you see it; everyone has to decide that for themselves."

"In other words, there is no law about it, no standard that distinguishes, as I once heard someone say, what is art and what is trash. You asked about what I did. I make sure that everything that happens in a courtroom, everything a witness says, every remark the prosecution makes, every piece of evidence that is introduced, complies with the rules. I suppose you could say, Mr. Kramer, if you'll forgive me for putting it like this, that there has to be a reason for everything done in a trial; and, as you just admitted, there isn't any reason at all in modern art, the only standard whatever anyone happens to like at any particular moment in time. The law can give an account of itself; modern art cannot."

"You clearly don't know anything about art, Mr. Antonelli," he sniffed. "You can't limit art by some narrow definition."

"But of course you can. In fact, you must," objected Giuseppe Gambarini. "The same thing happened to music as happened to art: the madness of the twentieth century. What Picasso and some others started in painting, Arnold Schoenberg tried to start in music with his tone deaf orchestration."

One of the other guests, Lucas Fairweather, who prided himself on his ability to do several things at once, had never stopped eating while he listened to what the others round the table were saying. Bending over his plate, he watched with bank teller eyes as the conversation moved back and forth.

"You both miss the point," he said, wiping his mouth as he sat back. "Art, music, everything is a function of time and place. The art of Rembrandt, DaVinci, the music of Bach, Beethoven, what they did reflected a particular culture, a particular place in history. You cannot understand art, or music, or anything else unless you understand history and what it means."

Gambarini raised an eyebrow. In his early sixties, he had the cheerful cynicism that comes with age and deep intelligence. The world was full of fools, none of them less forgivable than the ones who thought they knew more than others did.

"You are suggesting, then, that Mozart's music cannot be understood on its own, that you have to know when and where he was born?"

Long before Fairweather became the president of the University of California he had taught classes to undergraduates. He smiled at Gambarini the way he must have smiled at them, forgiving them the understandable ignorance he was there to correct. Gambarini's dark eyes glowed with amusement.

"You can certainly appreciate what you are hearing. I think there is no question about that. But understand it? - No, I don't think you can. You have to see the development, how it changes over time."

"And has it changed for the better, or for the worse?" asked Tangerine, with a look that, for a moment, seemed to render him speechless.

"Better? Worse?" he mumbled.

"Yes," she insisted. "This development you were talking about. Is it a good thing? Is post-modern impressionism, for example, an improvement on Rembrandt, or DaVinci; is Schoenberg.... No, let's leave him out of it. Let's bring this development up to the present day. Is heavy metal, is rap music, an improvement - is it better - than Beethoven or Mozart?"

"Those are value judgments. Everyone has to decide questions like that for themselves," he said, with the pious certainty of a lifetime of academic achievement.

"That is exactly right," agreed Rupert Kramer, anxious to throw his weight into the balance. "Everything is question of interpretation. No two people are going to see the same thing the same way.'

"Or prefer the same music, or the same art - is that what you are trying to say?" inquired Tangerine, with a brilliant smile that had him nodding his agreement before he knew what he had been asked. "Everyone decides for himself, and if more people like rap music than Mozart, that is what they should hear; and if more people like pornography than pictures Rembrandt painted, that is what the museum of modern art should hang on its walls."

"I've been to the museum," interjected Craven's wife, Isabel, who had been sitting quietly when she was not helping in the kitchen. "That's pretty much what they do."

"Art," replied Kramer, looking down his nose, "is free expression; it is what the artist creates."

"Art," said Guiseppe Gambarini, " and by that I meant all the arts, including music and poetry - literature - as well, was not thought of as creative until about five hundred years ago. The Greeks, the Romans, everyone until the beginning of modernity with the Renaissance starting the end of the 15th century, thought that art was imitation. They were called the 'imitative arts,' the attempt to copy nature, to show in various forms the essence of what something really was. Music - the only thing about which I can presume to speak with any authority - followed the ordered rules of harmony; painting and sculpture tried to portray in close detail the form, the figure, of a human being, or what with your own unassisted vision you saw in the natural world around you. When someone painted a tree, it was supposed to look like a tree; everyone who looked at it knew what it was. If no two people could agree what it was, the artists was considered a failure. Music, for its part, had to correspond to the harmony within a well-ordered soul. And harmony, I need hardly add, can never be the kind of noise whose only purpose is to inflame the disordered, not to say violent, passions of the crowd."

"Doesn't that show how much progress we have made?" argued Fairweather. "We've gotten rid of all those restrictions. We aren't bound by an pre-determined rules. We're free to experiment, to explore new ways of expression."

"Progress? Toward what?" asked Gasperini. "What we have done, what modernity is all about, is the rejection of nature, nature as having an order of its own. What does nature mean today, what has it meant since Machiavelli and Hobbes, Descartes and Bacon, started us on this modern project in which we give the law to nature and not the other way round. What has modern science done except to lower the horizon, make everyone believe that comfortable self-preservation is the only worthwhile goal for human beings? We have lost all sense of what human excellence really means. There is nothing we look up to, nothing that inspires great effort and sacrifice, nothing worth great risk. Until the beginning of the twentieth century, a university education, at least in Europe, meant a classical education, the study of the great works of the human mind read in their original Greek and Latin. The purpose of a classical education was not just to make men, and women, too, learned, but to teach them how to live. They read Plutarch and learned how the greatest men in history lived their lives. You head a world famous university, Mr. Fairweather. How many of your students know Greek or Latin? How many of them study Plutarch, or any other ancient writer, even in translation?"

Fairweather glanced around the table, certain everyone would agree that the comments of this Italian musician, while no doubt interesting, had no relevance to the requirements of the modern world and a modern education.

"The university still teaches classes in Greek and Latin; we still have a classics department. There isn't much demand; students are more interested in what will help them prepare for the kind of jobs they are going to have, than spending their time studying what, I think you'll have to admit, have at best a kind of curiosity value."

"I should have thought the encouragement of curiosity was the main function of a university," remarked Giuseppe Gambarini's extraordinary wife. "What is the point of being young, if you're always thinking about how you're going to get ahead in the world?" Her lips trembled with silent laughter, as she added, "When I was a girl in school, I never thought about that kind of thing. There were only two things that had an interest for me: old books ... and young men."

"I can imagine," said her husband, with a droll expression on a face that had become more handsome, and more distinguished, as he grew older.

Observing the way the two of them carried on - the teasing, charming, marvelously seductive by-play, no matter what was going on around them - I exchanged a glance with Tangerine, knowing that we both hoped we were watching our own future. And then, suddenly, I caught the significance of Fairweather's last remark.

"The demand. You still teach Greek and Latin, and there is still a classics department, but there isn't much demand. Mr. Gambarini described the European university of the 19th century in terms of what it saw as the purpose of a university education; what you describe has no purpose at all - it's whatever anyone who enrolls wants it to be. If I follow what you're saying, the modern university, like modern art and modern music, is whatever anyone wants it to be?"

He would not go quite that far. Logic was one thing; the privilege of his position was another. He was the president of a world famous institution; it had to be something more than the creature of the moment, driven by nothing more important than the demands of the workplace for trained personnel.

"There is a core curriculum. There are requirements that every student has to satisfy," he protested, in a thin, condescending voice.

"Unless you're there on an athletic scholarship," interjected Albert Craven, who seemed irritated. That was strange by itself: he almost never lost his temper, especially when he was presiding over a dinner table discussion in his own home. 'We have, at Berkeley, the school I attended, the school from which I graduated, become such a slave to the need to have a winning football team that we don't require anything from our so-called student athletes except that they can play. That is the only requirement for admission. Isn't that right, Lucas? Isn't that what we have now become - a university that would rather win a national championship than the Nobel prize for chemistry or physics?"

Now I understood. Albert was on the board of trustees, but I did not know about this unresolved issue or how strongly he felt about it. Fairweather's face reddened, but only slightly. He had not made his way through the academic bureaucracy without learning how to become a master of the bland assurance that this, like every dispute, was based on a misunderstanding.

"Athletics is an important part of college life," he insisted. He might have been a high school principle talking to the boys. "It provides a chance at a higher education for some who might not otherwise ever have that chance, and it gives the entire student body something to rally around."

"Which is the reason we pay the football coach a couple million a year; the reason we pay assistant coaches, some of them barely able to graduate from college themselves, hundreds of thousands. No, Lucas, this isn't something that can be ignored. This is a total disgrace!"

"It's what everyone wants," replied the president of the

university, with a cold smile that had, in his experience, brought an end to any further discussion.

Albert Craven was too polite to object. If I had any virtues, politeness was not one of them, but even if it had been, Albert was the last person I would let go undefended. The dinner dishes had been cleared away and coffee had been served. Stirring milk and sugar into my cup, I started to laugh.

"If you ever commit murder, Mr. Fairweather, I hope you'll let me represent you."

He stared at me, incredulous that I, or anyone, could even think such a thing possible.

"I have to confess," I went on, looking down the table at him, "it's a defense I had not thought of before: a defendant who can claim that he murdered because - how did you put it? - 'Its what everyone wants.' It's really quite ingenious, and it is perfectly connected with what all of you - almost all of you," I added, glancing at Giuseppe Gambarini - "were saying tonight: Everything is a matter of perspective, how someone happens to see a work of art, or hear a piece of music. There is no better or worse; everyone is entitled to their own opinion. This even includes what it means to be educated. Should the university teach this course or that, should it admit students who could not graduate from high school because they can play football?- everyone's opinion is as good as everyone else's opinion, which leads inevitably to the consequence that the only measure, the only means of deciding anything, is to let the majority decide. So, good - kill someone and if a majority think the victim deserved to die, the killer goes free. Think how much time and money that will save. No more trials, no more costly lawyers."

Lucas Fairweather was shocked. Art, music, education, that was one thing; but murder, the taking of a human life? No one could argue that that could ever be thought the right thing to do.

"There are no standards - everything is permitted - when it is nothing more serious than the human mind or the human spirit, but when it comes to what happens to the human body, when it is a question about human life and not human degradation, then we suddenly forget everything you think we should believe and act as if there is, and can be, only one known standard? Let me tell you something, President Fairweather. I have been doing this a long time. A murder trial is serious business. Murder is serious business. We used to have lynch mobs who would break into jails so they could hang someone accused of a murder they thought needed instant punishment. We don't do that anymore. What we do instead is convict people on television before the trial has even started, and then riot in the streets when the jury - the only people who have actually heard all the evidence - doesn't return the verdict they want. This is what happens when you teach a generation, more than one, to think that the only standard is whatever at any given moment they happen to want. It's what happens when the only thing you think worth teaching is what everything thinks they already know!"

To my astonishment, everyone except Fairweather seemed to agree. It may have been nothing more than the normal inconsistency of the way we live, this refusal to follow out to their ultimate conclusions the basic premises of our own assumptions, that Rupert Kramer was suddenly so eager to express his own disappointment at the way a verdict in a murder trial had been received.

"The Friedrich trial," he reminded everyone. "You got Justin Friedrich off. The jury found him not guilty of the murder of his wife, Allison. They were both friends of mine. Allison was on my board. She chaired the fund raising committee. I could not believe it when she was killed."

He had been looking right at me, but now he lowered his eyes, embarrassed by what he was about to admit.

"I thought he was guilty; I thought he must have done it. Don't misunderstand. I never thought of Justin as violent; I never would have thought him capable of murder. But when he was arrested, when he was accused, when he was put on trial…, then, yes, I'm afraid I assumed he must have done it, murdered Allison."

He looked at me now as if he had misjudged me, which meant that I had misjudged him. I had not thought him capable of changing his mind.

"If it had not been for you, Mr. Antonelli - he would have been convicted for a murder he did not commit, which doesn't mean he isn't paying a price for what happened."

I thought I knew what he meant, but I was not sure, and I did not want to guess. Albert Craven did not have to guess: he knew.

"No one wants anything to do with him," he explained, as everyone turned to him, waiting to hear more. "He's innocent, no one doubts that, but his wife was murdered, and he was accused, and that makes people ill at ease. No one want to get too close. That would have been true in any case, but after everything that came out during the trial - the way they lived, their disregard for all the normal decencies - he's become a social pariah, an outcast. People will still talk to him if they run into him at a restaurant or a social event, but he doesn't get invited anywhere - I mean, any-where he used to like to go. With all the money he has, there are still people…."

"He's made a very generous contribution to the museum," Kramer was quick to point out. "And he had the decency to make it in Allison's name. We're naming a wing in the museum after her. But, innocent or not, his life will never be what it was before."

"Perhaps it will be better," suggested Giuseppe Gambarini. "Now that he's on his own, free from false friends, he may begin to take himself seriously."

No one, it seemed, had considered that possibility, nor the one Tangerine now offered.

"Whoever killed Allison Friedrich wanted her husband to go through a trial. Do you think," she asked me in front of everyone, "that this was part of the reason: to destroy his life?"

I remembered - I would never forget - the look on the face of James Michael Redfield as he sat with us that night and without apology told us everything, or almost everything, that had been behind Allison Friedrich's murder. I gave the only answer I could.

"I really can't say what the killer really wanted.'

"That was well done," said Tangerine, an hour later, as we were walking to the car. "'I really can't say.' I don't know why I asked you that. It just came out."

"I think you're right. It would fit. When you destroy some-one's life, you do more than that: you tell a story to an audience, another example of the corruption you insist is everywhere."

She took my arm as we walked down the quiet well-lit street. The air was cool and clean and the sweet smell of an April night was everywhere.

"Tell me who you liked, and who you didn't," laughed Tangerine, and before I could say anything started with a list of her own. "I'll leave that awful Fairweather - strange, isn't it, how some people fit their name so perfectly? - he's not on the list. He's in that category called: 'didn't like and don't remember' - Don't want to remember, with that empty-minded smugness of his. Leave off Albert and Isabel because we know them already. That leaves.... Well, that's fairly easy, isn't it? I'm in love with the Gambarini's - both of them. We're invited, by the way."

"Invited? To what, when?"'

"Their place, next week. But about Rupert - I knew him a little when I was married. Everyone knew him. Everyone with money likes to collect art. They're all rich, but not rich enough to buy Old Masters or any of the great Impressionists like Monet or Cezanne. They buy post-impressionist art because it is much more affordable, especially, as most of them do, when they buy the work of someone who isn't all that well-known. They've seen how well others have done when they bought, years ago, Jaspers, or Michael

Cooper, or any of the other famous ones before they were famous. Rupert is who they go to when they have a question about who they should buy and how much they should pay."

We had reached the car, two blocks down the street from Albert Craven's pastel painted house.

"And your list, how is it different from mine?"

I told her that I would have had a hard time deciding between Fairweather and Kramer, the university president and the museum director, which I liked least, but that I had changed my mind and Fairweather now had last place all to himself. I started to tell her how much I liked Guiseppe Gambarini and his gorgeous, elegant wife when my cell phone rang.

"This is my private number. How did you get it?" I asked, with more anger than I meant to show. Tangerine gave me a worried look. "If you want to see me, you can do what everyone else does: call my office!"

"Who was that?" asked Tangerine, as I put the phone back in my pocket. From the look in her eyes I knew she had already guessed.

"James Michael Redfield. He wants to see me tomorrow."

Chapter Seven

I wonder now if it was a premonition, a sense that something was about to happen, or that something already had, that made me wake up as early as I did. The view outside the bedroom's sliding glass doors was like an endless series of picture postcards, each one a look at the same scene: the bay and San Francisco, Alcatraz and the Golden Gate Bridge; and every look different than the one before. When I had gone to bed, sometime after midnight, the city was as bright and shiny as the star filled sky. This morning, a little before six, the city and the bay were enveloped in a grayish white fog bank under the rising red gold sun. I trudged out to the kitchen and made myself a cup of coffee.

It was the phone call, the voice of James Michael Redfield telling me that he wanted to see me, that echoed like a warning in my mind. There have been times in my life when, without any reason at all, I suddenly knew what was going to happen. I would be on my way to the mailbox, thinking of nothing, and then, with a feeling of absolute certainty knew that a letter I had not expected was waiting for me. I would pick up the phone and hear myself speak the name of the person I somehow knew was calling. It happened to me now. I turned on the television, knowing that someone had been murdered, and that, somehow, I would be involved.

A few minutes later, Tangerine wandered into the kitchen, rubbing her eyes.

"You're up early. Couldn't you sleep?" She put her hand on my shoulder, bent down and kissed my on the side of my face.

97

"Are you going in early today?"

"I think I better," I said, as I got up from the table. "Something happened, late last night."

Her eyes flashed open.

"Redfield! What's he done?"

I started to act the lawyer, always ready to counsel caution.

"Maybe nothing; it may not have had anything to do with him."

"It may…?"

The look on her face told me that it was no good: There was no point pretending that I did not think the same thing she did.

"Lucas Fairweather was murdered…late last night."

"Where? - Berkeley or San Francisco?"

"Berkeley, in his office, on campus. He must have gone there after he left Albert's place last night."

Tangerine sat down, trying hard not to seem worried.

"Redfield called you just after we left Albert's, when we got to the car. Lucas Fairweather left just a little before we did."

She knew as well as I did what it meant; or, rather, what it might mean. Either Redfield wanted to see me for a reason that had nothing to do with the murder of Lucas Fairweather, or he had called in advance of a murder he knew was going to happen.

"If he did this, if he is behind this murder, the way I know he was behind the murder of Allison Friedrich, he'll want you to represent him if he's charged, won't he?"

"I don't know what Redfield wants, but it won't be to represent him in a trial. You saw what happened in the Friedrich trial, you've met him, you heard what he said about what the killer wanted. Do you really think he would do anything that would make the police, or anyone else, think he was responsible?"

She got up from the chair and stood in front of me, staring into my eyes as if she were searching for what she knew I could not tell her.

98

"He never said anything to me about this, or anything else he might be planning. He knows how the privilege works; he knows that it's limited to what he tell me about things that have happened - the past. It doesn't apply, it doesn't hold, for what he says about what he might be planning to do in the future."

"I know that," she said, stroking my face with her soft, warm hand. "I don't know the rules, other than what you've told me, but I know you'd never let something like this happen. Even if there was a rule that said you couldn't, you'd find a way around it: You'd never let anyone get killed."

I wondered about that as I drove across the bridge on my way to my office in the city. I had been lucky, luckier than most lawyers who practiced in the criminal courts: I had never had a client who, after he had been found not guilty, went out and killed someone. There were no serial killers still loose because I had managed to get them acquitted for a murder early in the series. It was the one thing I had always feared: the responsibility that, despite all the reasonable sounding arguments about the duty of a defense lawyer to do everything he could for a defendant without any thought for what he, or she, might do later, I would feel if someone I helped go free then committed murder. I had always assumed that it could only happen if I defended someone I knew was guilty of murder, someone who, given the chance, would kill again. It never occurred to me that it could happen like this: a client who used murder as a method of instruction, a way to teach the world what the world did not want to learn.

Redfield had not made an appointment, and when he had not called my office by the early afternoon I began to wonder, or rather began to hope, that his call the night before had been purely coincidental, and that, contrary to my fear, the murder of Lucas Fairweather had nothing to do with him. I had enough to keep me occupied: phone calls I had to return, the preparation for a dozen cases, some of them close to the date for trial, appointments with clients and prospective clients that went on all morning and late into the afternoon. I was just getting ready to leave when my secretary called to tell me that Redfield was here.

"Did he have an appointment?" I asked.

I was certain that he had not bothered; I was not certain I was going to see him unless he had. Redfield, of course, had anticipated that possibility.

"He said he didn't have an appointment," explained Millie Davis, who had been with me now for years. "He apologized and said that if you didn't have time to see him, he understood and would take the next appointment you had available."

I could tell from the tone of her voice that she was impressed, that she thought - and why would she not? - James Michael Redfield of a different class from my normal clientele, a different class from nearly anyone she had ever met. He had that effect on people. She would have thought me worse than a fool, ill-mannered, if I had insisted, without good reason, that he come back some other time.

He was all grace and charm when he strolled into my office dressed, as usual, in a suit and tie. He sat in the wingback chair in front of my desk as if I were visiting him.

"It's good to see you, Mr. Antonelli. I'm sorry I didn't call first." Frowning, he shook his head, scolding himself for his failure to treat me with the respect he thought I deserved. "That was unconscionable," he said, as his chin came up a slight fraction of an inch, enough to emphasize how seriously he took the obligation to be completely honest with me. "I've never been able to tell the whole truth to anyone; most people, almost everyone, are too much a slave of their own beliefs to understand it, or not to feel offended. You and I have a different understanding; or rather, a different set of rules. I can tell you anything without any worry what you might think. There is no reason to lie to you out of simple politeness. I should have called, and I might have, but the truth is that once you told me I had to, I knew I could not."

I was not in a mood for a mindless game of power.

"You couldn't call because I told you that you had to make an appointment to see me? Good for you. What do you want?" I asked, sinking back in my chair and crossing my arms over my chest. I eyed him with deep suspicion. "Are you here to tell me that you may be in trouble, that you might be arrested, charged with the murder of Lucas Fairweather?"

"No, not at all," he replied, looking at me as if the mere possibility was absurd. "What did you think of him, by the way? You had dinner with him last night, didn't you, along with a few others at your partner's home in the Marina?"

Moving my index finger slowly back and forth across my upper lip, I watched him carefully. Other than a slight, almost imperceptible smile on his mouth, a smile that seemed to brag his indifference to all morality, nothing changed. He might have been talking about the weather for all the care he showed telling me he had me under surveillance.

"You show up at a restaurant in Sausalito; you know where I had dinner last night. I don't know what it is you think you're doing, Mr. Redfield, but it ends here." Reaching inside a desk drawer I pulled out the envelope he had left with me the last time he had been in my office. "I never cashed this," I said, handing back the retainer he had given me.

"It hasn't been opened. You never even bothered to look?" he asked, as apparently amused as he professed to be astonished. "I can pretty well guarantee you that it is the largest retainer you, or any criminal defense lawyer, has ever been given. And you don't want it? Good for you, Mr. Antonelli, good for you. I knew you were exactly the lawyer I wanted!"

"The lawyer you no longer have," I said, as I got to my feet.

Redfield did not move from his chair. He sat there, looking straight at me. I had the feeling he was trying to decide how far to go, whether to tell me what was in his mind, or tell me nothing at all and let the story, whatever the story was, takes its own course. Finally, though I don't think he had decided anything, he got to his feet, but instead of turning to leave he walked across the room the windows opposite the book lined wall.

"There is really no place like it, is there?" he asked, staring at the bay, glistening in the distance. "I've been everywhere: I've lived in Paris, I've lived in Rome - but San Francisco! It's the only place I never want to leave. I was born here. Maybe that's the reason. Whatever the reason," he went on, turning to face me, "it's the only place I feel at home. Perhaps you think I am something of a hypocrite, believing, as I think you understand, that corruption is endemic, and that, for reasons which you perhaps don't yet understand, it has to be exposed. You might well wonder how I can, at the same time, be so drawn to the place. It is an old story. It is all about democracy, how everyone is free to live in whatever way they like, which means, inevitably, that a great many will live in ways that are really disgraceful; but it also means that, at least if you keep quiet about what you're doing, you have the chance to think, to discover how you should live, and how you can help others find their way as well."

"Even if you have to murder someone, and have someone else go on trial for your crime?"

"You don't know that I did any such thing. For all you know, I stumbled upon certain essential facts, and, as a good citizen, shared what I discovered with the only person in a position to put those facts to their proper use. For all you know, Mr. Antonelli, I might be a modern day Svengali who watches various charlatans and fools plan their own sordid schemes of violence and revenge and then tries to turn their various idiocies to the kind of good purpose I tried to describe when I happened, quite by chance, to run into you and your beautiful friend at a restaurant in Sausalito."

"For all I know," I replied, "you may have murdered Allison Friedrich yourself, and left her drunk husband to take the blame. For all I know, you've done it again: murdered Lucas Fairweather and done it in a way to make sure someone else has to face the possibility of losing at trial: another person who might spend their life in prison or face execution for something they did not do. You're protected by the privilege, Mr. Redfield - Why don't you just tell me what you've done?"

"There are certain matters, Mr. Antonelli, that should never be discussed with anyone unless they have acquired sufficient insight to at least credit the possibility that what you have done you have done with good cause. Until that time comes - if it ever does - it is better if I only say enough to let you read between the lines, as it were. You're not my priest; I did not come here to make my confession. I did come to tell you something about Lucas Fairweather, however. The police haven't arrested anyone yet; no one has been accused. When someone is charged, I would like you to represent him."

"I told you: I'm not your lawyer. I'm certainly not going to represent someone just because you might like me to."

Holding the envelope with the retainer in his hand, he tapped it twice against his other hand and asked me if I was sure I did not want it.

"In that case," he said, when I refused again, "I'll donate it to charity. Do you have a favorite? Anything to which you would like me to make a contribution?"

I told him it was his money and he should do whatever he wanted with it.

"I still think you should keep it. Unlike Justin Friedrich, the defendant in the Fairweather murder trial isn't likely to have the kind of money necessary to pay your fee."

It was maddening, the blithe way he seemed to ignore what anyone else would have taken as an emphatic rejection.

"I'm not going to do it, Mr. Redfield! I'll have nothing to

do with anything having to do with the murder of Lucas Fairweath-er."

He nodded as if, finally, he was ready to take my word for it. He started for the door and then, suddenly, looked back at me.

"The only thing I can tell you with absolute certainty, Mr. Antonelli, is that if you don't agree to defend the person who is go-ing to be accused of murdering President Fairweather you will have to live with the knowledge that because of your refusal an innocent man has been sent to the gas chamber."

I dismissed this as a hollow threat.

"There are a lot of good lawyers. It doesn't take me to get an acquittal for someone who didn't commit the crime."

"Yes, but if you had not been representing Justin Friedrich the murder weapon - the gun -, and the sales receipt that proved he could not have bought it, would never have been discovered. And if you're not the lawyer in the Fairweather murder trial, Mr. Antonelli, I can almost guarantee that there won't be any last minute discovery of the evidence without which the defendant will have no chance of an acquittal."

He smiled and held up the envelope.

"I'll think of something good to do with this."

I sat there for a long time, going over in my mind every-thing Redfield had said, back to the beginning when he first came to see me. Everything now took on the aspect of a carefully con-structed plan; there was nothing random about any of it. It had been too well-orchestrated, the parts too well-connected. He had not decided on a second murder because he had committed, or ar-ranged, the murder of Allison Friedrich; they were, each of them, the necessary steps in whatever he was trying to accomplish in a scheme of his own devising. That much seemed relatively clear. It was also clear by now that he was determined to make me an unwilling accomplice in his plan. Murder was not only a means to an end; what he really wanted was a trial, a trial in which the defendant was all but certain to be convicted for a crime he had not committed.

It was really quite ingenious. A hundred investigative reporters working for years could never uncover the various corruptions of American society with anything like the dramatic effect of what could be brought to light in a murder trial. Murder sold papers, violence in any form was the stuff of movies and television and more than half the bad novels ever written. Americans were in love with death, violent death. It was at the root of what, deep down, nearly everyone feared the most. The Friedrich trial had attracted such wide attention because it involved the wasted lives of the useless rich. Like violent death, money had become an American obsession. Lucas Fairweather was the president of one of the best known and most highly respected universities in the country. If the desire for money had no limit, if everyone, however much they had, always wanted more, it was difficult to to find anyone who did not believe that the best way to learn how to get it was a college education. The dinner table conversation at Albert Craven's had shown how this was a mere shadow of what education had meant before. If the Friedrich trial had been about money and what too much of it does to people, was it possible that the Fairweather murder would be used to put American education on trial?

"You're still here?" said Albert Craven, as he slipped quietly into the room.

Clasping his small hands behind his back, he paced slowly back and forth, three steps in one direction, three steps in another, staring at the floor with a grave, deeply worried expression on his smooth, unlined face. There was something he wanted to say, but he was not sure quite how to say it.

"Yes," I said, firm and emphatic.

He stopped and looked up.

"Yes?"

"What you want to tell me, what you're not sure you should

ask. Redfield was here, left half an hour ago; Redfield who you know, because you were here when I opened that gift-wrapped package, left the gun, the murder weapon, that cleared Justin Friedrich. I can't talk about it, but there was only one thing you could have assumed about the murder of Allison Friedrich. And now, the day after Lucas Fairweather is murdered, Redfield is here again. I know what you must be thinking, and you know that I can't...."

"Say any more than that. Yes, Joseph, I understand." He plopped down in the wingback chair. Looking quite miserable, he threw up his hands in frustration. "No, that's a lie. I don't understand anything. What does he want? What is he trying to do?" Leaning forward, he fixed me with a penetrating gaze. "And what the hell is he trying to do with you?"

"He wants me to represent....I don't know who he wants me to represent: whoever gets charged with the Fairweather murder."

Albert Craven had made a fortune practicing civil law. Unlike most lawyers, he had an eye for detail: the one word out of place, the sentence that changed the meaning of what to everyone else seemed obvious. Other might think a contract that was 99.9 percent perfect an achievement; Craven thought it worse than a disaster, a lawsuit waiting to happen. He could read between the lines, not just the written lines of a document, but the spoken words of a conversation, better than anyone I knew. Though he was usually too polite to do it out loud, he could often finish your sentence quicker than you could yourself.

"And whoever is charged won't be the one who really did it," he remarked, with a sharp nod of his head. "He wants another trial like the Friedrich trial. What are you going to do?"

Sitting back in the chair, he crossed his legs and with his palms turned up began to weigh in the balance the advantages and disadvantages of two possible decisions.

"In the end, it all comes down to one question, doesn't it?

If you don't take the case, if the accused is represented by another attorney, does Redfield let an innocent man be convicted? You have no legal responsibility for what happens. You don't have to take this, or any other, case. You turn down cases all the time. You...."

"Have never been in a situation like this. I doubt anyone has. The real question, Albert, isn't what Redfield might do; the real question is whether I'm prepared to let someone's life depend on his decision, when I'm almost certain what that decision would be."

Craven did not doubt that Redfield would carry out his threat. After murder, why suppose the thought of an innocent man paying for the crime would be some kind of deterrence?

"Then you're going to do it, defend whoever has been set up to take the blame?"

"It may be the only choice I have."

I got up, took two steps and stopped. I stood there, trying to puzzle my way through a maze, every turn, every opening, one I had to take. I was trapped. There was nothing I could do, except go on with it, continue the journey, and hope that somewhere along the line Redfield would make a mistake and give me the means of my escape. All I knew at the moment was that though I did not yet have a client, I had a case.

"What can you tell me about Lucas Fairweather?"

"The public version? - What I had to tell the reporters who called today to get my reaction as a member of the board of trustees. Or the truth?" he asked, with a raised eyebrow that expressed perfectly the cynicism he felt. "After that conversation last night at dinner, you don't really have to ask, do you? Do you know what the secret is for being a successful - notice I don't say good - college president? - The simple ability to listen patiently to the various heads of department when they are explaining the particular expertise involved in their fields. Fairweather, and he was just an example of the type, would listen with more than sympathy and an apparent understanding, he would beam with encouragement as the head of the physics department would describe their work in quantum mechanics. He would not understand a word of what he was being told, but how often does the head of the physics department get to talk to the head of the university, how often does he get to feel that he has made a favorable impression on the source of money and power in the university. Do you know what you need to be president of a university? - The ability to play the Wizard of Oz. You want to know what Lucas Fairweather was really like - a charlatan and a fraud, with this important difference: he did not realize he was either. He thought, he really believed, that he was a scholar, a serious intellectual, because, years ago, a young assistant professor at some place in the east, he wrote a couple of published papers on some minor and forgotten episode in 19th century American foreign policy."

"But he didn't stay a teacher; that isn't why he was hired," I remarked. "I remember when it happened; I remember you were opposed."

Tucking his chin, Craven gave me a sardonic glance from his lowered eyes.

"Opposed, lost in a landslide vote; opposed, without any thought that it would be more than a protest; opposed, if only to prevent unanimous approval of what, in my dotage, I continue to insist is the destruction of the university and what it means, or what it is supposed to mean. You don't have to be as much a purist as your new good friend, Giuseppe Gasperini, to think the university has lost its way. Berkeley used to be all about the improvement of the human mind; now its all about mass entertainment - all those expensive televised sports that gets everyone so excited - and teaching how to make life more comfortable through medicine and technology. When I was a student there we used to protest against any connection with government; we hired Lucas Fairweather because he had been Secretary of Health and Human Services. No one was better equipped to make sure the university got all the federal funding it possibly could. We don't choose people to head our universities because of the example they can set as serious scholars and serious human beings; we get the best fund raisers we can find."

He had been speaking faster, and with more intensity, than usual. Shaking his head, he began to laugh.

"I better be careful. Maybe I'll get arrested. If anyone had a motive to murder him, it's probably me."

"Who - besides you - would have had a motive? I don't mean a real motive, one a real killer might have, but is there anyone who would seem to have a motive sufficient to cause them to want to murder Lucas Fairweather, anyone easy to frame?"

"You know the old line - the reason academic politics are so vicious is because the stakes are so low. It's a line used to dismiss the importance of what is in dispute, but what no one seems to realize is that it also shows how little important a motive has to be. It could be anyone. Someone on the faculty denied tenure, someone in the administration passed over for promotion, a disgruntled student in danger of flunking out, an outraged parent whose child was not admitted. But is there one person in particular who stands out? Someone, again, who did not do it, but would be easy to blame; someone who, once you heard who it was, you would immediately think it made sense? Is there an obvious...?"

Craven fell into a worried silence. There was someone.

"Alan Boe. I should have thought of it right away. The reason I didn't is because it is impossible he could ever murder anyone. Just impossible! He's a legend; everyone knows who he is; everyone on campus, I mean. He teaches philosophy. He's in his late fifties, early sixties. There is standing room only when he lectures, and standing room only when he speaks in the faculty senate where he has become the main opponent to everything the administration has done, is doing, or ever will do. He's almost a cult figure. He's a throwback, a serious man, a serious student, someone who never stops asking questions. He keeps trying to remind the university what it is supposed to be about; the university keeps trying to ignore him."

Pursing his lips, Craven looked down at his hands, pondering whether it was possible, and, if it was, what might happen.

"If that is Redfield's game, if Alan Boe is charged with Fairweather's murder, then I hope to God you defend him. The trial of Alan Boe....I would come every day, just to watch. It would be an education for all of us," said Craven, feeling, strangely, better than he had before. "I think he would actually look forward to it! Have you ever defended anyone on a murder charge who thought going on trial for his life was more fun than anything he could think of doing? Just put him on the stand and let him talk. You won't be able to stop him; it'll go on for weeks. He'll still be talking when the jury goes home," he added, as he got to his feet, rapped his knuckles twice on the corner of my desk and turned toward the door.

He stopped before he got there and turned back.

"I hope it isn't Boe; I hope it isn't anyone. I hope they catch the real killer. I hope they somehow catch Redfield and put an end to whatever it is he wants to drag you into. Be careful. I don't think we have any idea what Redfield may be capable of doing."

Tangeine was not quite as worried, but she did not know, and I could not tell her, everything that Albert Craven knew. She knew enough, and could guess a lot more, when I told her that Redfield had come to visit.

"I gave back the retainer he had given me, and I told him that I would not represent him anymore."

We were having dinner on the deck outside. The lights from the city, glittering in the darkness, seemed almost close enough to touch. Tangerine glittered brighter than any city, even San Francisco, ever could.

"And it didn't change anything, as far as he was concerned, did it?"

She was quicker, smarter, a better lawyer, had she become one, than I had ever been.

"Why don't you tell me what happened," I suggested, as I poured myself a second glass of an Italian pinot grigio. "I'll just listen."

She knew I was joking; she showed me why that was my mistake.

"He explained everything before, the night we were at dinner at the Spinnaker. First, the Friedrich murder and trial, now the murder of Lucas Fairweather and the trial of whomever Redfield makes sure gets accused. And in both trials, Joseph Antonelli for the defense. You defended Justin Friedrich because everyone knows you're the best there is; you'll defend whomever gets charged with this for the same reason, and one other: Redfield wants you to do it, and he has the kind of leverage to force you into it. You're too damn honorable to let someone go to prison, or worse, for something they did not do, and the only way you can stop it is to play along with Redfield because he otherwise won't do anything - the way he did with Friedrich - to make sure there is an acquittal at the end. You realize, this isn't going to stop. He'll keep doing it, over and over again, until he makes whatever point he's trying to make. He'll use you, over and over again, and believe me, if and when he decides to stop, it won't be before he has managed to destroy you the way he has the lives of everyone else he has decided to murder or ruin! The only chance you have - the only chance we have - is to destroy him first."

Chapter Eight

It is a strange feeling reading about a murder when you are the only one, other than the killer, who knows what happened. It is like watching children play blind man's bluff, each one certain he has got it right, and all of them wrong. Lucas Fairweather had been murdered sometime between eleven o'clock and midnight. The same security guard who found the body had seen the chancellor in his office an hour earlier. That narrowed the time period within which it happened; it did nothing to narrow the list of possible suspects. Fairweather had died from a blow to his head from a two foot tall marble statue kept on the credenza directly behind the desk where he worked. It was not, as one might have imagined it to be, a statue of an ancient philosopher or a literary figure such as Homer or Shakespeare; it was an elegant work of abstract art that bore no obvious resemblance to anything, or anyone. Laying next to the chancellor's dead body, it was covered in blood and small bits of brain. Whatever fingerprints might have been on it had been wiped clean. There were no suspects, at least none that were reported in the papers.

The inevitable question was whether Fairweather's death had something to do with his position as chancellor of the university, or something in his personal life. Few things are as deadly dull as the policies and politics of a university; few things sell more papers, or increase a television audience, than something sordid having to do with sex. Rumor is to scandal what a match is to fire, and nothing is easier to start than a rumor about the victim of a homicide. When it was discovered that Fairweather had been the subject of more than one complaint of sexual misconduct, the same people who pretended shock could not wait to hear more about it.

Even the unpredictable becomes predictable when you know how the story is going to end. In a murder case, rumor follows a logic of its own. The immediate reports are all about the murder itself: the chronology of violent death Outrage is a given; sorrow, and even anguish, for the victim and those close to him - his family, if he had one, his friends, if he had any - comes right after. Then attention is paid to the investigation, whether the police are making any progress, whether they have any leads, whether there is any hard evidence that might point in one direction or another. And then, inevitably, the questions start. How could something like this have happened? What was there about the victim, what flaw in his character, what misdeeds in his past, what illicit activity was he involved in, what reason, good or otherwise, might someone have had to want him to die?

"Nothing while he was here," said Albert Craven, when I mentioned what I had been reading in the morning paper. "Nothing was ever brought to the board's attention," he added, rubbing his chin. "And, so far as I know, no one on the board had heard anything about what is now coming out about what happened when he was Secretary of Health and Human Services, or what happened before that. Three different lawsuits!" he said, shaking his head, a grim expression on his round, smooth face.

Craven was sitting behind his new glass and steel desk. He had the uncomfortable, and slightly embarrassed, look of a classical pianist handed an electric guitar and asked to play it.

"Yes, you're right, Antonelli. I hate this damn thing. There's nothing wrong with it; it's very functional. Isabel keeps telling me it has beautiful lines. And, yes, you can remind me how ugly, how really grotesque, that Victorian monstrosity was, but you know," he said, sitting back, his head tilted up, "I got used to it. If

I had ever stayed married long enough, it's what I might have felt about a woman who over time lost her youthful beauty. But this? - It's an object, dead metal and dead glass. There is no history in a thing like this!"

Craven's gaze turned inward. A thin, rueful grimace snapped across his mouth, and he immediately slapped the glass top of his new unwanted desk with his open palm.

"History! We've lost all sense of it. Lucas Fairweather taught American history and had less understanding of it than what, half a century ago, every kid in high school knew. We can't learn from the past, because everyone now thinks we are here to judge it. Washington and Jefferson were slave owners. That is all you need to know. That both of them thought slavery an abomination, that Washington freed his slaves in his will - that he added a provision that it would not happen until his wife, if she survived him, had died, so that there would be no possibility that any of their slaves would be separated from their husbands or wives or children - is seldom reported and never remembered. That Jefferson included in the original draft of the Declaration of Independence a paragraph condemning the slave trade and condemning the British government for imposing slavery on the American colonies, has been all but forgotten. They had slaves; they are to be forever condemned. We are like dwarfs who make fun of giants because they don't look, and act, just like them."

Sinking low in his chair, he crossed his arms and stretched out his legs. He looked at me for a long time in a speechless conversation that more than words ever could expressed not just a deep sense of disappointment but a feeling of inevitability. He reached toward a pile of thick books stacked neatly on the side of the glass topped desk.

"Tocqueville, Democracy in America," he explained, as he opened it to a bookmarked page. "I asked Fairweather what he thought of it, whether he agreed that it was the best book ever written about America, whether he agreed that, written in 1830, it explained better than anything else what has happened - the driving force, if you will - in the American experience. He said he thought he had read a few excerpts from it in an undergraduate course. A few excerpts, and the man had a Ph.d in history! And as for its continuing relevance, though again, he had not read, much less studied, it, his answer was what he was telling you at dinner: the only thing important is the present, what people today think, including what they think about the past."

The bookmark was a small sheet of notepaper on which Craven had scribbled some quotations from Tocqueville's famous book.

"If he had read Tocqueville and remembered only this, he might for once in his life have actually learned something: 'When everything is more or less level, the slightest variation is noticed. Hence the more equal men are the more insatiable will be their longing for equality.' It's true, isn't it? Think how sensitive we have become to every perceived difference, every suggestion of disparate treatment. It becomes the way - sometimes the only way - we look at the past. Every previous generation stands accused of bigotry and prejudice because distinctions were made we find intolerable. We assume that everyone is the same, that there is no distinction, no acceptable distinction, between what people want. Which brings us to the second thing Fairweather could have learned from Tocqueville, the thing that a university should more than any other institution make it is business to fight against: 'If ever the thoughts of the great majority of mankind come to be concentrated solely on the search for material blessings, one can anticipate that there will be a colossal reaction in the souls of men.'"

Placing the notepaper back in the book, Craven closed the volume and looked at me in a more hopeful manner.

"As I have gotten older I notice that I find more encouragement when I read someone like Tocqueville. It reminds you what a great human being is capable of doing. That is what is missing now: the sense of what greatness really means."

His eyes shot open and he grabbed the book again.

"Here, this helps explain it," he said, excited that he had remembered. "'Classical historians taught how to command; those of our time teach next to nothing but how to obey.' When I was a freshman at Cal, we read Thucydides in the course - the required course - in western civilization. Now, if they mention Thucydides, or any other ancient historian, chances are it is to dismiss them as representative of the kind of inequality that white men taught. And that, finally, reminds me of one last observation Tocqueville made nearly two centuries ago that, as it seems to me, explains a great deal about the present condition of at least American politics, if not American life altogether: In 'America suicide is rare, but I'm told madness is commoner there than anywhere else.'

"Change the date, tell everyone that Alexis deTocqueville was alive and living in France, you could start a war inside the American university. It would take all day to list the names he would be called, all of them variations on the same theme: that Tocqueville did not believe in democracy. The shame of it is that no one, before or since, has ever discussed with more intelligence how to save democracy from itself." He picked up his copy and handed it to me. "Read it, even though, as I happen to know, you have read it before. It's one of those rare books you learn more from each time you work your way through it."

I was always interested in what Albert Craven told me, and always surprised by how many different things he knew, but I wanted to know more about Lucas Fairweather and what might have been the reason why James Michael Redfield had chosen him for his latest victim.

"I don't know. It obviously has to do with his position. But what, exactly? If I had to guess, it would be that he sees it - the murder and the trial - as a way to expose the mindlessness of higher education in this country. That's why…."

"Why what?" I asked. "What were you going to say?"

Craven became quite serious. He did not want to talk about it. He bit his lip and looked off to the side, amused at his own reluctance to say out loud what he was thinking for fear it might call down the vengeance of the gods and be made true. He bent toward me as if we were two conspirators who could not afford to be overheard.

"Remember what I told you before, when you asked if anyone immediately came to mind as someone who might be blamed?"

"Alan Boe, philosophy professor. How could I forget? You said you would come to court every day, just to watch."

"I got a call last night, someone at the university. He told me the police were interviewing several people and Boe is one of them. The terrible thing is that it makes perfect sense. I don't mean that he would have done it. But if you wanted someone the direct opposite of Lucas Fairweather, the direct opposite in every important regard, no one else is even close. They had diametrically different ideas about what a university is supposed to be; and in terms of how they lived, what they thought important, it is night and day. Fairweather was being paid more than a million a year, had a free house, a car and driver, a golf course membership. Boe made considerably less than a tenth that amount, and from what I've been told gave most of it away. He didn't live in that 'ten thousand fold poverty' that Socrates claimed, but close enough. Socrates! That is what it would be: a second trial of Socrates," said Craven, the smile on his mouth broader and more emphatic with each word. "The difference is that Socrates represented himself, and Boe - if it was to be Boe - would have you."

"Which is about as far from Socrates as you could get," I remarked, as I got up from my chair.

"Perhaps; but remember: Socrates lost and was condemned to death, and you always win."

Craven's glass and steel desk was in the corner of his large office. There were bookshelves on the wall behind him and on the wall to his left as he sat facing me. There was a gray marble fireplace on the long wall on his right, with a sofa and two easy chairs in front. Thick oriental rugs were scattered over the floor. There were pictures everywhere, paintings done by artists he had known, and photographs, dozens of them, tracing in a kind of random fashion the history of the city: the destruction from the earthquake of 1906, the Golden Gate Bridge under construction in 1937. Everything of importance that had ever happened, everyone who had played an important part in the city's life, could be found in the photographs that marched from a point low to the floor to a point near the ceiling. If you looked at them closely, if you took the time to stand on your tip toes, or bend down to your knees, you would find, on most of them, the signature of the photographer or the once famous person whose face had been captured forever on film. Albert Craven had known everyone, and everyone had known him. People gave him things and thought themselves honored when he accepted.

"Someone I know, an author who writes the kind of serious novels not that many people read anymore, wrote a novel about Machiavelli. He told me he stayed as close as possible to the historical record. There is a line near the beginning that could be said about Alan Boe. The young Machiavelli is at home. There is a knock on the door. Angelo Ambrogini, known throughout the world as Poliziano, has come to tell him that Lorenzo de Medici - Lorenzo the Magnificent - the ruler of Florence, wants to see him. Machiavelli, who is telling the story, describes Poliziano, 'as ugly as Socrates and nearly as wise.' That may be the best description of Alan Boe ever written.

"That would paint a picture of its own: the contrast, the extreme difference, between them. You would notice both of them in a crowd. Boe because he looks like nothing you have ever seen;

118

Fairweather because he looked like a fashion model for the kind of clothing worn by wealthy middle-aged men. Beauty and the beast, if Fairweather had been a woman. Poor Boe! The more I talk about it, the more certain I feel that Redfield has chosen him."

The telephone rang. Craven picked it up and listened. He started to laugh, but quickly stopped.

"Yes. When I see him, I'll tell him. I'm sure you'll be able to reach him later today. Yes, absolutely; I'll tell him you called and how grateful you are."

He hung up and for a moment stared at the telephone. The grin on his face diminished and then disappeared.

"That was Rupert Kramer, calling to tell you that the museum just received the gift that was sent in your name. It is the largest single donation anyone has given the museum of modern art. I didn't know you were such an admirer of post-impressionism."

"Redfield! He told me he would donate that retainer to a good cause!"

"And you never looked to see how much it was? I'm not sure you shouldn't have kept it. I have a feeling he means to keep you rather occupied. Yes, I know: you told him you weren't willing to represent him anymore. Redfield is probably a murderer; he is certainly a genius. You're too much a part of this plan of his - whatever it turns out to be - to let you decide when you get to stop."

Another week went by and there was still no arrest, no one charged with the murder of Lucas Fairweather, but there was a new story, or rather a new rumor, about why he might have been killed. He had not resigned his position with the government to become chancellor of the University of California; he had been forced to leave. Had he not been a close friend of the president, he would have left in disgrace after having been caught having sex with a certain congressman's wife on the table in the secretary's private dining room. What one person in Washington knows, everyone eventually knows, and what was only whispered while Fairweather was alive became the kind of thing everyone was all too eager to talk about once he was dead. Fairweather, it was now concluded with the confidence of final wisdom, had been a notorious womanizer who had not been beyond physical coercion to get what he wanted. The usual stages of grief were upended and set aside. Anger and resentment took the place of acceptance, and Lucas Fairweather became a victim in only the technical sense. Had he not been murdered, he might have been lynched. When the police finally made an arrest, the immediate assumption was that the killer must have had a good reason. Alan Boe thought he must have had a good reason as well, if only he could remember what it was.

"Bishop George Berkeley - curious coincidence, the name. Not coincidental at all, as it turns out. Berkeley was named after him, but not because of his metaphysics. It was because he wrote the line, 'Westward the course of empire takes its way.' Did you ever read him? - We don't know, that is to say, we can't prove that we are really awake, that we're not dreaming. They say I killed - murdered, that sounds more interesting than killed - the chancellor. I don't remember doing that, but perhaps I did - when I was awake, and I'm dreaming now; or, of course, the other way round. But - I'm sorry, Mr. Antonelli - I couldn't resist. Don't worry about Bishop Berkeley. No one has in a very long time. It isn't very serious stuff. We may not be able to prove we're not dreaming, but that is hardly relevant to what we as human beings have to do, is it?"

'As ugly as Socrates and nearly as wise.' The quotation Albert Craven had used from someone's novel about Machiavelli leaped into my mind and before I knew it a smile shot across my face. I had never met Boe before, and I felt as if there had never been a time when I had not known him. It was not that we had anything in common; I had every reason to think that we did not. Strange as it must seem, that was the reason I felt this way. He was, quite simply, an impossibility, so different from anyone I had ever met that I wondered for a moment whether I might have created him myself, a figment of my own delusion.

"You for some reason seem not to find me astonishingly good looking, Mr. Antonelli. Don't worry about this. I live with disappointment. There are advantages in a face like mine. It keeps the attention of an audience. It has a mesmerizing effect on college students. They wonder if my bulging eyes will suddenly leave my face altogether, jump across the room to see them closer, penetrate the outer layer of their pretended indifference and discover all their young uncertainties. And my ears!" he exclaimed, with the eagerness of an earnest child. "I can hear what you haven't yet started to say. My rather large, misshapen nose - well, enough of that. Tell me a little about yourself. You don't have to tell me it was inevitable that we would meet. I know that already."

"You know that…?"

We were sitting in a small, square, windowless room where lawyers could confer with their clients who were in custody. Boe was wearing the standard short sleeve v-neck shirt and matching draw string pants. Both were too large. He was short, perhaps five foot eight, with broad shoulders and the kind of arms and hands you would have expected to see on a truck driver or longshoreman. His fingers, however, were not calloused, but smooth and almost perfectly flat from the first knuckle to the tips, as if they were, all ten of them, pressing against a hard surface.

"That it was inevitable that we would meet - here, in this grim place; now - this day, this moment. The proof is simple: we're here!"

He threw out his hands and stared at me with eyes the like of which I had never seen, eyes that seemed to reveal a new, and different, depth the longer he looked at you, as infinite in their meaning as two facing mirrors. He pulled his index finger over his mouth and the tip of his nose. His eyes flashed open.

"Have you ever wondered about this? About all the things that had to have happened, not just in our lifetimes, but in the history of the world, to make this one simple thing possible? Easy example: if Columbus had not discovered America, neither you nor I would exist; a million - more than a million - chance occurrences, and all of them, when you look at it retroactively, necessary. Necessary, that is to say, if this thing we call history - history with a capital H - has a meaning. Have you read Hegel, Mr. Antonelli?"

The question, his question, seemed to amuse him. Pushing back from the metal table he lowered his chin over his crossed arms. He looked at me, smiling, as he waited for my answer. I felt like a student in a college class again: I had sense that what I was being asked had some tremendous significance and I did not have the slightest idea what it might be. I actually felt myself gulp.

"No, I haven't...read Hegel, I mean."

He was magic. He made it seem as if that was the most intelligent answer anyone could have given, that it was more than he could have hoped for. I felt, in that moment, enormously proud and started to laugh at my own confusion.

"Sometime, you might; but whatever you do, don't try the Phenomenology. Not unless," he laughed, "you find yourself, like me, at what may be the beginning of a life sentence." His eyes shut halfway; he became as serious as if he were studying something on the printed page. "Hegel isn't as difficult as everyone thinks; not as difficult as the Phenomenology is to read. If you're interested, read his Philosophy of History. It is reasonably straightforward. Try to understand it this way. Hegel begins with a seemingly simply question: When we look back through history, beginning with the Greeks, then the Romans, then Christianity, and now the modern world, does anything make sense? All these revolutions and wars, all this carnage and violence, is it just a 'tale told by an idiot signifying nothing but sound and fury,' or was it all the necessary steps in a journey. Hegel insists it was all necessary, what had to happen before human beings could reach the point where they were truly free, where they were no longer slaves to custom and tradition, where they could finally understand that every individual - not just one man, or a few - had the right to determine the condition of his own existence. History, for Hegel, ends with him. Notice what happens. Everything before Hegel, all of history - the history that has meaning because it is the development of reason - has meaning, in the way we look at things today, because it is progressive, each generation building on what other generations built before. That means that history - everything before Hegel - is defective because, by definition, it is still on the way to completion. More than that, it means that only the present is in position to judge the past. The past is incapable of understanding itself. This means - and this is crucial - that thought itself is a prisoner of time. Thought is a function of the time and place the thought occurred. The works of Plato, the works of Aristotle, are nothing more than a reflection of ancient Greece and Athens.

"Hegel, you see, is the foundation of how we view history. Hegel is in every respect dead wrong. I know you aren't here to discuss Hegel, or any of the other things I teach, but it sometimes helps to put things in context. This trial may end up being more about history than anything else."

I opened my black leather briefcase and took out a yellow legal pad.

"You write with a fountain pen! The only thing better would be if you used a quill!," cried Boe, with gleeful wonder. "Someone who still writes longhand. I would have hired you based on that fact alone. Hired you? I don't even know what you charge. Whatever it is, I'm sure it's beyond my capacity to pay."

He said this with a shrug of indifference. It did not matter what his defense might cost because he could not pay for it. It was my business if I thought this a problem. It was not any of his concern. I could stay, or I could leave, but though that seemed to be his attitude, I don't think he believed that I would not handle his defense. Why would I let anything as unimportant as money stop me from the chance to spend more time with him? In anyone else it would have been sheer pretension, the boorish arrogance of a self-important fool; with Boe, it was a kind of reward, an acknowledgement that you were more serious about what you did than the money you might make from doing it.

I began, or tried to begin, at the beginning. I asked him what he had told the police.

"When you were arrested, did you tell the police anything, or did you tell them that you wanted a lawyer?"

He looked at me as if I were an errant child, one whose mistakes, however, he sympathized with and was willing to forgive.

"I told them everything they wanted to know; I answered every question. It only seemed fair. They answered all of mine."

"All of yours? You asked them questions?"

"Yes, of course; how else does anyone learn anything?"

I put down my pen and leaned back in my chair. I forgot about the murder of Lucas Fairweather; I forgot about James Michael Redfield's sinister manipulation; I forgot about everything except Alan Boe and his questioning by the police.

"I asked them - there were two detectives: Grayson and Huddleston - if they had ever thought about how much better things would be if the chief of police was gone. They confessed - they seemed to like the idea - that it had crossed their minds. And then I asked them if they had ever, even for just an instant, had the thought - the fugitive thought - that it would not be such a terrible thing to kill the chief themselves. They looked at each other, and, if they had not had the idea before, it did not seem like a bad idea now. That is when I made my confession."

"Your confession?" I laughed, though I could not have explained why. "You confessed to the murder of...?"

"I confessed to having the same thought, having it more than once, almost every time I heard the chancellor speak in the faculty senate. I confessed to that. And because we were, the three of us, guilty of the thought, we should all go to prison together. Then I asked them another question: why, if they had the thought, had they never done it? This is a serious question. Why not murder someone? What holds us back? Is it the fear of getting caught, the fear of punishment; or is it a different kind of fear: the fear of what others will think of us, fear for our reputation? Or is it, finally, because we understand that this isn't who we are, men who cannot control themselves, who have to resort to violence because we lack the intelligence - the reason - to do anything else?"

"What did they say to that?" I asked, amused, and utterly bewildered, by what this strange goggle-eyed apparition was telling me. "What was their answer."

"They didn't have an answer. They tried to make a joke of it. They said they were afraid that whoever took the chief's place might be even worse. But, to their credit, they did not try to make a joke out of my question. They agreed it was an interesting question to ask. And so they asked me, if I had not killed the chancellor, what had stopped me. I told them the truth: Lucas Fairweather was not worth it. And then, of course - they were detectives after all - they asked me, if Fairweather was not worth it, who was? Who did I think worth murdering. I'm sure they felt compelled to ask this, to see if I thought murder was sometimes okay, because that would mean that despite my denials, I could have murdered the chancellor. I said there were of course people who should be murdered, and that I knew they were of the same opinion."

"Were they - of the same opinion?"

"They didn't think so - at first."

Boe was a prisoner, accused of murder, sitting in a windowless room that seemed to have been constructed for the specific purpose of producing a sense of utter hopelessness, and he was as full of energy and enthusiasm, as full of life, as anyone I had ever seen. Every word, every eager sentence, careened off the walls like a jazz player's brass trumpet.

"They didn't think so - at first?" I asked, as I began to shake with laughter.

Boe threw up his hands, his astonishing eyes darting in what seemed a dozen different directions at once.

"Yes, of course; because it is obvious that murder is sometimes not merely justifiable, but worthy of the highest praise. Hitler. If someone had murdered him, would anyone call that wrong? Rules are important, Mr. Antonelli, as I need not tell you; but the exceptions are what have to be understood."

I picked up my pen and tapped it gently on the thick legal pad on which I had yet to write a line.

"Was that the end of it? Did the detectives now start to ask you questions about what had happened, what you were doing the night of the murder?"

He quickly shook his head, eager to go on with his story.

"I asked them that, given that I was innocent, that I had not killed the chancellor, or anyone else, how they would feel if I were nevertheless convicted. Judging from the look on their faces, I think no one had ever asked them this before. They said - and I thought this quite honorable - that if I was innocent they hoped I would not be convicted. They explained that they were only following the evidence. I had been seen coming out of the building."

"You were in the building, at the time of the murder, sometime between eleven and midnight?"

"Yes, I was there. I'm there, near there, almost every night at that time. It's when I walk across campus and try to think about whatever I have been studying that evening."

"But why did you happen to go into the building? I take it you don't do that every night when you are out for your walk? You need a key."

"I was just passing in front when I heard a woman scream from somewhere inside. That's the reason I went in: to see what was going on, to see if I could help. And it was not locked. I

126

had just started up the stairs when a woman bolted past me in the dark, bumped into me, almost knocked me over. I started after her; I thought she must be panic-stricken, that she must need help, someone to call 911. But suddenly the alarm bell went off and all the lights came on and security guards were running toward me. I explained what had happened. They took down my information, and then let me go on my way."

Chapter Nine

Giuseppe Gambarini thought the whole thing criminal.

"I knew Professor Boe, not personally - we've never met - but by reputation. No one here seems to know much about him - the newspaper reports refer to him only as a teacher in the philosophy department - but in Europe, where we still take seriously the great minds of the past, everyone knows him as the greatest living authority on German philosophy from Hegel to Nietzsche. There isn't a graduate student in philosophy or political science who has not studied his writings."

Gambarini's gorgeous wife, Sophia, flashed a brilliant smile.

"But Giuseppe, just because someone isn't Italian doesn't mean he cannot be an extremely intelligent murderer. I mean," she asked, exchanging a glance with Tangerine, "the only murderers who are very interesting are….Well, perhaps Giuseppe is right. We Italians are a little spoiled. We had the Borgias, and as if that weren't enough, Machiavelli then taught the world murder as policy. Yes, I agree: in America it doesn't seem likely that someone as well-educated, as deeply learned as…."

The four of us were having dinner in a small restaurant in North Beach, one of those out of the way places only people who live in the city know about. It was Sunday, the night before the trial of Alan Boe for the murder of Lucas Fairweather was scheduled to start. I was grateful to get away from the frenzied anticipation of what might happen, the endless questions and answers that might occur at trial, - what a witness might say, all the different ways what he said might be dealt with - everything a kaleidoscope of shifting images and sounds, the fragments of what became, as the trial drew closer, my own disordered mind. Giuseppe's remarks, and Sophia's response, gave me something to think about, a central thread that held everything together.

"I should have done that,"I blurted out. "I should have read what Boe has written."

"Why?" asked Tangerine, tilting her head in curiosity. "What would you learn from what he wrote about 19th century German philosophy that would help you defend him?"

"It might help me understand why he was chosen."

"Chosen?" asked Sophia, tilting her head exactly the way Tangerine had done.

It was uncanny, how the two of them, a generation apart, sometimes seemed the mirror image of each other. They laughed at the same things, and usually at the same time, and then, with a kind of sixth sense, would look at each other in silent confirmation of their shared reaction to what someone else had just said.

"Chosen," she repeated. "Someone chose Professor Boe to be the accused, the defendant in the trial you start tomorrow?"

"Yes," said Tangerine, with a flash of anger in her eyes. "Chosen by the one responsible, the man who was behind the murder of Allison Friedrich. This is the second murder he has either committed himself or arranged to have done. Someone who...." She turned to me, afraid she might have gone too far, but not sorry if she had. "It isn't anything Joseph has told me. I promise that it isn't. I've met him, listened to what he said about why Allison Friedrich was murdered and why her innocent husband was put on trial." Turning to me again, Tangerine smiled softly. "That's all right, isn't it? You haven't told me anything you shouldn't; I can tell them what I know myself?"

Gambarini did not understand, and when I explained what

the lawyer-client privilege meant he tapped his fingers together as he thought through the consequences.

"The priest in the confessional. Although not quite," he remarked, remembering a distinction. "A priest can never tell anything a penitent tells him, even if he hears him confess that he is planning to murder someone; or even, for that matter, blow up a city. There is a reason for the difference." A slight smile signifying grudging admiration for the consistency of a belief that, though raised a Catholic, he no longer shared, curled across his mouth. "When you confess to a priest, you are confessing to God. If you tell the priest you are going to commit a crime, you are telling God, and God has the power to stop it."

"Which means, my dear Antonelli," said Sophia, "that you may have to play God yourself."

Her husband looked at her with curiosity. He knew she understood the distinction he had just drawn between the obligations of a priest and a lawyer; she knew that, unlike the priest, the lawyer could, and in certain circumstances was required, to reveal what a client said concerning what he intended to do, as opposed to what he had done.

"Someone who doesn't tell you what they're going to do," she explained, a shrewd glint in her large, luminous eyes, "but tells you about the intricate scheme by which someone was murdered and an innocent man was put on trial, and gives you every reason to think he is doing it again. God isn't going to do anything about it."

Lifting an eyebrow, Giuseppe nodded his agreement, the way, I imagined, he would have responded to a musician in an orchestra with a thoughtful suggestion about how something should be played. Gambarini was an orchestra in himself. Everything - his hands, his fingers, his eyes - was always in motion, keeping time, as it were, with the measured movement of his words. Long, lean, with gray hair that curled over his collar in back, wearing a dark tailored suit with an open collar white dress shirt, as elegant sitting in a cafe as on the podium in a concert hall, he spoke in a slow, unhurried voice that seemed to echo with five centuries of music, history, and culture.

"Two murders, two trials, both men innocent, the first one acquitted, and you're the attorney in each. That cannot be coincidental. It would seem that you are the central character in a drama still being written." He looked at me with a new, and different, interest. "Your situation seems to be extremely precarious. You have become a character in someone else's work of fiction."

"Someone else's?" asked Sophia, puzzled, but also, because she knew the subtlety of his mind, more than a little amused.

"What I learned from Alan Boe's remarkable book, what he wrote about Nietzsche: we invent ourselves, or someone else does."

"Nietzsche!" laughed Sophia. "That's all he talked about for months! You should have seen him," she said, waving her hand back in front of her face as she tossed her head. "Nietzsche this, Nietzsche that! He was like a schoolboy suddenly, passionately, in love - not with a girl, that would be too prosaic, but something as godlike as God himself!"

Giuseppe Gambarini watched with amused affection the antic exaggerations of the woman whose exuberance had, ever since he first met her, made even dull things seem exciting.

"It wasn't my fault," he insisted, dryly. "Ten, or twelve, years ago - I don't remember exactly when, except that I was scheduled to conduct the Berlin philharmonic orchestra the next season. One of the selections was to be Richard Strauss' Thus Spake Zarathustra. Like everyone else of my generation, I had read some of Nietzsche when I was a university student. I had perhaps read a few pages, a few sections, of Nietzsche's Zarathustra. But now I thought I should try to get a deeper understanding of what Zarathustra meant. Let me explain. I could read what Richard

Strauss had written - the music, his composition; and I could take an orchestra through it. But what if there was more to it than what Richard Strauss thought; what if he had in some important respect failed to get hold of what Nietzsche was trying to say? This may seem unnecessary and even beside the point. The music is there. Anyone who can read music can play it. But music is the universal language, the only one we have, and Richard Strauss had written what, by the title alone, is an interpretation of one of the great works of the human mind, one of the last great works ever written. Strauss interpreted Nietzsche. I now had to interpret Strauss. That meant, or at least it seemed to me, that I had to go back to the original source to see whether what Strauss had done should be, not exactly corrected, but changed in emphasis. Boe helped me see this. It was something he said about translations in that book of his. Too many translations, especially translations from the ancient Greek, try to put everything in terms of the way things are understood at present. Instead of a literal translation, using the same English word for each Greek word, we end up with a translator's interpretation of what he thinks Plato, for example, must have meant. That helped me see the problem. Did Richard Strauss give a literal translation of Nietzsche's Zarathustra, or was his composition his own interpretation of what Nietzsche wrote? It is music, not a philosophical critique; but music, great music, is always philosophical. It is always a search for wisdom, an attempt to plumb the depths of the mystery of our existence. So, yes, I studied Nietzsche and, among other things, discovered how close great writing is to great music. Read Nietzsche, listen to Beethoven, you sit there, mesmerized by what you hear, carried to places you did not know existed, transported out of yourself and then brought back, changed into someone different, better, than you were before, determined, in ways you had never thought possible, to try to do something great yourself. Because you now know that you will never again be satisfied with settling for anything less than that."

Her fingers spread as wide as they would go, Sophia was gesturing with her hands, smiling and laughing at the same time.

"This is what I had to listen to - for months! He never stops. You won't believe this," she cried, looking first at Tangerine and then at me, "but he means what he says! Once he started, he could not stop. The next year, he was scheduled to perform Wagner. So what does he do? He has us stay in the same hotel - the same suite - where Wagner wrote the opera he was going to play! You think this isn't strange? The hotel is in Palermo. We live in Palermo. We stayed there for a month. Sometimes I walked home, just to remind myself what it was like to live in more than two rooms."

"But you always came back at night," Giuseppe reminded her.

Throwing back her head, she gave him a wicked, scornful look.

"I was always tired - after the way I had spent my afternoons."

"Not that tired, as I remember," he replied, with a droll, roguish grin of his own.

"At your age, it's a wonder you remember anything !" she shot back, her eyes full of excitement and full of life.

"Did it help, staying where Wagner stayed when he wrote the opera you were going to be conducting?" I asked, seriously interested.

He glanced around the small, neighborhood restaurant. There were perhaps a dozen tables, all of them, and the chairs as well, a hard, burnished black; all the tablecloths a soft white, almost almond, color. The pictures on the walls were scenes of the Italian countryside and the Italian sea.

"This is an Italian restaurant. The food here is very good. That would tell you two things of importance if you have not been here, but nothing close to what you know - what you feel - sitting here. If I didn't know Wagner's music, if I hadn't known something about Wagner's life, if I had not read what Nietzsche wrote about what he finally realized Wagner was trying to do - make the kind of large, grandiose music that would attract the attention, by appealing to the emotions, of the crowd, use music to create a mass movement and become a popular idol - staying in Wagner's room in a hotel would have been little more than a tourist's curiosity. As it was, it gave me a sense - and I cannot explain this any better than to say it was like tracing someone's footsteps along a path you have never traveled - of how all the things that have the greatest effect, the things that change how people think, how they feel, are always done in private, someone working alone where no one can intrude. I would sit there for hours, listening in my mind to the music he wrote; listening as if, as in a way I was, I was hearing each new note as it first came into existence. You do the same thing," he said, smiling at me with the certainty of a thing foretold. "You know what it feels like to be in a courtroom, what it is like to ask questions of a witness, to talk to juries. The place where something happens - you can describe it to someone, but you can only know what it feels like to be there, doing that kind of work, by being there yourself. Don't you agree?"

"Giuseppe is right, isn't he?" asked Tangerine, eager, as always, to see the connections that often pass unnoticed. "But more than the courtroom - where the crime took place. How long did you spend on the sailboat where Allison Friedrich was murdered? Hours, half a day, and now…Berkeley, the chancellor's office."

"You were there? Of course, you would have done that," said Gasparini. "Did you discover anything that helps?"

"Yes."

They all looked at me, waiting to hear what it was. I started on my dinner, as if there was nothing left to say.

"Joseph Antonelli - you're the worst!" laughed Tangerine.

"Yes, I discovered something; no, I won't tell you. I save

134

all surprises for trial."

"You're worse than the worst!"

"That means," said Sophia, with a sly smile of approval, "that he is best at being bad. And if that is true, my dear Tangerine, I think you have nothing to complain about. But now, prove it, Joseph - be the worst of the worst, or the best of the bad, and tell us, reveal your secret, so we can all become silent conspirators in whatever plot you are preparing, this surprise you are going to spring on everyone in court."

She was so much like what I imagined Tangerine might be like in twenty years, I almost wished I was suddenly much older.

"Scuff marks," I reported matter of factly and went back to my dinner.

"Scuff marks? On the floor?" asked Giuseppe, wondering why that might be significant.

"On the chancellor's desk."

They looked at one another, thoroughly confused.

"I'm sorry; I really can't say more than that."

"You mean you won't."

"Sophia will be there watching; I'll come whenever I don't have rehearsal. So, I agree, Joseph: don't spoil the surprise. But that isn't the only thing you discovered, is it? How do I know this?" he said, turning suddenly to Tangerine. "I don't know. It's the music, perhaps. After a while you know before you hear it that a note isn't right, that something is missing. Am I right, is there something else?" he asked, perfectly confident I would agree.

"It's possible; it depends on what the scuff mark means. I'm not trying to be difficult, but it isn't as straightforward as you might think. It depends on whether I can use those scuff marks to get a witness for the prosecution to change his story."

Giuseppe studied me with a kind of cheerful intensity.

"Change his story to tell the truth, or change his story in a way that by showing he has been deceptive will discredit his testimony?"

"Both, I think; but I won't know until it starts. You're right, by the way: being there, having a sense of how things work, of what goes on when someone has a thought or takes an action, makes all the difference. I could tell you who the witness is, I could tell you what he is going to say; I could tell you what I am going to ask him, how that single scuff mark will - or might - change everything, but it would not be half the truth of the way it will happen. I don't know that yet, and I won't know - I can't know - until I am right in the middle of it."

A strange look of what seemed nostalgia took possession of Gasparini's kind, thoughtful eyes.

"Nietzsche could have written what you just said. What am I saying? - Nietzsche wrote what you just said: We don't think the thought, the thought thinks us. It's Descartes' classic line, the one every schoolboy used to learn: 'I think, therefore I am.' Nietzsche asked: Who is this I? A thought comes to us. It is what intrigues me most about what you do, a lawyer in a courtroom. The action unfolds, each question produces an answer, each answer produces another question. It is, is it not, like watching a play that writes itself? A play, however, that like any great play depends for its success on a great actor. And that is what you are - isn't it? A great actor who also happens to be a great playwright."

Shoving to the side my only half-finished dinner, I leaned forward on my arms. This was far too interesting to even think of eating.

"It's what a trial really is: a story - two stories: yours and the prosecution's - stories about what the evidence means, or what it could mean. You're right: it isn't just who has the better story to tell, but who can tell the story in a way that makes twelve people you've never met want to hear more, makes them want to believe what you're telling them, believe that they can trust you, that you would never tell them anything you did not believe yourself."

136

"And do you?" asked Sophia, with the sympathetic interest that was almost never missing. "Do you always believe what you tell a jury?"

I looked away and with narrowed eyes shook my head, wondering if I really knew the answer. Then I looked back.

"Yes, always. I have a talent for self-delusion. There have been cases I was forced to take to trial because there was no offer of anything less than the maximum sentence the defendant could get if he were convicted at trial. Those are easy cases. The defendant is guilty; there is nothing to lose. An innocent man isn't going to be convicted, and a guilty one might go free. And every time it happens, every time I take a guilty man to trial, once the trial begins I start to wonder how any jury could possibly convict on the basis of what the prosecution is able to prove. When I get to closing argument, that is all I think about: what the prosecution has failed to prove. I know he's guilty, everyone knows he's guilty; but the prosecution did not prove it. That is what I do - play my part in the play, as Giuseppe was describing it, use, more often than not, the prosecution's own witnesses to tell the story the jury needs to hear."

"And then the guilty man goes free, and you go home and sleep well that night, because you won," remarked Sophia, with a look that said she was not at all sure.

"No, that wouldn't be true," replied her husband. "I imagine there have been times when Joseph hasn't slept well at all."

With his thumb under his chin and two fingers stretched along the side of his face, Giuseppe smiled to himself. He reached for his glass and took a long, slow drink, and then, putting it down, rubbed his lower lip with the fourth finger of that same hand.

"There must have been a case in which you were at least tempted to let a guilty client get what he deserved."

I could think of half a dozen.

"It's a temptation I've managed to resist."

"Not a temptation in the trial that starts tomorrow, I'm sure. Do you think you'll have any difficulty winning?"

We were like practiced liars with too much respect for each other not to tell the truth with our eyes.

"It shouldn't be too difficult. Everyone in the university knew that Alan Boe despised Fairweather, and that Fairweather was intent on driving Boe out of the university. Boe had led public protests, spoken to a rally of more than ten thousand students and faculty outside the administration building two weeks before the murder, insisting that if Fairweather did not go, the university would be destroyed. Boe was seen outside the building between 11:30 and midnight the night the murder occurred, and he admitted to the police that he had gone inside. Blood - Fairweather's blood - was found on his clothing. The woman he claims bolted past him on the stairway has never come forward and no one has been found who saw her. All in all," I added, with a shrug and a smile, "it shouldn't be a problem at all to win this case."

"Because of a scuff mark," said Tangerine, wondering what I was really up to.

"No, because of Alan Boe."

"Is he really that...?"

"Yes, and a whole lot more. I'm not surprised," I said, looking across the table at Gambarini, "what you said about his reputation, the depth of intelligence in what he has written. I wouldn't be surprised by anything you, or anyone else, might tell me about him. He is completely and utterly unique. He told me not to worry about the trial, that he was looking forward to it. He had never been put on trial before and he thought it would be - and I swear this is the word he used - a 'wonderful' experience. I felt obligated to tell him that it might not be as wonderful as he thought, that innocent men were sometimes convicted. His eyes - the strangest eyes I have ever seen - actually lit up. If that happens, he said, do what you can to get me life in prison. Think of all the time I'll have to study and write. No students taking courses because they have to fulfill some requirement; no faculty who, because they are specialists in their respective field, know more and more about less and less. I think he was teasing me, and he even tugged on my sleeve and said that if it was not too late it might make sense to change his plea to guilty. He seemed a little disappointed when I informed him he would have to stand in front of a judge and describe what he had done. His only remark was 'some lies are noble.'"

"Did he say that? Did he really say that?" laughed Gasparini with such full throated enthusiasm that the other conversations in the restaurant all stopped. "Plato's Socrates: the noble lie by which to convince others to do what is right. I think I'll cancel all the rehearsals. This is something I have to see."

"You know you won't!" cried Sophia, her eyes shining with gleeful malice. "You wouldn't cancel a rehearsal to attend my funeral, if they were scheduled for the same time!"

He fixed her with a bright, decisive smile.

"But that could never happen. I could always change the time of the funeral."

"You see," she said to Tangerine, "what I have to live with! What he doesn't know is that there could not be any rehearsal - none of the musicians would bother to attend: they would all be in mourning, too distraught to even think of playing."

Giuseppe Gambarini sighed.

"It's true, at least among the musicians in the orchestra at home. They're all in love with her. I never let her attend rehearsal - they can't keep their eyes off her."

"Perhaps he's not so bad after all," purred Sophia.

"But I would if I could," he assured me. "I would love to watch this trial of yours from start to finish. I'll be there whenever I can. But, let me ask you, do you know already who the judge will be, and the prosecutor?"

"Yes, both. There have been a couple of hearings; routine

matters, mostly, things that have to be decided before trial. The prosecutor is one of the best around; the judge....well, the judge is a problem. It's odd, in a way: they're both women; but that is the only thing they have in common. Eleanor McFarland has been prosecuting cases for thirty years or more. She's in her sixties, heavy-set, everything about her, from the way she speaks to the way she moves, deliberate, methodical, and nothing, not a word, ever out of place or out of order. She makes everything she does in a courtroom look easy. The judge, Michelle Longstreet, makes everything she does look hard. She can't sit still, she's always bustling about, shifting positions in her chair, bending her head to one side and then the other. She's in her thirties, one of the youngest judges, and as ambitious as they come. There is talk - more than talk, it's the working assumption of everyone who knows her - that she wants to be governor. They say she's very smart; there isn't any doubt she's remarkably good-looking. Stanford law, good-looking, ambitious - and too important to bother about the law. Whatever way she rules on a question today, chances are she'll rule the other way tomorrow. She seems to think that way neither side can complain they weren't treated fairly. She's afraid of McFarland; she's intimidated by anyone who knows more than she does. But it's more than that. I think she feels in McFarland's presence a little like a fraud, someone who has not earned her way; someone who knows that this other, much older, woman should be sitting on the bench instead of her."

The restaurant had gradually emptied out. Other than a young couple at a table in the corner who were so much in love they would not have noticed if an earthquake had brought the roof down on top of them, we were the only people left. It felt like a Sunday night before school when, as a boy, I was always hoping that, just this once, the clock would not move. I loved being in trial; it was what I had spent most of my life doing, trying cases; but I hated the uncertainty that always held me by the throat squeezing tighter and tighter, as the day of trial approached. Talking about it gave me a confidence that, left alone, I did not feel. I started to go on about the tension I had noticed between the prosecutor and the judge, the imbalance between their abilities, as well as their ambitions, when Sophia asked a question that, precisely because it was obvious, cut to the heart of the issue.

"Doesn't that help you? If they don't like each other, isn't the judge more likely to favor the defense?"

"She is supposed to favor the defense. In a murder case - in any criminal case, really - when there is any doubt how a ruling should go, the defense should have the advantage. The burden of proof is on the prosecution. They have to provide evidence that leaves no doubt."

I stirred my coffee with a spoon, my cheek red with embarrassment at this mindless textbook answer to an honest question.

"That's how it is supposed to work," I said, in a quiet, chastened voice. "It's usually the other way round. In this country - if I'm not mistaken, it's different in Italy - if a defendant is acquitted, there is nothing the state, the government, can do. There is no appeal. A trial court judge can rule out evidence that should have been allowed, make it impossible for the prosecution to win, and that is the end of it. Only a guilty verdict can be appealed. That's why a lot of trial court judges bend over backward to deny any motion the defense makes, why a lot of them will sustain any objection made by the prosecution to a question the defense asks and overrule the same objection when its made by the defense to a question the prosecution asks. But that's all right, because you know what is going to happen. The problem with Longstreet is that she is so completely unpredictable. You have no idea what she is going to do, because she has no idea what she is going to do."

"Which means - does it not? - that she is predictable after all," remarked Sophia, with the bare whisper of a smile on her lips. "As predictable as any woman who cannot make up her mind. Do you know what you do with such a predictably unpredictable woman? - Ignore her."

"That might be difficult. She's the judge."

"Ignore her!" repeated Sophia, laughing. "You'll figure out a way. From what I hear, you've managed to ignore every other woman in your life until you met Tangerine, and there has not been a man born yet who could ignore a woman looks like her. Ignore her. Ask Giuseppe if you don't know. He ignores everyone, even sometimes me, if you can believe it!"

It was good advice. I had often followed it before. I had ignored judges, and even gone out of my way to antagonize them, to force a jury to choose between an overbearing magistrate, blind to everything except the belief that the defendant must be guilty because accused, and a defense lawyer who was only standing up for what was right. But whatever her failings, Michelle Longstreet was not anything like the arrogant, self-righteous fools I had sometimes found staring down at me from the bench with cruel condescension and a misplaced sense of their own importance. Still, though the manner and the style were far more attractive, there was underneath it all that same sense of entitlement, that same belief that she was the master of her courtroom and everyone who came before her slaves. Ignore her, two words, but spoken by Sophia Gambarini, who had a style and manner few others could ever match, they made me suddenly look forward to Monday morning and the trial.

Chapter Ten

The jury could not keep their eyes off him. No one could. Everyone stared at Alan Boe, transfixed by an ugliness that, far from concealing, only concentrated their attention on the shining brilliance of his strange, almost unworldly eyes, eyes that glowed with laughter and seemed to take in everything at a single glance. When before the jury was sworn Judge Longstreet asked if any of them were personally acquainted with the defendant and none of them did, he jumped to his feet, bowed slightly, and with a smile that would have rivaled an accomplished 18th century courtier, told them what a pleasure it was to meet them.

"Mr. Boe, you're not to address the jury, now, or at any other time during the trial," cautioned Longstreet, trying to appear firm and decisive.

"I thought you were introducing us," replied Boe, who continued to stand. He smiled again at the jury and tapped his finger three times on the counsel table. "Would it not have been rude of me to stay silent? Wouldn't you have thought me an ill-mannered boor?"

His eyes, I swear, were magnetic. Longstreet forgot where she was.

"Yes, I suppose....No; no one would have thought that. I'm sure they wouldn't have..." She remembered where she was. "You're not to address the jury, Mr. Boe. Do you understand?"

"Not at all? Not even when I am a witness, sworn to tell the truth, testifying in open court? Who do I then address, if not the jury? Can you tell me that?"

Longstreet blinked, and then, twisting her head to the side, had to think about what he had asked.

"Of course that's what I meant. When you testify - if you testify, because, as I'm sure your lawyer has explained to you, you don't have to testify, you -"

"I'm going to testify," interjected Boe, with eager insistence. "There isn't any question about that. I'll do it right now, if you like. I'd like to do it right now. I'll answer any question anyone might care to ask. One question: Is there any time limit, any rule on how long my answers can be?"

I was sitting next to Alan Boe's now empty chair, staring up at the ceiling and trying hard not to laugh. In any other trial, with any other defendant, I would have grabbed him by the sleeve and pulled him down into his chair and in no uncertain terms let him know he was not to do anything without my express prior approval. But Alan Boe was not like any other defendant; he was not like anyone else at all. He was unique, a force of nature, and the more the jury got to see him as he really was the greater the chance they would come to believe he was just about the last person in the world who would ever murder anyone. Boe would have thought it the worst kind of failure: you cannot win an argument with the dead.

"Is there any time limit?" repeated Longstreet, her bright eyes shadowed by a doubt as to the meaning of a question she had never been asked before.

"Yes, your Honor," said Boe. With his feet spread wide apart and his hands clasped behind his back, he looked a little like Napoleon asking questions of his generals. "Because, sworn to tell the truth, that sometimes requires a fairly lengthy exploration of all the known alternatives."

"The known...? All right, Mr. Boe; I think we have done enough with this. Now, please, take your seat. You should discuss with your attorney, Mr. Antonelli, any questions related to your testimony, if you decide to testify. It's time to get on with the trial."

He did not move. He stood there, peering up at her as if he were waiting for her to say something more. Aware that everyone in the courtroom was watching what threatened to become a test of wills, Longstreet started to become irritated.

"Sit down, Mr. Boe! I won't ask again."

"You wouldn't have to ask twice if you would simply answer once. The question is whether there is a limit. And there is, isn't there, if not on my answers when I testify under oath, but on the court's patience when I question what it does? Thank you, your Honor," he said, and with a brief, polite nod at the jury, finally resumed his place in the chair next to mine.

The first witness called by the prosecution was the coroner. Question by question, Eleanor McFarland took him through his findings, establishing that Lucas Fairweather had been bludgeoned to death, the back of his skull shattered, by a marble statue which was covered with his blood. The second witness narrowed the time within which the murder had occurred. Melvin Hoskins, a campus security guard, had, as part of his normal nightly routine, checked on the chancellor's office at around eleven o'clock.

"What did you find? Was Chancellor Fairweather in his office when you checked?" asked McFarland, standing broad shouldered at the end of the jury box, directly in line with the witness.

"The chancellor was there," replied Hoskins, with a tight, nervous smile.

He was a small man, with straight black hair parted neatly on the side. He looked at the jury, remembering too late that he was supposed to have done that when he began his answer. McFarland, a large woman who, because of the power of her mind and the force of her personality, seemed even larger than she was, showed him with the kindness in her gray eyes that it was nothing to worry about.

"When did you next check on the chancellor's office?"

Hoskin looked immediately at the jury, but instead of starting his answer, he looked back at McFarland. He seemed to draw strength from her. He was not young, and he was not old; he was in his middle-age, more comfortable roaming the corridors of an empty building late at night than answering questions in front of the silent, searching gaze of several hundred strangers in a courtroom. His voice, not very strong to begin with, faltered and failed, forcing him to repeat himself after every few words he managed to get out. Eleanor McFarland did her best to be understanding.

"I know it's difficult, having to give testimony in front of all these people. Just take your time. Tell us in your own words what happened next."

Clutching the arms of the witness chair like a shipwrecked survivor, he took a deep breath.

"I check every office every hour or so. He was there - Mr. Fairweather - when I opened the door to look around, like I said before. I came back, about an hour later. The lights were still on. I did not see the need to open the door again, but then - I can't explain it - I just decided I ought to take a closer look. I opened the door, and there he was, slumped over his desk, the statue on the floor, blood all over it."

Eleanor McFarland nodded slowly, sympathizing with what he had had the misfortune to discover. Her eyes stayed fixed on him as she tried to keep him on track. She wanted him to concentrate on every detail of what he had seen.

"Was there anything else - the body, the statue, the blood everywhere - anything else you noticed?"

There was something. I could tell it from the tone of her voice.

"Boe."

"I'm sorry….Boe? The name of the defendant. What do you mean?"

"The name - his name - written on the datebook on the chancellor's desk. it was written in for that night."

This was even better than I had hoped, too good not to use right at the beginning of my cross-examination.

"You say you noticed that the defendant's name was written in the chancellor's datebook, and the datebook was laying there, open, right next to the chancellor's dead body - Is that what you testified?"

Melvin Hoskins scratched his neck. He was certain I was trying to trick him into saying something and had no idea what it might be.

"It isn't a trick question, Mr. Hoskins. I swear it isn't. The chancellor had a datebook, and the defendant's name was written in it - Is that true?"

"Yes," he sputtered.

"Do you remember on what line? You said it was 'written in for that night.' Was it for any particular time, as best you could tell?"

"No, it wasn't written like that; it wasn't written straight across, but like this," he said, as he held up his finger and drew it downward. "Through the lines."

"I see. So he wrote a name, the defendant's name, not the way you would for an actual appointment you had with someone, but to remind yourself that you had something you needed, or wanted, to do concerning that person - Would you agree?"

"I guess," he shrugged.

"When you checked the chancellor's office - the prosecution did not ask, but can we assume that eleven o'clock was not the first time you checked his office that evening?"

"No, it wasn't."

"Because you check every hour, from the time you start at - what time?"

"Nine o'clock."

"Was Chancellor Fairweather in his office the first time you checked that evening?"

"No, and he was not there at ten o'clock either."

"Which means he must have come to his office sometime after that, but before eleven - correct?"

"That's right."

I had started pacing, slowly, back and forth in front of the witness stand, listening intently to each answer, looking up only to ask the next question.

"When you first saw him, at eleven o'clock, he wasn't there with the defendant, Alan Boe, was he?" I asked as casually as if I had been asking about the weather.

"No. Boe - I mean Professor Boe - wasn't there."

"Yes, because the chancellor was there, working alone in his office, late at night - correct?"

There was no reply, just dead silence. I stopped pacing and looked straight at him, a knowing smile on my face. And in that moment, Melvin Hoskins knew he was in trouble.

"You liked Lucas Fairweather, didn't you, Mr. Hoskins? I understand he treated you very well, even paid you out of his own pocked for the help you sometimes gave him. That's true, isn't it? - You liked him. He was good to you, probably treated you a lot better than some of those other people who worked in the administration building, the kind who like to look down on anyone who doesn't have a college degree. You liked him, and you didn't want to be part of anything that might be damaging to his reputation. Isn't that correct?"

Eleanor McFarland was on her feet, objecting.

"If there is a question in all this, your Honor, I haven't heard it."

Any other judge would have told me to ask a question; Michelle Longstreet had to give the appearance of being thoughtful. Pursing her lips, she tapped her fingers methodically on the bench.

"I'm afraid I have to agree, Mr. Antonelli. Perhaps you could -"

"The chancellor was not alone when you checked his office at eleven, was he, Mr. Hoskins?" I asked, with such sudden force that he started answering before I had finished.

"No, he wasn't alone, he was with -"

"A woman, a young woman, and they weren't exactly engaged in conversation, were they, Mr. Hoskins?" I asked, with all the righteous anger I could invent. "What were they doing, Mr. Hoskins? What did you see when you suddenly opened the door?"

His eyes had gone wide with wonder at what he thought I knew.

"He had her up on the desk. He was - the chancellor was - fucking the hell out of her! That's what I saw, and that's why I shut the door and got out of there and didn't go back until an hour later!"

His words, the sound of his voice, were drowned out as the courtroom exploded in a sea of noise. Longstreet sat there, gavel in hand, too stunned to remember what she was supposed to do with it.

That evening I had dinner with Tangerine in the city. I had to see Boe in jail later on, and there was not time to go home to Sausalito. We went to one of the places on Fisherman's Wharf were the tourists go. There was less chance of running into anyone we knew, or anyone who might recognize us. With a view across the bay, it was as good a place as any to put the trial, and everything connected with it, into perspective. Tangerine could hardly wait until we sat down to ask the question she had been dying to ask from the moment Melvin Hoskins left the stand.

"How did you know?"

I kept studying the menu, pretending that I did not understand.

"How did you know that Fairweather was not alone? How did you know he was with a woman?"

The waiter came over to our table and took our order. I watched him write it down. He was as nervous as Melvin Hoskins had been. I did not need to look around the restaurant, I could feel everyone stop what they were doing to look at Tangerine. There was something to be learned in the fact that, for opposite reasons, Tangerine made everyone around her stare exactly the same way Alan Boe had done. It was the literal meaning of 'extraordinary.'

"How did you know?" she persisted.

"You know already. I told you last night at dinner."

The blank expression suddenly dissolved. She started to laugh.

"The scuff marks on the desk!" she cried, leaning forward so no one else could hear. "High heels! Of course!" She looked at me a second way, a doubt that it could have been that easy. "But that was a guess. You couldn't have known for sure what those scuff marks meant. And you certainly couldn't have known that poor Mr. Hoskins walked in on them. So how…?"

I took a drink, the kind of wine they buy by the bottle and sell by the glass. It did not matter what it was. Looking across the table at her I would not have noticed if I had been drinking champagne.

"I knew that a woman had been there. She ran into Boe when she was running down the stairs. I knew about Fairweather and women. What better way to get to him, what better way to get to him that late at night? Remember who is behind all this; remember Redfield and what he is capable of doing. Fairweather did not go back to his office to work; he went there to meet that woman. What were the chances that Hoskins, a security guard, would find Fairweather sitting at his desk, alone?"

"But how did you know that Hoskins felt the kind of gratitude to Fairweather that would make him want to conceal what he had seen?"

"Because he had not told the police. There did not seem to

be any other explanation. You're right: I could not be absolutely certain about any of it. But then, when I watched him testify, the way he answered McFarland's questions, how cautious he tried to be. Some of it was nerves, but there was something else. He was holding something back. I could have been wrong, I could have misread everything, but there are two rules in cross-examination."

"Two rules?" she asked, her eyes bright with anticipation.

"The first is - and everyone knows this - never ask a question unless you know what the answer is going to be."

"And the second?" It was all she could do not to laugh out loud.

"Ask it anyway. Just for the hell of it. See what happens. But be quick enough to make sure that everyone thinks you know what you are doing. Because that way, if the answer really hurts your case, the other side will start to worry that you know something they don't."

She looked at me hard and long. Her fingers grasped the edge of her glass. The smile that curled along her lips became a dare.

"Except that you don't really believe that at all, do you? The 'just for the hell of it' part - that I know you believe. But the rest of it - that doesn't apply. Your instinct is too good. You know when to take a chance. Look at the chance you took on me."

"The chance? What chance - that you would laugh in my face when I told you to divorce your husband and marry me?"

"The chance that I may not be what you think I am; the chance that I might not always be able to stay completely sane."

"Completely sane...? You're one of the few really sane people I know."

There was a strange vulnerability in the way she looked at me, a confession that because of how others saw her she thought herself a fraud, and that anyone who could see past her astonishing good looks would discover the fear and trembling of a woman without any other qualities, a woman who was not sufficiently sure of herself to be certain she might not one day shatter.

"Look around, what do you see?" I asked her.

"A restaurant, crowded with people."

"And when we walked in - and even now, some of them - what were they all looking at? - You. And you know it, you've always known it, every time you walk into a room everything stops. That is what you're missing, what you never get to see - You, walking into a room. Everyone else does, but you don't get to. If you could, you might begin to understand that the way you look is more than the way you look."

"The way you look is more than...?"

"It's how I pick juries - How they look. It's how you make a judgement about anyone: the look they have. You don't do it from a photograph, from a picture; you do it when you see them yourself, when they're in the same room, the same place, when they're sitting in the jury box. You see it in their eyes, how they hold themselves, how they react, the way they move. Trust me: I'm never wrong. I didn't fall in love with your photograph; I fell in love with you."

"Would you love me if I were ugly?"

"Probably not," I replied, briskly, suppressing a grin. "Why? Were you thinking of changing?"

"It would be worth being ugly, if I could be like Alan Boe. He's really quite remarkable, isn't he?"

Pushing back from the table, I bent my head to the side and gave her a long, searching glance.

"I don't know that I could ever guess how remarkable, how unusual, he really is. You were there today, watching. What did you think? No, tell me this instead: After what you saw, after what he did, can you imagine him as a murderer, someone who would kill Lucas Fairweather?"

"No, not in a thousand years. Could you?"

"No, never. I've never seen anyone do what he did today. He took over the courtroom. He is a defendant in a murder trial. He's supposed to just sit there and try to look interested. I was the one doing that. Longstreet did not know what to do with him; I'm not sure any other judge could have done any better. And it wasn't because Boe had decided he was going to do this; I don't think he thought about it at all. It is who he is, what he does. The jury - I've never seen anything like the way they reacted - would have declared him not guilty on the spot, if they had been given the chance. That is what has me, not so much worried, as confused."

"Confused? About what?" asked Tangerine, staring into the glass she held with both hands just below her mouth.

"About what James Michael Redfield has in mind. Fair-weather's murder, then this trial. Why Alan Boe? It can't just be to expose what Fairweather really was; it has to be about Boe. But if he knows anything about Boe, he had to have known that, far from feeling punished, Boe seems almost delighted for the chance to experience what it is like to be put on trial."

"That's it! He wants the world to see what Alan Boe is like; he wants the world to see what someone like that can be!"

"But why? - For what reason arrange a murder just to provide what a courtroom full of spectators might find entertaining? It has to be more than that?"

"Why don't you ask him?"

"Redfield?"

"Why not? He seems to think he can arrange everything, control everyone, as he sees fit." She sat straight up, her mouth drawn tight at the corners. "This trial won't be the end of it. We've talked about this. Why not talk to him, ask him questions, put him on the defensive? Maybe he'll make a mistake. You told me the privilege only covers what he has done in the past; it doesn't cover anything he might tell you about what he intends to do next. And it doesn't cover anything he tells you about the Fairweather murder, does it? You told him you weren't his lawyer anymore."

"Redfield won't make that kind of mistake. But, you're right. He'll keep doing this unless I can figure out a way to stop him. He may have already made one mistake. The guard, Hoskins. The woman is the killer. She seduced Fairweather. That would not have been difficult. She tells him she can meet him later that night, after he gets back from dinner in the city at Albert Craven's place. She has sex with him, and afterward, when he's completely relaxed, she probably wanders around his office, examining the various things he keeps on the credenza behind the desk where he is sitting. She did not know - Redfield must not have known - that Hoskins stopped every hour or so to check on the chancellor's office. Boe told the police that a woman had run past him on the stairs. Hoskins' testimony proves the woman was there."

We finished dinner, and for a few short minutes stood outside, listening in the cool California night to the water lapping against the pier. Tangerine leaned against me, her face pressed against my neck and I wondered at the fool I was not to go straight home with her.

"You better go, Joseph Antonelli. Serve your time in jail. My only worry is that once Alan Boe starts talking you might forget to leave."

It was impossible, I thought to myself as we said goodbye, but she was almost right. Alan Boe - what he said and how he said it - was irresistible.

"Listen to this, Mr. Antonelli; I think you'll find it interesting," said Alan Boe, when I entered the small, square windowless conference room. He had somehow managed not just to be there before my arrival but to bring a book with him. "This was written in the 1930's:

'From a metaphysical point of view, Russia and America are the same; the same dreary technological frenzy, the same unrestricted organization of the average man. At a time when the farthermost corner of the globe has been conquered by technology and opened to economic exploitation; when any incident whatever, regardless of where or when it occurs, can be communicated to the rest of the world at any desired speed; when the assassination of a king in France and a symphony concert in Tokyo can be 'experienced' simultaneously; when time has ceased to be anything other than velocity, instantaneousness, and simultaneity, and time as history has vanished from the lives of all peoples; when a boxer is regarded as a nation's great man; when mass meetings attended by millions are looked on as triumph - then, yes, through all this turmoil the question still haunts us like a specter: What for? - Whither? And what then?'"

Closing the pocket size book, Boe nodded twice emphatically.

"And here we are, nearly a century later, and nothing has changed, except that the same tendencies have become more pronounced, to say nothing of the fact that no one now seems to think there is anything wrong. But perhaps it has always been like this: everyone, or almost everyone, busy with their everyday lives, worried about what is going to happen tomorrow or next week, or maybe, some of them, next year. History for most of us begins with ourselves, when we were born. Ancient history goes back as far, but seldom farther, than our grandparents' lives. Greek, Roman, early Christianity, the Middle Ages, the Renaissance - a few short paragraphs in a college textbook, and that only for those who took a course on western civilization."

Boe threw up his hands in mock despair.

"You see, I can't help myself; I have this constant compulsion to tell anyone I can get to listen how much trouble we're in. Yes, I know: you think it odd that I would concern myself with something other than the trouble I am in myself. But, remember, I'm not that important; what happens to me is hardly worthy of notice. And I'm not guilty; even if I am convicted I have nothing

to regret. Consider how really fortunate I am: I get to know what
it is like to be put on trial. Do you have any idea how valuable
this experience is to me - To be put on trial like Socrates? It isn't
quite the same, of course. Socrates was accused of corrupting the
young and not believing in the gods of Athens. I'm only accused
of murder. By the way, that was the reason I asked the judge if
there would be a time limit on what I said when I was a witness in
my own defense. Socrates had a time limit. It probably would not
have made a difference; although, you never know. Trials were
different. The defendant was his own defense; he spoke directly to
the charges, gave his testimony about why the accusation was not
true."

It was so engrossing that it took a moment before I realized he was finished. The strange part was that I was not sure
that he knew he had stopped staying out loud the words that - and
this I was sure of - were still running through his mind. His eyes
were eager with anticipation, because whatever you said in reply,
no matter how dull and commonplace, would give him the chance
to find something remarkable about it, something he could use to
show you how much intelligence those otherwise unremarkable
words of yours contained.

"What can I do for you, Mr. Antonelli? I hope what I did
today didn't embarrass you." He said this in a way that left no
doubt that his refusal to abide by the normal rules of courtroom
behavior had been no mistake; it had been a deliberate challenge.
"Rules are important, but they lose their meaning if you don't know
the reason for them. Is there a rule against a defendant asking questions?"

"You're represented by an attorney; it is assumed that...."

"Yes, precisely - assumed! But is there a rule that prohibits
a defendant, whether or not represented by counsel, from asking
questions? If I were representing myself, I certainly could do so.
One of the determinations whether someone has the mental capaci-

ty to stand trial is whether he can assist in his own defense. That is
what I was doing - was it not? - assisting in my defense. But, don't
worry: I won't do it, at least not very often, and I certainly won't do
it, if you ask me not to."

He had done something no one I had represented had ever
done. He had made me forget that I was his lawyer, and made me
remember the boundless curiosity of my long vanished youth. I
was a spectator entranced by a performance, interested only in what
was going to happen next. But then, in the silence that followed,
staring into eyes that seemed a double mirror of endless depth, the
habit of my profession, what had after years of experience become
second nature, brought me back to the prosaic details of the case
that could not be ignored. But even then, the question I asked was
not one I would normally have asked someone on trial for his life.

"Why do you think you're on trial? Why do you think
someone wants you to be on trial for the murder of Lucas Fairweather?"

He thought about it. He did not shrug his shoulders or
shake his head or do any of the other things by which we ordinarily
show our confusion, or our ignorance. He explored, as he might
have put it, the known possibilities.

"I walk there every night, and always at the same time. It
is a settled routine. I have been teaching at Berkeley for so many
years that my habits are fairly well-known. If someone wanted to
murder the chancellor, they would know that if it were done close
to midnight, I would be in close proximity. That, I think, is what
they call opportunity. As for motive, I had none: I never would
have considered the possibility. But someone else, looking at what
my history has been at the university, the arguments, the disputes,
the organized attempt I was part of to get rid of Fairweather before
he did any more damage - what he, for his part, was planning to
do: the budget cuts, the reorganization, all of it designed to further
diminish the already laughably reduced course offers in philosophy

- might be thought sufficient motive by some."

"That isn't exactly what I meant," I said, tentatively. He was my client, on trial for murder, but there was only so far I could go. "Let me ask the question this way: never mind that someone could try try to put the blame on you. Other than the fact that you walked past the chancellor's office every night, other than the fact that you might seem to have a motive, is there any reason you can think of why someone would want you - Alan Boe - to stand trial for the chancellor's murder? Is there any reason," I went on, peering into his light filled eyes, "why someone would want, not just Lucas Fairweather dead, but to have you put on trial for his death?"

His eyes flashed with instant recognition.

'Who would have a motive to put me on trial for murder? That would be interesting, wouldn't it? Why do you think that? You have a reason. I've learned that much about you, Mr. Antonelli - There is something you know, and you're not ready - or perhaps able - to tell me. It's all right," he remarked, before I could start to explain. "I don't need to know. There is nothing you need to tell me."

This self-imposed restriction lasted perhaps half a second.

"But someone doesn't just want me to be blamed for a murder - they want a trial." A smile rippled across the uneven contours of his large, ungainly mouth. "Perhaps one of my former students wants to see if I really meant it when I used to say that the noblest death in history is what happened to Socrates, and that I could only envy the way he conducted himself in his trial. But, no, that would not be possible. I'm afraid I'm not much help." His eyes flashed a second time. "That means the woman, the one who ran into me, the one who got blood on me, the one who must have murdered the chancellor, did not do it on her own. You're saying she was hired by someone to do this, murder him and frame me?"

"Hired, or persuaded; I'm not sure how she was convinced to do it, but yes. She knew she could get Fairweather to meet her alone in his office. She probably waited after she killed him until she could see you from the window on the second floor and then start screaming to bring you running."

"But she made a mistake - correct. Mr. Hoskins, the security guard."

"Yes. She couldn't have known that Hoskins would open the door and see her with Fairweather. This helps. It confirms you story about a woman being there."

"But that is all it confirms, isn't it? It's still just my word that she was running down the stairs and that was how the chancellor's blood got on my hands and clothing."

I was thinking about something else, the other trial, the first one that James Michael Redfield had arranged.

"I can't tell you everything, but I can tell you that this is the second trial in a sequence. The first one happened a few months ago. Justin Friedrich was put on trial for the murder of his wife. Perhaps you read about it. He was saved at the last minute, just as the trial was ending, when someone left at my office the murder weapon, a gun with the sales receipt marked with the time and place of purchase. It proved that Justin Friedrich could not have murdered his wife. The murder, the trial of an innocent man, were the work of the same person who, I have every reason to believe, arranged the murder of Lucas Fairweather and made certain that you would be put on trial for it."

"What is the connection between the two? What did whoever did this want to achieve in the first trial? I'm assuming the same person gave you the evidence you needed at the end of the trial. If he did not want the defendant convicted, what was he after?"

"To reveal the corruption in the lives of the useless rich. Or so he suggested."

"Then the connection may be obvious."

"Obvious?"

"I am perhaps uniquely qualified to reveal the utter, and almost complete, corruption of higher education in America. You see," he said, his bulb like eyes shining with an uncanny brightness, "I knew this trial would be something to look forward to."

Chapter Eleven

Eleanor McFarland sat hunched over a thin black binder, reviewing the notes she had made for her next witness. There was another, vacant, chair next to her, the place for another, junior, member of the district attorney's office, but McFarland preferred to try her cases alone. A lawyer who knew what she was doing had to work that way. There was no time, and no need, to consult with someone sitting second chair, if at the end of a trial that might last for weeks, or even longer, you were going to be able to stand in front of a jury and without so much as a note to rely on convince them that the evidence left no choice but to convict, or, if you were on the other side, acquit, the defendant.

There were not many lawyers who did this anymore. Eleanor McFarland was one of the last who still understood that if you read from notes there is something missing. It suggests that you are not yourself sufficiently convinced, that you lack the passion of real conviction, if you have to stand there, written notes in hand, or worse yet, with a chalkboard outline, to give your closing argument. Others in the electronic age might have an attention span measured in seconds; Eleanor McFarland could still recite from memory whole passages from Shakespeare's histories.

"Is the prosecution ready to call its next witness?" asked Michelle Longstreet. Trying to accomplish two things at once, she smiled at the jury as she slid onto her chair at the bench.

McFarland did not look up from what she was doing.

"Is the prosecution ready to call its next witness?" again

161

asked Longstreet.

She began to arrange the books and papers she had brought in with her. She stopped, and looked down at McFarland, who had not moved.

"Is the -"

McFarland lumbered to her feet and without so much as a glance at Longstreet, faced the jury.

"The prosecution calls Detective Oliver Grayson."

Longstreet glared at her. McFarland did not notice, or rather, made a point not to appear to notice. There is no advantage in antagonizing the judge presiding over a trial you are trying to win. This was not tactical, it was personal; personal, but perhaps not deliberate. It seemed inadvertent, a slight born of indifference. Eleanor McFarland did not respect Michelle Longstreet. She showed the deference due a trial court judge, but only when she remembered that it was something she owed the position.

Oliver Grayson took the stand, looked out at the crowed courtroom, and then looked at the jury. It was what he would have done in any trial to get a sense of things, a feeling for the people in the room. Having testified in more trials than he could count, his expression was serious, professional. Then he looked at the counsel table where I was sitting next to Alan Boe and for a brief instant came alive. Too late to stop himself, he smiled, and then immediately looked away.

"Detective Grayson," began McFarland, "you were the lead investigator in the murder of Lucas Fairweather?"

"Yes, that's correct: I was," he replied. His voice, a sharp staccato, seemed to match the quick, precise movements with which he punctuated his speech.

"Would you describe to the jury what you observed when you arrived at the scene?"

"My partner, Detective Huddleston, and I got to the chancellor's office at half past midnight. The security guard, Melvin

Hoskins, had discovered the body of Chancellor Fairweather. He called 911 and two uniformed officers were there in a matter of minutes. They called us. Nothing had been touched. The chancellor was laying face down - actually face to the side - on his desk. There was a deep gash in the back of his head, and a lot of blood. A statue, about two feet in length…."

Holding up her hand to stop him, McFarland signaled to the clerk to bring the statue, now encased in a cellophane wrapper, to the witness.

"Is this the statue you were describing?"

"Yes, this is the statue; the murder weapon, if you will."

Holding it in both hands, he lifted it up so the jury could see it better.

"It seems to have a rather sharp edge, especially where it comes to a point. Is it heavy?"

Grayson balanced it in his hands as if he were trying to guess its weight. McFarland motioned for the clerk to again approach the witness.

"Would you please hand it to the jury. And would the members of the jury," she went on, looking over to them, "pass it around so each of you can see for yourself how lethal a weapon it could be."

I was on my feet, but instead of shouting an objection, I just stood there, my hand on my hip, an eyebrow raised in amusement.

"Mr. Antonelli," asked Judge Longstreet, "do you have an objection? Is there -?"

I ignored her. I did worse than that: I held up my hand to stop her, the same way McFarland had done with her witness. I waited until, a moment later, McFarland turned to see what I was doing.

"You have the murder weapon," I congratulated her. "Now if you only had the murderer!"

Nothing bothered Eleanor McFarland. She had too much

the sense of her own ability to let anything get to her. More than that, she had a rare appreciation of how things should be done in a courtroom: not the arid rules of procedure that dull-witted judges like to enforce and dim-witted lawyers do not know how to break, but the way that, with a little daring, a trial can be made into a drama full of unexpected twists and turns. She kept looking at me, a faint, though definite, glimmer of acknowledgement in her eyes, as she insisted in a clear, forceful voice that, "Perhaps your Honor might want to remind Mr. Antonelli that only a sworn witness can testify in a trial."

"I'll try to remember that," I replied, before Longstreet could decide whether she wanted to follow the prosecution's advice.

McFarland had already turned back to her witness.

"The chancellor was dead; the statue which had been used to smash his skull was there, on the floor. What else did you observe?"

Grayson proceeded to describe in detail everything about the room, including the fact that there was only one way in or out.

"So the murderer must have come in that way and then left that way. Was anyone seen leaving the chancellor's office that night?"

"Not leaving his office, but someone - the defendant - was seen inside the building; or rather, leaving the building, at the same time the security guard discovered the chancellor's body."

"The security guard," repeated McFarland, with a pensive expression on her large, square face. She had her hand on the railing of the jury box, her gaze steady and unrelenting, the look of someone who only wanted the truth. "The security guard, Melvin Hoskins - you talked to him?"

"Yes, of course; that night, at the scene, and then, a few days later, he came to our office."

"Did he - either time you talked with him - say anything

about a woman being there that night with the chancellor, anything to make you think Lucas Fairweather had not been there alone in his office?"

"He told us that he checked that office every hour, that Fairweather had been there when he checked at eleven, and that when he went back, a little before midnight, Fairweather was dead."

"As you know, he testified under oath that a woman was there when he checked the office at eleven, and that when he went back, an hour later, it was because he heard someone screaming. Can you account for why Mr. Hoskins did not tell you that?"

"No, I can't. We didn't ask him if anyone had been with Fairweather. In that sense, he did not lie. Maybe we should have asked. He's worked there a long time. Maybe he thought he shouldn't say anything bad about the dead. He's quite religious. He always has his Bible with him. But do I know for sure why he didn't say anything? - No."

"Did he tell you he heard screaming?"

"He said he thought he heard noise."

"Have you - have the police - attempted to find this woman, the one who was seen having sex with Lucas Fairweather?"

"We've tried; but no one saw her. There isn't any record of phone calls, emails, anything that would give us a clue who she might have been."

"There is a record - there is a witness - to the defendant being there, though, isn't there?"

"Yes. He was seen leaving the building at the time of the murder."

"With blood on his hands and shirt?"

"Yes, that's correct."

"Tell us, Detective Grayson, in all your years of experience, have you ever heard of someone who has just committed murder screaming for help?"

"No, I don't think so."

"A woman screams for help, and scared to death that the murderer is going to kill her next, runs away. Isn't that what all the evidence seems to suggest?"

I objected, but McFarland had made her point, and no ruling from the bench was going to make the jury forget what they had just heard.

There were more questions, and more answers, until, finally, McFarland got to what had happened when the defendant, Alan Boe, was first interviewed by the police.

"What did he tell you? Did he confess that he had thought about murdering the chancellor?"

I wondered how much she knew, how much Grayson had told her about the extraordinary conversation he and the other detective had had with Alan Boe, that conversation in which they had been forced to answer as many questions as they had asked. The police report had described only what Boe had said in response to what he had been asked. If all she knew was what she had read in the standard deathlike prose in which police reports were invariably written, she was in for the surprise of her life.

"Yes," replied Grayson; "he said he had often had that thought."

"Did he also tell you that there were at least some occasions on which, in his judgement, murder would be justified?"

"Yes, he said that too."

Finished with the witness. McFarland returned to her chair. I did not move from mine.

"Mr. Antonelli, do you wish to cross-examine the witness?" asked Longstreet.

My elbow on the table, my left hand pressed against the side of my head, I held my fountain pen point up in the fingers of my right. Tapping the bottom of the barrel against the hard surface, I stared at Grayson with a smile of disbelief.

"What you just said: that Alan Boe admitted he had sometimes thought about murdering Lucas Fairweather, that he said there were times when murder would be justifiable - that's true: he said that. But what you did not tell us," I said, as I put down my pen and slowly got up from my chair, " is that you - and your partner, Detective Huddleston, as well - have had the same kind of thoughts yourselves. Isn't it true, Detective Grayson, that the defendant asked you if you had ever thought about murdering the police chief, the man you work for?"

Ever so slightly, Grayson raised his eyebrows; ever so slightly the corners of his mouth broke in the direction of a grin. He remembered what had happened, and he was not disappointed to discover that I knew it as well. He was there to do his job, a witness for the prosecution, but if I could turn him into a better witness for the defense, a witness for Alan Boe, he would not mind at all.

"Yes, he asked us that."

"And you admitted that you had thought of murdering the police chief. Have you done it yet - murdered the chief - or is it only in the early, planning stage?" I asked, with a broad smile. Some of the jurors were smiling as well. Who had not fantasized about killing their boss at one time or another?

"Things haven't gotten that bad," allowed Grayson.

"Which means they could! Never mind; I won't force you to answer that. But, this second so-called admission: that murder can sometimes be justified. He went farther than that, didn't he? He told you that murder was sometimes necessary, didn't he?"

"Yes, he said that."

"And he gave you an example, didn't he? Tell the jury what it was."

"Hitler. He said if you murdered someone like that you won't be a criminal; you would be a hero."

"I'm sure we all agree. When he said that, it was part of his response when you asked him if he had murdered Lucas Fairweather. He told you he didn't murder the chancellor, didn't he?"

"That's correct. He said he hadn't done it. He said Fair-weather wouldn't be worth it. Those were his exact words. That was when I asked him who he thought would be worth murdering, and he said Hitler."

"He denied murdering Fairweather, and then he asked you a question, didn't he? He asked you how you would feel, given that he was innocent, if he was convicted. Tell us, Detective Grayson, in all your years as a homicide detective, has any defendant ever asked you a question like that before?"

"No, it was a first."

"And do you remember your answer, what you said when he asked you that question?

I looked straight at him, and he looked straight back at me, and I knew he would not lie.

"I told him that if he was innocent, I hoped he would not be convicted."

"During your interview with the defendant, was there ever a time when you thought he was being deceptive?"

"No."

"Which means, does it not, that you believed him when he said he did not murder Lucas Fairweather!"

"Objection!" cried McFarland, rising straight up from her chair

I raised my hand, signaling I was done. The jury, and everyone else, knew what Grayson's answer would have been.

Eleanor McFarland was unfazed, unmoved, and unimpressed. The only thing important was evidence. It did not matter how anyone felt about someone; it did not matter, even if it was a police detective who thought it, that the defendant seemed like someone who would never lie. In thirty years of trying cases in the criminal courts, thirty years of prosecuting murderers who, if they had not all sworn they were innocent, would never have gone to trial, she had learned to discount anything and everything that was not susceptible to hard, unquestioned proof. The moment Grayson left the stand, she called her next witness: William J. Merrick, vice-chancellor of the university.

"He knows nothing," whispered Alan Boe, as the vice-chancellor was sworn in.

"About...?"

"Anything," he replied, shaking his head. "It's worse than that: he think he knows everything."

William Merrick was one of those people who would look aggrieved if you asked him for the time, unless he thought you someone of importance, when he would practically leave scratch marks on his watch in his hurry to tell you what you wanted to know. He was part of the new phenomenon in higher education: a college administrator who had never taught a college course. Both as an undergraduate and a graduate student, he had majored in education and obtained the necessary degrees. There was something sanctimonious about his devotion to a cause that almost no one in American did not share. Like a great many of his colleagues who held administrative posts in American colleges and universities, he thought that making less than those who held similar positions in the corporate world showed the kind of sacrifice he was willing to make, and all the proof needed to dismiss any complaint that he was making so much more than anyone engaged in teaching. When he described the death of Lucas Fairweather as "a tragic loss to the entire university community," Alan Boe had to stifle a laugh.

"He's now the acting chancellor. The only thing he thinks tragic is that he had to wait this long to get it. Make sure to ask him if he ever had thoughts of murder." He gave me an impish grin. "No, don't bother. He only knows how to say what he thinks he is supposed to say. I'm really quite serious," he went on, turning in his chair to face me directly. "There are a lot of people like him now: they have no real feeling of their own. They react to things the way they have seen the way others react. Everyone is an abstraction; everyone reacts the same way. Everyone -"

"Mr. Antonelli! Will you please instruct the defendant to be quiet! Mr. Boe, I've told you before: you are permitted to speak only when you are called as a witness. I won't warn you again."

Before I could stop him, he was on his feet, his bulging eyes full of mischief.

"I'm not allowed to speak with my attorney?"

Longstreet was not used to being questioned. She had the feeling that whatever she said, it would only lead to another question. This strange gnome like creature would never stop.

"Two things, Mr. Boe: First, you may speak with your lawyer, but only at the appropriate time. Mr. Antonelli, not you, will decide when that is. Second, you are not to question the judgement of this court - period! Do you understand?"

"I understand your decision; I do not understand that it is correct."

"Mr. Antonelli!" cried Longstreet, out of patience. "For the last time, will you please control your client!"

I threw up my hands in mock frustration.

"I've tried everything, your Honor; but despite all my efforts, I've never been able to get him to do anything - except tell the truth!"

Her mouth dropped open, her eyes were set on fire.

"I'll hold you in contempt; I'll…!"

Boe fell back into his chair and bent forward, all his attention on the just sworn witness. Eleanor McFarland, who had watched with studied indifference the defendant's antic behavior, took a step toward the witness stand as if everything was exactly as it should be.

"Mr. Merrick, I wonder -?"

"That's Dr. Merrick," he said, with a thin smile of such mindless condescension that for one of the few times in her life Eleanor McFarland let her irritation show. Drawing herself up to her full height, she taught him who was in control.

"I'll try again. Mr. Merrick, I wonder if you would tell the court what, to your knowledge, was the relationship between the defendant, Alan Boe, and the chancellor, Lucas Fairweather?"

In a perfect example of what Alan Boe had tried to tell me, Merrick pursed his lips and appeared to think about how best to respond.

"I believe it is fair to say that they were adversaries, when it came to the affairs of the university."

"Adversaries? Can you be more specific?"

"The chancellor has overall responsibility for the university. In addition to tens of thousands of students, there are thousands of faculty, administrative personnel, all the people who take care of the feeding and housing and safety of everyone - faculty and students - who are on campus. It is a massive undertaking - complicated, difficult, full of constant challenges. Chancellor Fairweather had to supervise this entire operation. Professor Boe taught classes in the philosophy department. He thought he knew more about the way the university should be run than the people - including especially the chancellor - who had to meet this responsibility every day. It is easy to question what others do when you have never had to do it yourself."

His voice was grating, his manner insufferable. McFarland tried to ignore it and hoped that everyone else would as well. She listened patiently until he finished and then, in the quiet, friendly way of casual conversation asked whether, beyond that general sense of their different perspectives, anything had happened that had made things between the chancellor and the professor more personal.

"Yes, you could say that! He led a riot, a bunch of hot-headed students and disgruntled professors - a mass meeting they called it - in front of the administration building, demanding the chancellor's resignation and the entire revamping of the governing structure of the university. They were out for blood. Boe led the chant: 'Death to administration,' 'Destroy the university and start again' - slogans like that."

"Was that the end of it, that demonstration, or where there other occasions when the defendant expressed his dislike of the chancellor?"

"Every time there was a meeting of the faculty senate, Boe would be there, questioning everything the chancellor said, opposing everything the chancellor asked for. More than that, he threatened the chancellor - did it directly; told him that something bad was sure to happen if he did not make way for someone else, that he had no place in a university, certainly not one that took itself seriously."

McFarland nodded to herself, as if everything the vice-chancellor was saying confirmed the defendant's obvious guilt.

"What, if anything, did the chancellor do to protect himself against these attacks by the defendant? What -?"

"Attacks?" I yelled. "There isn't any basis for that characterization, your Honor. Neither this witness, nor any other witness the prosecution has produced has said anything about a threat to the chancellor, much less a physical attack on him!"

"Sustained!" ruled Longstreet, with unusual speed. "Be careful, counselor," she added, with a baleful glance at a woman whom, because she had to respect her, she did not like.

McFarland paid no attention. She simply reminded Merrick of the question.

"What did the chancellor do?"

"He took a closer look at what the philosophy department did, and decided that very little of what they taught was any great help to our students; that it was out of touch with the needs of a modern, world class institution. It may make some sense to teach the few students still interested a course or two in the history of philosophy - although they could do just as well with the courses

172

offered in the history department on intellectual history - and obviously we would want to keep the courses on logic and perhaps the philosophy of science. Those continue to be helpful, especially students with an interest in computer science. But the rest of it! - We're not living in medieval times. There is no reason to go around asking how many angels can live on the end of a pin!"

Pausing, he glanced around the courtroom as if he were addressing an alumni meeting. He announced that as part of its determination to modernize itself, the university would be following the suggestion of Chancellor Fairweather. The department of philosophy would be closing as a separate entity. The courses still thought worthwhile would be combined with the general curriculum of the humanities department.

"I told you he was a fool," said Alan Boe, in a voice he did not even try to disguise as a whisper.

"Did the defendant know this? Did he know that this is what the chancellor intended to do?"

"Yes; I imagine that is why Professor Boe decided to murder him!"

A trial transcript tells you what was said at a trial; it does not tell you anything about how it was said, or, as happened now, the way I shook my head in disparagement at the idiocy of the witness. The court reporter's rapid fingers lack all instruction when it comes to recording the contempt, the unfeigned derision, that I lavished on the small minded vice-chancellor as I approached him to start my cross-examination.

I got halfway down the jury box, stopped, shook my head again, then turned to the jury and with a caustic smile let them know I was sure they thought the same thing about this pretentious, overbearing, bureaucrat. My glance moved from one juror to the next, as I repeated, word for word, what Merrick had just said.

"'Yes; I imagine that is why Professor Boe decided to murder him.'" Slowly, and with what I made seem an effort, I turned my head. "You - the acting chancellor of the university - 'imagine this is why Professor Boe decided to murder....' You - the acting chancellor of the university, a place where until today most of us thought was dedicated to the pursuit of truth, 'imagine' someone guilty, and apparently see no need even to heard the evidence, much less consider it. Tell us, Mr. Merrick, how long have you been vice-chancellor?"

The look of mild interest, the common mask of his profession, had not changed. Nothing could ever make that happen. Praise him to the skies, send him to the devil, there was always the same impervious expression.

"Eleven years, next September," he said, with what he doubtless thought the appropriate, modest, measure of pride.

"Eleven years - and in all that time never once had a conversation with Alan Boe, have you?"

"No, I don't recall that I ever have," he replied, without any obvious regret.

"Yes, I'm sure you have been too busy, helping to run the university. But you have a doctorate - a Ph.d in education - correct?"

"That's correct: I have a doctorate."

"Its pretty much a requirement, if you want to work in higher education, isn't it?" I asked, as if I were only curious.

"Yes, you're correct: a Ph.d. is a prerequisite for any position in college education."

"A Ph.d. - that stands for what, exactly?"

"It means 'doctor of philosophy.'"

"I see. Thank you. Doctor of Philosophy. Then you and Professor Boe have the same background; you studied the same things?"

I glanced over my shoulder at Alan Boe. His large eyes had become larger still, filled with wonder at what I seemed to be suggesting.

"No; I'm afraid we would have studied different things. His training is in philosophy in the academic sense."

"'Philosophy in the academic sense'? Well, I'm sure it doesn't matter; you both have Ph.d's - both doctors of philosophy. You must have things, serious things, in common, if words mean anything. You just testified you've never had a conversation with him, but you must have read his book, the one about 19th century German philosophy. Tell the jury what you thought of it."

He dismissed it as politely as he could. He had not read it, but he understood it was considered "an important contribution to the literature."

"An important...? You haven't read what, I am told, every serious scholar in Europe regards as the most important work on the subject written in the last fifty years?'

"It isn't my field."

"It isn't your...? You mean, because it is 19th century German philosophy - Hegel to Nietzsche. I understand. You head one of the great universities in the world. If you haven't an interest in what one of your own professors has done, is that because you're interest in philosophy goes farther back in time? Can we assume that you spend most of your time studying Greek philosophy: Plato, Aristotle?"

"When I was an undergraduate, I took a course in which we read about what the Greeks taught."

"Which philosophers have you read? - Never mind. You've never read anything, have you? Never read a dialogue of Plato, a treatise of Aristotle; never read a page of Descartes, or a paragraph of Locke or Rousseau. The truth, Mr. Merrick, is that you know nothing at all about philosophy, but are all in favor of getting rid of what you don't know anything about - correct?"

"I think that an unfair characterization. I cannot be expected to be fully conversant with everything taught in the university; I cannot -"

"The chancellor - Lucas Fairweather - he had a doctorate, too, didn't he; and he did not know any more about Alan Boe than you do - isn't that correct?"

"Well, I don't -"

"You never had a conversation with Alan Boe, and neither did Lucas Fairweather - did he?"

"Not that I'm aware of."

"Boe was a problem, though, wasn't he? He made a lot of trouble; he made the case against what the university had become public - speeches in the faculty senate, speeches at rallies right outside your building. That's why Lucas Fairweather wanted to get rid of him; that's why he wanted to eliminate the department - to get rid of someone with whom he could never win an argument - isn't that correct?"

"Again, I don't agree with your characterization; I don't agree that the chancellor was in any way afraid of Professor Boe. I certainly don't agree that the chancellor - who could be quite persuasive - was afraid of losing an argument. But you're right, when you say that the chancellor was intent on modernizing the curriculum. It's what I said before, Mr. Antonelli," he added, with the thin, condescending smile that made him feel important; "it's the reason I imagine he killed him."

I smiled back.

"Had you ever read his book, you would know that Alan Boe would never be fool enough to think the university would be better off with you as chancellor than Lucas Fairweather. Now tell us about the women."

"The women...?"

"Yes, the women. You were aware that Lucas Fairweather had been having sex with a woman in his office the night of his death, were you not?"

He was careful. He answered the question, and nothing more than that.

176

"I've heard what the security guard said."

"You weren't surprised to hear that, were you? You've known for some time that the chancellor was sometimes visited in his office late at night by women - that's true, isn't it, Mr. Merrick?"I asked, making it sound as if he were being accused of a cover-up of Fairweather's indiscretions.

"No, I....There were rumors; people were starting to talk. But did I have any direct knowledge...? No, I did not."

"But you were aware that the reason he left his position with the federal government was because of his involvement with someone else's wife - correct?"

"I've been made aware of that."

I walked over to the counsel table, opened a file folder, found the document I wanted, and walked back to the witness stand.

"Are you familiar with this document?"

As soon as he glanced at it, his face tightened and his eyes went cold.

"How did you...? Yes, I'm familiar with it."

"This is the report of an internal investigation into the conduct of the chancellor, Lucas Fairweather. Please read the last sentence: the recommendation that was made."

I almost felt sorry for him. He looked like a student caught cheating, hoping he would get off with a warning, worried he would be sent home in disgrace. Fumbling through the pages, he got to the last one. When he began to read that last, damning, sentence, his voice, always so even and controlled, seemed strangled.

"'Because of the chancellor's repeated violation of the university's rules against sexual exploitation of faculty or students, Lucas Fairweather should be removed from his position with as much speed, and as little publicity, as possible.'"

"And would you now go back to the first page of the report and tell the jury to whom this report was submitted?"

Merrick bit his lip. He did not need to look at the report.

"The report was submitted to the chairman of the board of trustees and to me, as vice-chancellor."

"Is it not true, Mr. Merrick, that this investigation was begun at your insistence, that you had become so alarmed at what you knew was going on that you thought that if something was not done, Lucas Fairweather would involve the university in a scandal from which it might never recover?"

"I did what I thought I had to do."

"One last question. What is the date on which you received this report? - Nearly three months before Lucas Fairweather was murdered; three months in which you did nothing. Why was that, Mr. Merrick? Was it because you wanted to be sure you had enough support on the board of trustees to make sure you would be chosen the chancellor's successor?"

"No," he insisted in a hollow sounding voice. "It wasn't like that. It wasn't about me; it was about making sure we could get him to agree to leave voluntarily, so we wouldn't have to deal with the kind of scandal you just mentioned."

Merrick thought he was through, that he could take literally my remark that there was just 'one last question.' He had his hands on the arms of the chair, ready to get up.

"'One last question,' about that, Mr. Merrick. You're not done yet. In all your years as a college administrator, how often have you heard of someone on the faculty committing an act of violence on someone in the administration? I don't just mean murder - any kind of violence?"

"I don't remember it ever happening."

"And how often do you imagine," I said, emphasizing the word, "someone commits murder in this country out of jealousy, or out of a desire for revenge? How often, Mr. Merrick, do you imagine that the husband, or the boyfriend, of a woman has murdered the man his wife, or his girlfriend, was sleeping with? How

178

often, Mr. Merrick, do you imagine, a woman who has been taken advantage of by a man in a position of authority and power has committed murder because of what was done to her? There were two people in the chancellor's office that night between eleven and twelve, a member of the faculty and a young, attractive woman. Which of them, Mr. Merick, would you imagine might have had a reason to kill him?"

He looked at me with a blank expression; he had not heard the question. All he could think about was what had just happened to his career, the destruction of his own complacent dream as the leader of a world famous university. Alan Boe tugged my sleeve.

"You've done more in ten minutes than I was able to do in ten years to save the university from its own bad judgment." His eyes filled with laughter. "Which only means that whoever they get next will probably be even worse."

It was nearly five o'clock, and except for the hour and half recess at lunch we had been at it all day. Caught up in the action of the trial, asking questions, listening to the answers as I got ready with the next question, saying things I did not know I was going to say until I heard myself speaking the words, I could have gone on until midnight or even later, given the chance. I did not doubt that Eleanor McFarland could have done the same thing. Everyone else was tired, brought to the edge of exhaustion, by what, for most of the others in the courtroom, exceeded the limits of their ability to concentrate on a single, uninterrupted line of argument. When Judge Longstreet declared the court in recess until the next morning, only Alan Boe seemed reluctant to leave.

"I can't tell you how much I am enjoying this, Mr. Antonelli. Its even more interesting than I thought it would be; but it confirms what I suspected: the system is essentially unfair, isn't it?"

We were sitting at the counsel table. The judge and the jury had left. The courtroom crowd was slowly filing out the two doors in back. Eleanor McFarland was gathering up her belongings at the other counsel table a few feet away on our left. Alan Boe pushed his chair back and crossed one leg over the other. With his head bent back at an angle, he searched my eyes.

"Not many lawyers - perhaps none at all - could have done what you did today. It isn't fair, is it? With you as my attorney, I have what seems a very good chance of being found not guilty; with someone else as my lawyer, I probably go to prison. There is nothing very reasonable in this. If you were on trial - on trial for murder, a murder you did not commit - can you think of many lawyers you would want to represent you? At least you would have the alternative of representing yourself, but think of all those other poor souls who have to settle for some one who barely made it through law school and is practicing criminal law because it was the only job he could get. We call it the adversarial system, and we make the same mistake we do when it comes to our belief that if there are no limits on free speech, if everyone can have their say, the truth will always, ultimately, triumph. What we forget, but what anyone who sits in a courtroom, or watches a political campaign, knows, is that some people are more persuasive than others, and most of those who decide which side wins are not always able to recognize the truth when they see it. And, by the way, it is not true to say that with all its faults, it is the best system possible. The British do it better. The judges takes an active part, ask questions of a witness if he thinks it necessary to bring out the truth, and then, at the end, instead of the lawyers doing it, the judge summarizes the evidence and suggests to the jury what it means."

I kept looking at him, held a prisoner by his unrelenting gaze. There was something in that look of his, a sense that somewhere deep inside those eyes was the answer to every question you could ever think to ask.

"Would you really want Michelle Longstreet to do that?" I asked, as if I were only repeating the question he had invited me to ask.

"Yes! Why not? When you give someone something important to do, they tend to take their responsibilities more seriously, don't you think? Why am I asking that! You know this already. Look at this jury of ours. You see the way they watch, the way they listen. They may spend most of their time doing dull things at work; they may waste too much time indulging themselves in mindless entertainment; but look what they are capable of when given the responsibility of deciding whether someone is guilty or innocent of murder. Look at how they look at you."

He was about to say something more when, suddenly, he looked up. Someone was standing just behind me, on the other side of the low railing that ran across the courtroom in front of the spectator benches.

"Hello, Professor Boe," said a strangely familiar voice. "It's good to see you again."

Boe was on his feet, his eyes shining with recognition as he eagerly greeted the man he introduced as, "the best student I ever taught."

James Michael Redfield shook my hand as if we had never met before.

Chapter Twelve

Albert Craven was astonished when I told him what had happened.

"Redfield was Alan Boe's best student! I had no idea. That would have been twenty - more than twenty - years ago," he explained, as he dropped into the blue wingback chair in front of my desk. "Then that is the reason...."

He stared at me, expecting me to finish the thought, make the connection between the murder Redfield had arranged and a teacher who still, after all this time, remembered him as the most gifted student he had ever had. I had no explanation to offer, nothing beyond what had been guessed before.

"He was there, watching the trial, and you did not know it?"

"I don't know if he was there or not; he might have come in when everyone else was leaving. You know what I'm like in the middle of a trial: I know the place is crowded, but the only people I see are on my side of the railing. He was there to see Boe; he was not there to see me."

I loosened my tie and loosened my shirt and started to see it all over again: the sudden look of recognition on the face of Alan Boe, and something more than that: pride in his own achievement. Whatever Redfield had done, whatever he had become, he had as a young man shown the bright, shining promise that had given the extraordinary Alan Boe the hope that what he had come to know could be passed on to at least one other, remarkable, human being. The recognition had been instantaneous; there had not been the slightest hesitation. After an absence of a quarter century, Boe had known immediately that it was his former student, James Michael Redfield and no one else.

"Strange, and I don't think he was serious, but after I told Boe that this was the second murder and trial that had been arranged by the same person, he wondered whether one of his students wanted to have the chance to know what it felt like when Socrates was put on trial."

With his elbows on the arms of the wingback chair, and his hands laying flat against his legs, Craven rocked gently back and forth for a moment, and then, stopping, crossed his left arm over his chest and with his right hand stroked his small, fragile chin.

"It seems he was right after all. Isn't that what has happened? Alan Boe on trial, Alan Boe who has questioned everything the university now thinks important and what nearly everyone believes, and who wants to teach students to question the same things as well. What is that, if not the trial of Socrates all over again? And who besides Boe could draw in such stark relief the deficiencies, not to say the outright fraud, of today's higher education. Redfield may be a kind of evil genius, but he seems to know what he is doing. The document you used today - doesn't that prove it?"

"The document...? The report of the internal investigation? How did you know about that? You weren't there, and I just got back from court."

"I got a phone call," he explained, getting up from the chair; "just a few minutes ago. There is an emergency meeting of the board of regents tonight. There is a real firestorm. The vice-chancellor won't be acting chancellor. He'll have to resign and leave the university. The chairman of the board will have to resign as well. He saw that report, he knew what was in it, how damaging it was, and he kept it under wraps. He did not tell anyone about it. The scandal they were trying to avoid has now, thanks to what you did today in court, claimed them as its first victims. What everyone wants to know is how you happened to get hold of it."

I tapped my fingers on the desk, remembering how easily people are deceived.

"You can tell them, what they already think: that it was the result of a thorough investigation. Don't tell them it came in the mail, a plain manilla envelope delivered by the post office."

"Without a return address, I presume."

"No, it had one: it was yours."

"Glad I could help," he said, drily, shaking his head at Redfield's strange sense of humor. He stood next to the chair, leaning against the side of it. "What did he say to Boe, when he came up to him? Interesting that Boe would immediately recognize him after all this time. Unless, of course, they have stayed in touch. I wonder....I mean, if he was his best student, and if Redfield is now using him for his own purposes. Did they talk for any length of time?"

"I don't think....I'll ask him, but, no, I don't think Boe has seen him since he was a student. You could tell the way he looked at him. But there was something else: a bond, a closeness that time does not affect. They had not seen each other in years and after that first, initial greeting, they were talking as if they were picking up a conversation they had been having the day before. When Refield left, he said, 'I'll see you again, when the trial is over and we can go somewhere for a long lunch.' Boe laughed, and said he might have to visit him instead in prison. Redfield put his hand on his shoulder and told him that there was not any chance he would be convicted. He knew that Boe had not killed anyone; he did not tell him that he also knew who the murderer really was.

Craven straightened his tie, pulled his shirt-cuffs down to their proper place below the sleeves of his dark tailored suit and, confident everything was now in order, reminded me that I had forgotten what day it was.

"It's Friday; you have the weekend. You don't have to stay

here, getting ready for tomorrow."

I threw up my hands, laughing at my own incompetence.

"Longstreet adjourned for the day, until 'tomorrow morning.' The jury probably thinks we're back in session on Saturday. I told Boe I would see him tonight, and I told Tangerine we would have a long, leisurely dinner Friday, after the trial!"

"Have dinner with the most beautiful woman in San Francisco or see someone in jail - that would be a difficult choice!" exclaimed Craven, lifting an eyebrow. Then he became serious. "Not a difficult choice at all: you'll see Alan Boe."

"It's what we do."

"It's what you do," he said. "You take your clients to trial; I make sure none of mine ever see the inside of a courtroom. You get to talk about innocence and justice; I get to talk about how much cheaper it is to settle lawsuits out of court. You get to...."

"I know, Albert; I know!" I cried, waving my hand to signal that I had heard it all before. "I get to talk to interesting people - murderers, rapists, and thieves; you have to sit through endless lunches and dinners listening to rich people complain about the taxes they have to pay. You're right: I have it much better than you do, especially when you remember that most of these so-called murderers, rapists and thieves were innocent and most of the people you represent, who have never been charged with a crime, have cheated and lied most of their lives. Good God, listen to me! First the Friedrich trial, and now Alan Boe - all I can think about is how unfair everything is!"

Springing out of my chair, I placed both hands on my desk and stared straight ahead, angry, frustrated, full of resentment and bent on revenge.

"And I am sick to death of being used! First Friedrich, now Alan Boe. Redfield pulls all the strings. Well, this is one puppet who is going to pull back! He thinks he can hide behind the privilege, that he can have me as his accomplice as he goes around proving what he wants to show the world by arranging homicides and trials, and I won't be able to do anything about it! He thinks he has me trapped, that if I stand aside and refuse to take a case, he'll let some innocent person be convicted for something he did!"

It was cathartic; I felt better for having given voice to the anger I felt. I dropped back into my chair and turned toward the window and the darkening sky outside and listened as Albert told me not to worry, that everything would work out; listened as he told me all the things a trusted friend invents when he has no more idea than you have how to deal with a problem neither of you has had to face before.

When I called Tangerine, she laughed when I told her I had forgotten what day it was, and told me we could have dinner later, after I was finished seeing Alan Boe in jail. "But," she added, "you still have to take me dancing - tomorrow night will do."

"I can't do that," I replied. I could see her nose wrinkle; I could see her start to laugh. "I never learned how."

"Don't you remember the Sinatra song - 'dancing is making love, set to music.'?"

"You want to go someplace and dance naked?" I asked, as innocently as I could.

"I want to go someplace to dance.., and then, later, when we get home...."

"You'll have to teach me."

"To dance..., or the other? Or would you rather teach me? Or would you rather just have dinner and rest? Or would you...?" There was a brief, breathless pause. "Just get here as soon as you can. We have all weekend."

Alan Boe was waiting in the same windowless room as before, but this time without a book. He did not need one to occupy his mind. The thick, steel door made a harsh, clanking noise when the jailer unlocked and pushed it open, but it did not make him so much as blink; he was that far lost in thought. I sat down on the opposite side of the table, but he did not notice I was there. I might have thought him dead had it not been for an occasional odd twitch that seized the left corner of his mouth. There seemed nothing to do but wait. I pulled a yellow legal pad out of my briefcase and reached inside my suit coat for my fountain pen.

"And you would be right to think so," he said, suddenly, his eyes still unseeing. I thought he was, in some equivalent way, talking in his sleep. "Right to think what you were telling me before."

He had come back to life, talking as if nothing strange had happened; as if, in the middle of a conversation, I knew exactly what he was talking about.

"You said that this trial - my trial - was the second murder and trial arranged by the same person. It is Redfield of course. I knew it when I saw him; I knew immediately that he was behind everything; I knew it without any doubt whatsoever when he told me he was sure I would never be convicted." Reaching across the table, he placed his hand on my arm. "I'm sorry; you didn't know him. If you had, you would know what I'm talking about. I said he was the best student I ever had; he was a good deal more than that. He was not a student at all, in the usual sense; his mind was too quick for that."

It was a habit with Alan Boe to hold his thumb under his chin and press his index finger against his mouth while he considered what he was going to say. His gaze would become so intense you almost thought he might start a fire if he looked at anything combustible.

"How much do you want to know? You know who he reminded me of when I first met him? - Martin Heidegger, the German philosopher; because of something I once read by someone who was studying at the same university - Marburg, I think it was. Heidegger was a graduate student, working as an assistant to Edmund Husserl, one of the great names in phenomenology. This student, who was there to study under Husserl, attended a lecture Heidegger gave on Aristotle, and realized afterward that there was no comparison between the two, no comparison between Husserl, this established pillar of European philosophy, and Heidegger, still in his early twenties. No comparison, because Heidegger was light years ahead. Redfield came to my office after the first lecture he had attended and showed me all the places where I was wrong, or, rather, all the places where what I had said could be challenged. I've never met anyone like him, before or since. He is certainly capable of arranging to have someone charged with a murder he did not commit. The question is why would he want to."

"After the first trial," I said, as Boe listened with a kind of interest that made me wonder whether what I was saying was only an echo of what had already passed through his mind, "I was having dinner with Tangerine, the woman with whom I live, at a restaurant in Sausalito. Redfield, who somehow knew we would be there, came over to our table and told us that whoever had done this had done it to expose the corruption of the rich, their lack of morality, their self-absorption, the empty vanity of their lives."

Alan Boe nodded in agreement, and for a moment stared past me, troubled by what he had heard; troubled, but not surprised.

"He was with me for two years. That first course he took was the beginning of his junior year. He was in every course I taught during that time; not just the upper division courses for juniors and seniors, but in graduate seminars as well. He made the graduate students look like high school freshmen. Bright students can be arrogant, quite insufferable; they take a private pleasure in making other students feel inferior. Redfield was not bright; Redfield was profound. No one, even those doctoral students I mentioned, felt anything but admiration, and even affection, for him. He had that way about him. Students four, five, years older, looked up to him. Part of it was that he never criticized anyone; he only criticized himself, because, you see, he did not think he knew anything. He only asked questions, questions about everything. There is a line he loved. He found it in Rousseau, but you can find it other places as well, that it 'isn't ignorance, but error, that causes problems in the world.'

"He saw error everywhere and in everything. He had that kind of mind. He could grasp at once, as it were, what the perfected state of something was. You've heard often enough this utterly ridiculous statement: 'the perfect is the enemy of the good.' Redfield understood that the perfect is the definition of the good. Redfield understood a lot of things most people never learn. That, perhaps, was his problem. When we see how things should be, most of us are prepared to settle for whatever small improvements we can help bring about. There are of course others - the revolutionaries we have all read about - who think they can change the world, and if they change it at all, only make it worse. Redfield thought you could not do anything, unless you went back and changed the beginning. There is another line, this one from Hobbes, he liked to quote: 'where men build on false ground, the more they build, the greater is the ruin.'"

Tilting his head, Boe studied me with a sympathy that bordered on affection. A quiet smile flickered on his mouth.

"You became a lawyer; a very good lawyer, if I may say so: a lawyer in the best tradition. You make a lot of money, but I don't believe that you ever took a case because of what someone could pay. That's one of the reason's you're so good; not the only reason, mind you, but one of them. If you only did it for the money, you would not have the kind of interest that makes each case important. Redfield could not have become a lawyer: the fate of an individual, whether someone falsely accused might be sent to prison or even executed, would not be important to him. That is not to say he would think it should not be important to other people, especially to the one accused; but his interest would be in why whatever happened was thought to be a crime in the first place. Who decides, on what ground? - Not what justice requires, but what justice is.

"Have you ever read Machiavelli? Redfield studied both The Prince and The Discourses. He understood what nearly everyone who reads Machiavelli fails to understand: that beneath what some like to call the realism of Machiavelli's advice about what has to be done to acquire and keep political power is a conscious break with both Christianity and the ancient, pagan, teaching of Plato and Aristotle. Christianity has weakened men by dismissing the importance of what happens here on earth in comparison with the great rewards awaiting the meek and submissive in the world to come. The Church, as Machiavelli describes it, has 'made it evil to speak evil of evil.' The good are taught not to resist, with the result that the evil will always win. As for ancient, that is to say, Greek philosophy, they set a standard too high for human beings to reach, with the same unfortunate result. The ancients build marvelous looking castles on sand and mud. Even if they could be built, even if, to steal a page from Plato, philosophers became kings, or kings philosophers, it could not last. A new, and a different, foundation is needed. Machiavelli, and Hobbes and Locke after him, insist the only solid, the only strong and lasting, foundation is to be found in the dominate passion of human beings: the desire for life itself. Preservation, self-preservation, the desire to live even if it means the need to kill, is always there in all of us. It is the one thing you can always count on. The question is no longer what you build on, but, given this foundation, whether monarchy or a republic is best suited to achieve what the modern world, the world created by Machiavelli and those who came after him, hoped to achieve."

Boe kept searching my eyes, making sure I followed. I did not follow, not entirely; the words were familiar, but the thoughts were strange. Still, in Alan Boe's voice they seemed to make sense, the way that something you never had occasion to think about before starts to bring the kind of clarity you had not had before. It was his gift, this ability to make what you did not know so much

190

more interesting than what you thought you knew.

"Everyone believes in 'life, liberty, and the pursuit of happiness'; everyone believes in the right of everyone to live anyway they like, so long, of course, as they don't interfere with someone else's right to do the same thing. We all believe that, but until five hundred years ago, no one believed that at all. The debate was not about the rights of the individual, the limitations on what government could do; the debate was about what kind of regime was best. We believe that we are free to do whatever is not prohibited by law; they - I mean those who thought seriously about such things before Machiavelli - believed that what is not permitted by the law is prohibited. The rights of the individual did not exist; the individual had only duties. This still holds for both Muslims and Orthodox Jews. Read the Koran - everything, including every detail of daily life, is spelled out, that is to say, required.

"The right of individuals - that was the promise of modernity; it was also the curse. The rights of the individual led to mass politics, mass democracy; it led to the belief of the right of everyone to what has been called 'comfortable self-preservation.' It led to what, at the end of the 19th century, Nietzsche called the 'last man:' No one believes in anything; we all follow blindly whatever everyone else believes. Anyone who thinks differently than the crowd is handled with therapy and pharmaceuticals. Everything is reduced to mere existence, survival. The last man does not aspire to anything beyond what he already is; there are no standards by which to measure, no standards by which to establish, human excellence. God is dead; everything is permitted. One thing is as good, or bad, as any other; everything, whether high art or trash, great literature or the obscene distortions of a twisted imagination, equally an expression of human creativity.

"Redfield was utterly fascinated by this. He read Nietzsche the way others read popular novels: once he started, he could not stop. Nietzsche had that effect on most of those who read him in the early years of the 20th century; he had that effect on Redfield three quarters of a century later, when almost no one read Nietzsche, or much of anything else. Redfield did more than that. He did not just read Nietzsche, he questioned him. Nietzsche thought that the radical decline in the human condition could be traced back, not to Machiavelli and the beginning of modernity, but to Plato's Socrates: the teaching that there are things, the ideas, that never change; that everything else, all the things we experience with our senses, come into being and out of being, but what we grasp with our mind, the models, if you will, of those transitory beings like ourselves, exist for all eternity. On this reading, you can see what Nietzsche meant, when he called Christianity Platonism for the people: this belief in an eternal life outside this world we live in. Nietzsche thought the only way to restore even the possibility of human greatness, that is, the possibility of human beings the way they should be, instead of the 'last man' we have become, is to go back to the pre-Socratics, especially Parmenides and Heraclitus

"This is a long story, one it isn't necessary that you know. I am telling you this much because it is the only way I know how to tell you who James Michael Redfield really is, and why he may be doing what he is. As I say, he read Nietzsche. He also read Heidegger, whose work is a commentary on Nietzsche, and then he read Plato."

Alan Boe shook his head at the memory of what Redfield had done: studied Plato's dialogues with a more acute intelligence than all but a handful of scholars had managed to bring to the same task.

"He would stay up all night, reading, slowly, trying to catch the meaning of each word; trying to imagine what it must have been like, being part of the action of the dialogue, there to watch the reactions, the change of expression, of everyone involved. He would be sitting on the floor, outside my office door, book still in hand, waiting for me, eager to ask my opinion on some passage he had found particularly challenging. He spent months doing this, months attempting to understand how much, if any, of Nietzsche's powerful critique was correct; months trying to decide whether Plato was right, and that the peak of human excellence was human wisdom, and that wisdom was the endless search for knowledge of the whole. It came down to this: Is Nietzsche right that the human being is driven by what he called 'will to power,' that there is no order, no natural order, in the world, that everything is a human construct, that we created the gods we believed in, and that everything we believe is the creation - the fiction, if you will - of someone who gave the law to everyone else? Or is there an order, a natural order, in the world, that can be grasped by the human being, who alone is part of that same order and has the capacity to understand what it is, an order that is the standard by which every degree of deficiency can be measured?"

Alan Boe look at me with a smile full of nostalgia at what, alone in his experience, James Michael Redfield had managed to see.

"Moses," he said, laughing for some reason that escaped me entirely. "Moses," he said again, as if repeating it would reveal his meaning.

"Moses?"

"That was the example he used, the way he explained his belief that Nietzsche's understanding of Plato was, to say no more, incomplete. In the sixth chapter of The Prince, that work by which Machiavelli is known to the world, he includes Moses as one of those who've become rulers by 'their own ingenuity.' For Machiavelli, ingenuity meant that Moses ruled by force and fraud. He killed thousands of those who opposed him, led his followers to the promised land, and kept them in the desert for forty years so no one would still be alive who remembered Egypt. Nietzsche mentions Moses as well, one of those who invented a religion, that is to say, created the horizon, the boundary of what people think and believe.

That is how Redfield decided Plato was right. Everyone who reads Plato's Republic remembers that the necessary condition for that perfect city in which philosophers rule is that everyone over the age of ten has to be banished. It is the only way the citizens of this new city can be raised to believe what they have to believe to make it possible for those philosophers Socrates talks about to have the consent, the support, without which they could easily be overthrown. Everyone thinks this an impossible condition; everyone except Redfield. He remembered Moses. Banish everyone over the age of ten and keep their children. Why was that impossible? Moses had done exactly that, if in a slightly different way.

"Now, remember what started Redfield on this journey: Nietzsche's insistence that the world had gone dark, that humanity was in danger of losing its soul. Redfield did not study Plato out of some antiquarian interest; he studied Plato because he wanted to find a way out, a solution to the problem of what, with the publication of Oswald Spengler's once famous book in the 1920s, became known as the Decline of the West. He told me, the summer after he graduated, one of the last times I saw him, that the only answer was what Moses and Socrates both thought necessary; somehow start all over with people who had no memory of how they used to live. Whatever he is doing, whatever reason he arranged two murders and two trials, has to have some connection with that. I have no idea what that connection is, but one thing I can tell you with absolute certainty: James Michael Redfield was determined to do anything he could to change the world. This is not the fantasy of some delusional fanatic. There was something else he often mentioned, something he had found written by more than one great writer: how much could be accomplished by just one hundred people if they were all dedicated to the same cause. I do not know if he has a hundred, but we both know - don't we? - that he has at least two willing to commit murder at his command."

Chapter Thirteen

Michelle Longstreet had cut her hair, cut it so short that instead of falling to her shoulders as it had before, it now swept back on a line very near the top of her ears. It gave her a boyish look, and, from the way she swept into the courtroom, something like girlish pride. She glanced at the crowd of spectators, pausing like a fashion model on the runway, to let everyone get a better look; she glanced at the jury and did the same thing, waiting to make certain everyone would notice the change, and, noticing, approve.

Eleanor McFarland, sitting alone at the table reserved for the prosecution, rolled her eyes.

"Is the prosecution ready to call its next witness?" asked Longstreet, as she turned from the jury.

Her arms crossed in front of her, McFarland sat back in her chair, as if deep in thought. The pretty smile on Longstreet's face faded away.

"Is the prosecution ready…?"

McFarland looked up. She had not heard the question.

"Are you going to call -?"

"A witness. Yes. I wondered if you were going to find time to get back to the business of the trial," she remarked, with a smile of her own, one that vanished almost the moment it started. "No, your Honor, the prosecution is not," she went on as she slowly, every movement a burden, rose from her chair. "I don't mean we're not ready; I mean that the prosecution has called its last witness." She waited just long enough to raise her chin and throw her broad shoulders back. "The prosecution rests, your Honor."

Longstreet bit her lip to stop herself giving voice to the anger she felt at the absence of the deference she thought she was owed. It was a private, unspoken war of generations; a war, she understood, she could not win. Everyone's sympathies would always be with the older woman, a woman who had never much bothered about her own, gray hair, or, for that matter, much of anything about her appearance. Longstreet's gaze moved immediately to me.

"Mr. Antonelli," she said, with an unmistakably friendly glance, "is the defense ready to proceed?"

"Yes, your Honor," I replied, jumping up from my chair as if I could not wait to begin. "The defense calls the defendant, Alan Boe."

Alan Boe was beaming. The smile on his large, ungainly mouth stretched from ear to ear as he started for the witness stand. He did not get there. He stopped in front of the jury box, looked at each juror in turn, as if he were a lawyer about to give his closing argument, and then told them: "I hope you are finding this experience as interesting as I am."

They could not help themselves, those twelve jurors who, it is safe to say, had never seen anyone quite like him before; they had to like him. They nodded their agreement, and he nodded back, and then they sat there, watching in amazement as this strange creature, with whom, without their quite knowing how it happened, they had now formed a bond of goodwill, swore to tell the truth and nothing but the truth. I had never seen a jury watch a witness more closely, or with greater interest.

Sitting on the witness stand, he leaned forward, his elbows on the arms of the chair and his hands clasped together, his ankles crossed and his knees apart. He looked like a figure eight bent slightly in the middle. He stared at me as if it was all he could do not to laugh. His eyes, those brilliant eyes that seemed to cast a

light of their own, flashed with anticipation. He could not wait to
start. I led with a question that was not a question at all.

"Would you please state your full name for the record."

He turned to the jury, quickly, not so much to answer as to
take them into his confidence.

"Alan Empedocles Boe. Strange, isn't it? My middle name.
My father was a physician, but he had studied classics as an undergraduate. Empedocles was both a physician and a philosopher who
lived in Agrigento, Sicily in the fifth century B.C.. It is said that
he once cured a woman who had died, brought her back from the
dead. He is among those known as the pre-Socratics, philosophers
who taught, and wrote, before Socrates brought philosophy 'down
from the heavens,' to the problems of the earth. I understand that
I was simply asked to state my name, but a proper answer to any
question requires that you know the reason something is the way it
is. That, by the way, is not the only name I have. I am called, by
some of my students, 'Albo.' You can see it is a kind of abbrevi-
ation, a brief combination of my first and last names. But, again,
there is a reason for this that would not immediately be obvious. I
sometimes teach a graduate seminar on medieval political philosophy. There is a famous - I'm sure you have all heard of him," he
added, with a puckish grin - "Jewish philosopher from the end of
the 14th and beginning of the 15th century, by the name of Albo.
His main work is entitled 'Book of Roots.' And that is what some
of my more clever students started calling this seminar of mine:
'Albo's Book of Roots.'"

The jury sat there, their mouths hanging open, their eyes
wide with wonder, dazzled by what they had just heard. Boe looked
at me.

"Is this sufficient answer to your question, Mr. Antonelli?"

Sufficient answer? I had asked him for his name. Sufficient answer? The judge, Michelle Longstreet, stared at him in
dumb astonishment; the prosecutor, the redoubtable Eleanor Mc-

Farland, held her breath to keep her pose of studied indifference. The jurors had moved forward on their chairs, their eyes alive with the excitement of an audience at a performance better than anything they had expected. There was only one thing to do. I turned to McFarland.

"Your witness."

"My witness?" she asked, incredulous. "What do you mean - my witness? You haven't yet asked a question on direct."

"I asked a question,' I replied, smiling at her. "I asked him what his name was, and after the answer he has just given, I think the jury has heard enough to reach a verdict. Don't you?"

She smiled back, and then lowered her eyes as if she were thinking through her response.

"He hasn't denied that he murdered Lucas Fairweather. I think the jury might certainly remember that. Don't you?" she asked, looking up at me.

I took it as a helpful suggestion and turned to Alan Boe.

"Did you murder Lucas Fairweather?"

"No, I did not," he said, shaking his head at the utter absurdity of it. "Despite the many times I thought it might not be such a bad idea," he added, nodding twice in succession to underscore the point, and to mark the difference, the crucial difference, between the thought and the deed.

I nodded back, and without bothering with the usual announcement that I had no more questions of the witness, took my seat, ready, like everyone else, to watch the show.

The prosecution had what, in any other trial, would have been enough circumstantial evidence to make its case, but Alan Boe was not any other defendant. Michelle Longstreet, ambitious, intelligent, vain and entitled, a woman who had always been told she could be anything she wanted to be and had not yet in her relatively young life encountered anything, or anyone, to challenge that belief, might have thought she could match wits with him, but

Eleanor McFarland had a deeper understanding. She approached the witness with caution.

"You have been a member of the faculty at the university for nearly thirty years - isn't that correct?"

"Twenty nine years," replied Boe, looking straight at her.

"In other words, your entire working life."

"No."

"No? You worked somewhere else?"

"No - I've never worked. I teach students; I write about what I find most interesting. I would never call it work."

"I see. But you're paid for what you do: the university gives you a salary as a teacher, and you get paid for the books you write. Every time someone buys one, you get a royalty - correct?"

Boe's remarkable eyes lit up. He turned to the jury, anxious to share a secret.

"Those books I write, they are not what you might call 'best-sellers.' But, I have to admit the sales are pretty consistent: nine or ten every year. In fairness to myself, I'm told the people who buy them read them more than once. In fairness to the truth, I have to tell you that it is probably because it takes more than one reading to begin to understand what I have written. Now, you know," he went on, as if he were about to go back to the beginning and start all over, "there is that dialogue of Plato's - the Phaedrus - you should read it - the remark that you cannot know what a writing means until you have read through it to the end and then read it again from the beginning with the benefit of what you have learned."

McFarland had quite forgotten why she was there. She might not have remembered at all, had he not asked her if she had another question she wished to ask.

"Yes, as a matter of fact, I do."

She studied him almost as if she wanted to assure herself he was real, and not a figment of her own imagination. She looked down at the floor, and then, a moment later, looked up. He was still there, waiting, a smile of what actually seemed a smile of encouragement, a smile he might have used with a shy student reluctant to speak in class. Had it not been for her own self-awareness, her understanding of what she was trained to do - what she was there to do - she might have yielded to the feeling, a feeling I was certain she had, that Alan Boe could not possibly be guilty of murder, whether of Lucas Fairweather or anyone else. She took a deep breath, drew herself up to her full height, and pushed on.

Or tried to. Because just as she was about to ask her next question, he asked one of her.

"Have you ever had a case where in the middle of the trial you realized that the person you were prosecuting was not guilty? What did you do - what would you do - when that happens?"

"A jury - not the prosecution, not the defense - decides whether...." McFarland caught herself. "Your Honor," she said, calmly, her eyes still on Alan Boe, "would you please instruct the witness that he is here to answer questions, not ask them."

Boe held up his hand. He understood what was expected.

"When you were asked if you murdered Lucas Fairweather, you said that you had 'many times thought it might not be such a bad idea.' Why did you think that? Why did you think it would be a good idea to kill him?"

Alan Boe tapped his middle finger on the wooden arm of the witness chair three times. He pressed his lips together in a tight line across his mouth. He looked at Eleanor McFarland, seriously disappointed in what she had done.

"I said that I did not murder Chancellor Fairweather. Then I added, as a way to put in perspective the difference between a criminal act and the kind of passing daydream we have, I think, all experienced when confronted by remarkable, and in this instance almost willful, stupidity, that I had many times thought it might not be a bad idea. I did not - and you know I did not - ever say that I thought 'it would be a good idea to kill' him. The distinction will seem small only to those incapable of making the kind of distinctions that matter. Now, as to the question - your question - the one you were starting to ask: why would I have ever thought that the world - or, rather, to be precise: the university - would be better off if Lucas Fairweather were not a part of it, that question, after what you and everyone in this courtroom heard from the vice-chancellor, almost answers itself. Lucas Fairweather represented everything a university should be against. Lucas Fairweather did not know the difference between a university and a trade school. It is our great misfortune that nearly everyone now thinks Lucas Fairweather was right; our misfortune that, like Lucas Fairweather, we no longer know what it means to have a conscience."

McFarland was standing at the far end of the jury box. A few of the jurors turned to look at her; most kept their eyes on Alan Boe, afraid they might miss something if, even for an instant, they looked away.

"We don't know what it means to have a conscience? Is that what you are saying? That, like Lucas Fairweather - the way he treated women - we don't know the difference between right and wrong?" she asked, with a look of deep suspicion.

He had given her an opening, a chance to make him seem condescending, someone who looked down on other people, people like the twelve jurors who already had to think him strange. It was not much of leap from strange to unaccountable, someone you could not trust to act in any normal way; someone who might, after all, have done what he was accused of doing. Eleanor McFarland stood there in the attitude of a woman who deserves an explanation. But instead of a reply, Alan Boe just gazed back at her.

"You don't want to answer my question?"

"How old are you?"

"How old am...? I'm not here to answer your questions; you're here to -"

"Answer yours. Yes, I've heard that. But - tell me if you disagree - we're both here to learn the truth. Am I wrong about that?" he asked, with a quick, disarming smile.

"No, you're not wrong about….But we do that in a court of law by having the attorney's ask questions, not the witnesses."

"I asked how old you were, because you appear to be a very well-educated woman with a considerable amount of experience. You asked me how many years I have been teaching at Berkeley; if I knew how old you were - if I did not have to guess - I could perhaps answer your question in a way that would allow me to draw on your memory and not just my own."

"My memory, your memory - I don't think I quite understand."

"My question goes to whether I am right in assuming that you have lived long enough to grasp, not just the changes that have taken place, but their significance."

"The changes that have…," she started to say, but stopped. She was angry at herself, angry for letting him throw her off track, angry at again yielding, if even for a moment, to the fascination he seemed to exercise on everyone. She practically shouted her insistence that he answer the question she had asked.

"You asked two questions: Do we know what it means to have a conscience, and do we know the difference between right and wrong? They are, both of them, very long questions. Begin with this: when do we learn what is right and wrong? It isn't from books on ethics; we don't learn it from our teachers in a university. We learn it before we know how to learn; we learn it, starting the day we are born, from our parents; we learn it in the stories we are told as small children; we learn it in a way that becomes so much a part of who we are that most of us never question what we know - what we believe - to be true. That is the nature of our conscience: what we know without any doubt whatsoever is right and wrong. But there is always a tension between the demands of

202

conscience and what society thinks important and wants to protect. We all know this. Here, in the United States, money and fame have become, for a great many people, the only measure of success. Nothing else seems to matter. The worst effect of this addiction to wealth and its privileges is on education where, we are constantly told by people like Lucas Fairweather, the important thing is to train a workforce that can compete in the world market. What we learn from reading great works of literature, the sense of what it means to be human that we get from listening to great music - the music of Bach and Mozart and Beethoven - what we see about the human condition in great works of art; in other words what not that long ago was thought to be the importance of a decent education is now dismissed as at best irrelevant, something that can be picked up in your spare time, and at worst harmful to the main business of learning a marketable skill. We have become like those Athenians someone told Socrates had all gathered around a horse. 'Why?' he asked. 'Is the horse rich?'"

The courtroom erupted in laughter. Michelle Longstreet could not quite suppress a grin as she gently tapped her gavel and reminded everyone that this was a courtroom and silence was required

"This is the most serious danger we have ever faced," insisted Alan Boe, his eyes shining with all the certainty of a thing foretold. "We are speaking - you asked about - conscience. What I said is true: we learn the difference between right and wrong while still in our cradles, but the choice between them is not always easy, or as straightforward as we would like, as we get older. We do not live by ourselves; we live with others. We are part of a country, a society of human beings. If you look around, what do you see - a frenzied attempt to gain recognition, to have more than others, to show yourself to advantage, to rise above the crowd, but to do so by becoming what the crowd admires. Public opinion becomes the only opinion that matters, and because, in the age of television and the internet, public opinion can change overnight, there is scarcely time to think. Instead of timeless values - that sense of right and wrong, the basis of our conscience, our 'shared knowledge,' - everything has become provisional. The morning paper, for those who still have one to read, has become, as it were, a typesetter's nightmare in which before you have reached the end of a sentence the beginning is already being rewritten."

Eleanor McFarland stared down at the floor, nodding in a way that suggested she did not disagree. She was old enough to remember when a university education meant more than the acquisition of marketable skills. But there were some things that had not changed, and a jury trial, a murder trial, was one of them.

"You considered Lucas Fairweather a threat, a danger, to the university, what you believe a university should be. That is why, as you have now admitted, you had 'many times thought it might not be a bad idea' - isn't that the phrase you used to correct my characterization? - if he was to be murdered. You are now on trial for that murder, and -"

"A murder I did not commit!"

"A murder the jury will decide you did or did not commit. When you were questioned by the police, you said there were circumstances in which murder was justified - isn't that correct, Professor Boe?'

"Yes, I said that."

"The example you used, an obvious example - Hitler?"

"Yes, of course."

"Because Hitler was a threat to everything we believe - isn't that the reason."

"To everything we believe, and to the lives - the millions of lives - of everyone who stood in his way."

"Someone presents a threat to our way of life, to what we hold most sacred, to what we would die to defend - the death of someone like that would not be murder, it would be the act of a hero, someone willing to risk their own life to rid the world of someone who posed that kind of danger - would you not agree?"

"Yes, no question."

"You just told us that - and tell me if I misquote you - that what Lucas Fairweather, and others like him, wanted to do with the university was 'the most serious danger we have ever faced.' The greatest danger we have ever faced," she repeated, as she turned slowly to the jury. "The greatest danger." She let the words echo in the silence of the courtroom and then, shaking her head, she glanced at the bench. "The prosecution has no more questions of this witness."

I was on my feet before she reached her chair.

"Re-direct, your Honor."

Alan Boe still sat in the same figure eight position, leaning forward, more than willing, eager, to hear the next question. It did not matter what the question was. He had the answer before you asked it. Better than anyone I had ever seen in a court of law, he understood the connections between things, the single thread that held everything together.

"No, I did not consider Lucas Fairweather that kind of threat."

Eleanor McFarland was just sitting down. I had not asked a question.

"I beg your pardon - you didn't consider...?"

"Lucas Fairweather - I was asked a question by Ms. McFarland. She did not give me time to answer. That is my answer."

He bent his head to the side, waiting to see if I wanted him to explain. It was a matter of form, a polite way of encouraging someone to join the conversation. If I had said nothing, just stood there, waiting to see what he would do next, he would have begun without me, but made it seem that he was only responding to what he knew I wanted him to do. It was a teacher encouraging a student. I looked at the jury, and with a slight smile let them know I was as fascinated by Alan Boe as I knew they must be.

"You didn't consider Lucas Fairweather the kind of threat that would justify his murder. You didn't think of him as someone like a Hitler, whom everyone would have wanted dead - is that the answer you would have given, had you been given the chance to answer?"

"Yes, exactly. I meant what I said about the dangerous changes that have taken place, about the way the university - and by this I mean all universities - has forgotten that the purpose of higher education is to liberate the mind from the dominant prejudices of the times in which we live, to preserve the long tradition of the timeless standards by which we should measure what we think important. That requires, not the death of individuals who are incapable of that kind of understanding, but the existence of people who can bring back to life what we too often kill: curiosity about how those who came before us - Plato and Aristotle, Cicero and Julian - saw the world, saw it through eyes that had not been darkened by all the changes we in our ignorance think so beneficial. Kill - murder - someone who does not agree with that? I would have to murder nearly everyone alive!"

I could have listened - the jury, everyone in the courtroom, could have listened - for as long as Alan Boe wanted to go on talking, listened until the sun vanished from the sky and the moon took its place. It was the perfect time to bring things back to specifics, the reason why we were here, what the jury had to decide.

"I want to take you back to the night of the murder. Why were you there?"

"I walk every night, a mile or so, always at the same time, always the same route. Every night, for so many years, I don't know I'm doing it. It gives me exercise, and without having to think where I am going, allows me to think about what I am studying, what I am trying to write."

"What happened," I asked, "what happened that made you

206

stop walking?"

Alan Boe's eyes flashed, then narrowed and drew inward as he went back to what he had heard and what he had seen.

"A scream, a shout, from a window, a woman's voice. When I heard it, I stopped and looked around. For a moment I was not sure I had really heard anything, everything was so still, so silent, I thought it might have been my own imagination; but then I heard it again, a scream, a second shout. There were lights on in the building, the second floor; I knew, I was sure, that was where the screams had come from. Someone was in trouble. I started for the entrance - it was not more than twenty, or thirty, feet away. The doors were open and I started up the steps when a woman, a young woman, a woman in her twenties, came running down the stairs toward me. She bumped into me, and I grabbed her, tried to stop her, because I knew - or thought I knew - she was in trouble. She looked at me with frantic eyes, scared, terrified, I thought. 'He's up there," she cried, tossing her head toward the floor above. 'He tried to...and I....' That is what she said, and then she shook free of me and ran off, and I ran up the stairs to see what had happened and I found him, Lucas Fairweather, laying on the floor, his head all bloody. He was dead."

Boe looked at the jury, astonished, as it seemed, how easily, and how completely, he had been misled.

"Those few words she spoke to me, that look I thought was terror, when I found Lucas Fairweather laying dead on the floor I thought she had acted in self-defense I kept wondering how she had managed to get hold of that statue and hit him on the back of his skull with it while he was trying to attack her. It is what happens when you look at things, not with your own eyes, but through what others tell you."

Eleanor McFarland would say what she had to say in her closing argument and I would say what I could in mine, but the verdict had already been decided. It had been decided five minutes after Alan Boe took the stand; it was probably decided even before that, before the jury had heard any witnesses at all, when he started asking the judge how she was going to conduct the trial and told everyone how much he was looking forward to the experience. They might have acquitted him even had they thought he was actually guilty of the murder of Lucas Fairweather in the belief that whatever Alan Boe did had to have had a justification, even if they could not quite see what it was. He inspired more than trust, loyalty; loyalty to what by his presence you understood was the best any of us, any human being, could ever be. I heard later that when the jury reached the jury room they all just looked at each other and shook their heads. The picked a foreman and having concluded their deliberations were back in court less than ten minutes after they had left.

Chapter Fourteen

Alan Boe was a free man, but I was still a prisoner, wondering what was going to happen next, what James Michael Redfield was planning in this strange conspiracy in which I had now twice been forced to play a part. A trial exposing the empty lives of the rich and privileged, a trial revealing the mindless hypocrisies of higher education, how many people was Redfield willing to have murdered, how many trials of innocent defendants, to accomplish whatever it was he was after? Serial killers murdered people because it gave them a sense of power, a feeling of importance; Redfield, if Alan Boe was right, wanted to change the way we lived; Redfield, if Alan Boe was right, was at war with modernity. But however brilliant Redfield might be, could he really believe that a trial, even a series of trials, could have anything like that kind of effect? Could he really believe that everyone would suddenly change their mind about getting rich because of what happened in the Friedrich trial; could he really believe that an American university, especially one dependent on public support, would go back to the 19th century teaching of the liberal arts because Lucas Fairweather had been murdered and Alan Boe had been put on trial?

"You don't seem very pleased with how the trial turned out," observed Giuseppe Gambarini, peering at me from across the table. "You can't be disappointed with the verdict. Alan Boe is a free man, thanks to you."

It brought me back to the present. We were having dinner, the four of us, in the same small Italian restaurant where we had dined together before.

"Alan Boe is a free man because of Alan Boe. He did everything; all I did was watch. And, yes, of course I'm pleased. I would have been devastated had the verdict gone the other way."

Giuseppe kept talking to me, but his eyes were moving back and forth between his wife and Tangerine, who were carrying on a conversation of their own. With her low cut crimson dress and her radiant dark eyes, it did not matter what Sophia was saying. She could say everything important without ever speaking a line, or talk endlessly, the way she was doing now, when the words meant nothing and the look she gave you told you what she really meant to say.

"Enough!" cried Giuseppe, throwing up his hands in a gesture of mock despair. "I have trouble following one conversation, I cannot follow two."

"Then you should quit talking," suggested Sophia, a larcenous smile of studied indifference hovering over the half-circle of her wide full mouth. "And instead perhaps take lessons in how to listen."

"If only I knew a good teacher," he sighed, his eyes the bare whisper of a smile. "Or even someone who knows sometimes how to do it."

"What is the point of listening to what I know you are going to say?"

"You think you know me that well?"

"Better," she insisted with perfect confidence, "than you know yourself."

"That is no great achievement," he replied, briskly shaking his head. "I know nothing about myself. No," he went on before she could object, "it's true. I know nothing about myself; if I did, I wouldn't always be so surprised at myself."

Sophia, who had been leaning toward him, pulled back, her attention, all her attention, on him. They could have been sitting

210

alone in a hotel room, for all either of them seemed aware that any-one else was there. He held her, entranced, bewitched, as it were, by the absolute certainty with which he announced what seemed to make no sense at all.

"Surprised that I ever had the arrogance to think that you, my dear Sophia, might ever want to be with me; surprised that I had the courage to ask. But, more than that," he went on, turning now to Tangerine and me, "surprised whenever I start to put pen to paper and begin to hear the music playing that I have not yet composed. It is what I tried to explain when we were here before - the seemingly strange paradox that we do not think the thought, the thought thinks us. We say that a thought has 'come to us.' That means that the thought does not start with us. What could be more surprising than that? The other reason I say I don't know myself, is that, quite frankly, I have never been too sure what it means. And I don't quite know where it would stop.

"Where it would stop?" asked Tangerine, curious to know not just what Giuseppe Gasperini might mean, but why, unlike so many other people she knew, he thought it a question worth pursu-ing.

"Yes, where it would stop, because if you say I want to know who I am, the question has to be asked again: who is the 'I' who wants to know who I....You see where this is going. There is no end to it, an infinite regression, a note played once loudly that never stops echoing, if," he added with a glance at Sophia, "you listen carefully enough."

Turning back to me, he remarked, "If I understood him, that is what Alan Boe has been trying to teach: the meaning of that famous and completely misunderstood instruction to 'know thy-self.' It does not mean know what you want, what you happen to desire - it means to know your place as a human being in the order of things."

We sat there, talking and drinking, for more than an hour,

and each time the waiter approached we either waved him off or ordered another bottle of wine. Somewhere the other side of sixty, he went about his business the way he would have had he been practicing on an empty table. His eyes followed his hands and his hands followed the same routine they had no doubt followed for years, decades, centuries if he did not stop to die; he was San Franciscan through and through, one of those blank-eyed waiters who, ready with a reply to any question, always gave it with all the jaded monotony of an answer given a thousand times before. On what was perhaps the fifth time he came up, when we were once again too caught up in our conversation to care about dinner, Sophia shook her head in response to his tired -voice inquiry about whether we might be ready to order.

As he started to walk away, he muttered something about how we might have just stayed in the bar. Giuseppe tore into him, a fast moving torrent of the Sicilian dialect of Italian that made the waiter go ashen-faced with astonishment and something very close to fear.

"Yes, yes, I'm very sorry. Please, I apologize," said the waiter, his narrow, half-hooded eyes as wide open as they had perhaps ever been. "Take your time, take all the time you need. And, again, please - I meant no offense."

And as quickly as that he was gone.

"You didn't need to do that," said Sophia, but with a look of such profound regard as left no question what she really thought.

"What did you say?" asked Tangerine, fascinated by how immediate, and how explosive, his reaction had been to this idle, if ill-mannered, remark of a hapless waiter.

"He's Sicilian. I knew it first time I saw him, and I heard him speaking in Sicilian another time we were here. I probably shouldn't have said what I did - but...you know, what I wouldn't bother with if he had said it to me, when he said it to...."

Grasping his left shoulder with his right hand, he bent his

head slightly to the side. He was amused, and I think a little proud of what he had done. It reminded him of what life was like, not here, in America, where everyone has forgotten formality and the way women were supposed to be treated, but in Sicily, where he lived, and where he had been raised.

"I told him that I had conducted orchestras all over the world, but that I lived and worked in Palermo and I remembered what he had obviously forgotten: what the word respect means to a Sicilian, that he should know what happens to someone who treats with discourtesy a Sicilian woman, and I told him that I was embarrassed, embarrassed to know that there was a Sicilian anywhere who had forgotten what it meant to be a man."

"That would get you in a little trouble here," remarked Tangerine, with a sideways glance at me. " There isn't supposed to be any difference between the sexes. We're all supposed to pretend that there isn't any real difference at all. You can't be discourteous to a woman because she is a woman; you aren't treating her as an equal unless the same thing you complain of what be just as discourteous if it were directed at a man. Woman, you have to remember, is no longer the weaker sex. And if you don't believe that, you're sexist, and if you're sexist, nothing you have to say - about anything - could possibly be worth listening to."

With a smile that grew broader with each word he heard her speak, Giuseppe Gambarini bounced his head from side to side, the silent sing-song chorus to the latest form of the world's false wisdom.

"The carnival of the uninstructed, the manic certainty that denies there is a difference between men and women on the doubtful mathematical theory that where there is a difference equality cannot exist. It is like so-called modern music, Schoenberg and his imitators, this insistence that every note is equal to all the others, and that they should all be played, in some manner, the same number of times. What they forget, what they do not understand,

213

is that it is the way notes fit together that determines whether there is a harmony or just noise. If you play a certain note only once in a great composition, something Bach or Mozart or Beethoven wrote, that note holds everything else together. Take it out, forget to play it, the piece is ruined. That is how equality should be measured, whether each note, whether each of us, man or woman, fits together in an ordered whole. Yes, yes, I know - I am a hopeless reactionary, a reader of old books and old music, someone who does not believe in the modern fixation on the equality of everything, no matter how bad the choice. I mean, think about it - if Rap and Mozart are both called music, if they are an equally valid choice - what better proof do you need that we have all gone, in that wonderfully accurate phrase, 'start raving mad'? That is really at the heart of it: no one believes that there are objectively valid standards; everyone believes - or pretends to believe - that everyone has the right to choose whatever he or she wants: how to live, what to like, who they want to be, and because you grant that right, everything is up to the individual, and every choice is as good as any other. The question no one takes seriously, which is the very question every thoughtful person should take seriously, is whether any of that is true."

Giuseppe had been looking at each of us, his gaze moving in a steady arc from one side to the other. Suddenly, as if he had just solved a puzzle, he stared at Tangerine, his eager, light-filled eyes full of knowing laughter.

"Antonelli is my witness. What happens whenever you walk into a room; what happened when you walked into this restaurant tonight? Everyone turned to look. It is what we do, all of us are drawn to what is most beautiful. I imagine there are people who resent this, who think it shows that sexism is still too deeply ingrained, that it has somehow to be eradicated. And then, when these same people are asked to appear on television they put on their make-up and their best clothes and talk as if the word 'attractive' had nothing to do with anything inherent in human nature."

Sophia rolled her eyes and, pretending to suppress a grin, shrugged her shoulders.

"If that is true, if we are all so attracted to the beautiful the way everyone - at least every man with any life left in him - would be attracted to Tangerine, how do you explain why I am married to you? Or do you think the sexes are really that different?"

Her husband fixed her with a smile of perfect confidence. She did not look away; she did not want to. There was a kind of magic between them, a history of such extravagant dimensions that it was as if everything that had ever passed between them could be taken in, remembered, in a single, laughing glance.

"Perhaps it is because I make beautiful music, and not just in the concert hall."

"They told you, then - that I always play your music in bed?"

"Yes," he replied, still holding her close in that playful, antic stare. "Everyone of them - every member of the Italian army."

"They're no good at fighting," she said, throwing up her chin as her eyes blazed delighted defiance. "Someone had to give them something to do."

"So you see," he said, turning to me, "I'm married to a music teacher, but, please notice, one who understands the difference between good and bad music. Now, tell us what is going to happen next."

"Next?' I asked, though I was reasonably certain what he wanted to know.

"Yes what happens next. Someone chose Alan Boe to stand trial for something he did not do; the same person, I assume, who was responsible for the Friedrich murder. You told us that - or rather, if I remember correctly - Tangerine told us that the night we were here, the night before the trial of Professor Boe was scheduled to start. I remember perfectly: 'Two murders, two trials, both

men innocent, the first one acquitted' - and now both men acquitted - 'and you're the attorney in each.' And I remember, what is
more true now than it was then , that I said I thought you were 'the
central character in a drama still being written.' What is going to
happen next? Has the next chapter been written?"

"There isn't going to be a next chapter," insisted Tangerine.
There was a bitter edge to her voice, and something unforgiving in
her eyes. "There isn't, is there?" she asked me, suddenly not quite
so sure. "It's stops now, doesn't it? You can't let him...!"

It was like asking a fly caught in a web for assurances that
the spider would never weave another one. There was not anything
I could do - there was not anything, so far as I could tell, anyone
could do - to stop James Michael Redfield from doing a third, or
a fourth, or a fifth time what he had now with complete success
done twice before. The only choice I would have, if he did it again,
had someone blamed for a murder he did not commit, was simply
refuse to take the case and assume Redfield would not punish my
refusal by actually allowing an innocent man or woman to be convicted. It seems a strange reliance on the basic decency of someone
who had already committed, or caused to be committed, two murders.

"Tell me, what would you do if the person behind all this,
the one who is writing this drama in which you have been forced to
play a leading part, were caught? What would you do if
this same person who, once again, is really responsible, were
charged with committing these crimes?"

"What would I do? I would...." I saw the look in his eyes
and recognized the dilemma that would be created. "Would I represent him? Is that what you want to know? Would I be his lawyer,
would I take his case to trial?"

I wondered. Would I defend James Michael Redfield after
everything he had done? I honestly did not know. The temptation, of course, was to say that there were no circumstances under

which I would do it, that it was the last thing I would ever do, but there was another question, which was how far would I go to learn the truth, not what he had done, or how he had done it - arranged things in the way he had so that two different murders would lead to the trial of two innocent men - but why? What purpose had he had, what had he been trying to accomplish? I had spent my life trying murder cases in courts of law. I had become familiar with what I had thought very possible kind of criminal behavior, but I had never known anyone like Redfield. He was, in his own way, as unusual, as unique, as Alan Boe was in his.

"I don't know," I answered honestly. "It would depend."

Tangerine did not want to believe it.

"You don't know? You couldn't really defend him after what he…."

"Would it really matter what he has done?" asked Giuseppe.

Leaning back, his left arm thrown casually over the corner of his chair, a troubled smile, like an unsolved riddle, slipped sideways across his mouth. He looked at Tangerine, but the question he had asked was one he tried himself to answer.

"There was some time ago in Europe a scandal about a certain composer. He had without question committed a number of criminal acts. He was even thought responsible for the suicide of his wife. He was by all accounts a thoroughly despicable human being, but no one suggested that for that reason we should stop performing the music - let me add, the brilliant music - he had written. And of course no one suggests that a surgeon should refuse to save the life of someone because of what the patient has done. Consider that: suppose you are a doctor and the man who has raped and murdered your wife suddenly needs your help - he'll die without it. What should he do?"

"Let the bastard die," suggested Sophia, with a grim expression of utter defiance. "And hope he suffers."

"He has not that choice," persisted Giuseppe. "As a man, a

husband, yes; but not as a physician."

"A physician who was a man, a physician who was a husband, would do what you say: operate to save his life, and then, at the crucial moment, let the knife slip just enough," said Sophia, her large, magnificent eyes full of exuberant malevolence. "I know what you will say, but, remember, the law and justice are not always the same."

"A lawyer, then, should do the same thing?" asked Giuseppe, stealing a glance at me before continuing with Sophia. "Would you have our friend, the great trial lawyer - No, I mean that, Joseph. Everyone agrees: you are the best there is at what you do - You would have him take the case to trial, and then, to get justice for what his client has done before, have him - I think the phrase is - 'throw the case,' make sure the jury finds him guilty, even if he did not do it, even if he was not guilty, even if, as in the two cases we have been talking about - the Friedrich trial and now the trial of Alan Boe - someone else committed the crime?"

He let the question hang in the air, a question that would make a liar out of anyone who thought he knew what the answer had to be, a question that you could only hope you would never have to answer, never have to choose whether to help someone who had gotten away with murder avoid conviction for a murder he did not commit, or make sure he was convicted as the only way to stop him from murdering again. We sat there, the four of us, with suddenly nothing we wanted to say, because, suddenly, everything we had thought before now seemed quite probably wrong.

Raising his hand, Giuseppe signaled for the waiter. He was there in an instant, ready to do whatever it was our pleasure to ask. Giuseppe ordered in Sicilian for all of us. And then it started, course after course, each one the best thing I had ever eaten, and each one better than the last. The talk, following our appetite, left the dismal metaphysics of courtroom justice, the juggling conundrums of legal reasoning, and turned to the more interesting, and more noble, discussion of the loves and hatreds of men and women, the taunting, teasing confessions of the romantically inspired, the strengths and weaknesses of that rarest of things, the love affair between two people still married to each other. We watched, together, as it were, Tangerine and I, the way Giuseppe and Sophia Gasperini seemed to live inside a mirror of their own devising, each movement become, before you could bat an eye, a double image, everything they did, everything they said, the first or second part of a two half whole. If they did not finish each other's sentences, it was only because they were too busy beginning the next sentence the other was about to speak.

Dinner went on for hours. I did not want it to end, I did not want to start thinking again about that question, what was going to happen next; I did not want to start thinking about James Michael Redfield. Tomorrow, I told myself, tomorrow there would be time enough for that. I knew that I was avoiding it, that I was trying too hard to lose myself in the present moment, trying too hard to have a good time. I started drinking, more than I usually did at dinner, and the more I drank the easier it became to have another glass, and another one after that. Tangerine began to look at me with what I thought a trace, more than a trace, of disappointment. I began to look at her with growing anger and resentment. I reached for the wine bottle. Her hand was on my wrist.

"Don't."

"Don't?" I demanded. "You're telling me that I shouldn't...?"

"Shouldn't let Redfield get to you like this. Remember what you told me, when we first met? When you're in court, you're the defense attorney, all the advantage is with you. You know everything the prosecution knows and you know more than that: you know what the defendant has told you in private."

"What does that have to do with...?"

"Redfield does not know what you know. He does not

219

know that - as you often remind me - something always happens during a trial that no one expects and no one has anticipated. What I am trying to tell you," she continued, squeezing my wrist, "is that if there is another murder, if there is another trial - if you think you have to do it - he'll make a mistake, he'll do something you'll be able to use to turn everything against him. I know it, I'm sure of it. So, for God's sake, don't worry about what will happen next. Whatever it is, whatever happens, you'll know what to do with it."

There was not a word of truth in what she said. I had nothing like the kind of greater knowledge, I had nothing like the advantage, she insisted I had. She was wrong, wrong about all of it, but - and this was the only thing that mattered - she believed it, believed that somehow, some way, whatever happened, Redfield, or anyone else I came up against, would lose and I would win. The strange, if perhaps predictable, part was that because she believed it, I began to believe it myself.

At least until the check for dinner came. There was no check, because, as our good waiter explained, someone had paid it for us. There was a note, addressed to me.

"Who is it? What does it say?" asked Tangerine, as I opened the small envelope and read the card.

"James Michael Redfield. He has invited me to visit him at that company of his, the one no outsider has supposedly ever seen."

Chapter Fifteen

Despite what I had been led to expect, there was no fence, no gate, no security guard at the entrance, nothing, except a small sign with the letters AIE, to indicate that you had not simply made a wrong turn and found yourself at the end of a dead end street. What looked more like a narrow paved walking path than a road led under a canopy of tall majestic redwood trees for perhaps half a mile until, suddenly, after coming around a steep curve, there was a large clearing of several hundred well-tended acres, where, on the far side of a small blue water lake, a half dozen low slung modern steel and glass buildings were spread out among close cut green grass lawns. Reflected off the water, the late afternoon sunlight painted everything a soft scarlet gold.

There was no parking lot that I could see, in fact there were no cars anywhere. I pulled up next to what looked to be the main building. I started to get out of the car, but the door was already being opened. A young woman, twenty-three or twenty-four, was standing there, apparently come to greet me. She was astonishingly good looking, but what struck me most about her was the depth of her eyes and the quiet intensity with which she looked at me. From a distance you might have imagined her somewhere on a beach; seeing her this close you would half expect to be told she was the newest member of the physics department of some university.

"Good afternoon, Mr. Antonelli. Welcome to AIE. My name is Carruthers. Redfield has asked me to show you around."

"Carruthers?" I asked. She was very friendly, she seemed quite open, but the use of her last name, as if it were the only name she had, seemed a shade, not exactly pretentious, but self-consciously formal.

"We don't use first names here, and we don't call anyone mister or miss. Redfield wants it that way. He explained to us that it avoids any invidious distinctions between the sexes, and eliminates any suggestion of a hierarchy among those of who who work and learn here."

"You called me Mr. Antonelli," I reminded her.

"Yes, of course. You're a visitor, an invited guest, the first one I think we have ever had. We're all very excited to have you with us. Redfield told us as great deal about you. What I was saying, what I tried to explain to you: the names we use here - that of course is only here, among the members of the community."

I may have been the first visitor to the sheltered campus of AIE, but Carruthers conducted the tour with the ease of someone who had done it dozens of times before. This does not mean that I really understood everything she told me; I did not even quite understand the full significance of the name. AIE, she explained, tossing her head as if there was something humorous in it, stood for Artificial Intelligence Enterprises.

"Redfield says it is a contradiction in terms, that intelligence - if it is intelligence, and not stupidity in the form of logic - is the very antithesis of anything artificial; that intelligence is not a product of the human mind: it is the essence, the definition, of the human mind. That makes perfect sense when you think about it, don't you think so, Mr. Antonelli?"

I had no answer to this, or to any other question she was likely to ask, as she continued to describe what AIE actually did.

"We are the world's leading producer of advanced artificial intelligence. Whatever you have read about what artificial intelligence will be able to do in ten years, twenty years - we are there already, and then some. Let me show you something," she announced with all the eagerness of surprise.

I followed her into a windowless building without any visible markings: no name, no number, nothing but the memory of where it was to distinguish it from its neighbors. Like the entrance to the campus itself, there was no apparent security, no lock on the door, no armed, or unarmed, personnel to keep anyone out.

"This is what I mean," said Carruthers, sweeping the air with her arm to take in everything inside.

But all I saw was an endless series of cubicles, dozens of them, and a few white coated technicians - at least I assumed that was what they were - crouched over microscopes or staring into densely colored computer screens.

"This is the medical building," she explained, as if that would tell me all I would need to know.

"It doesn't look like a medical building."

Carruthers was nearly as tall as I am, with long, straight blonde hair, and smooth perfect skin. Her hands, with long tapered fingers, were like those of a concert pianist or a gifted surgeon She looked at me with what for a moment was a blank expression. Then she understood.

"You'll have to forgive me. When you haven't been anywhere else for as along a time as I have been here, you forget what others do not know. It is called the medical building because this is where the future of medicine is being written."

"Written?"

She led me down the central corridor to what looked like a lounge, a large, open circle with two or three leather sofas, a couple of tables, and a half dozen straight back chairs. An enormous, wafer thin screen hung suspended from the ceiling at the farther edge. Placing her right foot on a bronze cylinder embedded in the gray cement floor, she pointed with her index finger toward the screen. The screen came to life, the picture in three dimensions and a narrator's voice I recognized immediately as Redfield's own.

"This will explain what we do here," said Carruthers, whispering as if Redfield were there in person and she did not want to interrupt.

The presentation was short and to the point; three minutes that, if what he said was true, would make what we call modern medicine seem like a witch doctor's primitive remedies. The human being, or rather the body of the human being would, in a sense, be reconfigured. A microchip - eventually, if I followed Redfield's argument, a whole series of them - would be implanted, beginning almost at birth. Every function, every heartbeat, every breath, every brain wave, every cell, would be under constant surveillance; every change, every even the slightest variation from the normal, optimum condition, noted and subjected to an immediate course of treatment. The initial treatment would involve the use of the body's own defenses: anti-bodies, healthy cells, would be directed by remedial programs written into the microchips. When this was not sufficient, a second stage of treatment would start. Everything tracked by the implanted microchips would also be monitored by computers which, upon the need, would make contact with the necessary hospital or physician. There would never be a disease detected too late for treatment, and nearly every treatment would be far less invasive, and far less difficult, than what was now required when a disease like cancer had spread throughout much of the body.

It was all very clinical, a concise, but, so far as I could tell, comprehensive and in every way convincing, summary of what the new medicine would accomplish. It was only at the end, in his very last sentence, that Redfield said something that gave me pause.

"For those who think there is nothing more important than life itself, this will seem like paradise on earth; for those who think that there is some other purpose to human existence the question may be somewhat more complicated."

We left the medical building and moved on to the next one. It was almost identical to the one before: a series of cubicles, everyone working with one or more computers; but instead of medicine, they were developing a new form of education, one in which no one would have to learn anything.

"It is really quite simple," remarked Carruthers, as we walked slowly from one end of the building to the other. "When everyone, or almost everyone, worked on the land; when except for a relatively small number of nobles that made up the ruling class, everyone, almost everyone, was illiterate, no one went to school. Then, with the industrial revolution, the working class, the people - including women and children - spent all their working hours in effect tethered to a machine; scarcely any of them learned to read or write. But with the development of a middle class, the rise of merchants, the increase in the members of the so-called learned professions like medicine and law, formal education - schools and colleges - began to assume a new importance. During all this time, there were always at least a small group of men, and even women, who read serious works. They were part of a leisured class that did not have to spend their time just trying to survive. Universities taught people like these the languages, the sciences, the classics of literature and philosophy; they taught history, ancient and modern. Then, after the Second World War, there was a new, increased demand for a college education, but it was a college education of a very particular kind: it was education for a practical purpose, the knowledge, the skills, needed to have a successful career. Theoretical knowledge was all right, but the world needed engineers; literature was okay, but business administration taught you how to rise quickly in a large corporation. Everyone now had to go to college; without that degree you were never going to get anywhere.

"Then, a half century later, something quite unexpected happened: you could get a college degree without going to college;

you could get it online. But - and this is quite obvious, if you think it through - if you can give someone a college education, or what most people now think of as a college education: technical training of the kind of job they want - why can you not do the same thing for grammar school and high school. Why have schools at all? Everyone has a computer - let the computer do the teaching. Look around you. What do you see? What do you think everyone here is doing? - writing computer programs? No, not exactly. What we do here is design artificial human beings - teachers, or rather mentors, or what was once called tutors. The computer itself isn't necessary anymore. We push a button - here, look at the screen." She pointed to a small thin screen on a table a few feet off to the side. "Tutor!" she cried. A face appeared on the screen, waiting, as it seemed, to be told what was wanted. "Start the math lesson."

And suddenly I was back in class, but all alone, answering questions, being told when I was wrong and the corrections I needed to make.

"That is the difference," explained Carruthers. "Instant feedback. You are immediately told that you have made a mistake and how to fix it. That is just the beginning. Why, if you have a full-time tutor, someone who you can always have with you, someone who can always not just answer any questions you have, but explain the reasoning behind the answer - why learn anything, why go to school, when you can design your own education to fit your own particular need. If I wanted to be able to communicate with someone in French, instead of spending years in school learning the language, and probably never learning it well enough, I just tell my 'tutor' what I want said and he, she, whatever you want to call it, takes care of it for you. Instantaneous translation, always there at your command. Why bother with…." She stopped, and stared at me in embarrassment. "I'm sorry. I'm afraid I've gotten a little carried away. That is a much longer explanation that I should have given. You must…."

"No, quite the contrary. It's fascinating, especially when, unless I'm mistaken, Redfield isn't himself convinced that any of this is all that beneficial - is he?"

Carruthers only smiled.

"There are things that cannot be stopped. Technology takes on a life of its own. Redfield teaches that. And that is all the more reason to be as far in advance of that development as you can. You have to see where it is going if you are going to survive it."

"Survive? You mean it might kill us all?"

"Or something worse than that," she remarked with a strange, distant glance. "Come. There is lots more to show you and there is only a little time left before dinner, and just after that is when Redfield speaks."

I had not come to have dinner and I certainly had not come to hear Redfield give a speech; I had come to meet Redfield , and to tell him that the game was over: I was not going to be forced into another trial.

"He'll see you," insisted Carruthers, when I told her I was there to meet Redfield privately. "When he's ready."

We went to the next building, and the one after that, and I was in each place given the same kind of short summation of how AIE, which meant Redfield, was years ahead of everyone else, in transportation, economic development, entertainment, even in sports. I noticed that I had been wrong in my assumption that there were hundreds of people working there. The size of the buildings, the long line of cubicles, had the effect of a kind of double mirror, the same thing repeated over and over into infinity. In fact, I learned when I finally asked, there were only a hundred people working there, exactly one hundred, as it turned out, divided for some reason equally between men and women. They were all in their early twenties, all of them graduates of the better universities in the country, all of them under contract for five years.

"And all of you started the same time, all of you together?"

"Yes," replied Carruthers, with a puzzled glance, as if she could not quite grasp why this seemed in any way unusual. "We're all members of the same class."

We had left the last building and were walking past a small amphitheater next to the dining hall on the other side. Carruthers moved with a dancer's easy, balanced grace, her shoulders straight, her head held high. Her voice, soft and warm like the summer wind, seemed to wrap around you, take you inside the thought she was giving expression. It was a voice that inspired confidence, but instead of inviting intimacy established a distance, like the voice of a teacher you loved to listen to, but who, if you passed her in the hall, you would not think to speak to unless she spoke to you first.

"Member of the same class? There was another class before you then, and another one that will follow?"

"Two classes before; we're the third. I don't know if there will be a fourth. That depends on Redfield."

I stopped walking. She turned and waited to see what I wanted.

"This doesn't make any sense."

"It doesn't...?"

"Make any sense. What you just told me. You work at what, if I am not mistaken - what Redfield himself has told me - is one of the most successful high tech companies in the -"

"No, not one of the most successful - AIE is the most successful company of its sort, not just in this country, but in the world. We're the leading -"

"Yes, I know, I know. That's my point. You work for AIE, but you talk about it - the way you describe it - like a university, a five year graduate education, part of a class that when you're finished - when you 'graduate' - another class takes your place, another class that repeats the same five year curriculum."

"No, nothing is repeated here," she responded, shaking her head abruptly. "What we do, what we accomplish - what we discover, what we invent, the technical and theoretical breakthroughs - in our last year is what the next class will build on in their first year."

"That is what doesn't make any sense. Why wouldn't all of you stay; why replace all of you with another 'class'? After all the training, after everything you must have learned, all the work you must have done, why not keep everyone here, continue the work, build on what you have done?"

She looked at me with the vast sympathy of her superior knowledge, and I began to get impatient. For all the thorough detail with which she had described the various things she had shown me on her guided tour, I had had the sense that something was being left out, something missing that would have given a different meaning to all those neatly labelled facts of her's and their endless classifications. Everything had been too measured, too organized, too well-prepared. Her soft summer voice had calibrated the intervals of spoken words like a metronome marking time. She seemed to take my question under advisement, not what the answer was going to be, but how she was going to phrase it. She smiled, briefly, the silent laughter of a secret she might have been willing to share if only she had thought I were capable of understanding what it meant.

"We aren't here to change the world, Mr. Antonelli; we're here to save it. At least the part that is important," she added, as she gave me that same, brief smile again, and started toward the dining hall just a few short steps away.

The dining hall was a large, rectangular room, the two long facing walls floor to ceiling glass. At one end, in open view, was the kitchen where everyone took turns cooking. There were no hired waiters, no one to wash dishes; everything was done by the hundred men and women who, from what I had been told and what I had seen, were developing the most advanced artificial intelligence technology in the world. They all knew each other, and seemed to like each other. There were ten tables each with ten chairs and, so far as I could tell, everyone just took whatever seat happened to be available. Then I noticed in the far corner something I had not expected, a large play pen with nearly a dozen small children. I looked at Carruthers.

"Our children," she said, and without another word of explanation led me to a table next to the window at the opposite end of the room from the kitchen.

"Whose children?" I asked, as I took a chair.

"Ours," she repeated. "The children born here. We're their parents."

She noticed my confusion and decided it was forgivable. She nodded to the other eight people at the table, four young men and four young women, an equal division which, I realized, was for some reason true of all the other tables as well.

"To make sure we all can work together, that we stay united, dedicated to a common objective, we have everything in common. That means, in a real sense, each other. We sleep with whomever we wish, but always with the understanding that we do not keep things private, that we do not form attachments of the kind that become exclusive. One result, of course, is that occasionally someone gets pregnant and has a child."

It seemed too obvious, but I said it anyway.

"There is such a thing as birth control."

"Yes, but that assumes we don't want children."

"And what happens when, at the end of five years, you all leave. Who takes care of the children then?"

"The mother, of course," she laughed. "Who else?"

"What about the father? No matter how many men the mother may have slept with, DNA would tell you who he was."

"There is a rule against that. If we did that, then, as I said before, there would be a separation, two people would have something private together."

It all seemed quite strange, and yet, somehow, quite normal. Carruthers and, it seemed, everyone there appeared to be perfectly adjusted. They sat at their tables, laughing, having what again at least seemed a remarkably good time. Carruthers introduced me to the others at our table. As she had told me, they all went by their last name, only their last name, and they all insisted on calling me Mr. Antonelli. They exhibited the kind of cheerful formality I seldom encountered anymore.

"And this is Blankenberg. He is CEO this week."

Blankenberg was sitting directly opposite me. Slightly overweight with small, sloping shoulders and a rather pudgy face, his mouth was as narrow and bunched together as a parrot's beak. He had a habit of running his hand over his forehead to keep his long brownish blonde hair from falling over his blue button size eyes.

"And next week I get to clean toilets," he remarked, as he reached across to shake my hand. "It is one of the things we do here, Mr. Antonelli: we learn how to do all the thing necessary, all the things that have to be done. It would not do much good if we all sat around talking about theoretical physics, or applied mathematics, if we did not have a clean place to work."

"Or if we didn't know how to cook or how to clean up," added a young woman, Henderson by name, who sat next to him. While Blankenberg brushed aside a few strands of hair that had slid down to his eyes, she tapped her fingers together beneath a wide, slightly off-center mouth that when she smiled dropped to an even more acute angle. "If you are going to run a company, particularly if you are going to start one of your own - which is what many of us plan to do - then you should know how all the parts fit together. Redfield taught us that."

I gazed around the room. There was a steady drone of conversation, accompanied by a muted chorus of silverware and plates. I looked everywhere, but I did not see him.

"Redfield - where is he?" I asked, a little irritated. "When is he coming?"

The question for some reason seemed a source of amusement. Everyone at the table looked at each other, wondering why I did not know.

"Redfield is never here at dinner," explained Blankenberg finally.

"I was invited here to see him," I said, turning to Carruthers. "You told me he wanted me to go on a tour of the facility, that he wanted me to learn something about this place. I've had the tour. Where is Redfield? I understand you said he would see me when he's ready; he needs to understand I am just about out of both time and patience."

"He comes after dinner," replied Carruthers. "When he lectures."

"When he lectures?"

I got up from my chair, and because this was not their fault, I started to tell them how much I had enjoyed meeting them and that I knew they would all make a great success of their lives. Carruthers grabbed my wrist.

"You can't leave now. It's almost time. You need to stay. Redfield's lecture tonight is all about you: the two trials, what you did, how you managed to keep two people from going to prison."

I was now more determined to leave than ever.

"Tell Redfield," I said, doing nothing to conceal the scorn I felt, "that I don't have any more time for this. He can play his games with someone else."

The lights suddenly flickered and went out, and then, immediately came on again.

"Don't go," pleaded Carruthers, with a gentle, hopeful smile. "He's here now. Or will be. Outside, in the amphitheater."

Everyone, all one hundred employees, all of Redfield's students, rose from their places and made their way outside where they seated themselves on the rows of benches in front of the small, circular stage that was at its closest point not more than twenty feet away from the audience. The stage and the circular rows of benches were well lighted. Carruthers wanted me to follow her to a place in front, but I was not sure how long I wanted to listen to a lecture, especially one in which, if Carruthers was right, was going to be about what I had done in two trials in which, though I was sure he was not going to talk about it, Redfield had been responsible for the murders. I sat in an unoccupied row as far back as I could get.

Everyone was seated; everyone was quiet. There was no one yet on stage. They were waiting for Redfield, but two, three, minutes went by and there was still no sign of him. But still no one made a sound. There were none of the whispered conversations that invariably take place when an audience is waiting for a play, a move, any kind of performance to begin. There was no sound at all. The longer the wait, the greater the sense of anticipation seemed to be. It was palpable. It was, strangely enough, like being in an audience at a political rally, everyone waiting for the candidate, the man on whom they had invested all their hopes and dreams, the candidate they expected to see any moment, but for whom they would wait for hours, as long as they had to, because nothing now mattered except the chance they had to get that close to him, to hear from him directly al the things, the bright new promises of what, thanks to him, their lives could be.

Three minutes, four; I was beginning to shake my head at this remarkable, inexplicable hold Redfield seemed to have on this group of one hundred of what must have been some of the best educated young men and women in the country. I was not going to wait a minute longer. I got up and turned to go. But, suddenly, there was darkness everywhere. The lights had all gone out. And then I heard a voice.

Chapter Sixteen

Redfield was on the stage, a disembodied voice in the darkness. I could not see him, no one could, and it was all on purpose. It was no accident, the lights had not gone out of their own accord. No one in that audience could see him, the sense of sight had been taken away, and with that the sense of hearing had become more acute. We were like blind men listening, nothing visible, nothing of the normal shifting scene of appearances to distract attention from what Redfield wanted to say.

"We have with us this evening a guest, Mr. Joseph Antonelli, a very distinguished attorney who has, in recent months, been involved in two trials, both of which have taught us something about the deficiencies of the world in which we live. Because Mr. Antonelli is here, I will wait until another time to continue the discussion we began last time of that extraordinary work, *Greek Mathematical Thought and the Origin of Algebra*, written by Jacob Klein half a century ago, a book that, if you had to summarize it in a single line, demonstrates that the smallest countable number is two, because, after all, if there is only one of a thing there is nothing to count."

As I became used to the darkness, I could see in bare outline a figure seated on an armless straight back chair, sitting perfectly still, talking to an audience he could not see. He spoke slowly, the way someone might speak sitting all alone, rehearsing a speech he was still working on, trying to get it right. Was that the reason for the darkness? - to make it easier to think out loud. He seemed completely at his ease. He certainly was not making an effort to impress anyone; it was too private, too personal, for that. He might have been talking to two or three close friends huddled around a small table in a Paris cafe. It had the feeling of that kind of intimacy.

"I invited Mr. Antonelli because I have been for a long time fascinated with the tension between justice and the law. We have discussed this before - this sense we have that some things like murder, or like betrayal, are always and everywhere wrong; and then the sometimes radical differences in what, in different times and different places, people believe is right and wrong. In a Muslim country, or among orthodox Jews, or in ancient Greece or Rome, the basic rule was whatever the law does not require is not permitted; while here, in America, and in most of the countries that talk of freedom, the rule is whatever is not prohibited by the law is allowed. Freedom, for the ancients, meant the ability to act in the way in which you should; freedom for the moderns means that we can, if we wish - or even if we do not wish, because wishing implies a conscious decision - live our lives as slaves. And this gets us to the real significance of what Mr. Antonelli was able to achieve in those two remarkable trials in which he, quite successfully, made the case for the defense."

Had Redfield been speaking in plain view, had everyone been able to see him, had he been able to see us, he would at this point undoubtedly have made some gesture toward me, pointed out to his audience the person, the lawyer, he was talking about. In the dark, he did not need to; in the dark, the absence of that normal, polite and expected gesture had no need, no possibility, of interpretation. The words, and the words alone, carried all the meaning.

"The first trial, the trial of Justin Friedrich for the murder of his wife, Allison, put on public display the empty lives of the useless rich. It proved, for those with a mind to listen, that wealth without liberality destroys the soul. Remember what you have

235

heard discussed here before, what was once the working assumption of every well-educated man or woman, what used to be taught to children, what used to be part of a classical, that is to say a liberal, education: living well requires having what you need to live and having time for important things like study and contemplation. Wealth has a limit: the end or purpose it serves. Everything has that as its limit. The question, the only important question, is what is the reason, what is the purpose, what is the end for which we engage in the activity, whatever that activity may happen to be.

"Consider again, and never stop considering, the work we do here. What is the reason, what the purpose, what the end, we hope to achieve with artificial intelligence? Is it to make money, to meet a demand, to be so far ahead of the competition that everyone looks to use to try to force the future? Yes, in a way. The money is a means, a necessary means, to enable us to continue to stay in front of everyone else; it is also, more importantly, the means by which when you leave here at the end to this year you will have the financial independence to do serious work: start your own companies or become involved in public things - politics, government, diplomacy - or spend your lives in study, learning everything the modern world to its great misfortune has forgotten: that it isn't what you have, but what you are, that is important. If the Friedrich trial taught us nothing else, it surely taught us that.

"What it did not teach us is why they lived the way they did. These were two intelligent people. They had all the money - more than all the money - they could ever need. Why did they do what they did; why did they marry each other? It was quite apparent - you remember what we talked about during the trial - how everyone who knew them seem to consider it more a merger than a marriage. How many witnesses took the stand and told the same story: that instead of being among the wealthiest individuals in the city, they wanted to be the wealthiest young couple in town. This is how we are supposed to measure ourselves: by our combined net worth! Justin Friedrich was a drunk who chased other women; Allison Friedrich slept with other men. But they had money and that made them the honored guests anywhere they chose to go. So the question becomes not just why these two people lived the way they did, but why everyone else seemed to think there was nothing wrong with it. Nothing wrong with it! What am I saying? Everyone thought those two benighted souls were to be envied! - an example that, given half a chance, everyone would have liked to follow! When did vice become a virtue? When did this become the lesson we were all supposed to learn? That was what the second trial should have taught us, what Joseph Antonelli, more than anyone else, helped show us.

"The university is supposed to teach the most important things we can learn. The question no one seems to ask anymore is who teaches the university. That question was asked, as we have talked about before, in the 17th century by Thomas Hobbes who answered without false modesty that he would teach the universities what to teach. Who had taught the universities before, who was teaching the universities what to teach when Hobbes proposed to do it instead? - Aristotle, as understood by Thomas Acquinas. Greek philosophy made to conform to the requirements of Christianity. Hobbes, along with Francis Bacon and John Locke, to say nothing of Descartes and Machiavelli, produced a radical change, a movement away from the belief in contemplation of what might be most perfect on earth or in heaven, toward a method by which to improve the condition of actual living human beings. Science, modern science, took the place of both revealed religion and Greek philosophy.

"Philosophy and religion had spoken about the ends, or purpose, of human existence; the new science was concerned only with the means by which men could acquire more power over the world in which they lived. Science, in that once famous phrase of Francis Bacon, would 'alleviate man's estate.' Philosophy had taught what it meant to be a human being, what human excellence really was; science promised to end human suffering. Religion had promised eternal life; science raised the question how far the average life span could be extended. The university which had always been dedicated to the life of the mind, began, by the middle years of the twentieth century, to be more and more committed to the needs of the body, the way science could help in the production of new and better labor saving schemes and devices, how science could improve medicine, how technology could be used to help find new cures for disease, how death itself could be delayed, and even, perhaps, defeated.

"The university, still insisting that it was guided only by the search for the truth, had become prisoner to the modern illusion that science was the only way to discover it. Science, which by its own definition can deal only with facts and never with values, could not say, much less prove, that one way of life was better than any other. The university could not teach anyone anything about how they should live. The most important question anyone could ask, and everyone was left to decide it as best they could for themselves. The university taught nothing about what it means to be a human being. This bankruptcy of the American university was the real issue in the trial of Alan Boe, the trial that Joseph Antonelli conducted with such admirable skill.

"Alan Boe was not on trial; the university, what the university had become under someone like Lucas Fairweather, was on trial. Alan Boe was not just innocent of the murder of Lucas Fairweather; he was the only one who still understood what a university is supposed to be. What was the result of that trial? What did Joseph Antonelli achieve? He saved an innocent man, and that is important, but there was something perhaps even more important than that. The Friedrich trial had exposed the corruption of people who measure themselves, and others, by how much they can acquire. The Boe trial proved the corruption of those who think the main function of a university is to teach what is essentially the same thing: that there is nothing more important than learning how to make money. The two trials differ in this: Friedrich, the defendant in the first trial, was as much a slave to his own desires as his wife, the victim, had been to hers. Alan Boe, on the other hand, proved that there is still someone who knows how to think, who understands what it means to be free and independent, who is not afraid that no one else will agree with him, who would rather die than turn his back on the truth. The only person who did not feel sorry for Alan Boe after the jury found him not guilty, after no one could any longer doubt his innocence, was Alan Boe himself. Why would he feel sorry for himself? He had done nothing wrong. But the real difference is this: Alan Boe would not have felt sorry for himself had he been convicted, had there been no one at all who thought him innocent. Why would he? Whatever the verdict, whatever public opinion might be, the fact would have been the same as it had always been: he had not done anything of which he should be ashamed. That was the great advantage he has always had: he knows that he had never done anything he should not have done. That is the advantage that all of you will have. It is the reason you are here.

"One of the reasons. Remember what we do here, remember what AIE is all about. It is not to lead the world in artificial intelligence. We do that, it isn't very difficult, but we do it so that there will be a few people left - the hundred of you - who will have the position, and the means - to lead independent lives, who will understand that artificial intelligence is no intelligence at all. Who will understand that like nearly everything modern science has made possible, it is just the latest, though perhaps the most insidious, method by which to impose slavery on ourselves. Think this through, never stop thinking this through. Slavery is bad enough when we enslave someone's body and make them prisoner to our own will and domination. How much worse when we enslave their minds, and how much worse even than that when we arrange things so that they do it to themselves, give up their real freedom so they can have the choice what kind of addiction they want at any given moment to enjoy?

"What we are about, the reason we exist, the end we mean to achieve, is to preserve the conditions - and create them where they do not exist, if we can - for the kind of freedom that is possible only for those who have the ability and the desire to understand the world in which they live. That is, and will remain, our challenge. It is not enough to talk about being free from limitations, free from all restraint, free to do whatever we happen at any moment to like; the freedom that matters, the freedom that can change everything, is the freedom to pursue human excellence.

"There is one last thing that I want to leave you with this evening, a thought that some of you may wish to discuss with our distinguished guest. Let us suppose for a moment that in both the Friedrich trial and the Boe trial, the real killer, or killers, had been caught and that Mr. Antonelli found himself again the attorney for the defense. How would he have done it, what defense could he have used? I have a suggestion: tyrannicide. This will sound at first strange and perhaps absurd. But I wonder. Someone who commits tyrannicide, someone who kills a tyrant, was always honored as the greatest benefactor of the city over which the tyrant ruled. Neither Allison Friedrich nor Lucas Fairweather were tyrants; they did not rule anywhere. Perhaps our definition of the tyrant and tyranny are too narrow, or too limited. The tyrant who rules a city rules every individual in it; whoever tyrannizes one individual is as much a tyrant as one who tyrannizes a thousand, or tens of thousands. What is the reason someone who kills a tyrant goes free? Why is it not murder under the law? Because the tyrant is lawless, because he dominates improperly. Is that in any way fundamentally different than someone dominated by a lawless passion of greed or lust, who acting on those tyrannical drives tyrannizes over others? Perhaps

Mr. Antonelli has the answer. Or perhaps, if something like this - the trials of Justin Friedrich and Alan Boe - happen again, he might on that occasion gain some greater insight into the question."

That was the last thing he said, literally the last thing. There was nothing in the way of a summary, nothing in the way of closing remarks; not a word about when he would be there to lecture again; nothing, just a complete, inexplicable silence. He simply stopped talking. That did not mean that anyone knew it. In the darkness it was impossible to know if he was still there, thinking about what he wanted to say next. Everyone sat where they were; no one moved, no one thought about moving. A minute went by, then another, and then, finally, the lights came on, not all at once, but gradually, and only gradually growing brighter. The stage was vacant, the only thing on it an empty chair. I turned to Carruthers and realized immediately that, far from unusual, this was completely normal, this was how Redfield's lectures always ended.

"He always speaks to you in the dark?"

The question seemed both to surprise and amuse her.

"No one has ever seen Redfield. You wouldn't expect him to lecture any other way, would you?"

"No one has ever...."

I remembered what Albert Craven had told me, that first time Redfield had come to the office, that no one had seen the enigmatic genius behind the world's most advanced technology company, but I had assumed that he meant no one outside the company, no one outside the circle of employees and whatever close friends and colleagues Redfield might have

"You're telling me you wouldn't recognize him if you passed him on the street?" I inquired, just to be sure. "How does he run the company, how does he communicate with you and the others?"

"Mainly in writing, of course; sometimes by phone."

She said this in the way of someone describing a routine,

a habit by now so ingrained that the novelty, the strangeness, of it had long since been forgotten. It was Redfield's way, and like everything else Redfield did, there was a reason.

"He wants us - he wanted us - to learn independence, to become used to make decisions ourselves. He did not want us to worry what he might think when we saw him coming. He is not our employer, not in the usual sense; he is our teacher, someone who helps us see more clearly, and more quickly, what we might have missed on our own. You heard what he said tonight. That is our mission, the only one, really, that we have: to learn how to keep ourselves from becoming slaves to the technology taking over the world. He keeps emphasizing that; it is what he talked about the first night I was here, what he never stops talking about: the only people who understand anything that is made are the ones who make it." She gave me a long, meaningful look, before she added, "And, what is of great importance when you are talking about artificial intelligence, only those who make the thing will never forget that the thing is made. Because if you don't understand that, you begin to forget what has been created and who has created it. Which, in turn, as Redfield explains it, is the difference between the end and the means by which to accomplish it. Who, or what, decides the purpose for which you create whatever it is you invent. That is the question."

Carruthers had been entirely serious, and her explanations, at least in that moment, rigorously clear, but now, when she paused and noted the puzzled astonishment on my face, she laughed self-consciously.

"I'm sorry! When Redfield talks about this it all makes perfect sense. I'm afraid when I try to explain it, I get things all jumbled up."

"No, not at all," I replied, giving her all the assurances of my own limited capacity. "I think I followed what you were trying to say."

"Well, Redfield can tell you, when you see him, later this evening."

I did not have the chance to ask her what she meant. With a quick, polite smile, she shook my hand and then, reaching inside her pocket, pulled out a small envelop and handed it to me.

"Redfield left this for you. It will tell you where you are to go next. Goodbye, Mr. Antonelli. I'm glad you were Professor Boe's attorney," she remarked, as she reached up to unfasten the ribbon on her head and then shook loose her long blonde hair. "I knew you would be able to convince a jury that he was a completely innocent man. He has such a remarkable face, don't you think?" she remarked with a grave, wistful and strangely determined look in her large blue eyes.

"It was you!" I exclaimed with a sudden sense of recognition. "That night...you!"

But she was gone, banished with the others somewhere into the night. I stared all around, wondering if it had just been my imagination. A chance remark about the look of Alan Boe, the knowledge that she was one of Redfield's employees, one of his students which meant, or might mean, willing to subjugate her own will to his, a slave, to use the word I had heard so often that evening, to Redfield's strange, and uncommon, definition of freedom, and I was ready to accuse her of murder!

Chapter Seventeen

Redfield left directions to where we were finally to meet. It was not very far, two miles, more or less, father up the hills, at the very top of the ridge line. The directions had the aspect of a child's treasure map, long winding lines and then a sharp right turn onto an unmarked, and unpaved, road, even more narrow than the one I had followed to the headquarters of AIE, but not nearly as long, a hundred yards at most before I reached the clearing and Redfield's contemporary mid-century home that could have been designed by Frank Lloyd Wright.

Clusters of bamboo stood on both sides of the double front doors the other side of a twelve foot long wooden bridge that straddled a shallow pond lit from below. Large coy moved slowly and methodically back and forth, glistening like golden baubles in a rich man's shaded palace. One of the doors was open part way and I stepped inside onto gleaming hardwood floors and tan matted carpets. Sliding parchment thick walls, almost Japanese in style, divided place from place and everywhere the glow of indirect lighting banished brightness and shadow both. Bookcases, ebony black, lined the walls of the living room. A flagstone fireplace, opening on one side into the living and on the other into the dining room, stood at the corner between the two rooms. The shelves, instead of filled with books held only a few dozen; formal photographs of famous men and famous places took up all the remaining space. There was, so far as I noticed on that first, cursory glance, no picture of Redfield, no sign of anything by which he could be identified. The house might have belonged to anyone, at least anyone who lived a fairly anonymous life.

Outside, through a double set of double sliding doors, at the edge of a lap pool forty, fifty feet in length and eight or ten feet wide, Redfield was standing, his back to me, gazing out into the cloudless star-filled night. He had not heard me come in, and, forced this long to wait to see him, I looked around, taking another, slower view of the house, the place Redfield called home. It seemed, as I glanced across the living room, a perfect place for a single, private life. I could imagine living there myself, if I had been more a recluse and less interested in my own form of anonymity, the kind I had lived in the middle of the city. Redfield had every convenience necessary, and none of those that are not. There was no large television set fastened to the wall; there was no television set at all. There was no sound system, at least none that I noticed; no electronic devices of any kind, nothing of the 'smart' house technology, nothing that could by even the loosest definition be called artificial intelligence. The light switches were the kind you see every day, in place right on the wall. It was exactly what it must have been like when it was first built, fifty or sixty years ago. That is what really caught my eye. After all this time, it still looked new, a house that had been lived in, but only for a year or so. It must have cost a fortune to make it look like that.

Wearing a light brown sports jacket, pale gray shirt, tan slacks and loafers, Redfield shoved his hands deep into his pants pockets and stared down at the ground. A moment later, he looked back at the house and, when he saw me standing at the sliding glass door, started to smile, and then gestured for me to come outside. You would have thought we were old friends from the way he greeted me. He seemed genuinely glad I was there. We sat at a round glass topped table, and without asking if I wanted something to drink, he poured us each a glass from a bottle of French wine.

"Did you think my performance this evening a little too dramatic?" he asked, as his eyes flickered with acknowledgement at what he seemed certain must have been my impression. "You probably - no, you have to think that I am some sort of mad man, some demented egomaniac, trying to get even with the world." He seemed almost to take this under advisement, to wonder whether it might really be true. "Or perhaps I have not given you enough credit; perhaps you have now begun to realize what it is I'm trying to do."

"Why don't you tell me - what you're trying to do. I think I understand why you speak only in the dark, and even why no one who works for you has ever seen you. It forces you to listen more carefully when you sit there in the dark like that. And as to why you don't let anyone see you, I imagine that is for something like the same reason: it makes them take more seriously what you do communicate to them in writing or, I'm told, sometimes on the telephone. It's a little like being God - no one ever gets to see you, which is part of the reason everyone believes you capable of any-thing."

Redfield slid down in the chair, stretched out his legs and crossed his ankles. A brief, candid smile darted across his lips as he seemed to remember something.

"Years ago when I was still a student - it was in one of Alan Boe's advanced seminars - there was a young woman, a black woman, who was completely blind. That is when I learned it, what I saw watching her. We were all sitting around a long, oblong table. She - I'm afraid I've forgotten her name; forgotten her name but have never forgotten her - would speak and of course never look around, never look - and this is really the point - to see how others were reacting to what she was saying. She had this wonderful face, eager, alert, and as kind as any you have ever seen. Everyone was looking at her; you could not look away, she held you that close, but she of course did not notice. That was when I started to realize how much we are all confined by the looks we see, the way others look at us when we talk to them, and how, quite without our knowing it, we make adjustments in our own look, adjustments in the way we phrase things, in the way we try to change what we are saying or at least how we are saying it, to the response we see that we are getting. It works the other way as well. We sit there, in a seminar, in a gathering of any size, and our own expression, our own thoughts, change with the change we see in the expression of whoever is speaking to us. But not when a blind woman is speaking, not when the speaker speaks in darkness. Then the speaker is in a way speaking to no one, he speaks all alone, he speaks his silent thoughts out loud. He becomes like one of Shakespeare's characters speaking to himself, knowing all the time that he has an audience for the private musings of his mind."

Redfield laughed quietly into the night, and then took a long, slow drink from his glass. When he put down the glass, he looked at me with a different expression. He was deeply serious.

"It isn't a bad analogy for the way most people think - the constant changing of disordered minds almost blinded by the millions of discordant voices coming at them now from every side, all those shifting images that they keep watching on their computer and television screens. It is complete and total madness, and it has become the only permissible definition of not just progress but civilization That is why I did this: went into business, started AIE - to save, to try to save, something of what is important for the world to remember. Let me tell you a story," he said, leaning closer. "The first day I sat in on one of Alan Boe's classes, an undergraduate course in the second semester of his year long course in the history of political philosophy - imagine fifty or sixty students, all of them far above average in intelligence, all of them the highest, or near the highest, in their graduating class in high school; all of them, in other words, worse than ignorant, wrongly educated! The first thing Boe did was take a piece of chalk, stand at the blackboard and start a line at the top left corner. 'Ancient Greece,' he explained. And from that high point on the board he drew the line downward at a forty five degree angle. 'The Dark Ages' he announced. Then he drew the line back up, not as high as the Greeks, but close. 'The Renaissance.' Then, and he did this with a flourish, he drew the line almost to the bottom of the board, lower than the Dark Ages. 'The Present Day.'

"I became obsessed with what that meant, this strange new notion that instead of progress we had somehow gone backward, that instead of making things better science, which is really how the modern world became what it is, had made it worse. I did nothing but study, trying to learn, to understand, everything I could about the difference between the ancient and the modern world. What did Alan Boe mean? What did the Greeks know, what had we forgotten? That is what I thought about, that is what I studied, that is what...."

Refield stopped suddenly, and looked at me as if he thought he should apologize for getting carried away, for going farther than he had meant to go. I started to tell him that I wanted to hear the rest of what he had to say, but he had already changed his mind.

"I speak for an hour, five, sometimes six, nights a week. I am now always too full of lectures. Let me get to my point another way. You heard most of it this evening, the reason for our existence, why it is important that we have some people who understand that what everyone else thinks the greatest achievement of our time, is as perfectly useless as the rest of this technology we invent. We have to make sure that at least a few people stay free."

"And so you arrange to have a few people killed so you can use the trials of innocent people to illustrate the evil, the corruption, that you want this privileged group of a hundred to protect itself against?"

I asked this as if it were nothing more than the logical next question; as if, far from angry about what he had done, I was only trying to understand why he had done it. It was, however intended, a serious question, but when he replied he began by appearing to dismiss its importance.

"One of the things I learned in those long forgotten books I studied is that the acknowledgement of others is nothing more than vanity. What use, what value, the approval of the crowd, of people who haven't studied, who know nothing and for that reason think they know everything? There are three kinds of people, Mr. Antonelli, and only three. There are those - a few, perhaps one every century or so, though sometimes more; they sometimes come close together: the end of the 4th and the beginning of the 3rd century B.C. when suddenly, in quick succession, Socrates, Plato and Aristotle came into their all too brief existence. And then, nearly two thousand years later, the 16th and 17th centuries, Machiavelli, Bacon, Hobbes and Locke. I said there were three kinds of people. These are all part of the first group, those few privileged minds who are able to learn and understand things on their own. They do not need teachers; everyone else learns from them.

There is a second kind, and there are not many of these either, at it turns out, and fewer and fewer all the time, perhaps a few dozen, perhaps a few hundred, in any generation: those who can understand things when they are explained to them. Then there is the third, and last, kind," he went on, with a strange gleam in his relentless eyes, "those who cannot understand no matter who explains, the great, the overwhelming, majority of people in all times and places. All of us, Mr. Antonelli; nearly all of us. The great democratic majority who insist they know everything, that their judgment can never be questioned that everyone is equal in everything, that there is no better and worse. They can't understand, which means they don't understand that they don't. Unaware of their ignorance, everyone lives in a fantastic swirl of strange delusions. Everyone believes - in something, and whether it is religion or politics they know, they always know, they are right. Everyone, or rather almost everyone, because there are still some of us who have, sometimes quite by accident, been drawn to what those few great minds, the ones who were born with the gift of seeing things as they really are, born with the ability to see that what everyone else claimed to see was someone's made up fiction, have left behind. And if you are lucky enough to be drawn to the study, the serious study, of that small number, a dozen or so, of true philosophers, then you have only one obligation: to do whatever is in your power to make sure that there are others who will keep those thoughts alive, help others learn to understand what it is important to know."

Redfield looked past me, nodding slowly as if in agreement with what he had just said. He had made it seem almost commonplace, obvious, a description of the human capacity with which no intelligent observer could disagree, and yet, as I realized, it violated the cardinal principle of democracy, the belief that everyone had an ability to learn, the belief in the truth of the Enlightenment.

"Let's go inside," suggested Redfield, as he gathered up his glass and the half finished bottle.

I followed him across the brief patch of lawn to the sliding glass door. In the living room he bent his head toward the sparsely filled bookshelves.

"A hundred books. Too many. You could spend your life, and spend it well, with less than half that number, especially if you read them the way they were meant to be read - slowly, word by word, and then read over, and over again. There is a story - Alan Boe must have told it - about Averroes or Alfarabi or someone else among that handful of marvelous Arab philosophers from the early Middle Ages. Whoever it was one day ran excited through the town square exclaiming with perfect joy that after reading it for the tenth, or the twelfth, time - I don't remember the exact number - he had finally understood what Plato meant in one of his dialogues."

Redfield shook his head and laughed. "I was wrong. Half

the number of books is much too large; half of the half would be more than enough. Here, sit down. Let me fill your glass."

While he poured the wine first into my glass, and then into his, I gazed around the living room, struck again by the feeling of quiet contemplation, like a vast, private library in which anything more than a whisper would be an intrusion. The shuffling sound of Redfield's loafers on the hardwood floor, the sound of wine pouring into a glass, were separate noises, distinctive and almost too easily heard.

"You live here - alone?" I asked, when he took a seat on the sofa facing the one on which I sat. The fireplace was just off to the side.

"You're the only other person who has ever been here. As a guest, I mean. There is a woman who comes to clean, and on occasion to cook dinner. And someone comes to take care of the pool and the yard. I never see them."

"You never see anyone."

"I see a lot of people," he corrected. "I go all sorts of places; I talk to all kinds of people. I live a little like you do yourself, at least how I believe you lived, before you started living with Tangerine Winslow. She is really quite remarkable, as beautiful a woman as I have ever seen. But, before that, when you lived alone, you did not feel alone, did you?"

I was not much interested in talking about how I had lived; I certainly was not interested in telling him how I had felt about it.

"It was one of the reasons why I was so glad you decided to handle the Friedrich case."

"It was…?"

"You had no obligations, no responsibilities, no family to worry about. You spent all your time doing the one thing you like doing. You didn't have any other interests. You don't sit at home watching sports; you don't watch anything. You don't play games, you don't play golf; you have no hobbies," he said, emitting a short, mocking laugh at the habits of others. "You don't entertain; other than Albert Craven, with whom you work, you have no friends. You are, every minute of every day, a lawyer, a courtroom lawyer. If you didn't try cases you would have to shoot yourself. But you do try cases, and the only people who think about suicide are the poor bastards who try to prosecute the people you defend. You were - you are - perfect for what I wanted."

"What you wanted?" I asked, searching those impenetrable eyes of his for the key to the secret of what he was trying to do. "Whatever it is, it is going to stop. I'm not going to be used anymore."

He only smiled.

"I'm sorry you think you've been used. You really shouldn't feel that way. What you did in those two trials was something no one who had the privilege of watching them will ever forget. What you did for Alan Boe -"

"Alan Boe -! I did nothing in that trial. Boe was his own defense. I just sat there and watched."

"And marveled, too, I'll bet! Isn't he something? Do you know how much good that did, having him on trial? What better way to show everyone what an intelligent human being is really like? What better way to show how mindless the American university has become? Those hundred people tonight, the ones who work for me - Do you know why they came, why they decided to start their careers with AIE? Two reasons, two reasons only: the reputation of what we do, the most advanced technology company on the planet, and the money. They don't get paid a decent salary, they don't get paid at the highest level of salaries paid in Silicon Valley. No, they become independently wealthy the day they walk in the door. Think about it! How easy it really is," he said, as he rose from the sofa and with his glass in hand began to move about the room. "Artificial intelligence. Everyone likes to talk about the future, what artificial intelligence is going to mean. That future they're always talking about? - That future is our past. Did you notice, on that tour you were given, how few people there seemed to be, and how many cubicles, how much space there was? We are already using so-called artificial intelligence, that is what does nearly all the work. Have you ever - perhaps when you were a college student in biology class - watched through a high-powered microscope at a microbe as it begins to multiply, how it starts to grow faster and faster, how it increases exponentially? It is what we are doing now with programmed computer systems. We have learned how to start them off in a certain direction and then, from that point forward, let them design their own expansion. Carruthers showed you what we are doing with medical technology. She did not tell you how it will make all of us together far less healthy."

Redfield was talking in a slow, quiet, measured voice. There was a rhythm to his speech usually heard only from a stage actor delivering a soliloquy. I do not mean to say that it sounded practiced or rehearsed; it was simply, I thought, the reflection of his balanced, well-organized mind, everything carefully considered, not on the surface where it would take time, but somewhere deep inside that remarkable intelligence where it came far quicker than it took to speak the words.

"We all live now like the outpatients of a hospital, everyone sick or on their way to getting ill. Turn on a television set, what do you see? - Endless advertisements about the drugs you should take, drugs that may not cure you, may not make you healthy, but will keep you alive, even if for just a little while longer. What is the point of it? There is nothing any more that anyone thinks more important than mere existence, staying alive. What has medicine become? Not what it used to be, what it was supposed to be - a way to restore health, always with the understanding that when it could not be done, it was better if the patient died than live out a long, lingering death. Now medicine - modern science altogether - has two related objectives: eliminate as much suffering as possible and lengthen life by whatever means or methods can be invented. What for? What virtue in a long life free of any forms of not just suffering, but discomfort? Mozart died at thirty-six. Would you - would anyone in their right mind - trade the life he had, what he was able to achieve, for a so-called normal life lived for twice that many years? But that is what we are doing, with our emphasis on the length of time we live, instead of the kind of life we live. What happens when everyone thinks of themselves as patients, when we worry all the time about how we feel, instead of what we should be doing? And if that is how thing are now, imagine what is going to happen when from the very moment we are born, we are implanted with microscopic devices that monitor, and eventually treat, our condition; when we are all connected to a machine, a vast computer network in which we are under the constant scrutiny of a computer program - or, rather, a whole series of them, always communicating with each other, every little thing that happens, even the slightest change, given instant treatment. It would be better if we abolished machines and were left to live without any outside help. Science, technology, machines, medicine - the daydream of painless longevity, the dream of cowards."

Standing next to the still open sliding glass doors, Redfield crossed his arms and began to laugh.

"Everyone else's future, it's already part of my past. It isn't difficult to see where this is going - if you're not caught up in it, if you get far enough ahead of it, if you have gone far enough back into the past to see how it all started. If you read, if you study, what someone like Descartes was really trying to do - devise a method that would make it possible to use each problem that his new science solved as a way to solve the next problem after that: science an artificial construct of the human mind, imposing an order of its own on all the material that nature supplied; the workings of human intelligence codified, made, if you will, machine-like. That is what Descartes called human beings - machines that could be made to work. We talk about artificial intelligence; Descartes thought human intelligence artificial, something that could be made, or made over, by the invention of a method of doing things, his method, what we in our ignorance call the scientific method."

I listened, listened carefully, listened to every word. I was fascinated, more perhaps by the fact, the great overwhelming fact, that Redfield had mastered things I could not possibly understand, than by that knowledge itself. If I had had any doubts about what Alan Boe had told me about him, I did not doubt now that Redfield was different from anyone I had ever met. It was impossible not to be drawn to him, not to want to hear more about anything he wanted to say. I had to remind myself what he had done and why I had agreed to come.

"We have a hundred people, that is all; a hundred young men and women who now have more money than they will ever need. The company can afford it; we make billions every year. Those hundred men and women were among the most highly recruited college students in the country. I say among, because there were others we did not choose. It is only a seeming paradox that we turned down anyone who said they wanted to make a lot of money. We also turned down anyone who was not single. If they were married, they could not live the way they live here, everything in common, no real privacy. They have to live like that if they are going to learn that money is nothing more than a means, that the reason they will be made wealthy is so they can live free and independent lives, studying serious things and doing good things, helping the poor, helping raise the level of public life. But the main reason, the most important reason, is to make sure there will be at least a few people to continue the tradition, the belief that there is more to human existence than simply staying alive, that there is a reason why the human being was endowed with reason."

Redfield stared down at the floor. He closed his mouth, clenching his jaw so tight that for a moment his head trembled with the tension. He lifted his eyes just far enough to give me a search-ing glance.

"Your question - why those two trials ? The power of ex-ample, the clarity that comes when you can see - when a hundred of the most intelligent young men and women in the country can see - what happens when the requirements of the law and the re-quirements of justice are completely different; when they can see, not in the abstract, not in some history book, but here and now, what happens when a man and wife live like the Friedrichs did, and when someone as brain dead as Lucas Fairweather is put in charge of a university. It was never true that a picture is worth a thousand words; it was only when the words were written by someone who did not know how to write that people thought it was. What is true, is that an example is the best, because the most convincing, way to explain to those capable of understanding what something means.

"What you did in those two trials was far more valuable than anything you can imagine. I had to show them, teach them, the limits of the law. The law says not to kill, but there are some things worse than murder. The law says not to steal, but there are times when, to save someone from starvation, it is the only decent thing to do. We are taught from childhood that lying is always wrong, but lying about the deficiencies of others, lying to make them feel better about themselves is something Aristotle, among others, insisted was the only honorable practice. But these only point to the most important lesson that the law's limitations teach, what the Friedrich and the Boe trials in their different ways taught: what the law requires is not sufficient, what the hundred need to follow is a law of their own, a law more stringent, most demanding, than what the law requires of normal people."

Some things worse than murder? Was that going to be his defense? It was a phrase I had heard often enough, the justification used when someone killed someone and thought that, far from evil they had actually done something, if not good, at least explainable, and if explainable at least in some sense forgivable.

"Worse than murder? Are you trying to tell me that Friedrich and Fairweather both deserved to die? Is that your excuse, because if it is…."

"I could make the case, though I admit it would not likely have much influence with a jury in a court today. But there was a time, and there are still places, where adultery alone was punished with death, and whatever else you want to say about her, Allison Friedrich was certainly guilty of that, and a good many more times than once." With a sudden, sharp, cynical glance that vanished as quickly as it appeared, he added, "And given that Justin Friedrich had lived his life pretty much the same way, it might have been better if you had not managed to win him an acquittal. As for Lucas Fairweather, who knows all the things he may have done: his flagrant abuse of power, the women he mistreated, all the allegations of sexual abuse that caused him to lose his job in Washington. Although, as far as that goes, if I were called upon to give a justification, if I had to say what he had done that was worse than murder, it would be what he tried to do, what he would have done, to Alan Boe. Isn't the defense of others a justification for a homicide?"

"Defense of another's life, when someone tries to stop someone from murdering someone else."

"Which brings us full circle, doesn't it? We think life, mere existence, the only important, or at least the most important, thing. But there might still be an argument that murdering the mind, taking away the best mind from the very place where the best minds are supposed to be left free to function, is something infinitely worse, because when you do that, when you do what Fairweather was about to do, you take not just one life, you tear the heart out of a whole generation and maybe more than just one."

I had heard enough. I got up to go. Redfield got up with me and together we walked toward the door.

"I'm glad you came. I wanted you to see what we do, and I wanted to have the chance to tell you how much I admire what you have done. There is not anyone else I could have trusted to make sure Alan Boe was not convicted."

"He would not have needed my help if Lucas Fairweather had not been murdered," I reminded him, wondering as I did so why instead of anger I felt a strange, inexplicable sympathy for someone I knew was responsible for two murders. Redfield had that effect. It was uncanny, the way he could make you think that despite everything you knew, or thought you knew, there was in a way you did not yet understand, and probably never would, something just below the surface that would put a different, and a better, face on things. Perhaps it was nothing more than the sheer power of that remarkable intelligence. He seemed too much the solitary, a man who lived entirely inside himself, to have done what there was no question that he had.

"I'm not your lawyer, Mr. Redfield. You need to be very clear about that. There is no lawyer-client privilege anymore. If you do what you did again, I'll tell everyone. There is not going to be a third trial."

He held the door open, waiting until I passed through, waiting until I had stepped onto the wooden bridge over the softly lit pond.

"It doesn't matter about the privilege, Mr. Antonelli. There is going to be at third trial, and no one will have to do anything to convince you to represent the defendant. I doubt very much there is anything anyone could say that could stop you. Good-night, Mr. Antonelli. It is unlikely we will ever meet again, but I hope you believe me when I tell you that it has been both a privilege and an honor. I know I can always count on you to do the right thing. I hope one day you will have reason to think the same thing of me."

Chapter Eighteen

Tangerine, waiting at the door with a worried look, cheated her feelings with bright eyes filled with mischief. She taunted me with how inexcusably late I was.

"Three hours, Antonelli! Three hours! I could have run off with another man, changed my mind and come back, and you would never have known how close I had been to betrayal!"

I was mesmerized. The past, the future, time disappeared. I barely remembered how to talk, and the words, when I spoke them, were as new to me as they were to her.

"Sure I would," I heard myself reply, as I set my briefcase down on the floor and took off my coat. "You would have told me. Told me! - You would have bragged about your astonishing self-restraint."

She studied me with amused indifference.

"I can imagine what Sophia would say if Giuseppe ever said something like that to her - 'Brag about something that commonplace? I am every day tempted to run off with someone else!'"

"'Then why don't you?' - Isn't that what Giuseppe would tell her with one of those indulgent smiles of his, letting her know that he doesn't believe for a minute that she would ever even think once about leaving him."

With an almost perfect imitation of an Italian woman's sultry glance, Tangerine tossed her head and laughed.

"Why go to all the trouble, running off somewhere? Infidelity is so much easier right here, at home."

"In that case," I remarked with some laughing indifference of my own, "I'll leave you here to rest while I go somewhere for dinner."

She grabbed my arm as I walked past, tugging on it as if to stop me leaving.

"It's almost ten. You haven't eaten?"

"Not exactly. I was there, at dinner, in the dining hall at Redfield's company, but I barely touched anything. I was too busy listening to what I was being told." I pulled off my tie and picked up my coat, ready to put it on again. "Really, let's go somewhere. I know I'm late. I know I should have called. I don't know why I didn't, except I could not stop thinking about what happened, what I saw, what I heard. We'll go into the village; we'll find something. All I want to do now is sit in some quiet restaurant, look across the table at you, have a glass of wine and get drunk as hell."

"On one glass of wine?"

"I don't need to drink anything to get drunk with you."

She rose up on her tip toes and kissed me on the side of my face.

"That's the nicest thing you've ever said. I'll run off with you, anywhere you want to go, anytime you want - Tonight, if you like."

It made me remember the first night we met, at a dinner at Albert Craven's house, when she waited outside for me in her car.

"Like the night I said I might drive out to the airport and fly off to London or New York, and asked if you thought you might like to go?"

"And I might have gone, if I had thought you serious."

"You didn't think I was serious when I told you that I might not come back?"

A shy, teasing smile slipped cautiously over her mouth.

"I wasn't sure you were serious when you asked me to marry you."

"When I suggested you divorce your husband and marry me instead? I had not been that serious about anything in my whole life."

"Is that why you looked so surprised?" she asked, with a shrewd, knowing glance. "The first you thought about it was when you heard yourself saying it. It's true, isn't it?"

"Which proves just how serious I was. I didn't need to think about it; there was nothing to consider. Those words, that night, when I said them, came as naturally as breathing."

We walked down the narrow, twisting road to the main street of town. The towers on the Golden Gate were barely visible in the fog; the houses we passed were hidden behind a heavy gray swirling mist. Tangerine held my arm with both hands and every so often, for no reason at all, with a quick, easy step got in front of me and smiled with her eyes as she walked backward like a happy child.

"Look over there!" she cried suddenly. "What do you see?"

We were just the other side of the street from the marina, filled with power boats, and sailboats, motor boats and yachts, boats of every size and description .

"I have been on a lot of sailboats, other people's boats, never one of my own. Why don't we get one?" Grabbing my hand, she pulled me along behind her as she dashed across the street. "Get one ourselves and sail off somewhere, just the two of us, go wherever we want, stay as long as we like any place we feel like staying?"

I could think of nothing better. I was tired of spending my time worrying about what would happen if I lost a trial; tired of the endless back and forth: the questions I might have to ask, the answers that might, or might not, be given, the days of mind-numbing preparation for every hour I might have to be in court. I was a fool and I knew it; a fool to spend any time at all away from her.

"We might not be able to go too far," I replied, with a helpless grin. "I've never sailed in my life."

"We'll learn," she insisted, quite in earnest. "It can't be that difficult. I've seen enough of those who can to know."

It was late, but the Spinnaker was open and we found a small table next to the window in the bar. I was almost used to it, the first looks when we entered a room, then the second, more intense and longer stare, when they tried to remember who she was. Anyone that looked like her had to be someone they had seen before, in the movies, or on television, somewhere in that world of shining screen images that nearly everyone thought more real than what they saw in a restaurant or out in the street.

"It's what Redfield does," I said to her confusion. "His company, where I was today - artificial intelligence. The new way of teaching: every child with an electronic tutor, a face, a body, on a screen, everything generated by a computer program. That face - that artificial person - will become everyone's best friend, their most trusted advisor. And everyone will live abstracted from what is real."

The waiter took our order - a sandwich for me, a salad for her - and, as starstruck as everyone else, tried not to look, afraid that he might stare. I watched him make his way across to the kitchen and, just before he went through the door, glance back across his shoulder. He was lucky not to stumble.

"I think it's a very good idea," I said, suddenly.

"What is a very good idea?"

"Get a sailboat and just go."

"When?"

"We'll start looking tomorrow. Albert keeps that boat of his in the Marina. He'll know someone who can start to teach me how to do it. He might even know someone with a sailboat to sell."

"We don't have to go anywhere," she said, taking hold of my hand. "We can keep it here, in Sausalito; take it out whenever

262

we feel like it, sail out on the bay all day long and then come home and sleep in the comfort of our own bed, and wake up in the morning and decide if we want to go out again."

Never have San Francisco out of view, whether out on the bay or up on the hill. It was sounding better all the time.

The waiter brought our food and wine and Tangerine thanked him in such a friendly voice he almost blushed.

"You made one man happy tonight," I remarked, as I sipped gratefully on my glass.

"Maybe not as happy as I might make another one later this evening. - Now, you promised, tell me everything," she said, leaning closer. "Tell me about your meeting with Redfield. Tell me he isn't going to bother you - bother us - anymore."

I told her what I had seen, and what I had learned, during my private, guided tour.

"Carruthers told me -"

"Carruthers?"

"I don't know her first name; everyone uses last names only. There are a hundred people - that's all - who run the place. It's remarkable. They create the world's most advanced technology and use that same technology to create even more. A hundred men and women, young men and women, all of them in their twenties; they don't just work together, they live together; they have children together."

"Children? Together? What do you mean?" she asked, intensely curious.

"Nothing is private, everything is in common. They sleep with whomever they want, and if they have children they all take care of them. Until they leave, and then the mother takes them."

"What about the father?"

"It's up to her - if she wants the father to live with her. And its up to him - if he wants to. It isn't a question of support. Good God, they're all rich! They get paid millions from the day they

start. And if they want to start a company of their own, AIE provides all the financing they need. When they leave they never have
to worry about money; but five years they have nothing in private,
nothing that, strictly speaking, is their own. It is all to make them
think less of themselves and think more of how they should live -
more of what Redfield teaches them about how they should want
to live - with an endless curiosity, a willingness to look at things
without any preconceptions. They learn not to be the slaves of
what everyone else thinks and feels. That is the word I kept hearing
- slavery, the slavery of the modern mind. One of them made the
remark - it might have been Redfield, it might have been someone
else - that the serious question is not freedom from, but freedom
for, i.e. freedom to act in accordance with what the greatest minds
have taught."

I had started speaking too fast. I smiled an apology.

"I wish you had been there, sitting with me in the dark, listening to Redfield speak, when no one could see him, when no one
could -"

"No one could see him?"

"After dinner, five, six times a week, they sit in a small
amphitheater and listen to Redfield lecture. He does it in the dark;
you can't see him. It has a remarkable effect. It makes you listen
more clearly, more intently, that you have ever listened to anyone
before. Remarkable, that's all I can say. And they do it, for five
years, every week of every month of every year. They listen to
what Redfield wants to tell them, and they do it willingly, eagerly;
they look forward to it. This isn't some kind of cult, there isn't
any indoctrination; Redfield doesn't insist that they agree to anything he says. There isn't any official program, no party line. He
teaches them the history of human thought: the conversation, as he
put it, that has been going on for twenty-five hundred years, beginning with the ancient Greeks, the dozen or so great minds that have
helped determine what, and how, we think; the conversation that,

according to him, we are in danger of destroying by our own stupidity. And so, every evening, for an hour, sometimes two or three, sometimes even four, they sit listening, enthralled, by a voice, a voice from a man none of them has ever seen."

The fork in her hand suspended just above her salad, Tangerine listened in open-mouthed astonishment.

"No one has ever seen him? Yes, he would do that, wouldn't he? - Establish a distance between himself and the others, the ones he wanted to make sure looked up to him."

"And keep them from identifying too closely with him, or with anyone else. He doesn't want followers, he wants them all to become what he called 'second best.'"

I remembered with a smile Redfield's description of the three types of human beings. With rare intuition Tangerine sensed immediately what Redfield must have meant.

"They won't be able to add to that conversation Redfield talked about; but they will be able to follow it and judge who has the better argument. Is that what he is after: a hundred people like that?"

"As near as I was able to follow. I'm not sure I would have understood anything if Alan Boe had not told me what he did about Redfield. The 'gift for solitude,' was the phrase he used. Boe was not talking about the ability to live alone - Redfield has that all right; if you had been there with me, at his home, a home that looked like it was just built, a house that must be at least sixty years old - you would have seen it right away. It's more than living a secluded, solitary life; he lives entirely within himself. He doesn't need - he doesn't want - anyone or anything. He would be perfectly content to live in that place, that house, and never see another soul. He almost does that now. He goes places, he sees people, but only the strangers he sees in a restaurant or passes in the street."

Impatiently, Tangerine began to shake her head.

"None of that explains why he did what he did, why he

committed two murders; why he let two other, innocent, people go on trial. None of it explains why he wanted you involved, why …?" She stared at me with something close to terror in her eyes. "There is going to be another murder, another trial, isn't there? There is going to be…!"

Reaching across the table, I grabbed her wrist and insisted there was nothing to worry about.

"I told him I wasn't his lawyer, that I was never going to be his lawyer, that the lawyer-client privilege didn't exist anymore. I told him that anything he told me now, anything about any other crimes, I would report it to the police."

She kept looking at me. . There was no accusation, no suggestion of disbelief. She just kept looking at me, telling me with her eyes that I had not finished and that I would not be finished until I told the truth.

"I told him all that," I continued, as if I had only meant to pause, " and I think he believed me; but, yes, there is going to be another trial. He said it was a trial that I would want, that I would not let anyone else defend whoever…."

"Whoever?"

"That when I found out who was accused of murder, I wouldn't let anyone else come near it. That I would have to take the case."

Tangerine knew what I was thinking and dismissed it with a gentle, teasing laugh.

"I'll try not to murder anyone, at least for a while."

We sat in silence for a few minutes, picking at our food, wondering what Redfield had meant, and what effect if might have on us.

"No effect at all," she said, lifting her soft chin in a show of defiance. "Not unless we let it. And we won't do that, will we, Joseph Antonelli? Even if we have to take our new sailboat and live somewhere far from shore."

I was not thinking about that; I was thinking about what I had felt during the time I was with Redfield alone.

"It's the strangest thing," I confessed, furrowing my brow as I struggled to clarify the thought. "I know what he did, and still, for some reason, I don't quite believe it. Redfield is a genius, but an evil genius? - He's too much a genius, far too intelligent, for that. There is something going on, and I have a feeling it is right in front of my eyes, but like that lecture he gave this evening, everything is too dark and I'm too blind to see it. There was something else he said. The second-best people - you had it right - there aren't very many of them; there never are. That leaves everyone else, which means nearly everyone, all of us raised to believe what everyone else believes. Its the way we all think, the assumptions of our times. Technology has made it worse, made it more difficult to escape the prison in which, without knowing it, we all live our lives. All we see now are images, what we see on screens. Living in a world of fictional characters we become fictional as well."

"Some things are still real," replied Tangerine, a look of shy intimacy in her large luminous eyes.

We left the restaurant and, my arm around her shoulder, made our way up the street. We passed a quiet bar where, through a half open door, the plaintive wail of a jazz player's trumpet filled the night with the bittersweet nostalgia of broken hearts and unbroken dreams. The waves lapped against the rocky shore, a few abbreviated lights glittered from boats moored close by in the bay. The warmth of her hand, the silky feel of her soft, clean hair against my chin, her gentle quiet breath against my face, the touch that told me everything there was to know, the midnight jazz that with a life of its own kept playing in my head, I could have walked like this forever and never noticed that I had moved. Then, in what seemed the same moment, we were home, inside looking out, the lights of the city, the lights of San Francisco, dancing barely visible in the shrouded thick gray night. We fell into bed and did not sleep until the first red rising of the early morning sun.

Two nights later we had dinner with the Gambarini's at Albert Craven's home in the Marina. When I described what I had seen at Redfield's company, Giuseppe Gambarini was particularly interested in the number.

"One hundred?" His cultured mouth drew back at the corners in the curious expression of an alert inquisitor. "Exactly one hundred - not a few more, not a few less - always one hundred?"

"Is the number important?" asked Tangerine, exchanging a glance with Sophia who seemed as much in the dark as the rest of us.

Gambarini looked down at this fine, manicured hands. A serious, thoughtful look in his blue gray eyes, he considered how to explain what he was thinking. It was a look all the most important musicians of Europe had seen, the moment before he described with unparalleled precision exactly how he wanted something played. He lifted his head, smiled at Tangerine, who was sitting directly opposite him at the table, and then gazed into the middle distance as he again pulled his mouth tight at the corners.

"He has them there for five years, one hundred of the best students in the country. Now, without knowing for certain, it would seem a reasonably safe assumption that what they mainly studied in college was computer science, or some one of the other sciences, the requisite course of study for anyone who wanted to work for a technology company. And what does this Redfield do with them? He keeps them there for five years, teaching them - what? The limitations, and the dangers, of the very technology they are working on. He wants them - those chosen one hundred - to become free and independent, and not just in the financial sense. He wants them, he teaches them, to question all the assumptions of their time and place. Now, I was struck by three things. The first is the number, the one hundred. If you read certain historians, serious European historians, you will sometimes come across this number.

If you read Machiavelli, you may find something similar, a reference to how much can be accomplished if you have a hundred men all dedicated to the same thing, if you have -"

"Boe told me exactly the same thing!" I interjected. "I remember every word. He was describing Redfield's astonishing intelligence - what he had studied, what he had learned, how obsessed he had become with trying somehow to repair what he called the 'modern mistake,' - when he mentioned that Redfield had often remarked on what he had found 'written by more than one great writer: how much could be accomplished by just one hundred people if they were all dedicated to the same cause.'"

Gambarini nodded in a way that suggested that we were in agreement, and that what he was about to say was only the obvious consequence.

"Everyone spends their time taking care of what they have to: themselves, their husbands, their wives, their children, people they are close to. The more ambitious among us try for office or some other, larger, fame But who looks forward into the future, the distant future? Who does that anymore?" Lifting his iron gray eyebrows, he glanced around the table, drawing us more closely into what he thought a remarkable conformity to what Redfield, a man he had never met, was trying to do. "When the great cathedrals of Europe were built, those who planned them, those who started their construction, all knew they would never see them - it was a hundred forty years for Chartres or Notre Dame. Who would think of proposing something like that now? But a hundred - if you could find them, as this Redfield may have found them - willing to build something for a future they themselves might never see? There would be great power in that. Find them, find a hundred; or, better yet, train them, teach them - what Redfield seems to be doing."

Gambarini looked straight at me, a warning like a premonition in his even gaze.

"If he thinks in those kind of terms, then a trial, using murder as a means, becomes in the great scheme of things a matter of no great importance."

Albert Craven, sitting in his accustomed place at the head of the table, drank slowly from a glass of one of the expensive wines he served his guest and that he privately insisted was no better than what you could get in any halfway decent grocery store. He liked and admired Giuseppe Gambarini and was fascinated by the range of his interests and the breadth of his knowledge. He reminded him that he had forgotten something.

"You said you were struck by three things."

"The number, yes; but also the way the hundred live, an equal number of men and women; everything, including each other, held in common. The children born out of these temporary liaison raised in common, until they leave, when the mother takes her child -" He cast a quick glance at his wife, Sophia, sitting on the other side of the table next to me. "She decides if she wants the father to have any responsibility. But, did you notice, there is no mention of how she is quite certain who among the fifty men, the father might be? But leaving that little detail aside, when you consider everything else about the arrangements the remarkable Mr. Redfield has put in place, you realize that what he has done is so far from original, it goes back more than two thousand years. He has stolen a page out of Plato - Plato's Republic, to be precise - communism of, not just property, but women and children. And like Plato," he added with a look of shrewd appraisal, "he has - a point often missed in the discussion - restricted this having everything in common to what we might call a governing class: one hundred people who, with their money and their new education, can have an influence in the world out of all proportion to their numbers, an influence that might even, at some point in the future, become dominant."

"The third thing," insisted Craven when Gambarini, thinking about what he had just said, seemed to forget.

"Yes," he replied, his eyes glistening with the triumph of his own discovery, "the darkness, the way he and his audience - his students - sit unseen when he lectures. It is how Pythagoras taught his students, students who, by the way, were also students for five years. No one saw him, and everyone he taught swore an oath never to reveal to anyone what they had learned there."

I was about to ask Guiseppe what had happened to Pythagoras and his school, when Albert Craven got a telephone call.

"Yes, yes, I understand. I'll make sure he knows."

Craven put his phone away. There was a strange, puzzled look in his eyes. He turned to me as if I might know the answer to the riddle.

"It was someone who works in the district attorney's office. They have been trying to reach you, and when they couldn't, thought they should call me here, at home, tonight. Someone has been arrested for the murder of Lucas Fairweather."

"The trial - you represented Professor Boe, who was innocent," said Sophia Gambarini with a look of surprise.

I felt a sudden coldness run down my spine. My mouth went dry. I could barely get out the words.

"Did they tell you who it was, who was arrested?"

Craven shrugged his shoulders. Whoever it was, the name had meant nothing to him.

"A woman. Someone named Carruthers."

Chapter Nineteen

Redfield was right: I did not want anyone else to be the attorney for the defense. I had thought I knew why Alan Boe had been put on trial, why he had been chosen to play a part, an important part, in the lesson about corruption Redfield was so determined to teach. But then why had Cynthia Carruthers simply walked into the police station and confessed to the murder of Lucas Fairweather. And why, having admitted the crime, had she insisted she would not say another word until she met with her attorney? When they asked for the name of her attorney, she said that she did not have one yet, but that someone would probably be there soon. And I was, first thing the next morning.

Even in a prisoner's orange jumpsuit, Carruthers looked free. It was the clear, undaunted expression in her eyes. She may have just confessed to murder, but she seemed, not just indifferent, but almost oblivious of what might happen.

"It's good of you to come, Mr. Antonelli," she said with what I swear was the same expression with which she had greeted me when I stepped out of my car just days earlier at AIE. For a moment I thought she might start describing to me the new facility in which she now found herself a temporary guest.

We sat a small metal table bolted to the floor. There was a chair on each side. There were no windows. A guard stood outside a metal door with a small, square, thick wire protected glass opening, through which he could see, but not hear, what was going on inside. I did not bother to take out a legal pad from my brief-case. There were only a few questions I wanted, or needed, to ask. I asked the first one with the same formality with which I would have cross-examined a hostile witness. I wanted her to understand who was in charge, and that I had no tinterest whatsoever in what might happen to anyone else.

"Am I correct in believing that when you murdered Lucas Fairweather you were acting on the instruction of James Michael Redfield?"

Carruthers did not bat an eyelash; she did not hesitate at all.

"No, you are not: I acted entirely on my own. I did what I did for what I thought good and sufficient reason."

I must have shown my surprise. She was looking right at me, she had not once looked away, but her eyes flashed with sympathy for what she knew I had never understood and could not possibly have known.

"You decided…? But even if you did, you didn't decide to implicate Alan Boe! You didn't decide to commit murder in a way - at a time and place - when he would become the main suspect! You didn't decide that Alan Boe should stand trial for something he didn't do!" I insisted, growing warmer as I spoke. I was angry, as angry as I had ever been, though not as much with her, as with Redfield, for what now seemed even worse than it had before. "You didn't decide to wait until now to make your confession, instead of when it would have prevented an innocent man from being charged with murder!"

Carruthers was unfazed, unmoved, almost uninterested. She sat there, listening politely and respectfully, as if she were again sitting in the dark, part of Redfield's blind audience. The sympathy I had seen in her eyes was still there, the anger I had just displayed treated as nothing more than an error of judgment, as understandable, and as easily forgiven, as a student's grammatical mistake in a language he was only just starting to learn.

"I'm the one who decided to do what I did; I'm the one who decided I had to do it." She studied me, wondering, as it seemed, whether to ask me a question. "What I tell you stays secret, doesn't it?"

The privilege. It was there again. But she was not Redfield; she had confessed to murder.

"Yes, it stays secret. I can never tell anyone anything you tell me about something you have done. But be careful," I warned, more severely, because of Redfield, than what I would normally have done. "The privilege does not apply to anything you might be planning to do, a crime you intend to commit, like perjury, lying on the stand. Now, what is it you want to tell me?"

"Redfield did not have anything to do with my decision, but he told me there would be someone walking just outside, and that if I cried for help he was certain that person would come running."

"If Redfield was not involved in your decision, if you made the decision all on your own to murder Lucas Fairweather - why? You did not know him. You did not go to Berkeley; you've been at AIE for - what?- almost five years. What possible reason could you have to murder someone you did not know - unless Redfield convinced you it was something that had to be done and that you were the one who should do it?"

There was a flash, not of anger exactly, but of bitter disappointment in her eyes.

"I never said I didn't know Lucas Fairweather."

When I left her at the jail an hour later, I knew, or thought I knew, enough about what had happened to believe that, despite her confession, she had at least the chance of an acquittal. There was no question but that she had killed Lucas Fairweather; there was a real question whether it was murder.

"You're going to do it? - You're going to take the case?" With his elbows on his glass and steel desk, Albert Craven watched me with a pawnbroker's measured glance. "Is that any different than what Redfield managed to get you to do before?"

"Maybe, maybe not; I don't really know. But I don't see what he gets out of this. No one innocent is being charged with a crime and forced to go to trial. Cynthia Carruthers did it. She killed Fairweather. Where is the 'lesson' in that?"

Albert thought my ignorance nothing short of remarkable.

"The trial won't be about whether she did it; the trial will be about why she did it. Why am I telling you this?" He shook his head with the practiced tolerance he lavished on those too stupid to learn from their own mistakes. "Am I wrong? Is there any other choice?"

"You're not wrong. Everything hinges on that one question: Why she did it, why she thought she had to do it. The problem," I continued with a shrug, as I crossed my arms, sat sideways in the chair and stared out the window at the bright sunshine of the late afternoon, "is that I don't believe her."

"You think she's lying?"

"Not lying; just not telling the whole truth. It isn't even that; it's more a question of emphasis, how something can be interpreted. It is the reason she went there that night that, when you start to think about it, leaves something out. I didn't catch it at first, but it's there, and it may make the difference whether she walks out of court a free woman or spends the rest of her life in prison. It may also make a difference in what we think of Redfield and what he has done."

With surprising agility for his years, Craven jumped up from his chair and rapped his fist on the desk in a quick, eager staccato.

"Wish I was a trial lawyer! What a great case to try! You've never had a trial like this, have you? - One trial a sequel to the other. You defend the innocent man charged with a murder, then you defend the guilty woman, the only one who should have been tried. Better yet, before you step inside the courtroom your client has confessed. Do you know how dull my life is compared to that? For thirty, forty…never mind how many years, all I've done is what they too generously call 'office law,' drafting documents so that rich people can get richer still," he complained.

He walked back and forth, waving his small, fragile hand in the air, like an actor in a courtroom drama, his mouth moving in silent imitation of a speech to mesmerize every jury ever sworn. He stopped, stared at me, started to laugh, and then, still smiling, collapsed back in his chair. His arms dangling out to the side, he looked at me with the helpless guile of an old man who could still revel in older, banished dreams, dreams of what he had never really wanted to do and had always known he never would.

"Have you heard anything from Redfield?" he asked, again quite serious. Pulling himself up, he again leaned forward, his elbows back on the desk. "Anything at all?"

"Nothing since the day I met with him. I don't really expect I will, unless he shows up to watch the trial. And even then…."

Redfield did not come to the trial, or if he did, I did not see him. Everyone else in the city seemed to be there. There was not a seat left in the courtroom when the Honorable Christopher Douglas, arrogant, sinister and sharp-witted, moved with slow, measured steps toward the bench, his shoulders slumped forward, held down by a massive bulging stomach that made that short walk seem an effort. With his hand on the the edge of the bench, he hoisted himself up to his black leather chair. Everyone held their breath, waiting to see if the chair would hold.

Douglas hated lawyers and lawyers hated him. Like most people who think more highly of themselves than they should, he thought everyone else a fool. If a lawyer said something that was not directly on point, Douglas would tell the jury why such an obvious error was only to be expected; when a lawyer said something that was directly on point, Douglas would let them know that even an idiot could sometimes guess right. Like every demagogue Christopher Douglas knew how to appeal to the prejudices of the crowd.

Eleanor McFarland, who had prosecuted the case against Alan Boe, did not prosecute the case against Cynthia Carruthers. Anthony Barnes, just three years out of law school, had been given the assignment. Juries do not like lawyers who talk down to them; Anthony Barnes could not have done that had he tried. Mild-mannered, pleasant and inoffensive, with boyish good looks and an open, candid expression, he seemed so honest I began to wonder whether he might just be the biggest liar I had ever met. Like nearly everyone else of his generation, he talked twice as fast as he should.

The first witness was the first witness for the second time; the lead witness in the first trial for the murder of Lucas Fairweather was the lead witness in this. The same way he had done before, the coroner described how the chancellor had been "bludgeoned to death" by a blow from a marble statue to the back of his skull. It was almost word for word. I listened, and Carruthers, sitting next to me, listened as well. Finally finished, Barnes took his seat.

"You wish to examine the witness?" asked Judge Douglas in a lackluster voice while he stared up at the ceiling.

I did not rise from my chair; I did not say anything. Douglas took a deep, weary breath, a sigh of disgust. His eyes moved, but farther along the ceiling, not down to me.

"Question, counselor - Do you have one?"

"Oh, were you talking to me?" I replied as I slowly got to my feet. "I thought you must be talking to yourself."

The large, ungainly head of Christopher Douglas twisted around. He stared at me through the tiny slits of his eyes.

"When I ask you a question, you stand up and answer it!" he instructed in a voice that threatened to break.

I smiled.

"My apologies, your Honor, but I thought at first, when I saw you looking up like that, that you might be talking to God. The last thing I would ever do is interrupt someone's prayer."

Those snake-like eyes grew more narrow, and more lethal, still. His head sank deeper into his hulking shoulders. He started to berate me for my insolence, to lecture me on this ill-considered act of defiance, but, changing his mind, turned instead to the jury.

"You may have heard of him, he's very famous, Antonelli. There is a line he likes to use. He used it with you during jury selection, a line he quotes from Blackstone. He does that, quotes long dead people no one remembers anymore. It makes it seem that he must know what he is talking about. The line - 'It's better that ten guilty men go free than that one innocent man be convicted' - he would know about that. He's made a career out of doing just that - helping guilty men go free! But not in this courtroom, not so long as I'm on the bench. In my courtroom the guilty get punished and only the innocent go free." He looked at me again. "Do you wish to ask any questions of the witness?"

I smiled again.

"No, your Honor; no questions of this witness. But I do have one for you: Did I understand you correctly? - You really do believe that at least the innocent should go free?"

His thick lips stretched down hard at the corners, his fat nostrils flared. He stared pure hatred at me.

"Call your next witness," he said, finally

Anthony Barnes sprang to attention.

"The prosecution calls Melvin Hoskins," he announced, in a clear, unhurried voice.

Hoskins looked the same, a small man in his forties, with straight black hair parted neatly on the side, but he was not quite as timid as before and not nearly as nervous. His voice no longer quivered when he spoke.

Barnes took Hoskins through the same line of questioning

he had been put through before, except that this time all the emphasis was on what, in the first trial, the prosecution had done everything it could to ignore.

"It was your practice to check the chancellor's office every hour or so at night, when you were on duty?" asked Barnes, standing at the far end of the jury box.

"Yes, that's right."

"When you checked - when you opened the door to his office at eleven o'clock - was Lucas Fairweather there?"

"Yes, he was."

Hoskins kept opening and closing his hands, darting a glance at the jury, as if he could not quite remember whether he was supposed to look at them all the time or not at all. Barnes nodded, encouraging him to relax and take his time.

"When you opened the door, was Lucas Fairweather alone?"

"No, he wasn't," replied Hoskins, lurching forward, eager to answer. "There was a woman."

"Would you please tell the jury what they were doing?"

Hoskins stared down at his hands, which he now clasped together.

"They were together, on the chancellor's desk, having sex."

Barnes did not change expression, and he did not look at the jury. He kept his gaze fixed on the witness and continued the conversation.

"Can you describe the woman?"

"She was blonde - that's all I saw," he added with a quick, furtive glance at the jury. "That's all I saw, and as soon as I saw it, I got out of there and shut the door behind me. It was none of my business what they were doing."

I was already on my feet, waiting for the prosecution to finish. I was asking my first question on cross before Barnes had returned to his chair at the counsel table.

"None of your business! - Is that what you said?" I asked with a slight grin as I glanced at Hoskins from under lowered eyes. "That it was none of your business?"

I remembered, and he knew I remembered, what he had said the last time I had him on the witness stand. He looked over at the jury, then he looked back at me, waiting for what he knew was going to happen next.

"I don't want to embarrass you, Mr. Hoskins, but I have to take you back to when we met before, when Alan Boe was on trial for the murder of Lucas Fairweather." Standing at the corner of the counsel table closest to the jury box, I reached down for the trial transcript I had placed there earlier. "When you testified in that trial…." I looked up at Judge Douglas, sitting with his arms crossed and a baleful expression in his serpent-like eyes. "A trial in which an innocent man was found not guilty, you described what you saw in a slightly different way. You said, and I quote, 'He had her up on the desk. He was - the chancellor was - fucking the hell out of her! That's what I saw, and that's why I shut the door and got out of there and didn't go back until an hour later!'"

I put the transcript down on the table and smiled at Hoskins, letting him know there was no reason to feel embarrassed. Moving the few short steps to the jury box, I placed my hand on the railing and studied the faces of the jurors as I asked the next question.

"I reminded you how you described what you saw because there is a difference, an extremely important difference, between your two accounts."

Hoskins gave me a blank look.

"You told Mr. Barnes that you saw the two of them - Lucas Fairweather and a woman you did not really see, only that she had blonde hair - 'having sex.' You told the jury in the other trial that 'the chancellor was fucking the hell out of her.' My question is which was it: were they having sex, or…?"

He still did not understand.

"In the one case - what you testified today - the jury could easily conclude that you saw a man and a woman making love; in the other case - what you told that other jury - the conclusion could easily be that Lucas Fairweather was committing rape!"

It took a moment, but finally, in the stunned silence of the courtroom, Anthony Barnes understood what I had just done.

"Objection!" he shouted in a voice that, even shouting, managed to seem polite. "The defense is -"

"Sustained!" Douglas ruled before Barnes could even finish. He was furious, stabbing the air with his thick finger as he began to lecture me on what he thought a mortal sin.

"I asked a question," I said simply.

"You didn't ask a question; you told the witness, you told the jury, what to think."

"Then I'll ask the question a different way: Based on what you saw, Mr. Hoskins, can you swear that Lucas Fairweather was not committing rape?"

The courtroom exploded, the judge went balistic, the prosecutor looked puzzled, and I sat down, stared straight ahead and pretended that none of it had anything to do with me.

The prosecution's third witness was Oliver Grayson, the lead detective in the case. Barnes did not waste any time. He asked the only important question: he asked if Cynthia Carruthers had confessed to the murder of Lucas Fairweather.

"Yes, she did."

"And did she put it in writing, and sign her confession?"

"Yes."

Barnes asked the clerk to hand the witness a document that had been marked as an exhibit. Grayson identified it as the signed confession of Cynthia Carruthers and Barnes asked him to read it to the jury.

"'I, Cynthia Carruthers, confess that I killed Lucas Fairweather.'"

Barnes turned toward the jury with a look that told them that the case was over, that there was nothing for them to decide. He glanced at me, and for just an instant, letting down his guard, he revealed the smug certainty of his youthful ignorance.

"Your witness, counselor."

Counselor! I almost laughed out loud. So now we were equals, or really less than that because he was going to win and I was going to lose. He had not yet reached the age of reason and it was a question whether he ever would, the age when after practicing law long enough you learn that the verdict in a criminal case is the least reliable measure of whether an attorney is good at what he does.

"Thank you - counselor," I remarked, showing affability to mask my laughter. "Detective Grayson!" I fairly shouted, exuding all the cheerful confidence I could invent. "Do you know who the prosecution is calling next, who is going to testify after you? - Alan Boe, the man you were here to testify against before."

"I heard they were going to call him," replied Grayson in that rapid, drumbeat voice I still remembered. A slight grin lit up his face. "Never saw anyone quite like him."

Barnes was halfway out of his chair with an objection before he realized he did not know what, precisely, his objection would be. Sinking back down, he bent forward, waiting for what I was going to ask next.

"With him at least you got your hope."

"My hope?"

"When he asked you - remember? - how you would feel if he were innocent but still got convicted."

"I remember. And you're right - He was innocent and he got acquitted."

"This is a different trial, detective," warned Douglas. "Move it along, counselor; I've got better things than to do than listen to you reminisce about some trial you won."

Grayson looked sharply up at Douglas.

"Yeah, well, I'm damn glad he did, won that case, I mean. You may not mind if someone innocent gets convicted, but I sure as hell do, especially if its someone I arrested!"

Douglas's face went red with rage. He reached for his gavel, as if he were reaching for a weapon, but caught himself in time to hold it in both hands under his chin as if he were thinking about some point of law. He could insult and disparage all the lawyers he wanted, but a police detective, a highly decorated detective, a detective with nothing to fear from a bully in a black robe, was something else again.

"Again, counselor," he remarked, looking at me as if I had somehow earned his respect, "we need to stay on point."

I looked at Grayson, and Grayson looked at me. We had become, thanks to Alan Boe, nothing like the adversaries we once had been.

"The confession that you read to the jury. Was that all of it? She did not say anything else?"

"No, that was it; there was nothing more."

"She confessed to you?"

"Yes, to me."

"I want to make sure I understand. The defendant, Cynthia Carruthers, asked to see you - no one else? She chose you, and no one else?"

"That's right. I got a call, was told someone wanted to see me, a woman who had some information about the Lucas Fairweather murder."

"She asked for you. And she told you she killed Lucas Fairweather. Is that all she said? She didn't tell you why she did it, how it happened - anything?" I asked, resting my hand on the corner of the counsel table where I stood, just steps from the jury box.

"It was interesting. I asked her, or started to ask her, about what she said she had done, but she told me that was all she had to say."

"Just that - as her confession states - she killed him?"

"That's correct."

I picked up the transcript of the Alan Boe trial and turned to the page where Grayson's testimony began.

"When Alan Boe was on trial, you were asked about his contention that a woman was there that night. You testified - let me read your response - that 'we've tried, but no one saw her. There isn't any record of phone calls, email, anything that would give us a clue who she might have been.' That is the reply you made when the prosecutor asked if you had attempted to find the woman the defendant said he had heard screaming and then had passed on the stairs as he went to help?"

"Yes, that's what I said."

"And then you were asked - again by the prosecution - 'in all your years of experience have you ever heard of someone who has just committed murder screaming for help?' You replied, 'No, I don't think so.' I set the transcript aside. I could quote from memory what the prosecution had insisted was the only reasonable explanation. "And then, finally, you were asked this: 'A woman screams for help, and scared to death that the murderer is going to kill her next, runs away. Isn't that what all the evidence seems to suggest?'"

Crossing my arms, I stared down at the floor and slowly shook my head.

"'In all your experience....' Detective Grayson, in all your experience wouldn't a woman who had just been brutally raped, raped and forced to defend herself against such a brutal, unforgivable act, be expected to scream for help? Wouldn't a woman put through that kind of violent ordeal run away as fast, and as far, as she could?"

Grayson immediately turned to the jury.

"That is exactly what I would expect to happen."
"Based on your experience?"
"Yes, based on my experience."

Chapter Twenty

"I was there today, and you didn't notice, did you?"

I felt Tangerine's hand on my shoulder; I heard ice tinkling in the glass she was bringing me. I did not turn around, I did not look up; I stayed where I was, stretched out on a grey cushioned chaise lounge on the back deck, looking out at the sleek white sailboats that seemed not to be moving at all, a still color photograph of twilight on the San Francisco bay.

"I knew you were there," I replied, finally, as I reached up for the glass she offered. "I did not need to see you; I can always sense when you're there."

"Liar!" she cried. "In the middle of a trial you would not notice if I ran stark naked through the courtroom!"

"No," I remarked, doing everything I could to suppress a grin, "but everyone else would. Probably take them years to get over the excitement. Why don't you try it sometime? I promise to be your lawyer when they charge you with indecent exposure. I have the defense all ready."

"All ready? What defense is that, Mr. Antonelli?"

"That there was nothing indecent about it, that everyone who saw you do it can't wait to see you do it again," I replied, turning just far enough to see the blushing laughter in her eyes.

You didn't know I was there, did you?" She sat down next to me on the chaise. "I sat way in the back so you wouldn't see me. I didn't know if you wanted...."

"You to come? Yes, and no. I'm a little self-conscious, like a schoolboy, for God's sake, afraid of making a fool of myself in front of the best looking girl he's ever seen. But then, on the other hand, like that same idiot teenager, convinced that given half a chance he'll do something so exceptional, so extraordinary, that she'll suddenly fall as much in love with him as he is with her."

"Why are you laughing?"

"Because I just realized that I would probably think you were there when you weren't, do something to impress you, feel real proud about it, and then find out you hadn't been there at all! And all because when it comes to you I am a complete and perfect fool!"

I drank a little of the scotch and soda and watched a little more the silent sailboats on the bay.

"We should," said Tangerine, watching as well.

"We will," I promised. "You were really there today? What did you think?"

"The judge is unbearable, the prosecutor - I'd bet he did well in law school: smart, or rather book-smart; a pupil, not a student."

I was not sure I followed.

"A pupil does what he has to, studies hard, learns the material, gives back the answers the teacher wants to hear. A student studies hard - even harder - but because he is interested and wants to learn more, he doesn't always get the best grades. He doesn't confine himself to what he thinks the teacher wants. Instead of answers, he asks questions." Shrugged a quick apology. "You went to law school. What am I telling you?"

"They were called 'grubbers,' the ones - just like you described - who wanted good grades because they wanted to make money, to join a big firm and become a high-priced specialist. Barnes has a different ambition. He wants to become a well-known prosecutor so he can become a judge or run for office. And maybe he will. He isn't that bad. He knows what he needs to know; he won't make any serious mistakes. But, you're right, there is something missing. I think it is the capacity to have a broken heart."

Tangerine took a last sip from the glass of white wine she was drinking. She looked at me with the melancholy of nostalgia, the memory of what she used to think she was, or rather, I suppose, of what she used to think she could never be.

"I used to think I didn't have that either - a heart that could be broken - and then I met you."

Her gorgeous eyes glistened with a new vulnerability, the sense of loss you sometimes feel for something you have not lost but suddenly realize you could. She stroked the side of my face.

"Better change. We have to be in the city in an hour. We can't be late for Giuseppe's final performance."

I do not remember ever feeling tired during a trial; the truth is I don't remember feeling much of anything at all. I was always too caught up in the action, too involved in what was going on, to think about anything except the question, the answer, the question after that, all the endless dialogue that from start to finish was the only world I knew. There was not time to worry, or even be aware, of what I felt. Giuseppe Gambarini conducted the philharmonic orchestra with the same, total, concentration. The ceiling could have collapsed and he would not have heard it fall. His hands, his arms, and especially his eyes moved in the same harmony, and with the same emphasis, as the music; his baton, like the instruments of the orchestra, part of a magnificent, ordered, whole. At the end, the thunderous climax of Beethoven's Ninth Symphony, his face glowed with the kind of triumph that only comes when perfection has finally been achieved.

"What did you think?" asked Tangerine, quietly and with genuine interest.

We were sitting at a small corner table in a bar and restaurant just down the street from the concert hall, crowded with well-dressed men and women who had seen the same performance.

"Look at their faces," I replied. "Look at their excitement, the way everything stays, the pride, the feeling that we all somehow share in what we heard, what Giuseppe Gambarini did tonight."

"Do you remember that night, the first time we met him and Sophia, when we had dinner at Albert Craven's?"

"The night Lucas Fairweather was murdered."

"That long conversation in which Guiseppe talked about the loss of all standards, the belief that one thing is as good, or as bad, as any other, that everything is a question of individual choice. He proved it tonight, didn't he? - Proved that it is all wrong. There is a standard; there is a difference between better and worse. All you have to do is listen."

"That's the problem, though, isn't it? - There is too much noise, too many voices saying too many different mindless things." I sat back, a scotch and soda in my hand, remembering how little I had once cared for what I now thought irreplaceable. "I could not stand it as a kid. Classical music was boring. Now it's the only thing I listen to - that, and jazz."

Tangerine reached for my hand.

"Think how lucky you are. You may not have liked it as a boy, but you love it now. I imagine it has always been like this. Most people probably never have the chance to learn how good, how important, it is. Most people have probably always thought it boring. Especially now."

I knew what she meant. In their different ways, Giuseppe Gambarini and James Michael Redfield had talked about the same thing: the constant, relentless barrage of modern media, the constant, changing images, the constant, discordant, hard-driving music, that had all but eliminated the ability to think; the absence of any serious sense of self-restraint, the endless craving for something new, the immediate addiction to every new impulse become the newest need. They had both, in the different ways, tried to find, not just for themselves, but for others, an escape from the modern insanity.

"Gambarini, Boe, Redfield - all three of them at war with the present and in love with the past," said Tangerine in a calm, thoughtful voice. She glanced at the crowd packed around the silver chrome and green glass bar, the art deco look that tried to merge the present with the past in a way that symbolized the future. "Giuseppe said he had read Boe's great book, and that every serious person in Europe had read it, too. It's too bad they never met. Or is it? Which one would have been more intimidated by the other? That's not what I meant," she added, pressing her lips together, disappointed she had not been more clear. "Which of them would have been more reticent, more unwilling to express an opinion?"

"Gambarini. No question. Two reasons. I doubt there is anyone alive who could stop Alan Boe from saying what he wants. Giuseppe Gambarini, on the other hand, is too intelligent for words. What we saw tonight -"

"Part of it was sung," she reminded me, and then realized her mistake. "But you did not need to know German to know, to understand, everything that was meant." Her eyes were full of knowledge. "There is a third reason - Giuseppe would not say anything: he would be too busy listening, learning everything he could. That is why he is going to be there Monday, at the trial. You knew that, didn't you?"

"Albert told me. He'll be there as well. Everyone is going to be there." I laughed. "The whole world wants to see Alan Boe. Whatever else Redfield has done, he made Boe into a celebrity. There doesn't seem to be anyone who hasn't heard of him. They wanted to move his classes to a larger room to accommodate all the students who now want to get in. He refused. He said if he had known that was going to happen, he would have pled guilty and asked for life in prison."

Tangerine smiled with her eyes at a chance missed, something she now wished she had done.

"If I had known there was someone like him, someone that

290

alive, I would have gone to college. I would have given anything to know what it was like to sit in a classroom and listen to an Alan Boe. Instead...."

"Instead, you wee too damn good-looking, too damn beautiful to...."

"To think about anything except what I wanted, what I thought I had to have - Is that what you are trying to say?"

I might have lied if she were anyone else, if I had not been hopelessly in love with her, if she had not known, far better than I ever could, that every advantage comes with a price of its own.

"Yes, that's exactly what I am trying to say. Everyone wanted to be with you. No one could have resisted that. There is one great difference. None of it, even what you might have wanted at the time, meant that much to you. More than that, you always had contempt for the game, contempt for the way you used what you had."

Lowering her eyes, that same smile of forgotten regret played on her lips. She looked at me again, but did not speak. And when, finally, she did, there was something heart-breaking in her voice.

"I don't ever want to be with anyone but you."

I had to look away, afraid of what might happen if I did not.

"You're not calling Alan Boe as a witness?" she asked, in a soft, reassuring voice that invited me back. "The prosecution is?"

I took a deep breath and glanced around at the shifting colors of the scene, the women sparkling in their bright jewelry and their expensive shiny clothes, their eager, incandescent smiles, the throbbing, hard-beating sound of brief, thrilling conversations, the flying hands of a bartender with slick black hair trying to keep track of a half dozen shouted orders while as carefully as possible he served someone their long awaited drink.

"Welcome to San Francisco," I remarked, with a knowing grin. "This is what the city isa all about: expensive women and more expensive booze, glamour, glitter, great music and sometimes great romance."

"Great music, great romance," said Tangerine, repeating the words. "We have nothing to complain about, do we, you and I? We're luckier than most, luckier than Cynthia Carruthers. Is it true?" She leaned close so no one around us could hear. "Did Fairweather really rape her? Was it self-defense? Was it...?" She stopped abruptly. "Sorry. I know you can't tell me anything she...."

I was again, though in a different way, prisoner of the privilege. I could not tell her, I could not tell anyone, what Carruthers had told me.

"It will all come out. And it's a lot more interesting than what anyone, especially the prosecution, could possibly imagine. Anthony Barnes is in a box and does not know it. Prosecutors dream of the chance to cross-examine the defendant in a criminal trial. If he knew what I knew he would be praying that I would not call her. He's calling Alan Boe," I added like a conspirator sharing one of the secrets to success. "He thinks he has to. Boe is the only one who can put Carruthers at the scene. Hoskins, the security guard, did not get a good enough look at her. Boe is the only one who saw her."

"She confessed," objected Tangerine. "The jury heard it. Why does the prosecution have to prove anything beyond that?"

"That one sentence - it's all there is. She didn't give any details, nothing that could be used to tie her to the murder. They have a confession, but Barnes can't take the chance that she might recant, take it all back, insist she didn't know what she was doing. He might still get a conviction - he probably would get a conviction - but Boe's testimony makes any denial of hers impossible to believe. That's what he thinks, but then he doesn't know what I know."

"What I don't understand is why she let Boe go on trial, why she didn't stop it, why she waited until now to confess."

"Redfield. I can tell you that because she's never said it. She hasn't said anything about a lot of things. But it has to be Redfield."

"But Redfield didn't murder, didn't arrange the murder, of Lucas Fairweather. Because if she was raped, if she was...? Why are you looking at me like that? He was behind it, he was responsible for what happened? - Is that what you're trying to tell me?"

I still did not know what, exactly, Redfield had done. It was almost as if Carruthers was bound by some privilege of her own, a limit on how much she could tell me. Or would tell me, because every time I asked I got the same answer: it would all come out at trial. She must have reminded me a half dozen times that, as she put it, "When I testify, I'll be under oath." It was no answer at all. It did not explain why she would not tell me.

"All I know for sure," I replied to Tangerine, "is that Fairweather was murdered and that somehow I have found myself defending both of the people who have been accused of doing it. And in both cases the victim, Lucas Fairweather - who he was and what he did - is the central issue."

Tangerine's eyes flashed with inspiration.

"Lucas Fairweather the central issue - or Alan Boe?"

It was a fair question. Monday morning, when Boe was called at the prosecution's last witness, no one was thinking about Lucas Fairweather; every eye was on the mesmerizing ugliness of a witness it was hard to believe was even possible. He had barely settled himself in the witness chair before he turned to the jury and with a beaming smile informed them, "You're better looking than the jury I had for my trial. There were a few of them, if you can believe it, nearly as ugly as me!" I had to stop myself from laughing when Anthony Barnes, still without the faintest idea what he was getting into, tried to get the witness to remember where he was by asking him to state his full name for the record.

"Alan Empedocles Boe," he said, in a deep, clear voice. He

darted a glance at me, and then looked back at the jury. "Poor Mr. Antonelli has heard this before, but there is no second version of the truth, so he will just have to stand by while I explain once again the peculiar nature of my name."

And then he started. He had reached the part about the name his students had given one of his courses, Al Boe's Book of Roots, when Judge Douglas came unglued.

"You were asked a simple question: to state your name for the record. That's all! We're not interested in your peculiar biography!"

Sitting cross-legged the way he had before, Boe looked up to where Douglas sat glowering down at him.

"A simple question? Only for the simple-minded. A name means everything. It's what we are called; it is how others see us, and it is how, sometimes, we see ourselves."

Douglas stared at him as if he were not just unusual but quite probably mad.

"You, for example," continued Boe, his eyes moving all around in a strange, manic dance. "What you're called - 'judge.' It's the reason, the only reason, you have any authority, the only reason you get to speak. And as for whether anyone is interested in my 'peculiar biography,' as you so generously put it, shall we have a show of hands, shall we ask the jurors what they think?"

"Why you -"

"Why me? That is of course the ultimate question, the question why any of us happens to exist at this time, or at any time. I could give you, if you like, some of the answers that have been given, though I admit there isn't one of them that cannot be questioned. It is -"

Douglas struck his gavel with such force it was a wonder splinters did not fly.

"One more word, I'll find you in contempt!"

"Two, then, would be all right?" remarked Boe, undisturbed. He turned back to Anthony Barnes who was standing, paralyzed, waiting, like the rest of us, to see what would happen. "I assume you have other questions."

"Yes, of course....Yes, questions." Barnes fumbled through a sheaf of notes he was holding. "Yes. Would you tell the jury what happened the night Lucas Fairweather was murdered?" His face flushed with embarrassment. He realized the question was too general and too broad. He looked again at this notes. "Were you walking near the administration building, where Lucas Fairweather had his office, around midnight, the night the chancellor was...?"

"Yes."

"Did something happen that made you go toward the building?"

"Yes," replied Alan Boe, suddenly the soul of brevity.

"Please tell the jury what the...?"

Barnes realized, almost too late, what the answer would be, that Boe had heard a woman scream and that was the reason he came running. Trained in the erroneous belief that a lawyer should never ask a question helpful to the other side, he asked a different one.

"Did you see anyone running from the building? Specifically, did you see the defendant, Cynthia Carruthers, running from the building?"

"No."

"No?" asked, Barnes, staggered not just by the answer, but by the look of perfect certainty in Alan Boe's uncanny eyes.

"No, I did not see anyone running out of the building."

"You did not see the defendant, Cynthia Carruthers, there, that night, the night Lucas Fairweather was murdered? Just answer, yes or no," he insisted, when Boe seemed to hesitate.

Alan Boe's shoulders rocked with laughter; his eyes nearly shot out of his head.

"Yes, I did not see her; no, I did not see her. Which answer would you prefer?"

Barnes was speechless. He did not understand what Boe was saying. Finally, when he did, he looked at Boe with a new appreciation.

"Yes, I see what you mean. Let me ask it this way: Did you see the defendant, Cynthia Carruthers, the night Lucas Fairweather was killed?"

"Yes, I did."

"Where?"

"She was coming down the stairs, just as I started up. She looked scared, she looked -"

"Yes, I understand. But, again, just to be sure: You saw - and you're absolutely certain that you saw - the defendant, Cynthia Carruthers, coming down the stairs from the chancellor's office?"

"No."

"No?"

"I saw her coming down the stairs. I don't know where she was coming from."

"I see. Very good. When you saw her, did she have blood on her hands, on her clothes?"

"Yes, blood; but I'm not sure where it was - her hands, her clothes. She bumped into me, which is how I got blood on me. But she was moving so quickly, she was so scared, so -"

"Yes, I understand. She had blood on her. That's all," announced Barnes, as he started back to his chair at the counsel table. No more questions, your Honor."

Douglas leaned back, the tall leather chair groaning under his weight. Like a gambler calculating the odds, he tapped his pudgy pink fingers together, while he watched me as I stood waiting to begin, watched me as the seconds passed, watched me with a smirk on his face, daring me to complain that he was keeping me from doing what everyone in the courtroom knew I was waiting to do. He had forgotten that I was not the only one waiting.

"As I was saying before Mr. Barnes decided he did not want me to tell you everything I saw," remarked Alan Boe, in a voice that echoed off the walls and riveted everyone's attention. "She bumped into me - I should probably say we nearly collided. She was scared, as scared as anyone I had ever seen. She -"

"Damn you! Stop!" shouted Douglas, in a voice like shattered glass. "You're a witness. You answer questions - you speak - when I say you can!"

"I'm a witness, sworn to tell the truth! And I'm going to do what I'm sworn to do. You're a judge, who swore an oath as well, an oath to do justice - You might want to remember that!"

If Douglas's eyes had not been buried so far back in his head, they might have shot out of his skull. He was just about to shout something back, when Boe stopped him with a smile.

"Do you want me to tell the truth or not, your Honor?" he inquired, in a quiet voice that was now, suddenly, all good will and reason.

He was looking at Douglas as if he really wanted to know. Douglas, perhaps to his own astonishment, was disarmed, willing, even eager, to get back to work.

"Yes, of course; which is the reason I would ask you to wait for the attorney to ask you questions."

Boe's remarkable eyes moved, quick as light, to my waiting gaze. I was at the side of the counsel table, close enough to touch the jury box. My hand on the railing, I took a step toward him.

"The defendant, Cynthia Carruthers, was scared when you almost ran into her on the steps coming down from Lucas Fairweather's office on the second floor - correct?"

"As scared as anyone I ever saw."

"There was a reason you were there, running up those steps, wasn't there? You had heard her screaming from the open window of the chancellor's office, didn't you?"

"Yes. I was walking just outside. I pass there every night on my walk across campus."

"Let's stop there for a moment." I went to the counsel table, picked up the trial transcript and turned to the page I wanted. "You were here, in a courtroom, in another trial for the murder of Lucas Fairweather, weren't you?"

"Yes, I was."

"Tell the jury why you were a witness in that trial."

He looked at the jury with a wide, unembarrassed grin.

"I was the defendant, on trial for murder."

"You were acquitted, were you not?"

"I had a good lawyer," he replied. The grin on his face grew wider still. "I probably would have been convicted with anyone else," he explained, to the immense enjoyment of a jury, none of whom could take their eyes off of him.

"The real reason, Mr. Boe, is that you were innocent."

"It's true I didn't murder Lucas Fairweather; it is also true that I might still have been convicted."

"At your trial, you testified that - let me read it - 'I walk every night, a mile or so, always at the same time, always the same route. Every night, for so many years I don't know I'm doing it.' Just to be sure, is that the route you took that night?"

"Yes, the same one. There was no variation."

"You were then asked - I asked you - what happened that made you stop walking. This is what you said: 'A scream, a shout, from the window, a woman's voice.' You then said that then everything went silent. And then you, 'Heard it again, a scream, a second shout.' Is that how you still remember it? - Two screams for help?"

"Yes, that is what I heard: two screams."

"And hearing that - those two screams - you testified that you knew, 'Someone was in trouble. I started for the entrance - it was not more than twenty, or thirty feet away. The doors were open and I started up the steps when a woman, a young woman, a woman in her twenties, came running down the stairs toward me. She bumped into me, and I grabbed her, tried to stop her, because I knew - or thought I knew - she was in trouble.'"

I looked up from the page I was reading.

"The woman, the woman in her twenties - that was the defendant, Cynthia Carruthers?"

"Yes. I did not know her name; but, yes, it was her."

"You go on," I said, holding the transcript in front of me and I walked slowly toward the jury box; "you're describing what she looked like, the impression you had of what she was going through. After you said you knew she was in trouble - 'She looked at me with frantic eyes, scared, terrified, I thought.' Scared, terrified - is that how you still remember it?"

"As I said, as scared as anyone I had ever seen."

"And do you remember what she said, in that brief moment you encountered her on the stairs, scared and terrified?"

"She started to tell me about something Fairweather had done, or tried to do."

"Exactly," I assured him, and the jury. "This is what you testified: 'He's up there,…he tried to…And I…' Then she ran off. Is that what happened, is that what she said?"

"Yes."

"And when you ran up to Fairweather's office and found him laying dead on the floor, you did not think she had murdered him, did you? - You thought she had acted in self-defense - isn't that right?"

"Yes, that is what I thought, when I saw him laying there. I thought he must have tried to attack her."

I had no more questions to ask and Boe was excused as a witness with the thanks of the court. It was the first time anyone could remember Christopher Douglas saying thank you to anyone who appeared in his courtroom. The prosecution had no more witnesses to call, and when he asked me if I ready to call the first witness for the defense, he seemed almost interested in what I was going to do.

"Yes, your Honor. The defense calls William Merrick."

Merrick had not just lost his chance to replace Lucas Fairweather as chancellor of the university, he had been fired from his position as vice-chancellor. The cover-up of Fairweather's long history of sexual misconduct had effectively ended his academic career. There was not a university in the country that would touch him. He had the look of a beaten man. His former self-importance was all but gone. It was a little like finding someone with whom you used to work lying drunk in an alleyway outside a bar.

"Mr. Merrick, you were until very recently vice-chancellor of the university. In that capacity, did you become aware that the chancellor, Lucas Fairweather, had been the subject of an internal investigation at the time of his death?"

Merrick bit his lip and slowly nodded. He looked at the jury as if thought he might find someone who would understand the difficult position in which he had found himself.

"Yes, I was aware there was an investigation. The chancellor had -"

"Had been involved in 'repeated violations of the university's rules against sexual exploitation of faculty or students.' Is that the conclusion that was reached?" I asked, quoting the report Merrick had received and then done nothing about.

There was no reason to embarrass him with this. He was there, a witness, not for the prosecution, but for the defense; he was there to help me show what Lucas Fairweather had done and what he was capable of doing, a sexual predator without a trace of conscience.

"How many different instances of sexual misconduct did the investigation reveal?"

"More than half a dozen."

"And among them, were there any allegations that Fairweather had used force?"

"Two, but I should add that there was no supporting evidence, only the statements of the two women."

"Only the statements of...? In other words, afraid to come forward, afraid to risk....They were both young members of the faculty, were they not? - Afraid for their careers, they did not report anything to the police?"

"That is my understanding. In both cases, he - the chancellor - had used his position to - I won't say seduce - but to make them feel that he was romantically drawn to them. And perhaps he was. But then, when he wanted things to go further, and they did not, he - again according to what they said later - tried to force them."

I had only one more question.

"In the course of the university's investigation, was it discovered that Lucas Fairweather had lied about the reason he had left his position in the federal government?"

"Yes. He was forced out. He had been caught having an affair with the wife of another cabinet secretary. There were also rumors of other indiscretions."

"Indiscretions? I think before this trial is over," I said, turning to the jury, "you'll discover that what Lucas Fairweather did was considerably more serious than that."

Merrick was my witness. The prosecution thought they could use him for a better purpose. Anthony Barnes stood arrow straight, certain he knew the answer to the question he was about to ask.

"Mr. Merrick, you testified that Lucas Fairweather used 'force' with two women. But neither of them said he raped them, did they?"

"No; they said they managed to get away before he could."

Chapter Twenty-One

The single sentence confession that Cynthia Carruthers had given Detective Grayson was all she had told the police. It was nearly all she had told me. I had spent hours with her and had never quite been able to break through her disciplined facade. She had told me the first time I had seen her in jail that she had known Lucas Fairweather. What she told me about how she met him and what had happened had given me the beginning of a defense. But whenever I asked her to describe the night Fairweather died, she never told me the truth. She was not evasive about what she had done. A trained detective could not have been more clinical - or more detached. I had no reason to doubt Alan Boe's testimony that she had been scared, terrified, when she nearly knocked him over, running down the stairs; no doubt at all that in the emotion of the moment, having just killed someone, she would have been as frantic, as frightened, as he had said she had been. The emotion, and the fear, had long since passed; she was not afraid of anything anymore. And that was the point: she was not afraid. She was about to go on trial for murder and, in her own way, she seemed almost as indifferent about it as Alan Boe had been. She was not talking about what a great experience it was going to be; she had a different kind of interest, though I was never really certain what that interest was. It may have been nothing more than the curiosity of a remarkably intelligent woman. She kept repeating that whatever the law might call what she did, no one would think what she had done was wrong.

"Redfield often talked about this," she would remind me. "The difference between what the law and justice each require. The law says murder is not murder if it is self-defense; but the law - I'm right, aren't I? - says it is self-defense only when you have to kill to avoid death, or serious harm to your body. The law says nothing about the assault on your honor. Isn't that why you are trying this case to a jury, and not to a judge alone? - A judge has to follow the law; a jury can follow its conscience. Do you ever think about what that word means, Mr. Antonelli? Consience - with science, with knowledge; knowledge of what is wrong and what is right, what the law can never teach."

She talked a lot about what she had learned from Redfield, but it always came back to that same question: what justice really meant.

"You can't know there is something wrong with the law if you don't know that. It's the reason the Spartans had the law they had," she explained. Her eyes were full of the memory of what she had heard Redfield say. "Any citizen could propose any change to the law he wanted. It the change was approved, if the change was made, he was given a tribute for his wisdom. If it was not approved, if the change was not made, he was killed." She gave me a glance of more than usual significance. "As you can imagine, there were not that many times when anyone thought to propose a change. There is something else involved. If you were going to do it, risk your life like that, you had to have more than a clear idea of what justice meant; you had to have the ability to persuade everyone else - all those people who believed, who had been taught to believe, that the law is always just - that they had been mistaken, that the law was not perfect, that the law should be changed. If Redfield has taught us anything, he has taught us that. It is not enough to know something; you have to be able to get others to accept it. And if you think that through, you will understand how difficult, not to say impossible, that is. And you may come to the conclusion that, as Redfield once put it, 'a lie is sometimes the only way to tell the truth.'"

It could have come right from the mouth of Alan Boe, and then I realized that, in a sense, it had. Redfield had studied under him, and for five years Redfield had been teaching Carruthers and the others, the hundred chosen to keep what he called the 'conversation' alive. The trial of Alan Boe had been used to teach what a teacher could not teach, what only an example, a trial, a drama, could show. What lesson did she, what did Redfield, believe they could teach with this, a second trial for the same murder?

When, finally, Carruthers took the stand, the last witness in the trial, I still was not sure what she was going to say. I tried not to think about Redfield, I tried not to think about anything except what, as the attorney for the defense, I was there to do. I began with the question, the first question, I always asked a defendant charged with murder. I asked her if she had killed Lucas Fairweather. Her answer was one I had not expected and that in all my years of trying cases I had never heard.

"Yes, I killed him, but only after he had killed me."

Carruthers did not so much sit on the witness chair, as perch on the front edge of it. She could have taught posture to a ballerina. Her back was arched, her shoulder pulled back, her head held at regal height. The look on her face was as serious as I had ever seen on anyone. The jurors who had all bent forward the moment she took the stand, now leaned even closer.

"He killed you - Is that what you said?"

"Yes, he killed me; not my body - my soul." Slowly, with the kind of reserve that suggests reluctance to impose on others talk of your own misfortunes, she turned to the jury. "I knew Lucas Fairweather. I met him almost ten years ago, the summer after my freshman year in college. I was majoring in computer science at M.I.T. - Massachusetts Institute of Technology - and I had a summer internship in Washington D.C. with the Department of Health and Human Services. I was working on the department's computer system which was badly in need of modernization. Lucas Fair-weather was the Secretary of Health and Human Services. I was just an eighteen year old college intern. I never had contact with any of the top people in the department; neither had most of the career people I was working with. I had been there all summer. It was my last week. The Secretary had agreed to have a luncheon in his private dining room with the dozen of so college students who had worked as interns during the summer. Like everyone else, I was thrilled to have the chance to meet the Secretary, someone that important.

"Lucas Fairweather was even more impressive that what I had imagined. We were all just eighteen or nineteen years old, but he treated us, talked to us, as if we were the most important visitors he had ever entertained. He asked us each where we went to school, what we were studying, what we wanted to do when we graduated. He told us he hoped we would all give some thought to the possibility of government service, and - I remember this quite well - he told us that while we could make a lot more money doing other things, there was no price that could be put on the value we could give, and the value we would feel, if we dedicated ourselves to doing what we could for our country."

Carruthers lifted her chin slightly higher. A smile of apology, a look of regret that she could not keep her emotions entirely in check, made a brief appearance at the corners of her mouth and then, an instant later, was gone.

"He was what we all thought someone in his position should be: kind, intelligent, someone you could look up to, someone you could trust to do the right thing, however difficult it might be. I was a young girl, in a lot of ways younger even than my age. I had never been with a boy. I had gone out on dates, but I had never been, as they say, 'serious,' about anyone. I was not naive, but I was inexperienced."

I was standing at the side of the counsel table, watching the jury watching her. They followed every word, nodding, some of them, as they put themselves in the scene she described. Her voice was soft, compelling, a voice that made you want to listen.

"When the luncheon was over and everyone started to leave, he called me back. He told me that he understood nothing about computers and he wondered if I might be willing to take a look at the computer system he was using. It was not working right. He told me that he was in meetings all day, but that if I could come back sometime after six, I could spend whatever time I might need. He apologized for asking. He laughed, and said that you would think someone in the government would have been able to fix the problem, but that he had not found anyone who could. I was flattered that he had asked me. I was there at six o'clock, right on time. His secretary had left. He was there all alone."

Carruthers' face went rigid, her eyes tightened into a penetrating stare. Her mouth twisted into a scornful look of hatred and contempt.

"I sat at his desk, the chair turned to face the credenza behind it, where his computer was placed. He talked to me while I worked, telling me how he wished he were still in college, asking me what I liked most about it. He could not have been nicer. Twenty, maybe thirty minutes went by, and was talking, asking questions, all the time. He touched me on the shoulder and I thought it was just a harmless, passing gesture. Then he started asking me about the parties I went to at school, whether I had taken any kind of drugs; then he asked me if I wanted to, that there was not anything wrong if you once in a while 'smoked a joint,' that it was something he did himself, but that it would not be good if anyone found out about it. He looked at me, told me he thought he could trust me, that what he had just told me he hoped would stay secret just between the two of us."

Pausing, Carruthers gave the jury a meaningful look. They
306

knew, everyone in that courtroom knew, what was coming.

"You see how insidious this was. You see how he drew me into a conspiracy of silence. He was the most important person I had ever met, the most important person I would probably ever meet. And he had shared a secret with me! Of course he could trust me. I would never tell anyone what he had told me!

"He thanked me, said he knew he had been right about me. Then, in a show of gratitude, nothing more than that, he kissed me, kissed me on the forehead. He told me he liked the way it felt, and he kissed me again, this time on my cheek, and then, before I knew what was happening, he kissed me - tried to kiss me, because I pulled back - on my mouth. And then he grabbed my shoulders and told me that I would like it, if he did that, kissed me the way a woman was meant to be kissed. And then, when I started shaking my head, when I tried to turn away, he was all over me. He had me down on the floor, tearing at my blouse, pulling up my skirt, and then his hand was on my mouth and he was inside me, deep inside me, hurting me, hurting me bad, and he would not stop, and I knew he never would, that there was nothing I could do."

Ashen faced, Carruthers sat there, bolt upright, on the edge of the chair. She did not speak, she did not move.

"And then," she said, coming back to herself, "when it was over, he told me that what had just happened would not have happened if I had not been so intelligent and so attractive. There was nothing to worry about - that is what he said - it would always be our secret, a secret we shared together. And he was right. Lucas Fairweather knew what he was doing. He knew I would never tell anyone what he had done. He knew that I knew no one would believe me, and he knew that even if I thought someone might, I was too young, I had too much to look forward to, to want anyone to know that my first sexual experience was a violent rape committed by someone as famous and powerful as Lucas Fairweather. He knew I would not want to go through life a footnote in the criminal history of a high ranking government official!"

There were a hundred different questions that followed from this. The first, and in certain respects, the most important was why, after what Fairweather had done to her, had she gone to see him again. Why, after nearly ten years, and she decided to visit him in his office on the Berkeley campus? I knew what she had told me; I did not know if I believed her.

"If he had done this to you before," I asked, "why did you want to see him that night?"

Carruthers waited until I had finished the question, but instead of turning to the jury, she kept her eyes on me. I had the sense that she did this on purpose. The answer, for some reason, was meant for me.

"He did not know who I was. That was the first thing I wanted to find out: Did he remember me, or had there been so many women, so many young women, in his life that he had taken advantage of, that he had forgotten who they were. I did not just call his office and make an appointment to see him late on a Saturday night. I called, told his secretary that I was a journalist, that I was writing an article on the 'most important university presidents in the country,' and the 'innovations they were making in higher education,' new ways of teaching the new curriculum for the computer age. I saw him, in his office, Wednesday afternoon, the Wednesday before that Saturday night. I spent two hours interviewing him for an article I was never going to write, two hours listening to Lucas Fairweather describe how outmoded university education had become, and how difficult it was to convince some members of the faculty - the ones who taught the kind of courses that had no practical application - that the university had to change. I listened, I asked questions, I took notes, and I smiled. I smiled a lot," she remembered, smiling the way she had smiled then. "I nodded my agreement with everything he said. When we finished, I mentioned that I wished we had had more time, there were a lot more questions I wanted to ask. I told him I would meet him any time, anywhere, he wanted. He was busy the next couple of days, and when I suggested Saturday as a possibility, he said he had a dinner he had to attend, but he thought he could get away by ten at the latest. Would I mind meeting him here, in his office, a little after that. We both understood we were not talking about an interview. We both understood - he thought we both understood - why I was going to visit him in his office that late on a Saturday evening."

The next question was why. What was the reason she was not just willing, but wanted, to meet him that late at night.

"It had been almost ten years - nine years, seven months, to be exact - since he raped me in his office in Washington. He did not know me when he saw me. I had been a young girl; I was now a grown woman. My look was completely different. He had tried to act the seducer that day he did what he did to me. It was my turn to act the seducer with him. I showed up in his office like some paid for call girl knocking on the door of his hotel room. I sat on the other side of his desk and taunted him with his ignorance, teasing him with his failure to remember me. He thought - I knew he would think - that I must be referring to some conference, some gathering of university administrators where I was one of the reporters, perhaps one of those who had asked him a question or tried to get an interview. He laughed. He said he could not imagine ever forgetting me. But you have forgotten, I insisted. You don't even remember having sex with me. That got his attention. He was embarrassed, not that he had had sex with me, but that he had forgotten. He started to blame it on what he supposed must have been some drunken late-night encounter.

"'No,' I told him. 'It was not like that. I was an eighteen year old college student, a summer intern in Washington. We had sex in your office. You raped me and you don't even remember?'

"His eyes drew close together. He was trying to figure out why I was there, what I was after. I could tell that he remembered now, remembered what he had done to me. There was no remorse, no attempt to say he was sorry, only fear, and anger. He sat there, waiting to hear what I was going to do.

"'I'm going to tell everyone what you did. It is going to be in all the papers; it's going to be all over television. I'm going to tell the police. You'll be fired, you'll be sent to prison. You'll be known everywhere as the rapist - the serial rapist - I know you are!'"

Carruthers eyes opened wide with astonishment as she looked at the jury and told them what happened next.

"He was enraged, and excited. I mean that - excited. The memory of what he had done to me before, he could not wait to do it again. And he did. He grabbed me, threw me down on his desk, and for the second time in my life, attacked me. But I was not a child anymore; I was not ashamed of what had been done to me and I was not going to let him get away with it again. I was not going to let him rape me, rape anyone, ever again. When he was finished - he had such arrogance - he thought it was all over, that I would just walk away, vanish into the night. No, that isn't right. I think he thought that I would change my mind and want to see him again, that I would come back, that I was the kind of woman who would always come back, that no matter how upset, how angry, I might be in the moment, there was a part of me that would want more. He was disgusting, he was a disgrace. He was back in his chair, buttoning his shirt. That's when I did it, picked up that small marble statue and hit him with it. I killed him. If I had not done it he would have raped me again."

The courtroom went silent. The jurors, who had followed with rapt attention every word of Carruthers' testimony, looked at her with the same solemn expression seen on the faces of a family standing together at the graveside. Whatever the law might say about what someone can do to protect themselves, no one had any doubt that something of more value than life itself and been taken away from Cynthia Carruthers by the violence of the man she had killed.

Anthony Barnes was almost as caught up in the feeling of the moment as everyone else. The judge had to ask twice if he wanted to cross-examine the witness. Barnes asked a question, or tried to, but he had not spoken loud enough and had to ask a second time.

"You say that Lucas Fairweather raped you a little more than nine years ago, when you were an eighteen year old college intern, but that you never told, never reported it, to the police or anyone else. Is that correct?"

"That's right; that is what happened."

Barnes gave her a sharp look.

"Never told anyone in more than nine years?"

Carruthers pressed her lips together the way she often did when she had to think about something.

"I did tell someone, once; someone I respected, someone I trusted."

"Someone who is not a witness in this trial?"

"That's correct."

"Someone who could corroborate your story, or at least give it, indirectly at least, the support of having told this story of yours at least once before."

"I think, Mr. Barnes, that the jury can decide whether I am lying or telling the truth. Let me remind you, if you think I am lying, that there would not be a trial, I would not have been charged with murder, or any other crime, if I had not walked into the police station and told the detective what I did."

I do not know if Anthony Barnes knew what he was doing, or whether, as happens more than we might like to admit, the next question was out of his mouth before he had time to think what he was saying.

"And why was that, Ms. Carruthers? Why did you suddenly decide to confess? Why didn't you come forward when an innocent man, Alan Boe, was charged with this same murder and put on trial? Were you waiting to see if he was going to be convicted, and then decide if you wanted someone else to pay the price for what you did?"

I sat there, watching, wondering if Carruthers would tell the truth, the whole truth, the truth she had never told me, that the trial of Alan Boe had never had anything to do with providing the answer to who was responsible for the death of Lucas Fairweather, that it had instead been about raising the question about what a university was meant to be. Carruthers answered only what she had to.

"No, I would not have let Professor Boe be found guilty. I would have come forward."

"But he was acquitted. Why come forward now?"

"I could have come forward right away; I could have come forward when Professor Boe was arrested. And perhaps I should have. But if I had done that there would not have ben a trial. The world would not have learned...."

"Wouldn't have learned what, Ms. Carruthers?" demanded Barnes, certain he was on the verge of discovering something that would change everything to his advantage.

"I don't know, Mr. Barnes. I just thought that because of what Lucas Fairweather had done to me, there was a better chance it would all come out - what a really despicable man he was - if someone as interesting, and as closely connected with the university, as Alan Boe, had a chance to tell all the truth he knew."

The trial ended the next day, after closing arguments, at half past three in the afternoon. The jury came back with its verdict a few minutes before six. There was nothing left to do. I made my way out of the courtroom, ignoring as best I could the shouted questions of reporters always eager to get the lawyers' reaction to a verdict, and found Tangerine waiting for me on the sidewalk outside, at the far edge of the crowd. Taking her hand, we headed for her car, parked just a few blocks away. She did not say anything about the trial, the verdict, or anything else, until, ten minutes later, we were driving over the bridge. She knew I was still upset.

"They found her not guilty," she reminded me. "They were out less than two hours."

"Less than two hours," I repeated the same way I might have acknowledged a defeat. "If she had told the truth it might have taken even less than that to find her guilty."

"She lied? Is that what you're saying?" Tangerine kept her eyes on the road, but her hands, for a moment, tightened on the wheel.

"No, that's the interesting part. She gave an honest answer to every question she was asked. It is the questions she was not asked, the answer she did not have to give, that kept the truth, the whole truth, from coming out. She said, under oath, that she went to Fairweather's office to confront him, to tell him that she was going to tell the world what he had done to her when she was just a kid in college. She told the truth about that. She did go there to tell him that. But she also went there to kill him."

Tangerine's light filled eyes flashed; her head shook side to side in a quick, decisive motion.

"And you know that, because…?"

"Because of what she told me. Not that she went there to kill him - she never told me that - but because she kept insisting on the distinction, the difference, between justice and the law; because she kept talking about what a jury could do that a judge never could: decide what was right and what was wrong and ignore the law when the law was wrong. Because Redfield - who teaches nothing but that distinction - told her when Alan Boe would pass right in front of the building late at night. Because she did not suggest that she meet Fairweather anywhere except at his office."

"Whatever she might have intended to do, he attacked her.

He raped her. That was the whole basis of your defense: that she killed him out of fear that he was going to rape her again, that-"

"It gave the jury an excuse, a reason to do what they wanted to do - find her not guilty. He had raped her when she was a girl, and he raped her again that night. She could have left and gone straight to the police. She did not do that, she killed him instead. Revenge, pure and simple, and everyone on that jury thought it was the right thing to do. There is only one problem. Fairweather did not rape her that night."

We had reached Sausalito and were winding down the steep hillside drive to our brown shingle-sided home. I looked over at Tangerine. There was nowhere else I wanted to be.

"He didn't rape her. He might have, had she resisted - I don't doubt that. But she let him. That's why when Hoskins, the security guard, opened the door and saw them...."

"'Fucking the hell out of her' - I remember."

"Probably everyone does. Hoskins sees them together, but she doesn't yell, doesn't scream for help. She doesn't do anything, until Fairweather is finished with her, and then, when his back is turned, she does what she went there to do - get revenge, get justice, for what he had done to her, taken away her honor, as she kept putting it."

We walked to the door. I was about to open it, when I remembered what I had thought when the jury foreman announced the verdict.

"There should have been a verdict form that read 'unlawful but not unjust.' Any other verdict is wrong."

I opened the door and went inside. Tangerine went to check the mail while I made us each a drink.

"Not guilty. It's the verdict I would have given, knowing everything I know."

"What about Redfield?" asked Tangerine, as she set a small bundle of mail down on the kitchen counter. "Is he guilty of anything?"

"Aiding and abetting, strictly speaking; but only if he knew she was going there to kill him. If he only knew she was going there to confront him, if - and she testified that she had told someone about what Fairweather had done to her - he was worried what Fairweather might do, then it would make sense if he told her about Alan Boe's never changing habit, that whether or not a security guard might be close by, Boe would be close enough to help. And that would mean that instead of two murders, he would be responsible only for one, the murder of Allison Friedrich."

Tangerine thumbed through the mail. There was a large manilla envelope at the bottom of the pile. She looked up, startled by something she had seen.

"This is for you. Redfield's name is on the return address."

I sat on the living room sofa. On the far side of the Golden Gate the lights of the city were starting to come on. I had to force myself to open the envelope, to see what Redfield had done now. There was no letter, nothing written to me, only two dull looking documents. I was not sure what they meant, or why Redfield had sent them, a routine ballistic test. Then, suddenly, I understood.

"What is it? Why do you look like that? What has Redfield...?"

"Artificial intelligence. The ballistic test that matched the bullets in the Friedrich case. They did not really match at all. Redfield used his own advanced technology to infiltrate the system the police were using and made the computer in their forensic lab show what he wanted it to show. The bullet did not come from the gun I introduced as the murder weapon, but Redfield made certain that everyone thought it did. That is how simple it was, exchanging one image for another, the way we do everything now, believing everything we see on a screen."

"But that means...."

"That Justin Friedrich was guilty after all. He threw the

gun in the bay, just like the prosecution said. I got an acquittal for a guilty man. That is what Redfield meant that night at dinner at the Spinnaker, the night you met him. Remember what he said? That I was 'the best example there could possibly be' of all the corruption there was. 'What would you call a system in which innocence and guilt, life and death, depends on what you can afford?' That is what he said, and after everything that has happened, I can't exactly argue that he was wrong.

"Redfield did not murder anyone. He just used those who did to teach others - the one hundred he thinks can learn - the difference between wisdom and error."

The End

D.W. Buffa was born in San Francisco and raised in the Bay Area. After graduation from Michigan State University, he studied under Leo Strauss, Joseph Cropsey and Hans J. Morgenthau at the University of Chicago where he earned both an M.A. and a Ph. D. in political science. He received his J.D. degree from Wayne State University in Detroit. Buffa was a criminal defense attorney for 10 years and his seven Joseph Antonelli novels reflect that experience. *The New York Times* called *The Defense* 'an accomplished first novel' which 'leaves you wanting to go back to the beginning and read it over again.' *The Judgment* was nominated for the Edgar Award for best novel of the year. D.W. Buffa lives in Northern California. You can visit his Official Website at dwbuffa.net.

.